Eight Days OF CHRISTMAS

A Pineridge Novel

STARLA DEKRUYF

EIGHT DAYS OF CHRISTMAS

STARLA DEKRUYF

CITY OWL
PRESS

EIGHT DAYS OF CHRISTMAS
Pineridge, Book 1

CITY OWL PRESS
www.cityowlpress.com

Cover Design by MiblArt. All stock photos licensed appropriately.

Edited by Charissa Weaks.

For information on subsidiary rights, please contact the publisher at info@cityowlpress.com.

Print Edition ISBN: 978-1-64898-099-2

Digital Edition ISBN: 978-1-64898-098-5

Printed in the United States of America

For Jeremy. My best friend, my love, and my number one support.

And for my kids. Thank you for sharing me. I hope I have instilled a drive in you to never give up on your dreams.

CHAPTER ONE

ISABELLA

IsABELLA WHITLEY GRIPPED BOTH ARMRESTS AND PRAYED SHE WOULDN'T die in a fiery plummet to the earth. Only clouds filled the view out the plane's window, but the aircraft jolted sideways and up and down, so vigorously that she closed her eyes and did the most ridiculous thing given her situation.

She *laughed*.

The irony of the moment was almost as painful as it was comical. Because wasn't this what her life had become now? A life in complete disarray and full of turbulence?

Bob—the complete stranger in the seat next to Isabella who'd talked non-stop since the wheels lifted from the JFK runway—cleared his throat. "I-it's going to be okay. We-we're going to be fine. Promise."

Isabella rolled her eyes and glanced down at his fisted hands in his lap, his knuckles white. What did Bob know? How did he know everything would be okay? And why was he so positive anyway? He'd already confessed that his girlfriend had dumped him, moved out and taken their cat with her, and his father died after choking on a shrimp— all in the last few weeks.

The plane rocked angrily, and Isabella inhaled a sharp breath. Sure, her life currently sucked, maybe not as bad as Bob's, but she definitely didn't want to die by way of a plane crash.

"H-hey, you've been letting me talk your ear off," Bob mumbled. "Besides your name, I don't know anything about you. How 'bout you tell me about yourself?"

Isabella didn't open up to just anyone. And on an airplane headed back home for the first time in ten years definitely wouldn't be one of those times. People often mistook this as a sign that she was a good listener—people other than her ex-boyfriend, Harrison Blake, anyway.

Harrison used this as one of the reasons to end their relationship. His exact words had been: *It's like you've built a wall around your heart, and after four years, it's still impossible to get in. Someone broke your heart. Broke you. And I can't help you. If you ever want me to commit, you gotta figure this out.*

Technically, their relationship hadn't ended. Harrison asked her to move out of his modern apartment and suggested they *take a break*. But who really knew what that meant? Was this a Ross and Rachel break? Or were they free to see other people?

As the floor beneath her feet continued to rumble, Isabella found herself asking, "What do you wanna know, Bob?" If she did die today, she refused to prove Harrison right.

"So, you live in New York?"

She nodded, picturing Central Park, and took a calming breath.

"And w-what do you do for a living?"

"I'm a journalist. At *The New Yorker*."

Bob exhaled a low whistle. "Impressive."

Gah, had she said too much? She tried not to be paranoid, but with her career, she'd met an unsuspecting creep or two in her day. The few things Bob knew about her could be enough for him to locate any of her social media profiles or find her bio on *The New Yorker*'s website for that matter. From there it would only be a matter of time before he had her address.

Except as of now, she technically didn't have a home address. The thought of Bob showing up at Harrison's apartment provoked the bubble of a laugh in her throat. *Joke's on you Bob*. She didn't live there anymore.

Something inside her withered. Not having an address linked to her name was the opposite of funny—it was disturbing and downright pathetic. She'd worked tirelessly to reach her current position at *The New Yorker* and what did she have to show for it? A new popcorn maker she'd left at Harrison's apartment and a strict wardrobe of blazers and designer boots.

Since living in Manhattan for the past ten years, she'd relied on city transit and subways, so she didn't even have a car. She didn't own a single thing with her name attached to it. Currently, Isabella was crashing on Margo and Todd's old, lumpy couch. Her friends from college had a two-bedroom apartment with each of them occupying a room.

She wasn't complaining. She was grateful for a place to stay, even if it was a slightly dilapidated apartment building just outside of the city, while Harrison's modern and recently renovated building was in the heart of NYC.

Isabella couldn't dwell on the issue of technically being homeless, which was how she knew Dad would label it.

Dad. She probably missed him the most. He'd been so supportive and encouraged her to follow her dreams and attend Ithaca College. But when fate threw a wrench into Isabella's plans and she never returned after graduation, he'd been the most resentful toward her.

Scratch that—second most resentful. She'd have to wait to figure out a more permanent living situation after she returned to New York. Right now, her only focus was surviving the next eight days.

The aircraft rattled and Isabella clutched the armrests again. A baby cried somewhere toward the back of the plane.

Bob patted her shoulder. "Everything's gonna be alright." His stale coffee breath emitted across the small space between them. "Tell me why you're headed to Colorado?"

The plane leveled and Isabella exhaled a breath through her nose. She wasn't typically a nervous flyer. She flew often for work. But a lot was riding on this trip to Colorado. Her family was counting on her— Norah was counting on her.

Maybe by her opening up to Bob, she'd be on her way to proving Harrison wrong. She didn't *always* need to be one of those tough nuts to crack; she could be chatty and charismatic like Norah.

"My sister is getting married," she said. To little Landon Hoffman from next door. Isabella was still trying to swallow that news.

"That's nice. Good reason to travel at Christmas. Unlike me, who has to attend a big pharmaceutical conference…" Bob rambled on.

When Isabella had agreed to be Norah's maid of honor, she had no clue Norah had chosen the week of Christmas to get married. If she'd known, she might've said no. It was almost like Norah chose a Christmas Day wedding on purpose. That way Isabella would be forced to return to Pineridge, not only to celebrate her only sister's new marriage, but to endure the holiday as well, including Eight Days of Christmas—a Whitley tradition where they performed a specific holiday activity each day for eight days leading up to December twenty-fifth.

Norah had left Isabella no choice but to return home and withstand the eleven million questions from her family. No choice but to face Landon's older brother Leo—the boy who held the key to her heart for more years than she could count.

She glanced out the window. Ready or not—she was headed home.

Or maybe not.

Static blared through the plane's overhead speakers, followed by an announcement.

"Good afternoon flight 434, this is your captain speaking. I'm afraid I have some less than exciting news. Due to the snowstorm Denver is currently experiencing, ground control has directed us to make an emergency landing in Omaha, Nebraska."

"What?" Isabella flung herself forward in her seat as groans, disapproving comments, and moans echoed through the cabin. "Is he for real?"

"I'm 'fraid so." Bob gave her a soft smile.

"At any rate," the captain continued, "the good folks at American Airlines customer service will be more than happy to assist you with accommodations. Hopefully the ice and fog will let up in Denver so we can get you all on your way real soon. American Airlines thanks you for flying with us and, as always, don't forget to fill out a customer service survey online and give us a top-star rating."

Just how in the hell was she supposed to make it home now? The plane descended quickly, giving Isabella that queasy feeling in her stomach she despised. This was seriously happening. The pilot was actually landing the plane in Omaha, Nebraska.

"This can't be happening." Isabella closed her eyes, pinching the bridge of her nose.

"Omaha, huh?" Bob said. "Never been here before." He pulled his phone from the front pocket of his laptop bag, ready for when he'd have service. "Better check Yelp for the best places to find some grub."

As if this little emergency pit stop was the best thing to happen to him. Then again, maybe it was.

All around her, phones chimed, signaling service. She exhaled a few deep breaths before slipping her phone from her purse. She pushed her hair behind her ear and scrolled through her notifications. There was a missed call from Dad, a missed call from Norah, and several unanswered texts from Margo and Norah. But the text that stood out the most was from Harrison.

Harrison: Did you want the Pampered Chef cheese grater? Or the popcorn air popper? I know how much you love popcorn. But I did buy it.

Isabella's eyes burned. She squeezed them tight enough to see floating black spots behind her lids. He was really doing this now? He had some nerve. Dividing their things the week before Christmas? When she wasn't even in town?

Even though he'd sent the text two hours before, Isabella opened her eyes and tapped out a reply.

Isabella: Keep them both.

Isabella: On second thought, no. If you can't wait until I'm back to divide our things, then I want them.

She inhaled a deep breath, holding it in.

Isabella: I didn't know we'd made a decision yet. To divide our things. To be completely over.

She didn't expect a reply, at least not so soon. But regardless, it came.

Harrison: Just figured it would be easier this way.

Isabella: You mean easier for you.

Harrison: Why make it harder than it has to be?

Isabella: After four years together, breaking up shouldn't be easy.

No response—no surprise.

Isabella sent a quick text to Dad to let him know about the flight's detour to Omaha, and to assure Norah everything was fine and not to worry. She'd figure something out.

Eppley Airfield was fully decked out for the holidays. Garland dangled above wide windows, and glimmering lights wrapped around fake trees that lined the walls. All it did was cause a tight pressure in Isabella's chest. By the time she—along with her rolling suitcase and overstuffed carry-on—made it to the customer service for American Airlines, there was already a long line.

"Well, would you look at that line," Bob said, hot on her heels.

"Right?" Isabella huffed. "This is going to take forever."

"Why don't you come with me to get a bite to eat and then we can make our way to customer service afterward."

Isabella glared at him. "I don't have time to get a bite to eat. I have to get on another plane. And fast." In truth, missing the first few days of Eight Days of Christmas sounded amazing, but Isabella's family already saw her as the daughter and sister who abandoned them. Storm or no storm, she had to make it home within the next twenty-four hours.

"Whoa, okay." Bob put up his hands. "I'm sure you'll get on another plane. But not anytime soon. You heard the captain. There's a winter storm rolling through Denver. It's probably gonna be a while. Maybe not even until tomorrow."

Isabella grunted. She rubbed at the tension building between her eyes. She didn't have time for Bob and his rational thinking. Or this line. Or to be in the Omaha airport at all. "You go ahead. I'm gonna wait."

"Alright, alright. I think I might just do that." He backed up, and Isabella exhaled her relief. "Check you later, Miss Bella." He tipped an imaginary hat at her.

"It's *Isa*bella," she said flatly as he, thankfully, walked away. Despite it being Isabella's unlucky day, the customer service line for American Airlines moved swiftly. When it was her turn, she stepped up to the counter and held her head high. She needed to put on her game face. The one she used in the office. The one she used to get the story. The friendly-but-don't-mess-with-me face.

"Good afternoon, welcome to American Airlines. How can I help you today?" The customer service representative—Ben, his name tag read—had too big of a smile plastered on his face for how distraught Isabella felt.

"Hi there. My name is Isabella Whitley. I was on flight 434 en route to Denver, Colorado, but we were rerouted here due to the snowstorm. The reader board," she pointed above Ben's head, "shows all flights to Denver are canceled. But are you sure the info has been updated? Because I need to get on the first available flight. Please."

"I do apologize, ma'am. But as you just said, all flights to Denver have been canceled."

She gritted her teeth, resisting the urge to raise her voice. Ben was only doing his job, but desperation tingled through her unforgivingly.

"Right. I understand that. But when will the next one take off? I need to get on that flight."

"Again, I do apologize. However, I'm unable to give you that info."

She exhaled. "And why not?"

"Because I'm unable to see the future." His smile turned into a smirk.

Isabella recognized a smirk when she saw one. And he was definitely smirking at her now.

She narrowed her eyes and leaned across the counter. "I have to get to Denver. Today. Whatever you need to do to make that happen, *Ben*, do it." She forced out a strangled, "Please."

"Since it's already late afternoon, what I *can* do for you, ma'am, is give you a hotel voucher and hopefully we can get you on a flight tomorrow morning."

She leaned in closer, heat crawling up her neck and spreading into her cheeks. "I don't *want* a hotel voucher. I *want* on a plane."

He rearranged his expression into a jackass blank stare, as if looking straight through her. "Like I said, let me get you that hotel voucher and—"

Isabella slapped her hand on the counter. "Ben, I'd like to speak to your manager."

"Izzy?"

Isabella sucked in a breath. Her back went rigid while her stomach plummeted to the floor. "Oh please, oh please, oh please, no."

She turned around, slowly.

But nope, luck was still not on her side today. Because when she turned, she knew exactly who would be standing there. Not only because his voice was as familiar as her own skin, but because he'd called her *Izzy*. Besides her family, only one other person in this world called her by that childhood nickname.

Leo Hoffman.

"What the hell are you doing?" Leo stood in the customer service line a few patrons back, hands stuffed in the pockets of his black peacoat.

She swallowed, uncertain if she could find her voice to reply. "Leo?"

She had to still be asleep on the plane, having a nightmare. There was no possible way her luck was this bad.

"You think yelling at customer service is actually gonna get you to Colorado faster? Man, you haven't changed a bit." His face, while the same, was older, all sharp lines and dark brown scruff. And too beautiful to even be fair.

She could wake up now. Any minute.

"I just thought...I was just hoping...I," she mumbled, her mouth going dry. This was real, and she sounded like a blubbering idiot instead of the accomplished woman she'd grown up to be. His words registered. "Wait. Haven't changed a bit? What is that supposed to mean?" She glared. "And what are you doing here?"

"What does it look like?" he snapped.

Her brows pinched together. "You're flying somewhere?"

The Leo she knew never left Pineridge.

His gaze shifted to the people who had their attention trained on the two of them. "Just take your hotel voucher, Izzy. You're holding up the line."

Isabella reluctantly faced Ben and forced a smile, her heart raging against her chest. After all the ways she'd thought about avoiding her ex once she arrived in Pineridge, he was here. In freaking Omaha, Nebraska. With her.

"Look," she said to Ben. "I'm sorry. I know you're just trying to do your job. But you don't understand. I need to get home to Colorado today." She pushed back her unexpected emotions and cleared her throat, feeling the bizarre urge to open up to this guy and win him over. "My little sister is getting married on Christmas Day and—"

"That's still a week away, ma'am. I can guarantee you'll be there by then."

"But you see, my family has this tradition…" She pinched the bridge of her nose, her back absorbing the scrutiny from the other fliers. "They call it Eight Days of Christmas. They expect me to be there." She leaned forward and whispered, "I haven't been home for Christmas in ten years."

And the stupidly handsome ghost of her past had clearly appeared to remind her of that fact.

Ben inhaled a sharp breath. "Ten years? What kind of person doesn't go home for Christmas for ten years?"

Isabella's jaw dropped, and her first instinct was to give in to the fantasy of clutching the navy-blue tie around his neck and choking him with it. But she couldn't be angry with Ben, because he was exactly right. What kind of person didn't go home for Christmas for ten years? What kind of selfish person did that?

Her—that's who.

"Damn it." Leo groaned, now suddenly standing at her side, sporting that sexy, scruffy beard. "What are you gonna do, tell him your life story? It's a little late to get sympathy when you've already pissed someone off." He leaned over the counter, his phone in his hand. "Excuse me, Ben? Where's the airport's car rental located?"

Ben proceeded to give Leo directions while Isabella remained quiet, trying hard to be annoyed with him while also admiring his broad shoulders and obvious fit physique. He smelled good, too, like pine and citrus, and all man and… Jeez, this was a really bad scenario.

Leo took a few steps sideways, hiking a duffel bag over his shoulder. "You can either come with me and rent yourself a car and drive to Pineridge, or you can stay here and harass this nice guy and embarrass yourself further." He held up a palm. "Your choice."

"Whoa, hold on a sec." She shuffled next to him, getting out of the customer service line. "How far is it from here to Pineridge?" Isabella hadn't driven a car since she moved to New York. The thought of driving, especially through a snowstorm, caused her stomach to flip-flop.

"About six hundred miles."

She gasped. "Six hundred miles?"

Leo blew out an exaggerated and annoyed breath. "Yep. And you might want to hurry. Before all of the cars are gone." Leo stalked away from her, his attention fixed on his phone.

Isabella stood there stupefied, staring after the man who had once been her everything.

Pressing her lips together in a grimace, her mind battled over her options: remain stranded in the airport alone or chase after Leo and somehow persuade him to let her catch a ride with him.

With the flight information screens displaying *cancelled* for nearly every departure, her chest tightened while imagining driving through a death-inducing blizzard. In the end, the panic won.

She bit the inside of her cheek, gripped the handle of her rolling suitcase, and stomped off after Leo.

CHAPTER TWO

LEO

LEO HOFFMAN KEPT HIS FOCUS ON THE BUSY TERMINAL AHEAD. HE would've done a double take, glancing over his shoulder to make sure he wasn't hallucinating, but he didn't have to. He could feel Isabella behind him, just like always; her nearness making his skin tingle with awareness.

He walked faster.

Of all the people he could've imagined running into at the airport today, Isabella Whitley would've been the last person to cross his mind. Of course, he knew she was coming for the wedding and Eight Days of Christmas, but he assumed she would've made it to Pineridge by now. Not very shocking she would wait until the last minute, though.

That's what selfish people did.

Isabella hadn't always been so self-centered. As a kid, she'd been the complete opposite. She was the brave girl who saved a bat trapped underneath the Whitley's wood deck. The generous girl who brought her mom's famous stew to the homeless guy who sat on the corner of Oak and Third every time he caught a cold. And the attentive, lovestruck girl who huddled on the ice-cold metal bleachers every Saturday during hockey season to support him. She'd even somehow convince her family to join her. Isabella was persuasive like that.

Until she wasn't. Until she'd given up on him.

On *them*.

After watching her harass poor Ben, Leo suspected Isabella had lost those skills of persuasion. More importantly, something told him she'd lost a critical quality that went along with being persuasive. She'd lost the sweetness he'd loved about her.

They reached the car rental kiosk and Leo took his place in the long line, dropping his duffel at his feet, and searched on his phone for the best route from the Omaha airport to home. He'd made the drive a few times over the last couple of years but never in winter—never in the middle of a snowstorm.

Isabella stomped up behind him and exhaled loudly, but he ignored her. He didn't owe her anything. Especially not a conversation. That was the *last* thing he wanted. Unless she was finally ready to offer up an excuse for leaving him and never coming back.

When he didn't take the bait, she grew impatient. "So what exactly is your plan here?"

Leo didn't pull his attention away from his phone to bother glancing in her direction—she didn't deserve it—even if his hungry eyes craved to take in every inch of her.

Izzy—*as a woman*. It was something that, no matter how much he'd prepared himself by looking at pictures of her on Norah's Instagram, still took the breath from his lungs. She was gorgeous. But he'd had no doubt that she would be.

"Like I said, I'm going to rent a car and drive. I suggest you do the same."

They moved up a few spots in line, and he pushed his duffel bag forward with the toe of his boot. He took a couple of screenshots of the route in case he didn't have cell service along the way. He felt Isabella's impatience behind him, radiating like flames from a fire, but he forced himself not to look at her. Allowing her beauty to complicate his feelings for her wasn't an option. He hated this woman.

"How long do you think it will take to drive the six hundred miles?" she asked.

"Depending on the weather…eight to ten hours."

"Eight to ten hours?" she repeated, agitation in her tone. "And you expect me to rent my own car?"

"Yep."

"You don't find that a bit ridiculous, us renting two cars when we're going to the same place?"

He glanced over his shoulder at her, gritting his teeth. "No."

"You're probably right. We wouldn't last twenty minutes in a car together."

"Agreed."

The customer service rep called, "Next!"

Leo slung his duffel bag over his shoulder and shuffled to the counter. He slid his wallet from the front pocket of his jeans and handed his driver's license and credit card to the guy behind the counter.

"Afternoon, sir. This is your lucky day," the man wearing a navy-blue sweater vest announced.

Leo stared at him, incredulous. His flight had just made an emergency landing, putting him in an entirely wrong state, and he'd just ran into his high school sweetheart who had gutted out his heart six years ago. How lucky could he be?

"You just snagged our last car available."

Leo arched a dark brow. "I was actually hoping for a truck. Or anything with all-wheel drive I guess would be fine too."

"I'm sorry, sir." The rep tapped the keyboard, glancing at the computer screen. "But like I said, we have one last rental. It's not all-wheel drive but I can assure you it has all-season tires."

The way Leo saw it, he had two choices—pass on the rental and hope he got on another flight in the morning or take his chances on the tin can on wheels.

Scratching at the scruff on his chin he exhaled an elongated, defeated breath. "Fine. I'll take it."

"That's wonderful, sir."

Near him, a long, low sigh expelled from Isabella's throat. As the situation sunk in, he couldn't say he blamed her. His stomach tightened and he slid a glare in her direction. He couldn't deny she was alluring. The way the tip of her nose turned up slightly. The way those amber eyes sparkled in just the right lighting. And somehow, in the last several years, she had become more beautiful—with voluptuous hips, and a nice rack hidden underneath her fitted sweater. But despite all of that, the memory of her leaving, of breaking his heart, was fresh on his mind.

He dropped his head in surrender. He knew the right thing to do, but it didn't make doing it any easier. He couldn't leave Isabella stranded at the Omaha airport. If Landon and Norah found out, he'd never hear the end of it.

"Excuse me for just a minute." He held up a finger to the car rental rep and shuffled sideways to where Isabella stood, pinching the bridge of her nose.

"If you'd like to share my car, I suppose…you're welcome to." He clenched his jaw.

She stared up at him, blinking back the tears building in her eyes. The sight caused an obnoxious ache in his throat.

"We each drive halfway," he said. "And we split the rental fee fifty-fifty."

"Didn't we just agree that the two of us in a car together is a bad idea?"

"Oh, it's definitely a bad idea."

She bit her lower lip, causing his gaze to travel to her mouth. He couldn't help but remember how soft and satisfying her kisses used to be, how she could consume him with the simple caress of her lips against his.

All right. This wasn't just a bad idea. It was downright idiotic. And yet…

"Okay, fine. Thank you," she said, lowering her chin to her chest.

"License," he demanded, holding out his hand.

She set the card in his open palm before rubbing at her temples, exhaling dramatically through her nose.

The customer service rep gave Leo the keys for the only remaining vehicle and tossed a cheerful, "Happy Holidays," at him while he picked up his duffle bag and hiked it over his shoulder.

Leo made his way toward the car lot, grumbling as he went. Isabella scrambled after him, trudging along with a disgruntled rolling suitcase.

Typically, he'd offer to help. But this was Isabella Whitley, and she'd made it damn clear all those years ago that she didn't need help.

Most importantly, not his.

Stopping in front of the Ford Fiesta, Leo's chest heaved. What he wouldn't give to have his lifted Chevy four-by-four right about now.

"You gotta be kidding me." Isabella crossed her arms. "Is this thing even all-wheel drive?"

"Nope." He unlocked the doors and threw his bag into the backseat since the car was a hatchback and technically didn't even have a trunk. "I'll take the first shift."

"Just hold on a second." She pinched the bridge of her nose.

This must be a new habit, something she picked up while living in New York for so long. The Isabella he remembered wasn't so stressed out, not so tightly wound. This Isabella resembled a fluttering hummingbird—constantly moving, yet mesmerizing. Thoughts of ways he could slow her down, *unwind* her, assaulted his mind.

Leo pressed his hands to his hips and hung his head, forcing those thoughts away. "What's the problem now?"

"If we're going to do this, I think we need to set some ground rules."

He slowly lifted his head and stared at her blankly from across the roof of the car. Was she serious? He'd been the one to offer her the favor. And what was she so afraid of?

He ground his teeth. "What kind of ground rules?"

"Well, for starters, we should not only split the driving responsibilities, but we should also split the cost of gas. Fifty-fifty." She nodded matter-of-factly.

"You honestly thought I was going to pay for all the gas?"

"I don't know." She threw up her hands. "Jeez, Leo, you don't have to be such an ass about it."

He couldn't help himself, his mouth tugged at the corner into a crooked, cocky smile. "Okay, what else?"

"And…" she dragged out the word, hesitation in her tone. "We don't talk about the past."

Leo narrowed his eyes at her like he'd just sent a trail of burning fire licking across the roof of the car. "Don't talk about the past?"

"Right. No talking about past relationships. With other people," she paused, tucking her long, brown hair behind her ear, "or ours," she clarified.

He glanced over his shoulder, pinching his tired eyes shut while tapping the car keys against the metal roof a few times. "Fine." Under his breath, he mumbled, "you're a real piece of work." He slid behind the steering wheel and slammed the door shut, jamming the key into the ignition.

The back door flew open, and he watched in the rear-view mirror as Isabella struggled to get her suitcase handle down. Ultimately, she gave up and shoved the luggage onto the back seat, the handle still in the upright position. She climbed into the passenger side, scowling at him. Her long and still-muscular legs, all wrapped in fitted, dark jeans distracted him—but only momentarily. She was still the same girl who chose New York over him.

"What was that supposed to mean?" she snapped.

"What?" He hunched his shoulders and shifted the car into reverse, not bothering to wait for her to put her seatbelt on.

"I'm a piece of work?" She buckled in.

Leo groaned. "This is gonna be the longest eight hours of my life."

"You're telling me." She crossed her arms, staring straight out the windshield.

It wasn't Leo's intention to be a jerk. And again, it wasn't like he didn't know she was coming to town. She may have broken his heart six years ago when she unexpectedly decided to not come home as she'd promised after college graduation, but she'd never let her sister, Norah down.

He just hadn't been ready to see her today is all. Especially not at the airport. He thought he had one more day. One more blissful Isabella-free day.

Leo had been on his way home to Pineridge, Colorado, after completing two photoshoots in Michigan. He'd taken a job capturing engagement photos for an old friend who wanted their session done at Pictured Rocks National Lakeshore. He typically didn't take engagement or wedding photos any longer—he'd done so many of those when he first started his photography business six years ago that he'd felt like poking his eyes out. But accepting the favor meant he could take photos of the picturesque frozen waterfalls too, and he knew the prints would not only be a huge hit, but he'd make a killing.

He'd planned on spending today editing those photos, uploading a few of the best ones, and getting his colleague's opinion, along with his dad's. Leo had no clue that when he began his photography business—LH Photography—his dad would have a knack for editing landscape prints.

But the biggest storm of the season to hit Colorado had decided to come now of all times. What a bastard. Leo's last free day before celebrating the Whitley's tradition of Eight Days of Christmas along with the wedding plans would be spent trapped in a car with Isabella. And those epic images sitting on the flash drives would have to remain unedited until after Christmas. Where was the justice?

Leo had already promised Landon and Norah he'd stay at his dad's house all week and help with whatever they needed. Some days he felt like cursing the day his brother Landon and Isabella's sister Norah made their relationship official. But the two were perfect for one another. And it wasn't Norah's fault she just happened to be sisters with New York's resident ice-princess.

Leo maneuvered the matchbox car onto the main road and hopped onto the freeway entrance that luckily displayed wet asphalt. Snow piled the sides of the freeway in uniformed mounds, but the temperature gauge reflected it was too warm for the roads to be frozen.

He cleared his throat. "So, there's a large town in about two hours. I figure we can stop there and fill up. Use the bathroom and get something to eat, since I'm guessing you haven't had dinner yet."

When she didn't respond, he glanced over his shoulder and caught her staring at him. Her eyes flicked away, pink instantly staining her cheeks. Had he just caught her checking him out?

"And how do you know the town will even have a gas station? Google?"

"As a matter of fact, yeah. Google. But I've also been through all these towns, from Omaha to Pineridge."

"Seriously?"

He narrowed his eyes in her direction, while also trying to keep his focus on the road. "We had a lot of away hockey games during those four years of college."

"Oh, right." She sucked her lower lip between her teeth, and he glanced away before his body betrayed his mind. "I guess I forgot about those."

"Not surprised," he mumbled.

"What's that supposed to mean?"

Old, long-ago anger hovered at the surface where it had no business being anymore. "Nothing, just forget it."

"No, I want to know."

"Fine, you want to know?" Heat bit at his cheeks. "You're such a hypocrite. You bugged me about never wanting to leave Colorado, but you never wanted to leave New York. You couldn't even make it back home for a single game."

"And I told you I couldn't afford to travel back and forth often."

"Try never. In four years, you didn't come back once."

She stopped talking, her shoulders slumped in on themselves, and he felt the exhaustion in her body language.

"Izzy," the word exhaled as if on impulse. But he couldn't undo it now that it was spoken. He was tired. He'd forgotten how much this girl —this *woman*—got under his skin and made him plain tired. "It was a long time ago." He gripped the steering wheel harder, with both hands, his palms beginning to sweat. "And you're breaking one of your rules."

She crossed her arms and stared straight out the windshield again, bottom lip still tucked in between her teeth. It was a small, familiar gesture. One that reminded him, that somewhere in that grown-up, curvy body, was the Izzy he once knew.

They rode in silence for a while, the scenery of Nebraska nearly hidden by a light misty fog. The sun had already dipped below the horizon, and Leo's stomach growled, reminding him it was dinnertime. He didn't ease his grip on the steering wheel, and he could already feel a kink working its way across the tops of his shoulders. Isabella busied herself on her phone but suddenly she perked up.

"Hey, have you let your family know we're driving and won't be there until tonight?"

"I let them know *I* was driving. I didn't mention anything about *we*," he said.

"Great, thanks," she muttered.

After a few more minutes of Isabella tapping on her phone, she leaned forward and turned on the radio. She scanned through stations and static before landing on a clear one playing Christmas music. "Is this okay?"

"It's fine." He didn't take his attention off the road, but he didn't need to see the eye roll to know she was giving it. The way he saw it, he should be the one rolling his eyes at her, not the other way around. She should be thanking her lucky stars he offered her a ride, or she'd definitely be missing the activities for day one of Eight Days of Christmas. He had a good feeling that wouldn't have gone over well with her family.

Isabella rested her head against the headrest and faced the passenger window. Leo finally eased off the steering wheel some, his hands slick with sweat, though the tension in his shoulders was dissipating. Outside, the day slipped into night and the fog thickened. It was hard to believe that only a couple hundred miles away there was a devastating snowstorm occurring.

"So, what were you doing in Omaha?" she asked.

Leo glanced at her before returning his attention on the road. "Just work stuff." He decided against correcting her by mentioning that he hadn't been in Omaha. It had only been an emergency stop on his way to Denver from Michigan due to the snowstorm.

"Work?" She straightened in her seat. "What kind of work are you doing that takes you out of Colorado? I didn't think you'd ever take a job that would force you to travel." She didn't bother to hide the snark in her tone. It was there. Front and center. And they both knew why. The topic had always caused conflict between them. Some might even go as far as saying it had been the reason for their breakup six years before. Okay, Isabella would probably say that. But if anyone asked Leo, he'd say it was because Isabella left and never came back.

"I think we're slipping into the past again," he said.

"Ugh," she groaned, facing the passenger window again and crossing her arms tight in exaggeration.

"It was your rule," he reminded her.

"Yeah, yeah," she muttered, sounding a bit defeated.

And the thought of that caused warmth to expand in his chest in a weird, sort of twisted achievement. He didn't mind seeing her agitated.

She was sort of cute that way, all flustered. Besides, he wasn't ready to tell her about his photography business. Something about her being one of his biggest cheerleaders in pursuing that career path and now he'd done it, rubbed him the wrong way. He didn't want her to think she had anything to do with his decision of switching careers a few years back. He'd done it for his mom mostly, and himself. The satisfaction he felt in his choice was evident each time he held his camera in his hands and peered through the lens.

Nah, he couldn't give her the gratification of being right.

"Just settle in and stop talking. We've got a long drive, and I'm not arguing the whole way home." Again, he didn't look at her, but he could feel her glare.

Mumbling things he was pretty sure he didn't want to hear anyway, she leaned her head against the window, bringing her feet up, knees hugged to her chest. "Some things—*and people*—" she ground out "—never change, I guess."

Gritting his teeth, he let the quip slide, for both their sakes.

After several minutes of quiet, a soft, shuttering sound came from Isabella. That little moan she used to make while sleeping.

Leo couldn't help but steal a glance at the woman beside him, his heart pushing out a strained beat when he did. God, she was still so stunning it hurt. He wished he could reach over and touch her. Wished the past had unfolded differently than it had when it came to her. Wished he wasn't so damn bitter.

But he was, and all the wishing in the world wouldn't make that bitterness go away.

CHAPTER THREE

ISABELLA

ISABELLA AWOKE JUST AS LEO PULLED INTO A BRIGHTLY LIT GAS STATION, a kink in her neck. Snow fluttered against the windshield, accumulating since Omaha, but the roads seemed to be mostly wet. The sky had turned into night while she'd slept, her stomach aching and reminding her she should've eaten by now. A Subway adjoined the gas station convenience store, and if Isabella still knew Leo in the way she once had, this was what he meant by, *there's a place we can get something to eat.*

She left her things in the car, putting on her coat and shoving her wallet into the pocket, and crunched across the snow-covered parking lot. Isabella went inside the cluttered convenience store in search of the bathroom, pulling down her hood and shaking off the snow. She'd been holding her bladder so long, trying to not be a nuisance and make Leo stop often for a bathroom break. She had to hobble toward the back of the store where the restroom sign hung.

When she was finished, she glanced out the windows of the convenience store, searching for the rental car at the gas pump. Her eyes roamed the dark, foggy parking lot until she spotted the empty car parked in a spot near the side of the building. She searched around the store and found Leo in line at the Subway counter.

Isabella would rather have a nice, hot meal, considering the chill in her bones, but she was starving, so she stepped in line. When Leo turned around and waved her over, she hesitantly passed everyone in line until she reached him.

"Italian?" He gestured at the two sandwiches laying open-faced on the counter. "Is that still what you get?"

Her stomach tightened, and her heart slid into her throat. He remembered her usual sandwich. "Um, yeah," she muttered. "Thanks."

Leo nodded, giving her a tight half-smile.

But that gesture only made her angry again. He couldn't even give her a genuine smile. Leo used to have the best smile. If she was having a bad day, all he had to do was break those perfect lips into a grin and all the bad would melt away. All of those nights when she snuck out her window and climbed into his. He'd curve those soft lips and the worry of getting caught vanished. It had always been worth it, just to see that smile.

"Isabella?" Leo nudged her arm.

"Huh...what?" she said, coming out of the memory.

"I asked if you wanted chips." He stared at her blankly, and a bit annoyed.

"Sure. That'd be great." Snatching two bottles of water from the cooler, she set them on the counter. "And these." She unzipped her wallet and plucked out her credit card, handing it to the cashier. "This is on me. I'm assuming you paid for the gas?"

He nodded. "You can get it next time." The cashier handed him the bag with the sandwiches and chips stuffed inside. "And, thanks," he mumbled.

"Wow. How painful was that?" she teased, following him toward the glass double doors.

"What are you talking about?"

"Telling me thank you."

He stopped, holding the door open for her to exit first. And then, it happened. The slightest hint of the Leo smile she remembered broke across his face. It brought her up short. Stole her breath. For a long second, she stood inches from the muscular man she couldn't seem to get over, the space between them way too close.

But then he quirked a cocky brow. "More than you'll ever know."

"Am I honestly that terrible?" Isabella finally asked after she climbed into the driver's seat. When Leo didn't respond, she glanced at him. He had his head tilted, a sneer on his lips. "O-kay," she said, drawing out the word. "Never mind. Don't answer that."

"No, Izzy," Leo breathed out, running a large hand down his tired face. "You're not that terrible."

Tension filled the car like a hot, stuffy sauna, and the heat burned in Isabella's chest. There was so much being said in the silence around them that it felt suffocating. She wanted to relieve it. She wanted the ache in the pit of her stomach to finally dissipate. The one she'd held onto for the last six years.

Isabella unwrapped her sandwich, took a bite, and forced herself to chew. After she swallowed the first dry bite, she unscrewed the cap on her water bottle and took a long drink. Then she returned the water to the cup holder in the center console and put the key in the ignition.

"Why don't you eat before you start driving?" Leo suggested around a mouthful of his sandwich.

"I'm fine. I can eat while I drive."

"Oh boy, this should be fun." Leo reached for his seatbelt.

"Ha, very funny." She glared at him and backed out of the parking spot.

"You're a terrible driver. And you're even worse when you eat while you drive."

Rather than being upset by his comments, it only reminded her of just one more way Leo knew her. But what he didn't know was that she hadn't driven in ten years. And when Leo suggested renting a car and driving the six hundred miles to Pineridge on her own, in the middle of a snowstorm, she felt on the verge of a panic attack. She could do this, though. It had to be like riding a bicycle, right?

"I'm a fine driver." She turned out of the gas station, and the car jumped over the curb with a jarring thud. "Shut up," she muttered before Leo had time to say anything.

"How long has it been since you drove? Because Norah said you don't drive in New York." Leo took another bite of his sandwich, crumbs clinging to the scruff on his face.

"Oh yeah? And what else has Norah been saying about me?" Norah and her big mouth. It had been Norah's fault Isabella got caught sneaking out her bedroom window when she was seventeen. At least Mom and Dad didn't know she'd been sneaking into Leo's window. And she'd been doing it for years.

With a mouthful of food pushed to one cheek, he said, "It's not like Landon and Norah and I sit around talking about you, if that's what you're insinuating."

"It's not," she snapped. "Believe me, I figure the last thing you want to do is talk about me. Unless you want to talk about how much you hate me." There, she'd said it.

"Hell, Izzy, I don't hate you." He crumpled the sandwich wrapper into a ball and chucked it at the floor mat. "I don't...well, I don't anything you."

Well, if that didn't send a burnt poker straight through her chest.

She widened her watering eyes, fighting back the untamed emotion. "Wow...thanks."

"What do you want me to say?"

"No, no, you're right. I deserve that." Isabella forgot about her sandwich, suddenly no longer having an appetite.

"We're not supposed to be talking about this, remember? Your rule."

"Right. My rule." She stared out the windshield, the wipers clearing the falling snow. "Fine. Talk about something else."

"Or we could just listen to the radio." Leo fiddled with the radio, but every station it jumped through was nothing but static. "Great." He gave up, flinging back in his seat.

In a quiet agreement, they drove in silence.

Isabella hadn't been driving for more than an hour when snowflakes sprinkled like confetti against the windshield, making it hard to see the road. Her palms were slick with sweat, and she debated asking Leo to take over the driving shift. Was it worth killing them to prove she still knew how to drive?

She glanced at him, his attention fixated on his phone. He was probably texting his family and complaining about being stuck with her. Complaining about how terrible of a driver she was. Maybe he was reiterating how much he hated her and how unfair it was of them to force the two of them together during the wedding festivities.

Isabella was less than thrilled about all of this herself.

A road sign appeared in the headlights, half-hidden by flakey snow. Two more miles until the next rest stop. Finally, she'd get to use the bathroom again and get a break from the weather. The snow flying toward the windshield had taken on the look of a vortex, and she was being sucked into it.

Leo tore his attention away from his phone screen. "What's going on?"

"There's a rest stop up ahead."

"You gotta pee already?" He shifted in his seat, squinting out the windshield.

"Yep. Already. Sorry," she said flatly. "And the snow is seriously starting to trip out my eyes."

"I guess when you haven't driven in it for so long, you forget how." He sighed. "It's been so long, I bet you won't even recognize home."

Everything out of Leo's mouth sounded like a jab. It didn't matter what he said. Every comment was another reminder of the fact that she'd left ten years ago and never looked back.

He was right—but not entirely. It was true, Isabella had left ten years ago. Left Pineridge, left Leo, left her family. But she had returned —once.

No one knew about that trip. No one except for one person.

And that person was dead.

CHAPTER FOUR

LEO

THE SNOW WHIRLED AROUND THE CAR THICKER THAN LEO HAD SEEN IN A long time. The wipers did little to nothing in helping to clear the view. If he was driving his Chevy, and if he wasn't responsible for the life of Norah's maid of honor, he'd at least feel more confident. Christmas Day was a terrible choice for a wedding date. And piss-poor planning if anyone had asked him. But no one had asked him. Because if someone had, he would've also told Norah and Landon to elope. To have an intimate ceremony in Hawaii or the Maldives, anywhere but Colorado at Christmas.

"You sure you can see?" Isabella asked, wrestling out of her coat and tossing it onto the back seat.

She fiddled with the radio and finally landed on a station playing music. Christmas music. He didn't want to hear cheerful bell ringing right now.

"I'm fine," he said. He was from Colorado. Born and raised. He'd driven over a decade through winter conditions.

"The weather shows it's only gonna get worse later," she said as she studied her phone.

"And that's why we're trying to get there before it gets worse." He leaned forward, his vision focused and determined and not at all interested in Isabella's warnings.

"We still have a few more hours at least. The storm should be at its worst soon, but it's supposed to be clear in the morning. Do you think it might be wise to find a hotel and stop for the night? We can leave early in the morning, once the storm has cleared and it's light out." Her tone was laced with condescension.

The last thing Leo wanted to do was spend any more time with Isabella than he had to, never mind staying the night with her at a hotel.

"We're not stopping."

"But Leo—"

He groaned—loudly. "I live in Colorado. I've always lived in Colorado. I've been driving in the snow since before I could make a flip shot." Okay, so that was complete bullshit. He'd been playing hockey since he was three, and he'd learned how to do a flip shot when he was six. But it sounded good, so he went with it.

"This isn't just a little snow. This is ice. And a snowstorm. If you could just take your egotistical head out of your butt for one second—"

"Me? Egotistical?" His voice went up an octave. She had some nerve, firing off accusations like that. "Says the stuck-up New Yorker who's too good for Colorado."

"Stuck up?" She shrieked when the car fishtailed.

Leo ignored Isabella's advice of stopping for the night, along with her name-calling and continued driving, though he did ease off the accelerator. If they stopped now, they'd get caught in the worst part of the storm. But if they kept going, they could stay ahead of it, getting them home around midnight.

Isabella turned the volume all the way down on the radio and slid her phone between her legs so that she had both hands free to grip the oh-shit handle and the console. The only sounds heard in the car were the wipers swishing against the windshield, and Isabella's accelerated breathing.

Leo tried to maintain focus on the road but hearing her breathing like that was insanely distracting. It made his mind travel back to a memory he hadn't visited in so long it resembled a dream. His limbs tangled with Isabella's. Their hot, naked flesh pressed so close. Her sweet breath panting in his ear.

It felt so real, yet so unreachable.

The car slipped, grazing against a patch of ice. Leo gripped the steering wheel, jerking it in the direction of the slide. But it was useless. The car fishtailed and spun them in a complete 360.

Isabella screamed, and Leo instinctively stretched his arm across her chest. She clutched the handle tighter, and her phone flew off her lap.

The car finally came to a full stop. Isabella breathed hard, her chest writhing against his arm.

"Izzy, are you okay?" His words exhaled on a rushed breath.

"I t-think so."

His rib cage tightened. He felt like such a jerk.

"Are you?" she asked. "Okay?"

"Yeah. I'm fine."

They both glanced down at the same time. Leo's arm was still awkwardly outstretched against her chest, his hand curved possessively around one breast. He reeled back, pushing his fingers through his hair.

"Sorry," he muttered.

Isabella shifted in her seat. Cleared her throat. "Is the car…is the car okay?"

Leo glanced at the dash, at the lights and gauges, at the key dangling from the ignition and felt the rumbling of the car as it purred. He switched on the interior light before checking over both shoulders, spotting the luggage still intact in the back.

"I think so. I don't think we hit anything. Just ice."

The two of them gazed out the windshield in silence, except for the sound of his heart thumping loudly in his ears. The headlights shined through the snow giving them a view of a sheet of white. There was a complete absence of both sky and road.

Isabella unbuckled her seatbelt and fished around on the floor, eventually coming back up with her phone.

Leo pushed open his door. "Stay here, I'm gonna check out the car."

The bitter wind assaulted him, freezing snow pelting his face. The snow was too deep to maneuver through, but a quick glance at the front and back ends of the car confirmed the vehicle survived in one piece.

A rumbling sound approached, and he shielded his eyes against the storm. After a semi-truck passed, his shoulders sagged in relief upon finding they were at least safely on the shoulder. He hopped back inside the car, fighting against a gust of wind to yank the door closed.

"We're safe. Car's fine." He rubbed his hands together and breathed into them before grabbing the steering wheel and glancing over his shoulder at the road. He couldn't even see a single set of headlights in either direction.

Isabella grabbed his arm. "Please tell me you're not seriously considering getting back onto the road?"

"You got a better idea?"

"Are you interested in a hotel yet?"

"And how do you suppose we're gonna get to a hotel without driving to it?" He released the steering wheel and rubbed his sweaty palms down his thighs.

"If one is close enough, maybe we could make it." She tapped on her phone. "We have cell service. Let me check if there's a hotel close by."

"I know there's not much between here and home, and I think it's safe to say there's no hotel in the direction we just came. Unless you want to backtrack several miles to Denver?"

"No. Definitely not."

She spent a few more minutes with her attention fixated on her phone screen, but, like he said, he already knew what she'd find. Nothing. There were a lot of picturesque views on this stretch of the freeway, but that was it. He'd traveled this road many times for work, not to mention all of the conventions he'd attended in Denver. But Isabella was obviously still stubborn as hell, so he let her do what she needed just so he could prove he was right. Isabella finally glanced at him, her eyes heavy and sullen. Those full lips drooped at the corners. "The closest hotel is ninety-eight miles ahead. And if we backtracked, the closest one is thirty-six miles."

Leo held up his hands. "Not going to say, 'I told you so,' but I told you so. We're stuck."

"I'm sorry," Isabella said, not fully owning her words.

Because why would she? What was she apologizing for? Maybe

because she knew she was the last person Leo wanted to be stuck in a car with during the biggest snowstorm of the season. Or stuck anywhere with, for any amount of time. He decided he should maybe let her off the hook. At least a little anyway.

"What are you sorry for? I'm the one who was driving. I suppose I should've listened to you and stopped at a hotel earlier."

"It's not like you knew. I mean, you said it yourself, you've been driving through snow and ice for forever."

He tried to ignore the slight edge to her tone. "Yeah," he exhaled a mirthless laugh. "I'm such a pro."

Isabella smiled, and he felt a grin break on his own face. It was one of very few he'd allowed since the two of them reunited at the airport earlier that day.

"It kinda serves you right," Isabella hedged. "All that bragging you did about knowing how to drive in the snow. Like you're some kind of an expert. And now look at us."

"Okay, okay, you made your point." He pushed his seat back, giving his six-foot-four-inches frame more legroom to stretch out. "Guess we better get comfortable. I'm gonna have to turn the car off so we don't kill the battery."

"Wait." She turned to face him. "So not only are we stuck together, but we're going to freeze to death. Together." She breathed out a laugh. "How's that for irony?"

"We're not gonna freeze to death. We can't even stand each other. Do you think we'd let ourselves die together? You know we're both too stubborn to allow that to happen."

He wanted to be angry, but any bitterness evaporated when he looked at Isabella. She bit her lip and fidgeted with the necklace dangling from the sleek column of her throat. With the dim overhead light illuminating her, he couldn't help but stare.

His heart kicked against the cage of his breastbone in a way it hadn't in a long time.

Stupid, stupid heart.

She met his gaze. "What? I'm not going to complain, if that's what you're waiting for."

He just shook his head and leaned back in his seat. What kind of karma was this? Causing him to not only run into Isabella today, but also trapping him in a car with her, their bodies mere inches apart.

He sighed, trying not to think about bodies. Not his, not hers, and definitely not theirs.

Damn. This was going to be a long night.

CHAPTER FIVE

ISABELLA

Leo's reminder that the two of them were together now not because they *wanted* to be but because they *had* to be pinched in Isabella's gut.

They were stuck. Confined. Trapped. After six years apart.

After rummaging in his suitcase, Leo brought out a winter hat and gloves. "You *did* pack your winter clothes?" He had something resembling hope shining in his brown eyes, almost as if he wished she hadn't.

"Of course."

"I'm surprised."

And there it was. Another jab.

"This was my home too, Leo. You don't forget that kind of stuff."

He shrugged, stretching his knit hat over his dark brown hair.

"Believe me, you can't forget the cold," she said. "The frozen toes and fingers." She shivered just thinking about it. She could argue with him that New York was known for icy, cold winters as well, but she didn't have the energy.

"I'm also surprised you refer to Colorado as home," he added.

Great, another jab. But this time to her heart. Just because she hadn't been back in several years didn't mean she loved it any less.

"As long as my parents are there, it will always be home."

"I guess." He gave a half-hearted shrug.

Isabella bit the inside of her cheek—letting this go would be harder than she thought. She climbed onto her knees on the seat and reached in the back for her suitcase. She unzipped it and searched for her winter clothes. Hat, gloves, scarf, wool socks. When she glanced over her shoulder to ask Leo if he thought she'd need her long underwear as well, she caught him staring at her backside.

"Uh-hmm," she cleared her throat, narrowing her eyes in half-amusement, half-indignation.

"Sorry." He whipped his head in the opposite direction. "Wow, that was a blast from the past."

"Excuse me?" she asked, frozen in the same position. "I think my butt has changed in ten years."

"Not *that*. Just," he fumbled over his words as he yanked on his wool socks. "Old habits die hard and all that. Checking you out used to be a reflex. Guess it never went away. Sorry." Pink stained his angled cheeks, and a memory spiked in Isabella's mind—him blushing in tenth grade before their first kiss.

"I guess you checking out my butt is better than you shooting fire at me with your eyes." She set the clothing on the console in between them.

"What are you talking about? Have not," he huffed.

"Have to. And throwing jabs at me every chance you get." She slumped back into the seat and wound the designer scarf around her neck. The gray and black herringbone-patterned wrap had been a Christmas gift from Harrison the year before last.

Leo groaned, pushing his hands into gloves. "Have not."

"And I think you've been making it obvious, too. You want me to feel bad. And guilty."

"No, I don't."

"But news flash, Leo. I already feel bad. So rubbing it in doesn't help. Like it or not, the two of us are gonna be stuck together for all of the wedding festivities."

"Despite what you think, I'm not an idiot—I'm well aware of our situation."

Isabella pushed back her hair before she pulled her knit cap over her head. "I could just kill Norah for choosing to get married in the winter. Never mind the week of Christmas."

"At least we can both agree on that."

"I mean, who does that?"

"Two young, dumb kids who are selfish and in love," Leo said, chuckling.

"Right?" She crossed her arms, sealing in her body heat. "They're so young."

"And dumb," he reminded, pointing a finger at her.

"Right? And selfish."

"Right."

"If I didn't know better, I'd think Norah and Landon did this on purpose."

"Did what?" Leo pressed his head against the headrest, and Isabella stole a second to take in the sight of his straight nose and angled cheekbones, at the unfairness of how even more attractive he'd become with age. When she didn't speak right away, he lifted his head, catching her gawking.

She swallowed. "You know, planned their wedding on Christmas. To get me home. To force the two of us together for longer than a single day."

Leo narrowed his eyes. "They are selfish, aren't they?"

A bit of surprise shimmied through her. Were the two of them actually getting along?

"Okay, fine. Four can play at this game." Leo smirked, taking off his gloves. He reached into the backseat and rummaged around before bringing out a large glass bottle with amber liquid inside. "Wanna drink?" He waggled his thick brows at her mischievously.

She frowned, tilting her head. "I don't understand."

"You see," he said as he twisted the cap off the bottle, "I bought this whiskey for Landon as a bachelor present. It's a Hoffman tradition. But the way I see it is, he doesn't deserve it. Not after conspiring this little plan with Norah—sticking me with you."

"Wow, thanks." That comment actually hurt, twisting in her gut.

"You know what I mean." He held the bottle out to her.

"So you want to drink his present?"

"Exactly."

She shrugged. Why not? What else did she have to do? She had nowhere to go and nowhere to be.

Isabella took a swig, the malty liquid burning once it hit her stomach. She passed the bottle back to Leo.

"Cheers, to Norah and Landon." He took a drink.

Isabella reached for the bottle again. "Hear, hear." She pressed it to her lips and tipped it back. This time, the alcohol warmed her throat, without burning her belly. "May the two young lovebirds have a long, dumb marriage."

Leo chuckled and put his gloves back on. "Along with saying *screw you* to Norah and Landon, this stuff should help keep us warm."

"True." Isabella agreed. "I'm already starting to get cold."

"Here." Leo grabbed her coat from the back seat. She leaned forward and he tucked it over her shoulders. She peered up at him, and for the first time all day, they made eye contact. Not a stolen glance, but *real* eye contact. And it made the world stop.

A shiver of desire coursed through her. Leo always did have mesmerizing brown eyes. She could get lost in them. Make promises she knew she couldn't keep. Her eyes flickered away, breaking the trance.

Leo cleared his throat. Then he reached in the back for his own coat. "What about your long underwear, did you bring those?"

"Of course."

"Why don't you put them on under your pants. You'll stay warmer."

"You think I'm going to get undressed in front of you? I don't think I have enough alcohol in me for that," she teased, the whiskey easing her knotted tension and causing her words to roll off her tongue.

He narrowed his eyes. "Izzy, knock it off. Obviously, I wasn't planning on looking." He shoved his arms into his coat, acting perturbed. "But it's not like it's stuff I haven't already seen," he muttered.

Isabella licked the malty liquid off her lips after taking another swig from the bottle. "Like I said, I'm sure I've changed. It's been a long time."

"It has, and I'm sure you have." Taking the bottle from her, he took a long drink, gulping it down.

She watched his Adam's apple bob, and it created a simmer in her depths. "C'mon, aren't you the least bit curious?" She bantered, unable to help herself.

He choked on the whiskey, dragging the bottle from his lips and wiping the back of his glove against his mouth.

"I mean, you were already looking," she said suggestively.

"Curious? Maybe. Stupid? No."

Isabella snorted a laugh. "Leo, chill. I'm only teasing."

"Yeah? Well, it's mean." He handed her the bottle like he was mad. But his expression revealed otherwise. His face was open and his cheeks pink, reminding her of the boy he once was. The boy she'd loved more than life itself. The one she would've done anything for. Except, keep her promise of returning home after college.

"Besides," he continued after a long beat, "aren't you seeing someone? Some douche that drinks wine and cuffs his jeans at the ankles?"

She gasped. "He doesn't cuff his jeans at the ankles. Well, not anymore."

"And don't you two live together?"

The question threw her for a moment. Not only did it remind her of the heartache she'd been trying to forget, but she was surprised Norah hadn't told him. She assumed Leo knew everything about her life. Because she knew everything about his. Most importantly, how he'd dealt with his mom's death. And how he'd recovered after his divorce from Talia.

"Not anymore."

"No?" He raised a brow at her. It asked so much more than his words did.

"We're sort of…taking a break. One where we don't live together anymore."

"Wow." He tipped his head back, taking another swig from the bottle.

"Yeah." Isabella reached for her long underwear.

"Does your family know?"

"Nope." She unbuttoned her pants. "And I'd like to be the one to tell them. So if you could keep your mouth shut about it, that would be great. Now, look away."

Leo rolled his eyes but adjusted himself in the seat so that he faced the driver's window. "But you plan on telling them?"

She wriggled out of her pants, constantly checking to make sure Leo wasn't looking. She hurried and wrestled with the long underwear. It had been years since she'd worn them. Growing up in Colorado meant that, for a few months out of the year, they were like a second skin. "Yes, I'm going to tell them. I just figured they had enough going on with the wedding and Christmas traditions. Besides, my mom has been hassling me and Harrison to get married. Reminding me that we're already living together so we should just get it over with."

"Except, you're not."

"Right." She caught him staring at her reflection in the window as she yanked her pants back on, which was no easy feat. "You can look now. But you already knew that since you were watching me in the window."

He turned back around. "Reflex." He shrugged.

"Uh-huh. Sure." She eyed him skeptically, but the idea of knowing he couldn't help himself from checking her out caused a rush of heat throughout her body.

"You warm enough now?"

Oh, things were definitely warming up.

She bit the inside of her cheek. "I guess."

"I can turn the heater on once in a while."

"Or…" she said, catching her lower lip between her teeth.

With his hand on the keychain dangling from the ignition, Leo glanced over his shoulder at her.

"You could warm me up." *Oh dear God, what was she saying?* Her cheeks burned. Was the whiskey already getting to her? She knew she became more forward once she had a little alcohol in her, but this was Leo. "You know, body heat and all. And so we don't run out of gas."

"Right, body heat. Guess I hadn't thought of that." He dropped his hand from the key, eyes narrowed. "But…we should probably set some ground rules, don't you think?"

"Oh for sure, most definitely."

"If we do this, it's strictly to stay warm. No funny business." He raised a brow.

"Why would there be? We can't stand each other, remember?"

"Right."

He flipped off the overhead light. "Don't want to kill the battery."

But it was obvious to her, he was stalling.

Leo fumbled at first, uncertain where to put his hands, so she helped him out by taking his arm and tucking herself under it, nuzzling into his chest. "See, strictly warmth. No funny business."

"Good." He exhaled. "Better?"

"Much."

Leo's chest felt firm against her face. How much had his body changed since they were teenagers? Imagining the solid pecs beneath his shirt piqued her curiosity.

Back then, Leo had already been mostly filled out with muscle. He played as centerman on their high school's hockey team. He was good at it too. So good, he could've gone pro. Scouts from colleges from all over the country were coming to his games to watch him play when he was only a sophomore.

It had been the first time Leo allowed himself to dream about the possibility of leaving Colorado. After sneaking out of her bedroom window and climbing into his, the two of them would talk about what college team he'd play for. What pro team he could end up on. Where she could go to write. What magazine or newspaper would hire her. Where the two could buy a home and start a family. Somewhere with picturesque scenery so Leo could still dabble in his photography.

But then his mom got sick. And all his dreams—their dreams—disintegrated. He felt he had no choice but to accept the full-ride scholarship and play for the Denver Pioneers at University of Denver so he could stay close to home. Isabella had to make an impossible choice, to give up on her dreams as well and stay in Colorado with him or go to Ithaca College in New York. She'd chosen New York, and nothing had been the same since.

She and Leo sat frozen for several minutes, neither saying a word. But what words they *weren't* saying rang loud and clear anyway. The sexual tension was as thick as smoke. Isabella dared a move. She ran her hand up his torso to rest on his chest. He tensed, but she could feel his heart racing beneath her palm. The intensity of her desire for him was so shocking and at the same time made complete sense. He was familiar. He was home.

Her stomach tightened, and she felt like her body may go into convulsions if he didn't kiss her soon. It was a stupid thought. Why would he kiss her? He hated her.

"Hey, Leo?"

"Hmm?" He ran his chin over the top of her head, sending goosebumps dancing over her skin.

"I've been thinking."

"About what?" His question came out breathy, or maybe it only sounded that way to her ears.

"If we don't want to freeze to death together…" She hesitated. What *was* she thinking? She was usually more subtle than this. But not only was she freezing—this was Leo. And she had no doubt in her mind, as insane as it was, and even though the timing could not possibly be worse, she wanted him. "Maybe we need to do everything in our power to stay warm. You know, so we don't die?"

Leo stiffened, jerking his head back to look down at her.

She peered up at him, biting her lip.

"You do realize this is just the whiskey talking, right?" He scrubbed a hand down his face. "Jeez, alcohol still makes you frisky."

He knew her too well.

She ran her hand down his stomach, and he caught her wrist, gently though. "Izzy. Come on."

"You don't want to die, right?" She knew she sounded utterly ridiculous, but she also knew she was getting to him. She loved that she somehow still had this effect on him, even after all this time.

"No. No I do not." He took a deep breath and mumbled something unintelligible. After a long moment, he rested his gloved hand against her flushed cheek. "So what you're saying is, we need to sacrifice our dislike of each other, so we don't end up freezing to death…together?"

"Exactly." She smiled and pressed her body closer to him.

He held her gaze. His voice dipped low, "What do you want, Izzy? Tell me."

She swallowed, hard, summoning the remains of her liquid courage. She answered him by leaning into him and drawing her lips to his.

He didn't meet her halfway, and she nearly changed her mind. But again, this was Leo. She missed the way she knew his kiss, his lips, his tongue, and that was enough to propel her mouth forward.

He licked his lips right before she planted them with a kiss. It didn't take long for him to respond. He took charge of her mouth, flicking his tongue against hers and gripping her back, pulling her into a tight embrace.

Isabella took his face in her palms, but the bulky winter gloves were awkward. She tore them off, tossing them, and they landed on the driver's side floor. Leo ripped his gloves off as well. Then he reached for her again, guiding her over the console, though not with ease. Her knee banged into console and then the shifter. She yelped before she relaxed onto his lap, straddling him.

He slid the seat back, giving them both more room. She touched his face, grazing her fingertips over the ragged scruff and sending a zing low in her belly. Even though she'd kissed Leo probably a million times before, she'd never kissed Leo as a man. That thought, along with the feeling of his lips sucking hers was thrilling.

He reached for Isabella's coat, and she helped by shrugging it off her shoulders and slipping her arms free. He ran his fingers up her back, underneath her shirt and around to cup her breasts, sending a thrill through her blood.

Isabella pushed Leo's knit hat off his head, spreading her fingers through his long, soft hair. The whiskey, along with passionate kissing, had Isabella's body on fire. If they kept this up, they definitely would not freeze to death.

Leo reached for the button on her pants, flicking it undone with ease. She helped him wriggle out of his heavy jacket. He unzipped her jeans, but the layer of long underwear, all thick and bulky, would be a problem.

One time, when Leo and Isabella were teenagers, she'd fallen through the ice while they were skating on the pond in spring. Leo rescued her out of the freezing water, stripping off all her winter layers of clothing and using his body heat and a blanket to warm her until it was safe enough to put her in the bath. He told her he thought he was going to lose her that day.

"Remember that day I fell through the ice? You saved me that day. You always saved me," she panted.

Leo jerked his head backward and leaned against the seat. "What?"

"Nothing. Just forget it." She leaned forward and pressed her lips to the hot skin on his neck.

"Izzy, don't." He held her by the forearms, and whatever magic had drawn them together evaporated.

"I'm sorry, I didn't—"

"You're breaking your rule again." He picked her up and helped her —well, practically shoved her—back into the passenger seat.

"We have a past, Leo. Did you honestly think we could spend all week together and not talk about it?"

"Yeah, well, you're the one who made the rule." He found her gloves on the floor near his feet and handed them to her.

She snatched them out of his grasp. "It was a stupid rule. Made to protect my heart."

"*Your* heart? Give me a break."

"What? You think you're the only one who came away with a broken heart? That I got off scot-free?"

"You sure act like it."

"No, I don't. And how would you know? We haven't been together in six years." She shoved her arms back into her jacket.

"And whose fault is that?"

"Oh!" She threw her flustered hands up. "Here we go again."

"C'mon, Izz, you can't blame me for throwing it in your face. You're the one who made promises. You're the one who broke them." He pointed his finger in her face, which maybe hurt the most.

"Fine. You're right." She readjusted her hat, pulling it down further on her head and curled in a ball on the seat.

"And there you go." He raised his voice, zipping up his coat. "You just accept the blame."

"What am I supposed to do? Huh, Leo?"

"Give me an explanation!" he yelled.

Leo's shout shook the car and vibrated in her chest. Tears pricked the corners of her eyes, and the ache in her stomach felt unbearable. How had this night taken such a drastic turn?

"I can't," she mumbled.

"Right, what's new." He adjusted himself in the driver's seat, crossing his arms and leaning his head against the headrest.

She hugged her knees to her chest and faced the window, struggling against the tears threatening to break free. She didn't want it to happen, but she couldn't stop it—the hard shell sheltering Isabella's heart grew another layer.

CHAPTER SIX

LEO

Faint light filled the car, waking Leo early. When he pried open his eyes, he realized just *how* early. The sky was void of the sun. Possibly the moon was still shining. Instantly, he shivered, too aware of how cold he was; his bones felt frozen inside his body.

He tore off his gloves and wriggled the car key from his pocket, jamming it into the ignition. When he did, Isabella stirred in the passenger seat.

He glanced at her. Still freaking beautiful, damn her.

Her teeth began to chatter, and she wiped the sleep from her eyes. She shifted in her seat, finally noticing him next to her, and they accidentally made eye contact, which had led to all sorts of bad last night, so he looked away.

The horrendous memories of their alcohol-filled make-out sesh from the night before flooded his mind. What had he been thinking?

She groaned and pressed a palm against her forehead.

"My feelings exactly," he muttered, adjusting the heater settings and vents.

"What time is it?" she asked on a yawn.

"Early. But not early enough. We need to get on the road." He scrubbed his hands down his rough face.

"Fine with me. The sooner we get back on the road, the sooner we get coffee. My head is pounding."

Leo pulled his beanie down over his ears, cranked the defrost dial to full blast, and zipped his coat up to his neck before heading outside to clear the snow off the car. Semitrucks whirled by, beaming headlights through the dim morning. Without an ice scraper or snow brush, he improvised and used his arm to clean off the windshield.

He hopped back inside, and they both remained quiet as Leo merged the car into the sparse traffic. Silence was perfectly fine with him—concentrating on the winter road conditions seemed like a better idea than talking. Thinking was bad enough. If it had only taken a few hours with Isabella and a little alcohol to cloud his judgment, what would happen after an entire week?

They stayed silent until he spotted the first gas station adorned in twinkling, colored Christmas lights and with a small food mart attached. It was a relief Isabella hadn't tried striking up a conversation before then. He wasn't sure he was prepared to talk about last night.

Not yet, and maybe not ever.

"Good Lord, finally. Coffee," Isabella said.

While Leo filled the tank with gas, Isabella went inside the food mart, taking a small bag with her. He hurried and used the bathroom while the gas finished pumping. He pulled the car into a parking spot, checking the time on his phone impatiently—5:50 a.m. He debated on sending a text to his dad or Landon but decided against it. The last thing he wanted to do was wake them early. Dad was usually up by six thirty in the morning.

The passenger door opened, and Leo was about to exhale a dramatic, *Finally*, but before he could, Isabella handed him a Styrofoam cup embellished with mistletoe and candy canes. He raised an untrusting brow at her.

"Truce?" She smiled.

He wasn't amused by her choice of wording, but he was enticed by the coffee, so he accepted and tipped the cup at her. "Thanks." He took a sip and the bitter brew bit at his tongue. It was black—just how he liked it, but it tasted stronger than he preferred. Regardless, it was caffeine, so he gulped another drink while he pulled back onto the road.

"So," she hedged. "Do you think we should talk about last night?"

A blur of her tempting, naked flesh fogged his mind momentarily—the feel of her in his hands, on his tongue.

Leo clenched his jaw. "Nope."

ABOUT AN HOUR AND A HALF LATER, Leo pulled up in front of Isabella's childhood split-level home where her parents still lived. He realized only now, the differences in contrast to the Whitley's home versus Dad's dated one next door. For years Dad had been too busy with the business —Hoffman and Son's Electric—to maintain it. Lately though, he'd been allowing Leo to help him with smaller renovations on the house, like new windows.

But there were other differences too, like Christmas lights on the Whitley's home. Garlands draped across the front, hiding the gutters. A full set of reindeer stood in the thick snow in the yard. Mr. W. even had one of those blow-up Santas. In contrast, the Hoffman home was bare, not looking like it was Christmas at all. Mom had always been the one to rally Dad into decorating the home. She'd put up both the menorah and a Christmas tree to honor hers and Dad's traditions.

"It's showtime," Isabella said through sing-song sarcasm.

"Good luck," he muttered. It was the first exchange they'd had since the coffee truce.

She pursed her lips and glared at him before climbing out of the car.

He waited for a moment and peered out the windshield, watching as Mr. and Mrs. Whitley stepped out of the house and onto the porch. Mr. W. still wore his flannel pajama pants and slippers, his short, light brown hair sticking up, and Mrs. W. donned an apron tied at her waist, her makeup and hair impeccable as always.

Norah barreled out and pushed past them both, clomping down the paved walkway dressed in a pair of oversized snow boots. Leo hesitantly climbed out of the car in time to watch Norah tackle Isabella in a hug, nearly landing both of them in the snowdrift next to the driveway.

"Izzy, you're finally here!" Norah squealed.

"I know, right. *Finally*."

Norah released Isabella and ran toward Leo, flinging her gangly arms around his waist. "Thank you," she muttered against his chest. "So glad you're back."

"Yeah, me too." He patted Norah's shoulder before she released him, then he reached into the back seat for the luggage.

"Well, aren't you two chummy?" Isabella mumbled.

He wasn't sure if the snippy comment was intended for his ears or Norah's.

Norah rushed at Isabella, taking her by the hands and dragging her toward the house. "C'mon, Izzy, there's so much we need to do before Finn and Nina get here and little Ava wants to steal all of your attention. Starting with you trying on your maid of honor dress."

"No problem," he called to absolutely no one. "I got the luggage." He shook his head and grumbled under his breath as Norah pulled Isabella up the front steps and he tried not to be obvious about lurking.

Isabella stopped on the porch and hugged Mr. Whitley.

"Hey, sweetie."

"Hi, Dad. The house looks great." She gestured at the lights.

"Thanks. But I can't take all the credit. Leo and Landon helped."

"Oh yeah?" Isabella glanced over her shoulder to where Leo now stood at the bottom of the porch steps, luggage in tow—her luggage.

He gave her a tight smile. He'd play nice. Especially when the parentals were around. But she ignored him and moved onto greeting her mother. He felt like chucking her suitcase straight into the snowdrift. If Mr. and Mrs. W. weren't standing right there, he would've done just that.

"Hey, Mom, you're looking as beautiful as ever."

"Oh, stop it, always bringing the compliments. But never bringing herself for a visit." Mrs. Whitley hugged her.

Isabella jerked back and set a hand on Mrs. Whitley's shoulder. "Mom, I'm here now, aren't I?"

"Well yeah, because of Norah's wedding." She untied her apron, showing off a classic Mrs. W. Christmas sweater—a snowman with embellished button eyes. "If it wasn't for Norah getting married on Christmas Day, would you have made it home this year?"

It was awkward being present for their reunion. He shouldn't care what words they exchanged. But a small part of him felt defensive for Isabella. But why? For years, he'd looked forward to this moment—when her family would finally accuse her of abandoning them. Because he wasn't the only one she'd ran out on.

Isabella cleared her throat and squared her shoulders, taking on the resemblance of the woman he first encountered at the airport yesterday. "Why don't we just focus on the traditions and Norah's wedding."

Mrs. Whitley's expression remained tight, and she pushed her glasses up the bridge of her nose. Leo suspected she wanted to have it out with her daughter right then, right there. But instead, she pressed her lips together and gave a curt nod.

"Izzy is right," Mr. Whitley said, putting an arm around her shoulder. "She's home now, and that's all that matters." He finally took the suitcases. "Thanks, Leo."

Leo nodded. "Not a problem." A small lie. Isabella herself was an enormous problem. A growth attaching to his body. A huge pain in his ass. Getting her here was only half of the issue. Putting up with her for the next week would be even bigger. Did she even know he'd been invited to join the festivities of Eight Days of Christmas?

"And...now that she's here," Norah took Isabella by the hand, "we have wedding stuff to do. C'mon, I'll show you the dress. I think you're really gonna love it." As Norah dragged her into the house, Isabella glanced over her shoulder again, training her eyes on him like she was scared she would never see him again. Which was ridiculous.

In an instant, he was reminded of the night before. His hands on her hot, naked skin, her wet lips sliding against his as she straddled him, the soft lace of her bra—and the almost *huge* mistake.

"Oh, Leo." Mrs. Whitley took his hand, sticking an ice pick into his thoughts. "How can we ever repay you for getting Izzy home safely?"

"No payment necessary, ma'am." He turned to head back down the steps when a gentle hand gripped his shoulder. He spun around, and Mrs. Whitley gathered him in a tight hug.

"Thank you," she whispered into his ear.

He tried not to cling to the woman like a lifeline, but she had been the closest thing he had to a mother since he lost his own six years before. He inhaled her scent of cinnamon and jerked away.

"Like I said, not a problem." He rushed down the steps, making a beeline for the rental car to grab his duffel bag.

"So we'll catch you later then?" Mr. Whitley hollered while Leo had his head stuffed inside the car.

He retrieved his bag and locked the rental. "Here, would you mind giving these to Isabella?" He tossed the keys to Mr. Whitley who caught them in the air.

"You *are* planning on joining us for day one, aren't you?"

Leo started to cross the distance between the two homes considering how to respond. A constant shoveled path kept it clear for Landon and Norah to quickly travel back and forth. Why hadn't he and Isabella thought to do that when they dated?

"Yeah," he finally called over his shoulder. "I'll be there." Under his breath, he muttered, "with frickin' bells on."

CHAPTER SEVEN

ISABELLA

Isabella eavesdropped from the front entryway as her mom crooned all over Leo. She couldn't help but roll her eyes. Leo had always been Mom's favorite Hoffman, and apparently that hadn't changed.

"Are Mom and Dad always like that? You know, with Leo?" Isabella asked as she slipped off her designer boots.

"Like what?" Norah asked.

"Never mind."

She took in the familiarity of the home. The scent combination of gingerbread and cinnamon warmed Isabella's body and assaulted her mind with about a million memories. Christmastime at the Whitley home had always been a magical season. While Dad worked on decorating the outside, wrangling Finn to help him, Mom transformed the inside of the home. Her collection of snowmen figures covered every square inch of surface.

Matching stockings for each family member hung over the mantle above the wood burning fireplace. Reading over the names—Finn, Nina, Ava—Isabella's chest tightened. It had been two years since she'd seen her brother, sister-in-law, and niece when they'd visited her in New York. Ava was five already. Her throat went thick. Watching her niece grow up on FaceTime suddenly didn't sit right. "Izzy?" Norah called from the stairs.

Disoriented, Isabella shook her head. "Right." She followed Norah up the stairs and down the hall. In a way, it felt as if she hadn't ever left. And when she stepped into the bedroom she grew up in, she didn't think she had.

Isabella turned in a 360-degree spin. The same pink comforter with red roses and red ruffled bed skirt covered the daybed. The pink walls had posters from popular bands from the 2000s, and a heart-shaped bulletin board displayed photos of her and her friends. And Leo.

Valentine's cards and birthday cards sat in an inch of dust on the bookcase. She picked up a card and read the signature, "Love, Leo." A bubble of nostalgia arose in her gut. Her old bedroom looked as if it threw up Leo all over it.

Besides the treadmill crammed in the corner, the wedding decorations piled around it, and a plastic-protected dress smoothed out on the bed, the room looked just how she left it ten years ago. When she left, she'd been naive in her assumption that she'd be back and someday planning her own wedding. She figured she'd pack all this stuff and take it to the home her and Leo would share. Literally nothing had gone the way she'd planned.

"Okay, I think you're gonna love this." Norah slipped the white plastic off the dress and held up the long, frilly gown. "What do you think?" She bit her lower lip, her eyes wide, anticipation beaming.

The dress—while in Isabella's favorite color, red—was a nightmare. A *sleeveless* nightmare at that. It was an outdoor wedding; the giant white tent and standing heaters would do little to block out the cold. Standing outside and exposed to the Colorado winter conditions during a wedding ceremony in a sleeveless dress had to have been Norah's craziest idea yet.

"It's um…it's pretty."

"Right? I knew you'd love the color. But don't you love all the material?" Norah ran her dainty hand over the frills.

"Um, sure." Isabella touched the dress. It felt scratchy. What *was* this material? Rayon?

Norah smoothed the dress across the bed gently, gazing longingly at it. "Oh, Izzy, I'm just so glad you're here." She yanked her sister's hand and pulled her onto the bed, sitting next to one another. "I've missed you. There's so much I've needed you for."

Norah's sincerity ballooned in Isabella's tight chest. "Me? Why me? You've got Mom and Nina."

"They're great, don't get me wrong. But they aren't my big sister. C'mon, Izzy, you know I've always looked up to you."

Isabella did know, though she wasn't sure why. She'd taken a completely different course in life than Norah was obviously headed.

"You know how important your approval is to me."

Isabella's mind snagged on that last comment, causing her stomach to twist uncomfortably. Being happy for Norah was the easy part. She'd be happy if Norah was happy. But if Norah wanted her approval, that was something entirely different. Because if she could've been honest, she worried Norah was rushing into this wedding. Sure, Landon was a great guy who clearly loved Norah. But they were so young. So, so young. Or at least Norah was young. She was only twenty-two. Landon was twenty-six. Twenty-two couldn't possibly be old enough to know for sure that she wanted to spend the rest of her life with someone. Of all people, Isabella should know that. She was twenty-nine and wasn't even sure if the relationship with Harrison was worth trying to fix.

Isabella admired her little sister, taking in her long reddish-brown hair, her upturned nose that matched her own, and she cleared her throat, squeezing Norah's hand. "You know all I want for you is that you're happy."

Norah's eyes went glossy and dreamy. "And I am. I really am."

She looked it. So what could Isabella do but bite her tongue? She couldn't break Norah's heart and tell her the truth—that she thought Norah could very well be making the biggest mistake of her life.

Isabella forced a smile. "Then I am, too."

Oh, the maid of honor dress fit Isabella just fine. But it was hard to tell either way, what with the gigantic red sash-y bow across her chest and the layers upon layers of scratchy, frilly fabric. Norah always had impeccable taste, so what was the meaning behind these atrocious bridesmaid's dresses?

Isabella stared at her lone reflection in the full-length mirror in disgust. She tugged on the zipper from behind, attempting to free herself from the monstrosity because she couldn't stand to be in it a second longer, but it got stuck partway. After fidgeting with it several times, she gave up.

She cracked the door open and hollered down the hallway. "Hey, Norah? Would you come back up here for a sec? I need some help." She maneuvered her arm over her shoulder, inching her fingers down her back toward the zipper. The door pushed open, and she spun around. "Finally," she exhaled.

But to her horror, it wasn't Norah standing there.

Leo dropped his head and laughed. Out loud. Without even bothering to hide it.

She pinched her lips into a pout. "Shut up," she muttered, her face burning with embarrassment. "It's not funny."

"Oh, c'mon, it's a little funny." He grinned.

"Would you just come over here and unzip me, please?"

"Well, since you asked so nicely." He playfully narrowed his eyes. "Turn around."

Isabella hesitated, sucking her lips in between her teeth and turned, holding up her hair. The next few moments felt like an eternity as she waited for him to close the distance between them. She didn't so much as hear him approach as feel him though, his presence and scent and heat suddenly surrounding her.

She squeezed her eyes shut when she felt him grip the dress, felt his warm breath cascade down the back of her neck. He slid the zipper down slowly. She sucked in a breath, the zipper gliding even lower. Her eyes fluttered open at the touch of his gentle fingertips skimming the skin of her back.

Stealing a glance at him in the full-length mirror, his gaze suddenly met hers, his brown eyes dark and lustful.

"There you go. All done." He cleared his throat, but his voice sounded husky.

"Thank you." She faced him, pressing her hand flat against the top of the dress to hold it in place.

Leo's vision moved over her, head to toes, and back up, her skin burning under his gaze. He quirked a thick, dark brow. "Landon certainly has some interesting taste."

She shook her head. "Wait, what? What does Landon have to do with this?"

"You didn't actually think Norah chose these hideous dresses, did you?" He waved a finger at the dress.

"Well, she said she knew I'd love it. She said it was my favorite color. So, I just thought…I mean…I assumed." She turned and gazed at her reflection in the mirror. Leo was right. Norah would never pick this dress. But why would she let Landon pick out her bridesmaid's dresses? "Are you for real?"

"Yep."

"But why?" She stared at herself in the mirror again, slack-jawed, careful not to give Leo a view of her backside.

"Norah has let Landon have a say in almost every wedding decision. For some reason, he actually cares. And Norah thinks compromise is a big part of a successful marriage." Leo put up his hands. "But hey," he said, as he moved back to the door, "what do I know?"

There was something in his tone. A knowledge, maybe discernment. Because out of the two of them and Norah and Landon, Leo did know. He was the only one with experience in that department—even if he wasn't offering up advice.

"I'm sure compromise does have a lot to do with a successful marriage but letting him choose the bridesmaids dresses? I think that's a little too far."

"Yeah, you would," he said gruffly.

"What's that supposed to mean?" Her face heated, and she nearly released the top of the dress to slam her fists to her hips.

"Nothing, forget it."

"You're the one who's divorced," she spat out unintentionally.

He took a step backward. "Wow. Alright."

Isabella pinched the bridge of her nose, regretting her words. "Leo, I'm sorry."

"It's fine."

"No." She glanced down at her shuffling feet that still wore the fuzzy, thick winter socks from the night before. "It's not fine. I mean, at least you put yourself out there. At least you found love. You committed to it and saw it through. That's more than I can say for myself."

There was an excruciatingly long pause of silence between them. She chewed on her bottom lip, contemplating her next words. She and Leo would never get back to where they were, how close they were, and she didn't necessarily want that. But they needed to get along for the sake of family—for Norah and Landon. But how could they do that when they couldn't be in the same room for more than two minutes before they were either thinking with teenage hormones or bickering until they were both blue in the face?

"Finn and Nina are almost here," Dad called from down the stairs, interrupting their tension. "T-minus ten minutes until the first day of Eight Days of Christmas!"

"Guess I better let you change out of that dress. It's almost snowman contest time. The fun officially begins." His eyes twinkled with mischief, then he turned and walked out of the room.

"Hey, wait a minute." She rushed to the door

Leo stopped, then spun around slowly. "What is it, Izzy."

With one hand, she gripped the door jam, and with the other, held the top of the dress. "You're not planning on joining in the snowman contest, are you?"

"'Fraid so."

"Seriously?"

"Norah and Landon asked me if I would. What was I supposed to say?" He tugged at the collar of his Henley, like it was choking him.

"You say, *thanks, but no thanks*." She threw a hand up. "You say, *nope, absolutely not*." She took long strides down the hall toward him. "You say, *not until pigs fly*. You say, *not a chance in hell*." She stood in front of him, her hand still clutching the top of the dress and the other pressed to her jutted hip, her eyes trained on his.

"Why? Because it makes you uncomfortable having me here?"

She stared at him, silently.

"Look, I've been a part of this tradition and this family for a helluva long time. Years when you were nowhere to be seen. So no, Izzy. I'm not gonna skip out on today and let them down. Like you've been doing for years."

Isabella gasped, and tears stung her eyes. But she would not let them fall.

She took a deep breath and lifted her chin. "Fine. But just so we're clear, I don't need you reminding me of my mistakes, Leo. I live with them every day."

He arched a brow. "As do I." He turned for the stairs but paused, his hand tight on the newel post. He scrubbed his other hand over his unshaven face and looked at her. "Listen. Let's not ruin this for your family. Let's just go out there like the two sensible adults we are and have a good time." A small laugh left him. "Besides, now that we're no longer teammates, I'm looking forward to destroying you in this contest. I can almost taste the sweet victory." With that, he winked and vanished downstairs.

Oh, oh no. Sensible? Fat chance.

She flung herself around and stomped back to her room, the itchy fabric swishing against her skin. She was going to kick Leo Hoffman's arrogant ass.

BUNDLED up in all her winter clothing, including a pair of borrowed snow boots from Norah that were a size too small, Isabella waited in the driveway to hug Finn, Nina, and Ava after they exited their car. Seeing Ava in person rather than on Facetime revealed how much she'd really grown since her last visit to New York. Isabella longed to catch up with her niece and curl up in front of the fireplace, drink spiked eggnog, and visit with her brother and sister-in-law. But that would have to wait. Dad was way too excited to get the first day of traditions underway, even ushering Ava into the front yard after she'd hugged each family member.

"But Grandpa, I have to go potty," Ava whined.

"Dad, it's a two-hour drive from Denver. It's not gonna kill us to wait a couple of minutes." Finn nudged Ava toward the house and Nina relaxed her shoulders at this.

"Fine, fine," Dad muttered. "But hurry."

"Can't believe you actually made it home this year, sis," Finn sneered.

Oh goody, the digs just continue.

"And *I* can't believe you took an entire week off work. You sure the clinic can function without you? I'm sure there's tons of emergencies for an ears, nose, and throat doctor to tend to," she challenged.

"I own the clinic, so no, it can't really function without me. And I always take the week of Eight Days of Christmas off. You'd know that if you ever came home once in a while." Nina cleared her throat, and Finn relented. "In all seriousness, it's really good to have you home."

Isabella willed a smile.

Mom scattered the snowman tools and accessories out on the snow while the family, including Landon and Leo slowly gathered around. Isabella tried to ignore Leo. She eyed Great Grandpa's old bowler hat. If she was going to beat Leo, she needed that hat. Ava zipped out of the house, yanking her knit hat over her ears.

"Okay. Because it's nearly Norah's special day, I'm letting her choose the teams this year," Dad announced.

Norah beamed.

"Wow. This is huge," Landon said. "Well, don't leave us in suspense."

"Obviously, Landon and I, we make a good team. So I figured why not just do couples? Finn and Nina, Mom and Dad, Ava can join Grandma and Grandpa, and…" Her voice trailed while her eyes fixed on Isabella and Leo.

Isabella's stomach rolled, and her throat went dry. Why hadn't she seen this coming earlier? Of course Norah would force her and Leo on the same team. Isabella would rather be on a team with her five-year-old niece than him.

"You've got to be kidding me," she complained.

Norah dipped her chin "Sorry, Izz."

"I can be with Izzy," Nina suggested.

"No way," Finn protested. "Izzy always wins. I mean, she used to always win."

Isabella rolled her eyes.

"He's not wrong," Mom chimed in.

This was going to happen all week long, wasn't it? Isabella thought it was rough to hear jabs from Leo the day before, but could she survive an entire week of her family teasing her?

"And since you've been gone," Finn added, "Nina and I have won."

"Really?" Isabella glanced at Nina. How had she not known her sister-in-law carried a competitive trait? Sure, the occasional FaceTime and the few visits they'd made to New York to see her had been great. But she supposed that didn't mean she *knew*, knew her.

"You haven't seen anything yet." Finn high-fived his wife. "She's got skills. Just you wait."

"Izzy is fine," Dad said. "She and Leo are both adults. They can handle being on a team."

"Thanks, Dad," Isabella said. She was grateful for his confidence, but she could see the uncertainty in his eyes. It was a bit unsettling how well he knew her and Leo. As per their conversation literally ten minutes ago, they had clearly not grown up. She turned to him, trying to decide whether or not she could be mature about any of this. "We'll be fine. Right, Leo?"

"Oh, yeah. Just peachy." He smirked.

"See, that's our boy," Mom said.

Isabella whipped around. *What the hell was that?* Had Leo somehow replaced her in her own family? It felt as if everyone had pretty much said *forget you* to Isabella, and he was Mr. Boy Wonder. Screw that. If she wanted to regain the respect she'd lost, she would need to take back the title as winner of the snowman contest.

"Whatever," Isabella muttered. "Just say go so we can beat you all and get back into the house where it's warm."

"Those are some big words, missy." Mom shook a finger at her.

"That's right, Mom. Why don't you just give up and quit now?" Isabella already had her eyes on the perfect carrot laid out on the snow in a pile surrounded by buttons, scarves, and hats.

"Not a chance." Mom's smile shined through crinkled eyes.

"Whoa, Mom is bringing it this year," Norah said. "Guess we better not hold her back any longer. Alright, let's do it. Go!"

Isabella made a beeline for the perfect carrot. Not too big and without a weird squiggly shape. But when she went for the big black buttons, Finn went for them at the same time. She had to hip check him to get her hands on them.

"Oh, you wanna play dirty, huh? Okay, it's on." Finn snatched Great Grandpa Whitley's hat—which was of course the best snowman cap.

"No worries, we can still win with this." She picked up the remaining hat, a multicolored knitted hat that Norah made years ago when she'd been learning how to crochet. It had gotten stinky over the years of sitting outside wet from the snow. Her hopes of winning dwindled in her chest.

"Ha! Yeah right!" Finn laughed and took off toward Nina who was already busying herself with a good-sized snowball.

Isabella grabbed a scarf and hurried toward Leo who was just standing there, hands on his trim hips, watching her. "Well don't just stand there," she sneered. "You should've already been working on the bottom. You know you're the one who does the bottom while I grab the accessories. What's wrong with you?" She groaned, pushing past him and tossing all the materials into a pile on the snow.

"Uh, what's wrong with me is it's been a long time since *we've* done this." Leo stayed frozen in place.

"Don't start with me, Leo. C'mon, help me. We can't let them win." She knelt in the snow, grateful her old snow pants from her teen years still fit her, though they were a little snug over her full hips. She formed snow into a tight ball before rolling it across the yard.

Leo shrugged. "Fine. But if we win, what's in it for me?" He followed Isabella, working on the bottom of the snowman.

"Duh. Bragging rights. Just like always." She crumpled a handful of snow in her glove and threw it at him. He ducked, and it skimmed his shoulder.

He retaliated by crawling toward her, grabbing hold of her wrists, and pinning her to the cold ground, threatening her with a snowball to the face. She squealed, fighting against the pressure of his body against hers, her wrists caught in his grasp. It was difficult to deny the sexual tension building between them, but acting on it now, in front of her family, would not only be foolish but ludicrous.

Though when she desisted in her struggling, her body stilling, Isabella stared up into Leo's dark brown eyes, captivated by the way he was looking at her—with intent and desire. She couldn't pull her attention away.

"See," Dad mumbled from somewhere in the distance, "I told you Izzy and Leo could handle being on the same team." Then he chuckled.

Heat rushed at Isabella's cheeks. Leo cleared his throat and released her wrists. He helped her up to a sitting position, and she adjusted her jacket. He gave her a lopsided smile before returning to work on their snowman.

Leo crouched low and pushed the ball of snow across the yard in a straight line. Dear God, how had his ass gotten even better? She scrubbed a cold, wet glove down her face.

Keeping her distance from him was going to be harder than she imagined.

CHAPTER EIGHT

LEO

Isabella huffed while she rolled the body of the snowman. Leo averted his eyes so he wouldn't be tempted to appreciate how she filled out her snow pants in all the right places. With her so close, he lowered his voice and pressed her for an answer to his earlier inquiry. "Well?"

"Well, what?" She cocked her head, her long brown hair cascading over her shoulder.

"What do I get if I help us win?"

Isabella pinned him with a look. "Well, I'm definitely not gonna reward you with a kiss or a glimpse of my boobs this time, if that's what you're getting at."

He exhaled a mirthless laugh. Her face pinked, and not from the cold. He'd already gotten a kiss. Got more than a look at her boobs, too.

Mr. Whitley cleared his throat, loudly and dramatically. "You two know we can hear you, right? And this isn't something a dad wants to hear about his teenage daughter."

Oh, if that man only knew the things his daughter had done to Leo back in the day.

"I'm surprised you care," Isabella sneered, finishing the snowman's body. "Since it's Mr. Boy Wonder we're referring to."

Mr. Whitley ignored her.

Mr. Boy Wonder?

He couldn't help himself.

"I think I already got that reward last night," Leo mumbled, though barely loud enough for even Isabella to hear.

Inching toward him on her knees, Isabella rolled the snowman's head and paused. She leaned in close to him and whispered low, "Well then, let's say you've had your reward in advance."

Her breathy tone made his blood stir, and he grinned. Bending down, he picked up the body of the snowman and rested it on the bottom ball, assuring it was secure before Isabella set the head on top. They remained quiet, working side by side while continuing to assemble the snowman. Leo added the stick arms and a scarf. Isabella pushed on the button eyes and a carrot nose, topping the head with the hat.

When it was completely assembled, they stood back and admired their work while the others laughed and scrambled to finish. It looked good, but something was wrong. And by the way Isabella's face contorted, it was obvious she saw it too.

Leo crossed his arms. "It's missing something."

"It is," she agreed. "But what?"

The two of them mulled it over for a few minutes, Isabella fidgeting with the zipper of her winter coat.

"We're not gonna win. Not without Great Grandpa's baller hat," Isabella said, defeated.

Leo dodged a snowball hurtling at his head. He glanced around. The other teams were finishing up, and Ava and Finn chucked snowballs at one another. He and Isabella were running out of time. But then he remembered something he'd seen online last Christmas.

"Hey, I've got an idea." He took the head off the snowman and rested it on the ground.

Isabella gasped. "Whoa, wait a minute. What are you doing?"

"Just trust me." He disassembled the snowman, removing every accessory.

"Don't you think you should run this idea by me first? You know, your partner?"

Partner? She had some nerve referring to him as a partner. If they had truly been partners, she would've shared her intentions about never returning home after college instead of going rogue.

"Exactly. If I'm your partner, you should trust me." He couldn't hide the edge to his voice.

She pressed her lips together and crossed her arms defiantly. It took her a few moments to catch on to his plan. When she did, she helped him lift the last ball and put it in place. "Do you honestly think this will work?"

He nodded, maybe more confidently than he should. Isabella was the most competitive person he knew. And he wasn't positive this would get them a win. But he figured the last time they'd taken a risk, it had worked in their favor.

Their risk didn't disappoint this time either. When Mr. Vega, the longtime neighborhood mailman, came by at eleven o'clock to deliver the mail, he blindly chose the winner of the Whitley family snowman contest—the upside-down snowman created by Leo and Isabella.

"Hot cocoa time!" Ava dashed past her parents, heading straight for the front door. "Race me, Uncle Landon!"

Landon chuckled and jogged to catch up to her.

Smiling from ear to ear, Mr. Whitley patted Leo on the back as he and Isabella's mom passed, heading inside. "Excellent idea, son. Truly excellent."

"You're always so shockingly creative, Leo," Mrs. Whitley added.

Isabella rolled her eyes. "It's an upside-down snowman, Mom. That's not genius-level creativity or anything."

Norah smiled as she passed, too. "I dunno. Look's pretty genius to me, Izz." She winked at Isabella, who groaned like Leo beating her at anything was absolute torture.

Leo stood there with Isabella, staring at their work of art, while everyone dispersed into the family home. He pursed his lips, hands deep in his pockets, still primed to annoy the hell out of his ex. "I'm good with my hands." He shrugged. "What can I say?"

She faced him, a flat look in her eyes, and for a minute, he thought he'd won. Until a wicked smile curved one corner of her mouth.

She closed the small distance between them, looked him over, and said, "I'm better. In case you forgot."

"Are not."

"Am too."

"You liked my hands well enough last night."

"Leo, I would've liked this snowman's hands last night."

He couldn't help the smile that teased its way onto his lips. "You realize we're going to drive each other crazy this week."

She cocked a brow before sauntering away. "Fully aware."

"Long as you know."

"Oh, I know."

BACK AT THE HOFFMAN HOUSE, Leo finally unloaded his duffel bag, shoving his clothes into the dresser in his old bedroom. The tiniest hint of lavender filled the room, reminding him of Mom, and he wished he hadn't agreed to stay here for the week. The quilt Mom made him when he was a boy lay spread across the small twin bed. He ignored it and slammed the dresser drawer, crossing the hall into the bathroom.

Leo hopped in the shower, grateful for the vital breather from Isabella and their tension. He anxiously washed away the airplane germs and the heavy make-out session with her from the night before. If he could, he'd scrub away the old bogged-down feelings and emotions he thought he'd long since forgotten.

He'd known it wouldn't be easy spending time with Isabella this week, but Leo hadn't anticipated that so many feelings would percolate to the surface. What happened between them was so long ago. All his bitterness, hurt, and even lust should've died long ago. In fact, those emotions should be nonexistent. So what if he and some girl made plans for their future and then she broke off those plans with zero explanation?

Leo stepped out of the shower, dried off, and dressed in a pair of jeans and a vintage Colorado Avalanche sweatshirt. He sat on the edge of his bed and pulled on a pair of thick wool socks. The old bedroom had been stripped bare from all childish memorabilia long ago. All of his hockey trophies, band posters, and memories of Isabella—gone. They'd stayed up until right after his mom died. He'd wanted to tear everything down when the realization sunk in that Isabella wasn't returning. But he hadn't wanted to change anything and upset his mom. She'd been so fragile in those last few weeks and keeping things the same seemed to calm her.

But in a fit of rage, after Mom couldn't hold on anymore, he'd torn everything down. A couple of trophies had broken in the crossfire, a few posters torn, and photos of him and Isabella crumpled and ripped.

Leo pushed his hands through his damp hair and released a growl of a breath, attempting to push away the memories.

Landon popped his head in through the open doorway, hands resting on both sides of the doorframe. "Hey."

Leo glanced up. "Hey."

"Dad's home. We're gonna head over to the Whitley's for dinner. You about ready?"

Leo rested his elbows on his thighs. "Yep," he dragged out the word.

Landon entered Leo's bedroom and strolled around, crossing his arms. "Look, I understand this is weird for you. Hanging out at the Whitley's and with Isabella. But it really means a lot to Norah that you're there. And to me."

Leo pushed off his thighs and stood like he was heaving up much more weight than his own. "Yeah, I know."

He wanted to say more. That it was more than weird. It was uncomfortable, and frustrating, and awkward. But none of that mattered. He wouldn't let his little brother down.

Landon peeked through the Venetian blinds which coincidentally lined up perfectly with Isabella's bedroom window. "Did the two of you talk on the drive?"

"A little." Leo swiped at the drips from his hair on the back of his neck. There was a point on their drive when they'd talked. And another point when they'd done a lot more than talking. But telling Landon about that would only make things more complicated.

"Did she finally come clean about her reason for not coming home?"

Leo's gut pinched. "I didn't ask."

Landon released his fingers from the slats of the blinds and straightened. "You serious?" He shot him an incredulous look.

Leo clenched his jaw. He didn't want to get into it with Landon. The last thing he wanted to do was upset him. "What's the point?" He snatched his beanie from the bed and stuffed it over his still-damp hair.

"The point—" Landon approached him "—is that she wrecked you, bro. And you deserve an explanation."

Leo puffed out his chest and brushed past his little brother. "She didn't wreck me. I'm fine. Some might even say…peachy." He sent a smirk over his shoulder. Why shouldn't he make light of this?

"You're not fine. And you're definitely not peachy," Landon said to Leo's back as he followed him out of the room and down the hall.

Leo's pulse quickened, and he whipped around at the top of the stairs. "What do you want from me, man?"

"I want you to admit that she wrecked you by leaving the way she did. And I want you to demand that she give you an explanation."

Leo ground his teeth and spun back around, jogging down the stairs. "It's the week of your wedding. I'm not gonna ruin it."

"All I'm saying is, spending the entire week with her is gonna eat at you. I know you. You're gonna hold it all in and then blow up. And that might ruin our week—or worse, our wedding. So why not get it all out now?"

"I'm not gonna blow up. I told you, I'm fine."

Dad entered the foyer dressed in his best jeans and a flannel. His dark brown hair had more gray than brown these days. Holding a bottle of wine in each hand, he glanced back and forth between his sons with a raised and quizzical brow.

"Hey, Dad." Leo squeezed his shoulder. "It's good to see you. How was work?"

Dad gave him a hesitant smile. "It was fine. No drama. So, can't complain. But what's going on here?"

"Nothing." Leo perched on the bottom stair and stuffed his feet into his snow boots.

"Not nothing. Dad, tell Leo he needs to have it out with Izzy once and for all. Tell him it's not healthy keeping it all bottled up." Landon yanked his jacket off the coat rack.

Leo laced his boots. In a way, he'd already had it out with Izzy.

Heat filled his cheeks. "We sort of talked. We were stuck together all night."

Landon eyed him skeptically.

"There. Then it's settled," Dad muttered, still contemplating over the wine choice.

Leo shook his head. "Since when did you start calling her Izzy?"

Landon ignored him.

Dad ignored both of them, brushing past the hazardous topic as he always did. Just like he did with anything too stressful or confrontational. He'd been doing it since Mom passed. "I'm sure Leo will do what he thinks is right. Now, which wine do you think? Red or white?"

Leo sighed. "Whichever is fine, Dad. C'mon, we don't want to be late." He plucked his jacket off the rack and went out the door, an odd anxiousness tight in his chest. He needed to get out of this house.

"Hey, man? Leo?" Landon hobbled down the steps in unlaced snow boots, but Leo started walking. "Hold up. Hey? Did something happen between you and Izzy?"

Leo jerked to an abrupt stop, and Landon smacked into his back. Leo turned on him. "What do you mean?"

"You said you two were stuck together…in a car…all night long…" Landon waggled his brows.

Leo ground his jaw.

"Damn. I knew it." Landon's eyes widened and he shoved a fist into Leo's shoulder. "How was it?"

Even if things had progressed further the night before between him and Isabella, the last person he would discuss it with would be Landon. Izzy was about to be his sister-in-law. Something about that seemed wrong.

Dad passed them, his chosen bottle of wine in his grip. "C'mon boys. Thought we didn't want to be late?"

Leo's shoulders sagged in relief, and he stomped up the Whitley's front steps behind Dad. Landon sidled up next to Leo on the porch. "So?"

Nostrils flaring, Leo pressed his lips in a hard line. Talking to anyone about Isabella meant thinking about Isabella. Her smile, her delicious kisses, her scent on him. It would be great if he could go five minutes without thinking about her.

The Whitley's front door swung open. Isabella stood there smiling, wet hair, yoga pants hugging her curves, a cropped sweatshirt revealing one bare shoulder, and a sliver of skin at her waist.

"Hi, guys," she said, opening the door wider so they could enter. She tucked her dark hair behind her ear, her face still flush from her shower. And, well, damn it, she looked good.

"Hey, Izzy." Landon pressed a quick peck to her cheek and slid into the house, toeing off his boots.

"I brought wine!" Dad announced, holding up both bottles because of course he couldn't decide. He also gave Isabella a soft peck on the cheek before striding inside.

Leo stood there for a moment in the cold, freezing off his bits while he contemplated. He definitely wasn't going to kiss her, that was for damn sure. But then she grabbed him by the front of his jacket.

"Come on," she said, hauling him across the threshold before shutting the door behind him. "It's freezing out there."

She was close. Too close. Her scent and warmth hit him like a Mack truck. He paused, staring down at her. "Izzy. You look—" like temptation, like torment, like trouble "—really pretty."

He could've sworn her cheeks flushed deeper.

Her lips parted and her eyes moved over him. "Leo, I—"

"Auntie Izzy!" Ava hollered, and barreled toward them, her duck slippers squeaking with each small step.

Leo shuffled his feet, averting his eyes.

"What is it, sweetie?" Isabella asked.

Ava pointed above them, grinning. "Lookie. Mistletoe." She cupped a small hand over her mouth and giggled.

Simultaneously, Leo and Isabella glanced up. Sure enough, the kid was right. Mistletoe.

"Would you look at that," Isabella's voice came out raspy.

"You have to kiss," Ava said in singsong.

Leo rubbed at the back of his neck. "Oh, I don't really think that's necessary—"

"Kiss. Kiss. Kiss. Kiss," Ava chanted, growing louder each time.

"Okay," Isabella nearly shouted. "Fine. We'll kiss. Happy?"

Ava jumped up and down, duck slippers quacking again, clapping her hands together. "Yay!"

Isabella moved closer to him and lifted her gaze. "It's tradition, right?" She shrugged.

Sure. One small, meaningless kiss. He could do that.

Leo took a tentative step toward her, and his attention went to her mouth. She licked her lips, and his hormones soared. She lifted her chin, and he leaned in. Their mouths barely brushed together before they pulled away.

Leo gazed down at her, her eyes fixed on him, and he was caught in the moment. The crackling fire nearby, the tinny sound of "Jingle Bells" in the background, glowing lights wrapped around the banister. He was tempted to wrap his arms around her and kiss her harder and longer—

A soft giggle interrupted his fantasies.

Leo cleared his throat and pushed a hand through his hair, giving it a gentle tug. Isabella stepped away from him. He pinched his eyes shut. What was he thinking?

Quacking ducks and louder giggling was heard as Ava ran out of the room.

CHAPTER NINE

ISABELLA

Everyone meandered into the open-concept kitchen and adjoining dining room. Two slow cookers of Mom's famous stew, a stack of bowls, and homemade bread rested on the island. While bowls were filled, and silvery bells of Christmas music streamed from the other room, it felt like musical chairs—and if Isabella didn't hurry and fill her bowl, she had a sneaking suspicion she'd end up next to Leo. The two of them, sitting next to one another and sharing a meal, had warning signals blaring.

Isabella spun from the island, bowl brimming with hot stew, and took in the predicted scene. One empty chair remained. Next to Leo.

Her shoulders sank. Should she just wave the white flag now?

She placed her bowl on the table, hard, but was still careful not to spill her stew, and yanked out her chair and took a seat, spine stiff. With Landon on the other side of her, she was the center of a Hoffman-brother sandwich. Norah sat across from Landon, and Mom next to her, sporting one of her favorite Christmas sweaters from her collection—red knit with a giant snowman head on the front.

From across the table, Norah made eye contact with Isabella and mouthed, *sorry*. But it was fine. As she'd told Dad, she was an adult. She could handle one dinner with her ex. Even if the mere heat radiating off his body set her hormones on fire.

Isabella dipped her spoon into the stew. "Mom, it smells delicious." She inhaled the scent of onions and bay leaves. It reminded her of childhood and home, of a time when things were easy. When she had her mom and dad to take care of her and didn't have to make all the decisions on her own. So far, adulting sucked.

"Thanks, sweetie. Let's hope it tastes as good as it smells." Mom smiled, pushing her wired glasses up the bridge of her nose. "It is just so good to have you home."

"Are you sure?" Isabella muttered. "Because it seems Leo snuck right in and took my place as the middle child around here." She blew on a steaming spoonful of stew.

Leo snickered, his arm brushing hers for a split second. She scooted over an inch in her seat.

"Oh, you stop it now." Mom waved her hand.

"What? Am I wrong?" she glanced around the table, not fully expecting anyone to answer.

Nina was busy helping Ava cool down her stew, Dad and Mr. Hoffman were deep in a conversation about Pineridge's new stop light, and Landon had his head so far into his bowl, he looked as if he might drown in it.

"I mean, Leo is better at snowman building. As we all witnessed today," Finn said.

"I'm surprised he didn't move in here with you guys instead of back in with his dad after the divorce."

Leo stiffened beside her. His spoon hand stilled, and he slid her a cutting look.

"Oh, he didn't move in with me," Howard piped up. "He didn't tell you on your ride in from Omaha? He has a real nice place off Brushwood Road. You know, heading toward the mountain? It's a beautiful log home." Howard looked at his son and raised a brow. "You should take her out there sometime."

"Yeah, you should take me out there sometime," Isabella said, turning a glance on Leo before forcing a smile at his dad. "And no, actually, he didn't tell me that…" She'd just assumed that Leo moved back in with his dad after his divorce from Talia. He was there all the time, so it made sense.

"Guess it didn't come up." Leo leaned in close to her, his breath skimming against her bare shoulder. "We were busy doing things with our mouths other than talking."

A flush swept across her cheeks. "Leo, Ava is right there," she hissed quietly.

"What was that, sweetie?" Mom asked.

Isabella jerked her head around. "Nothing. Just that the stew is perfect. Just like I remember."

"Have you made it for your honey on cold nights in the city?"

"Um…no." Isabella tore off a piece of bread and shoved it in her mouth, unable to make eye contact with Mom. She needed to tell her family about Harrison, but now, in front of the Hoffmans, didn't feel like the right time.

"Didn't I give you the recipe? I could've sworn I emailed it to you. Pull out your phone, I can give it to you again. Type it up in that little note app of yours. I've got it all right here." Mom tapped her pointer finger to her temple.

"Not now, Mom. Another time, okay?" Isabella tucked her chin to her chest. A sense of Leo's attention fixed on her sent a shiver of longing through her. She brushed her fingers against her neck.

"It's no trouble at all. C'mon," Mom urged.

Isabella's shoulders sagged. How on earth would she get out of this?

"Listen to your mom, sweetie." Dad pushed out his small pot belly and gave it a rub. "The way to a man's heart is through his stomach."

Mom nodded in agreement. "If you want your city beau to propose to you, this recipe will do the trick."

"But I don't—" Straightening, Isabella prepared to divulge a little bit about her relationship with Harrison. About the break. About being homeless. Okay, maybe not about the homeless part. "You don't, what?"

Concern streaked Mom's face, and Isabella deflated. She just couldn't do it. As much as Mom hated that she and Harrison weren't married yet, she'd be devastated to learn that things between them were most likely over.

Underneath the table, Leo pressed his foot against hers, a reminder that she wasn't alone. She briefly closed her eyes and swallowed.

"Nothing." Isabella forced a smile.

"What does your boyfriend do over there in New York?" Mr. Hoffman asked.

She fanned herself with her napkin. Was it hot in here?

"He's an independent financial advisor," she finally said. "He works for one of the largest investment firms in Manhattan."

"Sounds fancy," Mr. Hoffman answered.

A little bit of pride wriggled through her. But she quickly wiped it away.

"And he's loaded," Dad blurted around a mouthful of bread.

"Dad!" Isabella chided.

"Dear, wealthy or not, that's not why she loves him." Mom fluffed her dark brown bob.

Finn leaned forward, resting his elbows on the table. "But I'm sure it doesn't hurt."

"Guys, c'mon, this is Izzy we're talking about," Norah said, finally coming to her sister's rescue. "She doesn't care about money. Besides, she writes for *The New Yorker*, guys. Our girl is doing just fine on her own."

Isabella's eyes widened, and she almost choked on a potato.

Raising a high chin, Dad said, "She is. And we're so proud of her."

"It really is something, seeing both of your childhood dreams come to fruition." Mr. Hoffman gestured his spoon in Leo's direction. "Though I'd be lying if I said I was completely thrilled for Leo. I'd rather him come work for the family business."

Isabella swung her attention from Mr. Hoffman to Leo, her pulse picking up. "Oh yeah? And which childhood dream is this?"

There was hockey, but wasn't twenty-nine too old to just be starting out in the NHL? And she'd know if he'd gone pro. Then there was photography, but Norah had told her Leo put his camera equipment away after his mom passed.

"You're joking, right?" Finn asked. "You haven't noticed the canvases on the walls?"

Her breath caught, and a heaviness landed in her stomach. He'd done it. Leo really had become a photographer? But why had he been so vague about his job the day before? When they were kids, she always encouraged him to follow his dreams and make a go at photography as a career. She'd been heartbroken when she heard he'd stopped completely.

Leo shifted in his seat, tugging at the collar of his sweatshirt where his Adam's apple bobbed hard.

"You did it," she said, her voice soft and shaky.

Leo averted his eyes. "I did. Right now I have a studio in my home. But I'd like to open my own place one day."

"You should show her your studio, son." Mr. Hoffman said, tossing his napkin on his plate before sliding out his chair.

"Oh, I don't know about that." Leo scratched at his neck.

"Maybe we can squeeze it in sometime this week, Izz?" Norah said, standing.

Leo gave Isabella a sideways glance. "I'm sure Izzy has more important things to do. Wedding prep and all."

"I'll make space on my calendar," Isabella said with a half-smile. "I'd love to see your studio."

"It's settled then." Norah beamed.

Dad pushed up from his chair and stacked a few empty bowls. "But only if we have time. We're on a strict schedule this week. More than usual, what with the wedding festivities."

"Don't worry honey, everyone knows how important the Eight Days of Christmas schedule is to you," Mom teased, pressing a kiss to Dad's cheek.

"It's been a nice evening, but I better be getting home. Work comes early," Mr. Hoffman said. "Too bad I'm not a Whitley, or I'd have an excuse to take a week's vacation like the rest of y'all."

"It also helps when you work for the school district and you're already on break." Dad winked.

"Well, Howard, you know you're always welcome." Mom gave him a pat on the back. "Let me walk you out."

"Goodnight everyone," Mr. Hoffman called.

"Goodnight," Isabella joined in with the others. "I'll clean up in here, you all go on and relax."

"Are you sure?" Mom asked.

"Absolutely. Now go." Isabella shooed Mom out of the kitchen, along with the rest of the family. When she turned around, Leo stood behind her. She inhaled a breath, placing her hand to her chest. "Why didn't you tell me?"

Leo shrugged. "It's nothing."

"It's amazing." She busied herself with picking up the dirty dishes from the table and carrying them into the kitchen. "Norah told me you'd given it up."

Leo went to the sink, filling it with hot water. "I did…at first. But then I figured my mom would've wanted me to pursue my dream."

"I'm sure she'd be so proud of you." She placed the dishes into the sink. There were years of words Isabella wanted to say to this man. But would they be enough? Could the right words be enough to erase the hurt and the betrayal?

"Yeah, maybe."

With him next to her, so close, her breathing quickened, and her chest fluttered. "For the record, I'm proud of you, too."

Leo responded with a grunt.

Isabella bumped her hip into his side. "I mean, if I hadn't constantly pestered you to keep at photography through college, your future could look very different right now."

The implications of her words hit in her chest, a shift near her heart. Her gaze traveled up to meet his, finding a look of longing, of need, of pain. She swallowed.

"Yeah, I think I know how different my future could've been," he said, that wall suddenly separating them once again. Except it felt more like a skyscraper now. He dried his hands on a dishtowel. "I'm tired, I'm gonna get going. Goodnight." He tossed the towel onto the counter and left the room, leaving her heart aching.

IT TOOK READING three picture books to Ava before she fell asleep, and Isabella could finally retreat to her bedroom for the night. She pushed aside the wedding decorations, rolls of burlap and red and gold ribbon, before dropping onto the bed in an exhausted slump. Staring at the ceiling, Isabella mumbled aloud, "First day of Christmas down. Only seven more to go. You got this, Isabella." She sighed and pushed her fingers through her disheveled hair.

She stood and picked up the hideous bridesmaid dress, grimacing before hanging it on the treadmill handle. Isabella shuffled to the bed and pulled back the welcoming covers. She couldn't wait to climb in between the flannel sheets and sleep for a solid twelve hours, at least. Out of the corner of her eye, she caught movement outside through the window.

She crept to the window seat and knelt, gathering the curtains and peeking through them. Leo's bedroom was directly across from hers. Through his open blinds, she eyed him while he paced back and forth, until suddenly he stopped, took a purposeful stride toward the window, and pushed it open. Isabella sucked in a breath, released the curtains, and pressed her back against the wall.

Had he just been waiting for her to look out her window?

Isabella exhaled a deep breath before kneeling on the seat, pushing back the curtains, and peeking out once again. This time, she found him leaning out his open window. She gasped, clutching at her chest. Then slid open her own window. "Leo! What are you doing?"

"What are *you* doing?" his voice growled through the crisp night air, sending a thrumming in her stomach.

"You scared me," she blurted.

"Sorry. I was waiting for you to come to your window."

Her body tingled at his words. So he *had* been waiting for her.

"That was presumptuous."

"Maybe."

All the memories of her childhood surrounded her, mocking her, and made her feel off-kilter. How many times had she spoken to Leo from this very window? Shouting *I love you* the loudest. Until Mom or Mrs. Hoffman came to tell them to be quiet or they'd wake up all the neighbors.

Mrs. Hoffman.

The thought of her sent an unforgiving pinch to her gut. She sighed. "It's cold, Leo. And it's been a very long day. Let's talk tomorrow, okay?" Isabella reached for the window, ready to push it shut.

"C'mon, Izzy."

"C'mon, what?" She leaned on the windowsill.

"I'm still waiting for an explanation." Those hard lines to his face went serious.

Even though she knew exactly what he was referring to, she still asked. "An explanation for what?"

"Why'd you do it?"

Isabella's palms began to sweat, and her heart raced. She glanced over her shoulder, hoping Mom would come to save her now. She couldn't offer him an explanation, not one that he'd be happy with. What she had to tell him wouldn't ease the pain.

Tears clogged in her throat. Isabella pathetically shrugged a shoulder.

"Why'd you leave me?"

The words coming from Leo's mouth, in his grown-up voice dug under her ribcage.

She swallowed. "I didn't leave you, Leo. I just…I just never came back."

Leo stabbed his fingers through his hair. Through those dark brown, sexy, longish waves. "I don't see much of a difference," he growled.

Her eyes burned. "I don't know. What do you want me to say?" She distracted herself by running a thumb along the chipping paint on the windowsill, willing herself not to cry. "I guess I assumed you'd move on."

"I did."

"Yeah, I know." She pursed her lips. "When was the divorce final?"

"A year ago this past March."

"I'm sorry," she mumbled.

"Yeah? For what? What exactly are you sorry for, Izzy?"

"For that." She hesitated, the tears stinging the back of her eyes, just waiting to break free and rush out once she was all alone. "For us. For everything."

"Yeah?" He sighed and hung his head, killing her with the agonizing silence for a beat that seemed to last a lifetime. "After six years of silence, don't you think I deserve a better explanation than that?"

"You do. I'm just not ready to give it to you yet."

Leo shook his head slowly. "Fine."

He slammed the window shut and released the blinds.

She flinched, her eyes filling with tears and her heart aching like it was breaking all over again. Just like it had all those years ago. And there was that irony again. Because there she was, in her childhood room where her heart had pumped only for Leo.

CHAPTER TEN

ISABELLA

Waking up to the sound of Leo's expressive laugh wafting through the entire house would've been spectacular—if Isabella had chosen a different life. Or maybe even manageable, if the two of them hadn't undergone that dreadfully uncomfortable conversation the night before. It was too early for mayhem.

She hadn't even had coffee yet.

Finding an old Ithaca College sweatshirt in her suitcase, she pulled it over her head before pushing her feet into a pair of red fuzzy slippers. The sweatshirt didn't match her reindeer-printed flannel pajama pants, but she was too tired to care. She trudged down the stairs cursing under her breath and wiping the sleep from her eyes. The scent of cinnamon swirled throughout the house. Between the glorious smell and the memory of the sweet and spice of Mom's cinnamon rolls on her tongue, she almost gave up on being annoyed that Leo was there.

Almost.

A canvas on the wall in the hallway snagged Isabella's attention. She doubled back to take a closer look. She recognized the picturesque setting easily. Blue River in wintertime, with thick, white snow covering the ground and rocks while ice coated the branches of the surrounding trees. While admiring Leo's talent, Isabella drifted back to a time of young love, when she and Leo would get up early and crunch through the thick snow just so he could get the perfect shot of the Blue River waking up.

"Hey, there's the sleepyhead," Dad called in singsong from the kitchen. "Everyone is already up and eating breakfast. We gotta get a move on. Day two awaits."

She tore her focus away from the canvas and covered a yawn with a cupped hand. It was too early for singsong. She lumbered into the kitchen, her heavy-lidded eyes widening as she took in Leo seated at the table with her entire family. His dark hair sweeping across his forehead, a brow lifted and his eyes lingering as he took in her appearance.

Ava jumped off her chair and flung herself into Isabella's unexpectant arms. "Finally, Auntie Izzy. Hurry! It's Christmas tree day!" She raced out of the room, her sleepy mom chasing after her.

Isabella shuffled past Landon and Norah sitting at the island, taking the last open wooden barstool and slumping onto it.

"I guess someone still likes to sleep in," Finn teased.

"It's barely eight o'clock. I'd hardly call that sleeping in." Isabella leaned against the wall.

"Try being an on-call doctor. You'd never survive." Finn flashed her a smug closed mouth smile.

She rolled her eyes. Finn couldn't help himself. He would find any way possible to squeeze his profession into any conversation. Yeah, we get it—you're a doctor. What did he want? A medal?

"Oh, you remember—Izzy was never much of a morning person." Mom scooped a hot cinnamon roll from a pan, the gooeyness dripping off the spatula. She set it on a plate imprinted with a holly border and slid the sweet pastry in front of Isabella.

"Oh, I remember," Leo taunted, pushing his chair out and standing.

She gasped. "I'm a morning person." She didn't have a choice. Not when Harrison woke her up blending his smoothies after his run. And especially not now, with Margo's cat using her as a scratching post at five o'clock.

The room erupted in laughter.

"What? I am." Her cheeks burned.

Patting her arm, Norah said, "We know you are, Izz. We're just teasing."

Leo carried his dirty dishes to the sink. "Thanks for breakfast, Mrs. W." He pressed a kiss to Mom's cheek.

"Anytime, sweetie."

Isabella narrowed her eyes into slits, watching the exchange. Leo ignored her, leaving the kitchen and strutting down the hall. He was definitely strutting, the way his hips shimmied causing his backside to shift flawlessly in those tight jeans was distracting, she'd give him that.

But not enough to keep her from losing focus on the pastry perfection in front of her. She glanced at the gooeyness. The frosting dripped down the flaky sides, causing Isabella's mouth to water. She hadn't craved Mom's cinnamon rolls in years. In fact, she'd nearly forgotten about them altogether.

That last thought sent a pang of guilt straight through her chest. She kept reminding everyone that ten years really wasn't all that long. But if she'd forgotten about Mom's cinnamon rolls, ten years was scary long.

"Thanks, Mom." She took her fork and pushed it into the flaky goodness. Before taking a bite, she glanced at the plate next to hers— Norah's plate. Piled with fresh fruit, it clearly lacked a giant sugar bomb. She nodded her chin toward Norah's plate. "What's with the fruit?"

"The wedding is in seven days. I can't eat Mom's cinnamon rolls and risk not fitting into my dress."

"What?" Isabella's voice went up an octave. "That's crazy. A cinnamon roll isn't gonna put on the pounds just like that." She snapped her fingers.

Landon leaned forward, talking around Norah. "It's no use, I've tried to tell her." He shrugged and took a sip of coffee.

He was using her favorite holiday mug. The one with the Santa upside down in the Chimney. She rubbed her hand against her heart.

"You'd be surprised. I swear I gain at least ten pounds every December," Norah said, popping a grape into her mouth.

"You? Oh please," Isabella scoffed, her vision roaming over her little sister's body dressed in a Christmas print long underwear set. It clung to her, hugging her curves. Which, if she was being honest, there weren't many. Norah looked like she stepped out of the Victoria's Secret catalog. Tall, long legs, and narrow everything. A cinnamon roll would do her some good.

"I don't expect you to understand. You haven't been home for Christmas since I was a kid. But just you wait. After a week of eating Mom's cooking, you'll see." She pointed at her with her fork.

Ignoring the pang that came with realizing that Norah was only twelve during Isabella's last Christmas at home, she turned her attention back to the pastry. It screamed for her to devour it. It wanted to be eaten, enjoyed. Maybe Norah was right, but Isabella didn't care. Who was she going home to anyway? Todd and Margo and their cat?

She looked defiantly at Norah, stabbed her fork into the pastry, and took a bite. The combination of cinnamon and cream cheese frosting exploded in her mouth.

"Mmm," Isabella said aloud, more dramatically than necessary. "This is so good."

Better than sex. Well, at least any sex she'd had in a long while.

Norah smirked, bumping a shoulder into Isabella.

It wasn't fair for Isabella to be the only one of them enjoying their breakfast.

She dragged the fork down the middle of the cinnamon roll and plopped half of it onto Norah's plate. "It's gonna be a long day, I think you'll need this as much as I will." She winked at her sister.

"Okay, okay. Fine." Norah took a small taste, her eyes fluttering closed in pleasure.

"See, worth it." Isabella inhaled another bite.

On the opposite side of the island, Dad cleared his throat. "If you decide to come up for air, here's a cup of coffee," he teased, pushing a steaming mug in front of her. "Cream and sugar, right?" His wiry brows raised in question.

"Yeah. Thanks." She took a sip and groaned with delight. How was Mom's drip coffee so much better than her usual New York's finest eight-dollar cappuccino? She had no idea. But it was.

Ava zoomed back into the kitchen, her feet clomping in snow boots. "Auntie Izzy! C'mon. We've been waiting for you forever."

"Hey, let the woman eat," Nina scolded. "She hasn't had Grandma's cinnamon rolls in a long time."

Ava's big brown eyes widened. "For ten years?"

Isabella's cheeks flushed. "I guess it has been that long."

"Whoa. That's longer than I've been alive."

"Yes, that's true." Isabella side-eyed her brother. What had Finn been telling little Ava? Leo entered the kitchen again, a beanie hiding that ridiculously sexy hair of his. But more interestingly, he carried a huge, shiny chainsaw in his large hands. "Brought my tools, Mr. W. Threw some extra straps into the back of the pickup as well. You sure my chainsaw is in better condition than yours?"

Isabella sucked in a breath and turned her attention back to the pastry, though it didn't appear quite as appealing. Why was he there again? He might as well live there. He seemed to be at her parent's home more than his dad's.

"Oh yeah," Dad said, admiring Leo's tree killer. "That's a beauty alright. Top of the line. It's definitely better than mine."

Landon jumped up, joining in with the men and drooling over the power tool. "I think I need to get me one of these."

"Sue would never let me spend that much on a chainsaw," Dad said.

Mom made a *tsk-tsk* sound, waggling her finger at him. "Now, now, that's enough," she warned. "Why don't you boys put that in the truck and the rest of us will be along shortly."

Isabella's mouth dropped open, eyeing Dad and Leo as they left the room. She turned on Norah, nostrils flaring. She jabbed her elbow into Norah's ribs, causing her sister to jump and let out a yelp.

"What was that for?" Norah rubbed her side.

Isabella leaned closer and whispered. "Why is Leo putting tools into his truck? What is going on?"

Norah bit her lip.

She narrowed her eyes. "Norah?"

"Okay," Norah relented. "I invited him."

Isabella groaned. "Why?"

"I thought it would be nice if he came with us to celebrate the second day of Christmas."

Isabella's stomach did a flip-flop. She pushed her plate away, part of the cinnamon roll left uneaten. Her appetite had vanished. "Norah?" she said through gritted teeth. "Please tell me Leo is not going to be joining us for *all* Eight Days of Christmas."

Norah averted her gaze.

"Norah," Isabella whined, closing her eyes.

"Sorry." While Norah's expression did reflect remorse, Isabella had a feeling she was enjoying this. Isabella and Leo might've been right on the Norah being young part, but they'd been wrong on the dumb part. It was obvious. Norah knew exactly what she was doing. And they'd definitely underestimated her.

Isabella picked herself up from the stool and leaned into Norah's ear, whispering, "I know what you're trying to do. And it's not gonna work."

"I don't know what you're talking about," Norah said in mock innocence.

"Oh sweetie," Mom said, "Spending a week with Leo will be fine. Just like old times."

Isabella grimaced. She felt as if her entire family was conspiring against her. Didn't they see that she and Leo had tried this before? And it ended. Badly.

"Now you better hurry. We're all piling into Leo's and Landon's pickups. You don't want to be the last one." There was a mischievous glint in Mom's eye and a smirk on her lips.

Isabella tilted her head, her mind spinning. Was this a warning? If she was the last one, what would happen?

She had a sinking feeling she knew exactly what would happen— she'd end up being stuck riding in Leo's truck. Over her dead body.

Isabella raced out of the room and jogged up the stairs. She tore through her suitcase, yanking out clothes for a trek in the snowy mountains. She tugged on a pair of long underwear, then a pair of jeans, a long-sleeved shirt with a flannel over it, and two pairs of socks. She shoved her feet inside her UGGs and grabbed her winter jacket, gloves, and a gray knit cap before tearing down the stairs and rushing out the front door. She hadn't even brushed her teeth or hair yet.

Winded and panting, Isabella's heart sank when she discovered she'd been too late after all. The passenger seat in Leo's truck was the only empty spot remaining.

"You've got to be kidding me," she muttered as she stalked toward the truck. She flung the door open and glared at Finn, Nina, and Ava who sat comfortably in the backseat.

"Sorry, Izz," Nina said, wincing. She was the only one who looked like she might actually mean it.

"We saved you the best seat!" Ava's huge smile stretched across her face. "The front seat in Uncle Leo's truck is the best. If you're really good and don't touch the radio, he'll give you a Tic Tac."

"*Uncle* Leo?" Isabella's stomach tightened while she glanced back and forth from Finn, Nina, and Leo. None of them offered an immediate explanation. So she repeated herself, because maybe they hadn't heard her the first time. "*Uncle Leo?*"

"It was just easier that way. You know, for Ava," Nina said. "Since Landon will be her uncle, Ava wanted to know why Leo wasn't her uncle too. We figured it was less confusing this way."

"Less confusing?" Less confusing for who? Because it sounded like grounds for therapy when Ava grew to be an adult and learned her family lied to her.

"It's not a big deal," Leo finally said.

"It feels like a big deal." Isabella unzipped her jacket as the fire inside her body lit.

"Well, it's not, okay?" Finn pushed his window down a crack. "Just drop it."

Obviously, it was a big deal if Finn noticed the tension.

"Fine." Isabella exhaled and reached for the radio dial. Music had to be better than the awkward silence enveloping the cab of the truck.

"Uh oh," Ava said, disappointment in her tone. "No Tic Tac for you, Auntie Izzy."

Leo chuckled. "She's a naughty girl," he mumbled, his voice practically purring.

Was he seriously using sexual innuendo in front of her five-year-old niece?

"Yup, you're naughty." Ava played with the long strings hanging from her knit hat.

Nina stifled a laugh.

"I'm glad you're all enjoying yourselves." Isabella crossed her arms and pouted out the passenger window.

AFTER THE THIRTY-MINUTE awkward drive up the snowy, winding mountain road, Isabella couldn't wait to get out of the truck. Sure, hearing her niece sing a near-perfect rendition of "Rudolph the Red-Nosed Reindeer" was adorable, but the tension between her and Leo was suffocating. She jumped down from the truck, and the snow buried her UGGs by a few inches.

Leo took the chainsaw from the back of the truck and waited for Landon to pull alongside them. Isabella wasn't in the mood to wait—she wasn't in the mood to talk to any of them—never mind accompanying them on a search for the perfect Christmas tree like one big happy family.

It didn't make sense to have Leo there anyway. They were there to pick out the perfect Whitley Christmas tree. Was he picking out a tree for his dad's house? Or his own?

Isabella turned 360 degrees, spotting nothing but snow, trees, and parked vehicles. The memories from the last time she was here flashed through her mind, the nostalgia creating an ach in the center of her chest. She took in the sight of the trees frosted with glistening snow and inhaled the crisp air into her lungs.

By the time she looked back to the trucks, she'd been so caught up in her mental rant about Leo and the stupid tree that she hadn't even noticed that she'd been left behind.

Apparently, her family had grown accustomed to not having her around. They'd completely forgotten about her and ditched her. Except she wasn't alone. Leo stood propped against the side of his truck, ankles and arms crossed, and a smirk plastered on his face.

Just perfect.

She groaned. "Seriously?"

"Afraid so. We're stuck together. Again."

Isabella threw her head back and shouted to the sky, "Why?"

This wasn't happening.

Leo crunched through the snow, making his way toward her. "Not sure. But we'd better hurry or they'll pick a tree without you."

"They wouldn't." Though her voice wavered. And her statement sounded more like a question. They wouldn't do that, would they?

"Why not? I gave your dad my chainsaw." He said, passing her. "And they've only been doing it for the last ten years."

"Ha, ha, ha," she huffed sarcastically and hurried to catch up to him. "How long is everyone gonna make those remarks to me?"

"Until they stop being funny."

She stuffed her ice-cold hands deep into the pockets of her coat, a bit relieved when she found her gloves tucked inside. She put them on. "Well, I don't think they're funny."

"Or until they stop getting a rise out of you."

"Ahh." She focused on her boots, the snow fluttering into the air with each step. "So I need to pretend they don't bother me?"

He turned to face her, walking backward. "You see, what I don't get is why would you need to pretend? I don't get how they bother you at all."

Heat coiled through her body, and she bit the inside of her cheek. "Why wouldn't they bother me?"

"Because you're the one who chose not to come home." Leo pulled his beanie tighter over his ears, turning back around.

Anger pricked her skin. "I didn't just choose to stay away. It's not like I wanted to."

"But you did. You had the choice, and you chose to stay away."

"Forget it," she huffed, clenching her hands into fists inside the fuzzy gloves. "I don't expect you to understand."

"Try me." Not looking at her, he slowed until she was alongside him and matched his pace to hers.

"You act like I hate my family. Like I didn't miss them. Like every year when day one of Eight Days of Christmas rolled around, I didn't have the urge to go build my own snowman." Isabella's heart raced. Her words poured out of her. And to the wrong person. She couldn't talk to Leo about why she never returned. He was the last person she should be telling. But she felt so enervated, she couldn't hold it in anymore.

"I know you don't hate them. But that's just it. That's what I don't get. I know it's the opposite. You love your family." He threw his arms up. "So why didn't you come back?"

She had no choice. She could continue to hold the secret in and be the bad guy. She'd been doing it for six years, what was a couple of decades more? She zipped her jacket to her chin and crammed the remorse inching up her throat back down. "Just drop it, okay?"

His stride picked up the pace, and his boots stomped louder next to her. "No. Not again. Tell me. Please."

"Leo," her voice cracked. She could not cry. Not here. Not now. The intense cold up in the mountains would probably freeze her tears right on her cheeks before they had the chance to fall. "Just stop," she pleaded.

"No." He grabbed ahold of her arm, forcing her to stop. He squared his shoulders. "Enough of this, Izzy. Come on."

That look in his eyes, eyes she used to adore, is what broke the dam.

Tears spilled down her face. "I did come back, okay? I came back!" she shouted.

There. She'd finally said it. But now, not only would she have to live with the consequences of the confession, but so would he.

Shock played out on his expression. He shook his head in disbelief. He didn't believe her. "When?" His question came out breathless.

She opened her mouth to speak but was unsure what she'd say. Should she explain everything now? While picking out the perfect Christmas tree with her family? Or wait until later when they could be alone?

As if on cue, Ava barreled toward them, knit cap sliding down her forehead and nearly covering her brown eyes. "Auntie Izzy, hurry! Daddy thinks we found the tree. But Grandma says you have to say it's okay before they cut it down."

Isabella sniffed, wiped her runny nose with the back of her glove, and cleared the grief from her throat. "Okay, on my way." She braved a smile.

Ava dragged both Isabella and Leo by gloved hands to where the others stood surrounding a tree. Saved by a child. At least, for now.

After Isabella had given her approval, Leo did the honors and cut the tree down. It did have the look of a perfect Christmas tree. Full all the way around but not too bushy so that ornaments weren't forgotten and accidentally tossed out with the tree once Christmas was over. Isabella and Norah had learned that lesson the hard way. One year, the two of them chose what they thought was the perfect Christmas tree, but the thing had been so bushy, they lost a few ornaments to the Boy Scouts who came to pick up the tree that year.

Finn and Dad each took an end of the tree, hauling it on their trek back toward the trucks. Ava sang "Jingle Bells," but the Batman-smells version, skipping through the deep snow the entire way. Isabella cursed her UGGs. Apparently, they weren't waterproof. Her feet were freezing. She could practically hear the nurses gossiping about her in the hospital while they amputated both feet. "Dumb city girl," they'd whisper. "She actually thought UGGs were a good choice to wear in the mountains of Colorado?" Then they'd all have a good laugh.

Isabella took measured steps, falling behind the rest of the family. As the cold in her feet turned them numb, the chill worked its way up her legs. Pretty soon, she wasn't positive she was even moving at all. She supposed it was a good thing she had the distraction of the earlier conversation between her and Leo weaving through her brain. At least she could focus on something other than the worry of freezing to death.

"Hey?" Landon called over his shoulder, annoyance in his tone. "What's the hold up?"

"Nothing," Isabella hollered back. "You guys go ahead. I'll catch up with you."

"Let me guess—your feet are freezing?" Leo asked while he strutted in front of her.

She lifted her chin. "They're fine."

"It's the boots."

"It's not the boots," she said defiantly.

"Her feet are just always cold," Norah said.

"Leo," Dad called. "Finn and I have the tree, go help Izzy out, will you? Can't have her getting frostbite on only day two."

"Sure thing, Mr. W." Leo stopped, waiting for her to catch up.

"I'm fine on my own." She took two small steps. "See." She gestured at her feet. "I moved, didn't I?"

"At that rate, you'll be doing good if you make it back in time for the wedding," Leo sneered. He pulled off his gloves, stuffing them into the pockets of his jacket. Turning his back to her, he hunched down. "Just hop on, will you?"

"No way. I said I was fine." This was ridiculous. Her dad asking Leo to save her. No thank you. She could save herself.

"Stop being so stubborn. For your dad's sake, will you just get on?"

Well, when he put it that way. She hesitated, biting her lip and worrying the cold would take her ability to move her arms next. "Fine," she huffed. In one swift motion, she jumped, hopping onto his back and wrapping her legs and arms around him like a spider monkey.

"Whoa, you think you could let me breathe a little?"

"Sorry." She released her tight grip, but she couldn't deny the intense feelings zinging through her veins.

He carried the weight of her while trekking through the thick snow with ease. "Déjà vu," he mumbled.

"Right."

"I wonder how many piggyback rides I've given you over the years?"

"Probably too many to count."

Isabella held herself snug against his warm body, a tingling sensation running through her depths. The memories of his piggyback rides raced through her mind like a familiar Christmas carol. That was one thing she used to love about their relationship. Not only did a serious vibe bounce between them, but they also had fun. They had a childlike relationship. One that probably came from knowing one another for so long, growing up as neighbors and being friends since they were kids.

They hadn't started dating until they were sixteen. The first time Leo came over to the house to take Isabella out on a real date, Dad had been so confused. He invited Leo in and started talking about the football game. But when he caught sight of Isabella in a dress with her hair in curls and noticed the cheesy smiles plastered on each of their faces, he frowned. Having Leo as his daughter's friend was one thing. Having him dating his daughter was something entirely different.

And now he was the family favorite, it seemed.

Leo slowed the closer he got to the truck. Isabella clung to him tighter, gripping his firm chest. There was a shifting feeling near her heart, a yearning to never let him go. But then he stopped and lowered her to the ground. She slid down the length of him, feeling the agony of their parting instantly and inhaling a long, sharp breath. Being back in Pineridge with Leo again was worse than she'd anticipated it would be. Just because she had abandoned him, didn't mean she'd lost her feelings.

Deep down, she knew she'd always love Leo.

But those feelings for him weren't so deep down any longer.

"You okay?" Leo pressed, eyes scanning her downcast face.

She took off a glove and swiped her fingers over her wet cheeks. "I'm fine." She pulled on the truck handle. "Thank you." She braved a smile and climbed into the passenger seat, slamming the door behind her before her heart visually cracked in front of everyone.

CHAPTER ELEVEN

LEO

THE WHITLEY'S EIGHT DAYS OF CHRISTMAS tradition had been something Leo joined on occasion growing up. The few years he dated Isabella, the traditions had been mandatory. After his mom died, they offered for the Hoffman men to join them, but it didn't feel right without Isabella there. Then when Landon and Norah got together, the Whitley's insisted, not taking no for an answer.

Leo found he didn't mind joining in, it was good for Landon to be part of a big family, and it was even nice for his dad. But some of the Whitley traditions lasted hours, if not all day. Like today—day two. The tradition didn't stop with simply driving up to the mountain, picking out a tree, and cutting it down. Nope. It also involved setting up the tree, decorating it, and stringing popcorn with cranberries.

While Mr. Whitley and Landon stood back admiring the tree inside its old, rickety stand, all Leo could do was think about the earlier conversation with Isabella. She'd come back? When? And how had he not known? He wanted to grab her by the arm and drag her into the other room and drill her with questions—demand answers. But did it honestly matter now? Would it change anything? What happened between them was water under the bridge. But if that were true, why couldn't he stop obsessing over it?

"It looks good to me," Mr. Whitley said.

"Sure does," Landon agreed. "Isabella picked out a perfect tree this year."

"She always picks out the perfect tree. She has an eye for it or something. Mom and I could never quite figure it out." Mr. Whitley studied the tree, tilting his head, lips curved into a pleasant smile. "Our trees were terrible the last ten years without her guidance."

"Pft," Leo huffed out loud without intention.

Isabella narrowed her eyes at him, and he narrowed his right back. Two could play this game.

It was unsettling the way her dad worshipped her. So what if she had a knack for picking out a decent Christmas tree. She'd been gone for ten years, and Leo had been the one here, witnessing the sadness conveyed in Mr. Whitley's eyes as he studied every tree—every imperfect, not-passing-Isabella's-inspection tree.

Yep. Water under the bridge he decided. He didn't care that Isabella had come back or her reason for not telling him.

His skin itched with a pressing desire to get out of there. His vision slid to the plastic bins packed full of ornaments scattered around the living room. This always took hours. Between the unwrapping of each ornament, followed by Mrs. W. telling the story behind it, and then hanging them all on the tree, it was an excruciatingly tedious process. One Mrs. Whitley didn't take lightly. And then there was the stringing of popcorn and cranberries. That was its own process.

He pushed the heels of his hands into his tired eyes, contemplating how he could get the hell out of there.

"C'mon, Mom," Isabella hollered over her shoulder into the kitchen. "Let's get this thing going."

Leo looked at her, unsure if he should thank her for hurrying this along, or if he should remind her how selfish she was acting. Mrs. Whitley had been waiting for years to share each of these traditions with her daughter. So he did neither.

"Here, let me help you with that, Mrs. W.," Leo offered, jumping off the sofa and taking the giant bowls full of popcorn from her arms.

"Thank you, honey," Mrs. Whitley patted his arm.

Isabella blinked at their exchange. Her unease by his natural interaction with her mom did something inside his chest. It wasn't awkwardness or anxiousness, it was more of a satisfactory expansion of warmth. It was obvious their relationship unsettled her. Maybe spending the rest of the day here would be more fun than he'd originally thought.

Mrs. W. knelt on the living room floor next to a large plastic bin and opened it. She meticulously unwrapped a fragile ornament with careful fingers and gasped, pressing a hand to her chest. Leo slid the stainless-steel bowls full of popcorn onto the coffee table before dropping himself onto the sofa. And so it began. The stories of first Christmases, baptisms, and graduations. He shifted, getting comfortable for the long afternoon ahead.

Ava hopped up from her seat on the floor when Mrs. W. unwrapped Finn's Baby's First Christmas ornament. Ava had been hanging it on the tree for the last three years Leo had been spending Christmas with the Whitley's. Her own Baby's First Christmas ornament was unwrapped next.

Ava snatched the ornament from Mrs. W. and ran over to Isabella, dangling it in front of her eyes. "Look! It's my own ornament. It even has my name on it. See." She spun it around so Izzy could read her name engraved on the underside.

"I do see," Isabella said. "That's pretty special. I love it."

She smiled brightly, genuinely, and Leo nearly flinched. It had been a long time since he saw that smile. And what it did to him, he didn't much like. It hit him in the center of his chest, digging underneath his ribs and aching deep.

"Grandpa and Grandma gave it to me when I was a baby."

"You better hang it where everyone can see it."

Ava found a low branch and hung it a little too close to the end. She turned back around, awaiting Isabella's approval.

Isabella winked. "Good choice." But as soon as the little girl skipped toward Mrs. W. for another ornament, Isabella pushed it farther back on the branch. Well would you look at that, the ice queen had a heart after all.

When Mrs. Whitley finished sorting through the bins of ornaments, divvying them up to each Whitley child to hang on the tree, she pushed off her knees. She stopped in front of Leo and held an ornament in her palm, smiling at him. "And here is yours." She kissed him on the cheek.

"Thanks." Leo accepted it and shuffled toward the tree. He smirked at Isabella who eyed him suspiciously while she hung an ornament.

"What? You thought they'd get rid of my ornament?" He asked, incredulous.

"Uh, no…I didn't. I…I guess I just forgot you had one."

"I hang it on the tree every year."

"Why don't you hang it on your own tree?"

His heart snagged on her words for just a moment. He shrugged, finding a high empty branch. "I usually don't get a tree."

Isabella leaned in closer, her shirt riding up and revealing the smooth skin on her bare stomach. Her body illuminated from the glow of the crackling fire. He had an impossible time not staring at her. He swallowed hard.

"Not even when you were married?" she asked.

He dropped his head and sighed. "Fine. You got me there. For those two years, we did have a tree. But it wasn't as if I was gonna take my ornament from your mom. That would be weird, don't you think? Not to mention rude. Your parents bought it for me."

She pressed her lips together, and they disappeared in between her teeth. She was close enough for him to catch a scent of the same perfume that had intoxicated his senses two nights before. He sucked in a breath and waited, but for what he wasn't sure. He'd already decided he wasn't going to press the conversation about why she never returned to Pineridge, or the more recently development—why she'd come back and not told anyone.

"Leo, I—"

"Izzy," Mrs. Whitley interrupted, breaking his trance. "Why don't you help me with the needles and thread?"

Isabella trained her eyes on him, and he hated the magnetic pull he felt for her. "Okay, Mom."

Leo backed away until he felt his legs hit the sofa. He dropped onto it, needing to put distance between them before he had the urge to drill her with questions or worse—pull her into his arms.

CHAPTER TWELVE

ISABELLA

Isabella pinched one eye shut and stuck her tongue out as she concentrated on threading a needle, keeping it long and tying it at the end. She poked it in the butt of a Santa Claus pincushion before doing the same with another needle and thread, prepping them for the popcorn and cranberries. She forgot how tedious the process was and poked her fingertip more than once, feeling less jolly with each prick.

Ava climbed onto the barstool next to her, her dark, curly hair in two side ponytails resembling pom-poms. Mom gave Ava a pair of flat-nosed safety scissors, who cut open two bags of cranberries and poured them into small stainless-steel bowls, only spilling a few onto the counter.

"Okay, Grandma. Cranberries are ready." Ava grinned.

"Nicely done, sweets." Mom picked up the runaway cranberries and tossed them into the bowls. "Now why don't you take them out to the living room, please? We'll be right out with the strings."

Ava hopped off the stool and skipped out of the room, a bowl in each hand while Mom cringed, awaiting a trail of spilled cranberries left on the wood floor behind her.

"Hey, Mom?"

"Mmm?" Mom dumped the extra kernels from the air popper into the trash.

"What made Norah decide to have her wedding on Christmas?" Isabella pricked her finger again and shook out her hand, muttering, "Ouch," for about the hundredth time.

Tilting her head, Mom gave an incredulous look. "C'mon, Izzy, you know why."

"Do I? Because if she would've asked me, I would've told her to have a destination wedding like Finn and Nina. A tropical vacation and a wedding—two birds, one stone. Now that's what I'm going to do."

She pushed another threaded needle into the pincushion, remembering the Hawaii trip nearly six years ago fondly. What she wouldn't give to be laying out on a beach right now instead of freezing her appendages off in this winter wasteland.

"You do know that if they would've had a destination wedding, Leo would've been there too, right?" Mom returned the air popper to the upper cabinet. The same cabinet it had always been in. "And what's this talk about, 'that's what I'm gonna do?'" She mimicked Isabella's voice. "You getting married or something and forgot to tell us? Not that I'd be surprised. Hurt? Yes. But surprised? Definitely not."

There it was again. Another jab at her expense. Fine. Let her family give her a hard time. If that's what she had to do to keep Leo from learning the truth, so be it.

"No, Mom. No wedding. Not anytime soon at least." And it definitely wouldn't be her marrying Harrison Blake. Especially since he was presently contemplating who should keep the popcorn popper. "I know, you're right. Leo would've been there, too."

Mom leaned on the kitchen counter. "Then what's so bad about coming home? At Christmas?"

"Nothing," her voice went up without intention, her belly stirring with conviction. "You know I always loved Christmas. But I've told you. I'm just super busy. Work always has me trying to reach a deadline or traveling." Isabella cursed under her breath after another needle prick. She sucked on the tip of her finger.

"For what it's worth, we're all happy you're home. It's nice. I know some of us have been giving you a hard time, but I think it's just been easier that way."

Isabella pulled her fingertip from in between her lips. "Yeah? Easier for who?"

Mom waved her hand in the air dismissively. "Oh, just let Finn and Norah have their fun."

Was she being serious? Because it wasn't fun. Not to her, it wasn't.

"It's not just them. It's you and Dad, too. And Leo."

"Honey, you need to talk to him." Interesting how Mom completely deviated from herself being in the hot seat. "He deserves a reason why you broke things off with him. Izzy, he was devastated."

Heat filled her cheeks, and her eyes pricked. "I was devastated, too."

"Okay." Mom pushed away from the counter and held out her palms. "You've never even told any of us what happened. But Dad and I believe you had good reason."

"I did," her voice cracked. She wanted to tell Mom. And Dad. And everyone. But how could she? After all these years, did it even matter?

"I'm sure you did. But…I still think you should talk to him. Not just for him, but for you too. It never really felt like you two had closure." Mom inspected the Santa Claus pincushion with all the needles sticking out of its butt, then eyed Isabella with one penciled, arched brow.

Isabella sighed. "You know if I would've come back here after graduation, we would've gotten married, had kids, and we would've stayed in Colorado forever. And you would've loved that, but Dad always told me to go. Go to college. Reach for my dreams. Never settle."

"So what are you saying? If you married Leo, you would've settled?"

"No." Isabella glanced over her shoulder, lowering her voice. "Never. But what's done is done. We just weren't meant to be together, that's all."

"Are you trying to convince me, or yourself?" Mom scooped up the pincushion and sauntered out of the kitchen.

"You, obviously," Isabella called, following behind Mom, sucking on her fingertip again.

"You keep telling yourself that, sweetie," Mom said over her shoulder.

Isabella inhaled a deep breath and held it in, a stiffness working its way into her neck. What did Mom know? Sure, Isabella would always love Leo, but they weren't meant to be. If they were, nothing and no one would've stood in their way.

In the living room, Mom handed a threaded needle to each family member. And Leo. At this point, it felt like he belonged in the Whitley family more than Isabella did.

Ava reached for a threaded needle, but Finn said no way. She pouted until Nina told her she could add the tinsel to the tree once the popcorn strings were finished. Oh yes, the Whitley Christmas tree had it all—popcorn-cranberry strings *and* tinsel.

Isabella took a seat on the carpeted floor next to Norah. The bowls of popcorn and cranberries sat on the coffee table within reach. She felt safe next to Norah. Or at least the safest she was going to feel in this family, she decided.

When she glanced at Leo stretched out on the sofa with his feet propped on the coffee table, she tried not to allow the length of him, the filled-out chest, and wide shoulders, to distract her from her annoyance of him. He already had his second row of popcorn started in the pattern of five pieces of popcorn and two cranberries. How had he already gotten that far? She needed to catch up. She hurried, stringing the popcorn onto her needle and thread in record speed, pushing two cranberries onto the needle next. There. She'd caught up to him.

But when she checked his string again, he'd already moved onto another row of cranberries. Isabella's stomach tightened. She was being stupid. She knew that. And yet, why was her heart beating fast and hard against her rib cage while she continued pushing the cranberries and popcorn onto the string, glancing at Leo every few seconds?

It didn't take long before Leo caught on. He looked at her string, then back up at her. They shared a look. And not an, *Oh baby, I want to pick up where we left off in the rental car* look. No, it was definitely confirmed —this had just turned into a competition. And it was on. Leo had already weaseled his way into the hearts of her family, she wouldn't let him beat her at popcorn and cranberry stringing.

It didn't take long for the rest of the family to realize what the two were up to.

"Oh, I see how it is." Finn slapped Leo's back. "You two are having a competition without the rest of us?"

Unfortunately, the interruption didn't stop Leo. He remained focused on the tedious task at hand. As well as on Isabella's progress. She, too, kept precision eye contact on the needle and cranberries.

"Hey, maybe the rest of us wanted to get in on that action," Landon complained. "What are the stakes?"

"No stakes," Isabella muttered, annoyed, her fingers continuing to fly.

"That's it. I give up!" Norah threw her string down. "That's about the hundredth time I've pricked my finger."

"Don't give up. You could win," Mom coaxed.

"I didn't even know we were racing." Norah pouted.

"I don't think the rest of us knew either," Dad said.

Isabella gave him a quick glance.

Dad eyed both she and Leo. "And if we did, we're clearly losing."

Norah picked up the remote and turned on the television. "Well, we can listen to some music while we let those two finish stringing the popcorn, I guess."

Leo snatched a new needle from the pincushion and began on his fourth string, smirking at Isabella. Heat flashed across her cheeks. Why couldn't he just let her have this one thing? He had to be so stubborn and couldn't handle letting her win. She held in her frustration, pushing two more pieces of popcorn onto the needle and laid the full string onto the floor before reaching for a new needle and thread.

"Why don't you just give up," Leo muttered.

"Not a chance in hell," Isabella whispered.

"Language," Finn warned, covering Ava's innocent ears with his hands.

Isabella winced but kept working, her heartbeat accelerating.

"There's no way you can beat me," Leo said.

"Wanna make a bet?"

"Okay you two, play nice," Mom warned.

"I've got ten years on you."

Oh, he went there, did he? Her body heated, flames licking up her neck. But she wouldn't let his comment throw her off her game. That's exactly what he wanted. And she needed to remind him just whose family this was. "Yeah? Well I did this for eighteen years. I could do it in my sleep."

Tension filled the room, but Ava was oblivious to it. She jumped back and forth between Leo and Isabella, commentating the entire time. "Auntie Izzy, you're losing. Hurry! Uncle Leo has four finished strings already. Go, go, go!"

"Alright," Nina said, laughing and pulling Ava out of Isabella's face. "Let's let the grownups play." She took her daughter by the hand and led her down the hall. "I think Grandma has cookies and eggnog."

"I sure do," Mom said. "Whoever wants snickerdoodles and eggnog, come with me. I think those two have the popcorn-stringing under control."

Isabella tuned out everyone as they scattered. She could vaguely hear the Christmas music still filling the room. The only thing sounding loud in her ear was her own quick breathing and her pounding heart.

Leo scooted to the edge of the sofa, closer to where she sat crisscross on the floor. He leaned close to her, the heat from his breath brushing against the bare skin of her neck, sending goosebumps shooting down her arms. "This is pretty hot."

"What?" Isabella's fingers froze, and she whipped her head in his direction, blinking rapidly.

"Are you into this as much as I am?" He waggled his thick brows.

"Are you serious? Did you get into my mom's rum for the eggnog?"

"No. Unlike you, I don't require alcohol to get a rise. And yes. I'm absolutely into this. I've been reminded of what I used to like about you the most. What I still like, God help me."

She gulped, her mind snagging on what he'd just said, like the words *get a rise* for one, but more importantly, he still liked her. "And what is that, exactly?"

"Your competitiveness."

"Really?" She gaped at him. "*That's* what does it for you?"

He shrugged, his fingers moving slower as they strung the popcorn. "I guess so."

"But not me practically throwing myself at you?" The words tumbled out of her mouth before she could stop them. She had absolutely thrown herself at him in the rental car, but she definitely didn't need to revisit the details.

"Oh no, believe me, that was hot, too. But this," he gestured in the space between them, "is much more intense. It's like foreplay. Remember how exhilarating it used to be when I'd beat you at something? How you'd sneak into my room later and tackle me in my bed, all to prove you could still own me in at least *one* way? Pretty sure that's what the whole car thing was about. Not that I'm complaining."

Isabella's cheeks burned, and as much as she scolded herself, her body hummed at his words and the tension winding between them. "I remember that going both ways."

"What, the after-battle sex or the car sex?"

"Both." She bit her lip, her mind replaying the word *sex* in Leo's man voice over and over.

His gaze drifted to her mouth. "Seriously, if your family wasn't in the other room, I'd—" his words dropped.

She simultaneously wanted him to finish that sentence and not finish it. "You'd…what?"

He rubbed his forehead, like he was contemplating the best words to say. When he pulled his hand away, red cranberry stains streaked his skin.

Isabella couldn't help but smile.

"What?" Concern crumpled his brow.

"Come here, you've got cranberry on your face."

"I do? Where?" He swiped at his forehead, but only made it worse. "Stop laughing and get it off. This stuff stains."

Isabella snorted another laugh, rising to her knees and moving closer to him. She wiped her thumb across the red marks. It helped, but the cranberry juice was already seeping in for the long haul. "Here, lick my finger and I'll use it to wipe your forehead."

He reeled back when she held her finger up for him. "What? Gross."

"How is that gross? You've licked worse things on my body." Their eyes locked, and she swallowed down the choking awkwardness of what she'd just said. She cleared her throat, imagining her face had turned ten shades of hell-fire red. "Anyway, do you want me to lick my own finger and rub my spit on your face? Because you better hurry. It's staining."

He hesitated, and she swore his eyes had darkened. He folded his hand around hers and drew her finger into his mouth. But instead of just licking it quickly, he held it there, giving it a long, sensual suck, his eyes never leaving hers.

What. Were. They. Doing. In her parents' living room, no less.

Her body didn't care. She tensed, her entire being answering to his touch.

A sigh escaped her lungs, but laughter from the kitchen snapped her out of her Leo-induced haze. She wrenched back her trembling hand, then hurried and rubbed her wet finger across his forehead, erasing the red stains.

"There," she breathed out a shaky breath, tucking her chin to her chest, trying to look anywhere but at Leo so her heart had a chance to chill out.

"Better?" His voice came out gravelly and rough, and he touched her chin.

So much for a strong will.

She lifted her gaze to meet his. "Yep. All better."

Leo took her hands and wrapped them around to the back of his neck. He peered into her eyes, and she sucked her lip in between her teeth. So many intense emotions rippled through her that she couldn't make sense of them all.

"That mouth," he whispered, running a thumb against her jaw, and sending a craving low in her belly. She closed her eyes and leaned into him, her lips hopeful and parted, waiting through pure agony.

He pressed his forehead against hers. "If you don't pull back, Izzy," he said, low and husky, "I'm gonna kiss you." His warm breath on her mouth made her thighs clench, that feeling in her stomach only intensifying.

She threaded her fingers into his hair, her thoughts battling in her mind. Should she let him kiss her or stop this now? A kiss would go further. Not here and now, of course. But later, when the house grew still, they'd find one another and collide. They weren't capable of any less.

Before she could decide one way or another, her phone chimed and vibrated against the coffee tabletop, bringing her out of the trance.

Like a moth to a bug zapper, eyes had a natural attraction to a text on a cellphone. Unfortunately, they both glanced at it at the same time, so there would be no way to hide it or lie about it. The message was enough to not only put a pause on their intimate moment but put a stop to it altogether.

Harrison: Call me. We need to talk. I want to work this out. I love you.

CHAPTER THIRTEEN

ISABELLA

AT LEAST BY DAY THREE WHEN SHE TRUDGED DOWNSTAIRS FOR breakfast, Isabella expected Leo to be there. And sure enough—there he was, sitting in *her* seat next to Norah, looking far too sexy in his fitted thermal shirt and dark jeans, especially given that it wasn't even eight o'clock yet.

She resisted the urge to check him out further, and headed straight for the coffee, muffling a yawn with her hand.

"Dang, Izz. What happened to you last night?" Finn asked from the dining room table. "You drink too much of Mom's eggnog?"

"Finn," Nina hissed.

Isabella glared at her brother. "I just didn't sleep good."

Dad stood in front of the machine wearing his flannel pajama pants and worn-out slippers. He poured coffee into a mug with a jolly Santa printed on the front and handed it to her. She accepted it like the glorious gift that it was and brought it to her nose, inhaling the heavenly scented roast.

The text from Harrison still sat on Isabella's phone unanswered. Seconds after it came through, her siblings burst from the kitchen, Mom's eggnog with extra rum in hand. There'd been no call to Harrison and no kiss with Leo, much as she'd wanted—needed—the latter. Between Leo's threatening lips and Harrison's abrupt text, it had been the missed kiss that kept her awake much of the night. She'd tossed and turned, getting tangled in the penguin-printed flannel sheets, resulting in crappy sleep. She didn't know what to feel or think, how to deal with the man from her past or the one in her present.

After waking up on the wrong side of the bed, she always felt better if she was a bit put together. She'd brushed out the rat's nest of hair from her jumbled night, washed her face with her favorite brightening cleanser, and dressed in a pair of black leggings and a flannel. This time she'd even come to breakfast with a bra on. Progress from the day before.

Isabella poured a splash of milk and two teaspoons of sugar into her coffee, stirring it while murmurs from her family at the table began again. She lifted her eyes to Leo who was watching her over the brim of his mug. His gaze activated that annoying clenching between her thighs.

It was too early to be trying to figure out the confusing men in her life. Certainly too early to be thinking about steamy kisses and bedroom eyes. Her vision darted to the floor. Dad's coffee-stained slippers with holes in the toes distracted her, reminding her of the Christmas gifts she ordered and had sent gift-wrapped to Mom and Dad's for the family.

"Hey, Dad? Did the packages I had sent arrive?"

"Good morning to you." He took a sip of his coffee.

She smiled, running a hand over her tired face. "Morning."

"Yes, just like every other year, I believe all packages have been received, wrapped, and accounted for. It's a snazzy system you've worked out." He elbowed her in the side like the two were in cahoots. The coffee in her mug sloshed and she held it out, praying it wouldn't spill. She needed every drop this morning.

"Well, I'd planned on shopping when I got here. Ya know, mix it up a bit? But I figured with Eight Days of Christmas and wedding preparations, I wouldn't have enough time."

"It's the thought that counts, sweetie," Dad said, cheers-ing his coffee mug into Isabella's.

"I guess we can thank Amazon." She took a sip of her coffee, allowing her eyes to drift closed for just a second so she could savor the delicious, robust brew.

"Hear, hear." Dad put his own mug to his lips and winked at her over the brim.

She knew she wasn't the perfect daughter, that she'd made mistakes over the years—plenty of them, but Dad understood her. And she was trying to undo some of the wrongs she'd done. This time, she wanted to leave Pineridge on good terms.

"So, is everyone up for some ice skating?" Dad asked. "We better get a move on."

"I am," Norah said in her usual singsong.

"Yeah, of course you are. You just want to show off your fancy footwork." Landon gave her a lingering kiss.

"Don't you know it." She patted his cheeks.

Leo swiveled to face Landon. "You see, what I don't get is how you're no good at ice skating. You grew up in Colorado. Our school had an ice-skating rink."

"Because, big bro. I spent my time on the basketball court, showing off for the ladies. Not on the ice rink like you. I was busy playing the field while you were freezing your ass off." Landon carried his empty mug into the kitchen.

"Technically, *playing the field*," Leo used finger quotes, "is a football analogy. Not basketball. Little bro."

"Whatever. You know what I mean." Landon wiggled his brows.

Leo followed Landon into the kitchen. "No. I don't think I do know what you mean. Please do educate us on what *playing the field* means." He squeezed Landon's shoulders from behind. "You know, in front of your fiancée's parents."

Landon's face turned a bright shade of red.

"Okay," Norah said, joining Landon in the kitchen and sliding her hand into his. "On that awkward note, I think it's time to go."

Dad side-eyed his soon-to-be son-in-law, but he wasn't fooling anyone with the smirk on his face. He adored Landon. Always had. Although, maybe not quite as much as he adored Leo. Which, if Isabella was being honest, was super aggravating.

"Are you sure you're up for today's festivities, Isabella? Maybe you should hang back and catch up on your beauty sleep." Landon snorted.

Norah jabbed an elbow into his side.

Shoulders tense, Isabella narrowed her eyes into slits. Who gave Landon the right to judge her? So she had a rough night of sleep. Who wouldn't after their ex dropped an *I love you* bomb?

"I'm with Landon," Finn said. "You don't look so good. And you've never really liked day three. You kinda sucked at ice skating"

She sighed. "Just because I was an unskilled skater doesn't mean I didn't like it."

"If that's the case, maybe Landon should sit this day out too." Leo smirked.

"Alright." Mom clapped her hands together. "Everyone is going. Everyone is participating. And we need to get an early start. Otherwise, the parking lot will be packed, and the rink will be overcrowded with out-of-towners who don't have any business being out there." She untied her apron and turned to Isabella, pouting her lips. "Sorry, Izzy."

"For what?"

"About the out-of-towner joke."

"Mom, I'm not a tourist. This was my home for eighteen years." She slammed her coffee mug onto the counter. "Ugh, how have you all forgotten that?" Isabella pinched the bridge of her nose and stormed out of the room without even eating breakfast.

She mumbled to herself as she stomped up the stairs, "Eight Days of Christmas, my ass. It's only day three and I'm ready to jump on the next plane out of here."

YOU WOULD THINK, once she had time to calm down, Isabella would feel better. But she didn't. Instead, at the outdoor rink, she sat on the lowest bleacher with her skates, still fuming. Besides the lack of sleep, the eggnog, and the tug-of-war on her heart, her family's teasing was grating on her. Mom had said she enjoyed having her home for the holidays, but she sure didn't act like it.

The chilled breeze in the air blasted her bare cheeks and neck with an unforgiving sting. The ominous, grayish-white sky depicted the definite chance of another snowfall. Isabella had hoped for at least a few days of her favorite Colorado winter days—clear blue skies and a bright sun beaming its warmth.

Pineridge had four ice rinks. The one at the high school and the elementary school where the Whitleys and Hoffmans skated at on the weekends, the indoor rink where Norah taught children's figure skating lessons and the outdoor one that tourists liked the most. Bright lights crisscrossed and draped over the rink, illuminating the ice at night. There was a food truck parked next to the skate-rental booth that sold coffee, hot cocoa, and pastries. Seating areas around a couple gas fire pits were gathered near the parking lot.

Isabella daydreamed about warming herself in front of the crackling fire, sipping on a rich hot coffee. She groaned out loud, seated on the hard, cold bleacher, and bent over, tugging on her skates. That part she'd never forget, out-of-towner or not.

"This seat taken?"

Isabella glanced up and there was Leo, an ice skate in each hand. She shrugged and bit down on the inside of her cheek.

He sat next to her, though hesitantly. "How you doing?"

"Been better." She worked at her laces, dangling in knots.

"Yeah, I bet." Leo pushed his feet into his skates. "You know, she loves you. She's just trying to roll with things. She's not purposely trying to make you feel bad."

Isabella kept her head down, her eyes stinging. "I know my mom, Leo."

"Do you?"

She glared at him. She wanted to say something sharp, something that would hurt, but there was nothing to say. The truth was that she used to know her mom. Maybe not so much anymore. And it wasn't just Mom. It was everyone.

She turned back to her skates.

"How's your ex?" he said. "Harrison, was it?"

Isabella glared at him again. She was already pissed about all of this with her mom and now he was going to bring up Harrison? "I wouldn't know. Haven't talked to him."

He raised his hands in defense. "Just asking. Jeez."

A moment passed, and she finally loosened the last knot and began tightening her laces.

"You never called him?" Leo's voice came out softer than it had any right to be.

She wrapped the laces around the ankles of her skates over and over a few times before tying them in the front. "I don't know why it bothers you if I call him or not. We're not together."

Leo's face hardened. "I know we're not together. We haven't been together in years. I was just trying to give you space to talk in case you needed to vent."

She couldn't do this. Not right now. Kind Leo was even worse for her brain than Sexy Leo. He made her want to curl against him and cry. Let it all out. But there was a lot to get out. Things Leo wouldn't understand, let alone believe.

Isabella stood, shakily, bracing her palms on the bench. "I meant me and Harrison. He and I aren't together."

"Oh." He cleared his throat, eyes focused on his perfect lacing technique. "I knew that."

It was mean, but she didn't know what else to say. She and Leo had gotten far too comfortable last night. Not as comfy as they'd gotten in the rental car, but last night was a different level. A different kind of close. Things with him could be too easy if she let them. Too easy until he required an explanation again, and she knew that time would come.

Isabella opened her mouth to speak, but decided against it, pushing away from the bench instead. She had to get away from him and those tender eyes or any restraint she'd summoned would evaporate.

Her body swayed backward before she jerked herself forward and caught her balance. She swallowed and hobbled a few steps. "Now, if you'll please excuse me," she said over her shoulder, "I have some skating to do."

Leo smirked, rubbing at his beard. "Good luck with that."

Outwardly, she rolled her eyes, but inwardly, her stomach coiled with nervous energy. She knew she'd need it. She hadn't skated in what felt like eons.

She reached the ice, waiting for a wide clearing of people before pushing off the toe pick with a gentle ease. Her legs were stiff, her knees curving inward, but so far, so good. If she just took it slow, she'd be fine. She made it an entire way around the rink without falling. She could do this.

But then Ava skated up behind her, bumped into her hip, and Isabella lost her balance. She stumbled forward, landing hard on her knees.

"Ouch! Son of a—"

"Sorry, Auntie Izzy."

Isabella exhaled a shaky breath. "It's fine. I'm fine." She pushed herself up onto the toe pick and used her palms as leverage, the cold, rough ice biting into her skin.

And then Ava was gone—skating off in a flash as if a zombie chased after her. Once Isabella got back on her feet, she hedged toward the side of the rink. It would be safer on the outskirts with the other mediocre skaters rather than close to the middle where the pros skated.

Shuffling her feet, she managed to make it to the outside lane, but when she got there, she regretted her decision. Small children clung to the wall while older skaters wobbled and fell. The so-called tourists and out-of-towners could be picked out easily. Crap, maybe Mom was right. Isabella *was* an out-of-towner and had no business being out on the rink.

But no, she wasn't going to give up so easily. She was no quitter. There had to be some technique cemented in her body memory, didn't there?

"C'mon, Izzy," she muttered under her breath. "It's just like riding a bike."

"That's a lie."

The deep timbre of Leo's voice slid under her skin, sending warmth zipping through her bones. She sucked in a breath and turned around.

"Perfect," she said on exhale.

Now he was going to see her fail.

Leo skated past her, then spun and skated backward.

"Why are you always here?" She groaned. "Don't you have somewhere to be? Work to do, maybe?"

He circled her, showing off his stellar moves. "Nope. Remember, I sort of own my own business."

She didn't take her attention away from the ice when she spoke.

"Oh, that's right. So your business must be doing well to afford a house in the mountains?"

He shrugged, clearly downplaying his accomplishments.

Her mind went to his marriage with Talia. Isabella hadn't known exactly why Talia and Leo hadn't worked out, only that they divorced. Norah had told her that Talia was somewhat greedy, of both money and Leo's time.

"But the business wasn't successful enough for Talia to stick around?" She was clearly prying.

"Why, Isabella Whitley, are you being a nosy Nelly?" he teased, sounding like her dad. He grinned that genuine Leo smirk, the one that used to send a vibration throughout her entire body. Maybe the one that *still* sent vibrations through her entire body.

But right now, she felt like smacking the smug grin right off his manly face. Okay, maybe a small part of her felt like kissing it off his face.

"Absolutely not. But it sure doesn't keep everyone from telling me about you. My parents and Norah especially." She shuffled her skates, her feet beginning to find their rhythm and memory on the ice again.

"I can't help it if they love me."

"And why *is* that? Why do they love you so much?"

He shrugged those broad shoulders. "I guess I'm just a lovable kinda guy, Izz." He smiled and spun before speed skating away, ice sprinkling the air behind his skates.

Ugh. Stupid Leo. Stupid wobbly ankles. Stupid cold feet.

Norah skated up alongside her. "Hey, sis."

Isabella planted a fake smile on her face.

"You're hating this. I can tell."

"You know, day three was always my least favorite."

"For you and Landon both." Norah gestured to where Landon sat on the bleachers. She giggled. "But I gotta love him."

"If you must," Isabella's words came out sounding harsher than she intended.

"You better watch it, or I'll trip you."

"I guess if you want a bruised and banged-up maid of honor at your wedding, that's your choice."

"True." Norah put her hands up in surrender and skated away backward. She proceeded to do figure eights.

"Show off!" Isabella yelled between cupped hands.

Norah spun and spun and spun. Faster and faster. Yep, she was definitely showing off. But for who, Isabella didn't know. Because she could care less, and when she glanced over at Landon again, she was pretty sure he could care less, too. Instead of having his attention fixated on his fiancée, his eyes were on a pretty brunette with a totally unfair ass, bent over, slipping on her skates.

Heat bloomed in Isabella's chest, anger brimming to the surface, but before she had time to do anything about it, she was falling—landing hard on her backside on the cold ice. But instead of ice, it felt like fire shot through her body. She groaned. And that was it. She was done. She'd spend the next few hours joining Landon and his wandering eyes on the bleachers.

Or better yet, from the cozy spot in front of the fire.

"Tough fall out there," Landon said after she dragged herself from the ice.

"Yeah."

"But I guess at least you're trying. I haven't even made it off the bleachers."

When Isabella sat down, it hurt instantly. A reminder of the fall. But the fiery pain slipped her mind and the earlier anger toward her soon to be brother-in-law returned. Landon was checking out other women right in front of Norah. She didn't want to imagine how he'd be after ten years or even a year of marriage.

"You know, you don't have to be good at skating," Isabella said. "Norah just wants you to share this with her."

Landon's eyes followed Norah as she gracefully skated around the rink. "I fall every time."

"So what? You just saw me fall."

"Yeah, but who do you have to impress out there?"

"Ouch. Point taken." Isabella unlaced her skates.

"I didn't mean that. I guess I just assumed you weren't trying to impress Leo. Unless you are?"

She yanked off one skate and wiggled her toes. "No, I'm definitely not."

"Are you sure about that? Because I can see the two of you together again. But Norah says your ex wants to get back together."

"Dang it, Norah." Isabella tugged off her other skate. She stretched out her chilled, stiff foot. "Is nothing sacred between sisters anymore?" She was regretting telling Norah and Nina about Harrison's text on the drive to the rink that morning. She didn't even know if she wanted to work things out with him. Three days ago, her answer to Harrison would've been easy. But now, being home and spending time with Leo again was seriously messing with her head.

"Sorry, 'fraid not. I'm also sorry about inviting Leo to join in with Eight Days of Christmas."

Turning and narrowing her eyes at him, Isabella said, "So I have *you* to thank, huh? All eight days."

All he could offer was a half-hearted shrug and a noncommittal smile.

"Ugh," she groaned, glancing over at Leo while he skated side by side with Norah. Five more days stuck with Leo Hoffman. Staring at his pretty face. Trying not to remember how good he tasted.

"Just like old times," Landon offered.

"Yay," was all she managed to say.

CHAPTER FOURTEEN

ISABELLA

CONSUMED IN STRIPS OF BURLAP, RED RIBBON, AND PINECONES, Isabella's eyes and fingers burned. She was pretty sure that after Eight Days of Christmas was over—if she survived—she'd return to New York banged up, bruised, and exhausted. Each day seemed to bring a new ailment with it.

"What's next?" Isabella asked, setting aside a tall glass cylinder after filling it with pinecones. She'd never made a centerpiece, and she could safely say she hoped she didn't regret that fact.

The Whitley's living room had been turned into a cross between a JoAnn Fabrics store and a Colorado forest. There were piles of twigs and pinecones alongside the rolls of burlap and red ribbon. Packages of tea lights and floating candles sat stacked in boxes on the coffee table. Along one side of the room, fake mini trees lined the wall while strands of white twinkling lights were strewn across the floor. Dad had wanted to use real trees, but Norah said that would be wasteful.

"Here." Norah handed Isabella another glass cylinder. "Fill her up."

Isabella groaned. "Seriously? How many of these do we need?"

"One for each table. So…sixteen."

"Sixteen tables? Eight chairs around each table? That's…one hundred twenty-eight people. You're expecting that many guests?"

"Yep. Why do you sound so surprised?"

"Because. Your wedding is on Christmas Day. I guess I assumed most people would want to be with their family."

"Well, a lot of these guests *are* family. You remember how big the Hoffman family is?" Norah placed tea light candles into white, frosted votive holders.

"I guess." She stuck long twigs into the cylinders that held the pinecones, attempting to arrange them like flowers in a vase.

All of the Hoffman family would be at this wedding? She'd become familiar with several of them since she and Leo had been friends and then dated for so long. Thinking of sweet Nana Hoffman made her stomach churn.

Isabella shoved more pinecones into another vase, pricking what she'd dubbed her Cranberry Finger. She'd poked that finger the other night enough times that it looked more like a piece of fruit than an actual part of her anatomy.

She exhaled a breath of curses. That was it—after her fall on the ice today, and all the wedding decorations, Isabella needed a break. She also still had to propose her idea of a bachelorette party to Norah.

"Okay, time for afternoon coffee."

"You know that's not actually a thing, right?" Norah arched a brown brow.

"What's not a thing?"

"Afternoon coffee."

"Oh yeah? I'll have you know it's most definitely a thing because I said it is. And it's more than a thing, afternoon coffee is a full-on religious experience." She pushed herself off the floor and pulled Norah up.

Norah laughed, tucking her long, burnt sienna hair behind her ear. "Whatever you say." She followed Isabella into the kitchen. "Nina said she'd help with the centerpieces after she put Ava down for a nap."

"She's five. Do you think she still needs to be taking naps?" Isabella asked.

"What do I know? I don't have kids. Yet."

Standing in front of the coffee machine, Isabella froze and turned slowly to face Norah, clutching at her chest. "What do you mean, *yet?*

Oh Norah, please tell me you're not…" she let her words fall, unable to finish the question. She knew her sister would have kids eventually, but she didn't need to rush it.

"No." Norah confirmed quickly. "But I mean…soon, I hope."

"But you're so young. What's the hurry?"

"It's not a hurry. We love each other. We want to start a family right away. There's nothing wrong with that."

"I guess." Isabella prepped the coffee maker, folding her lips together and telling herself not to press the subject further.

"Believe me. When you get married, you'll feel the same way."

"Maybe. But by the time that happens, I won't be young anymore." She hit the brew button.

"You never know," Norah said, retrieving two mugs from the cupboard.

"I'm nowhere close. Remember, Harrison and I are sort of on a break?" She shoved an elbow into Norah's side. "Thanks for telling Landon about that, by the way."

Norah hunched her shoulders. "Sorry. But I tell him everything."

"Yeah, yeah, yeah," she said, waving her off. "Because you two are so in love. *And just you wait until you're in love, Izzy*. Blah, blah, blah."

Norah smiled wistfully. "Something like that. But I wasn't talking about Harrison."

"Well, I know you're not talking about another certain Hoffman. Because that would be borderline insane."

Norah leaned a hip into the counter. "C'mon, would it be so crazy?"

By the way Norah's voice went up an octave, it was obvious just how crazy.

"Yes," Isabella said flatly.

"But everyone knows how perfect you two are for each other. Everyone but you two stubborn jackasses."

"We had our chance." She picked up one of the Christmas mugs and studied the silly reindeer with the big, bright red nose, getting lost in a memory of Leo. One where their limbs were intertwined, and he whispered into her ear that he'd never let her go. She swallowed the lump full of regret in her throat. "It just wasn't meant to be."

"Can you just keep your heart and mind open to it? For me? Please?" Norah reached out and squeezed the top of Isabella's arm.

She wanted to promise Norah on reflex alone. She couldn't look at her angelic face without promising her the moon and the stars. She would do anything for Norah. So how could she deny her now?

Isabella's shoulders sagged as she sighed and agreed. "Fine. I'll try to be open to possibility."

"Yay." Norah jumped up and down before yanking Isabella into a hug.

"But," Isabella said, rearing back. "Then you have to do something for me. Agree to a bachelorette party. Tonight."

"Tonight?"

"Yes. I've already invited Nina and Maddie and Taylor." Isabella stared at her sister, hopefully. "If not for yourself, do it for me. I need a break from all this." She gestured to the space around them. "From Mom and Dad and Finn's teasing, from Leo, from the wedding centerpieces." She shook Norah's shoulders. "Please, I'm begging you."

"Okay. Let's do it."

"Yes!" Isabella pumped a celebratory fist into the air.

CHAPTER FIFTEEN

LEO

AFTER SPENDING HOURS SKATING, LEO HAD GONE BACK TO HIS DAD'S house and unclogged the garbage disposal before taking a long, hot shower. Dressed in jeans and a navy-blue and gray flannel, he groaned as he stretched out on Dad's couch, clicking through some photos on his digital camera.

As great as it felt to be out on the ice today, he was relieved to get a break from Isabella now. He wasn't sure what was worse, feeling such intense attraction to her in those tight leggings as they hugged every inch of her curves, or feeling awful watching her fall onto the ice. He shouldn't care. Not about her body, in any regard. Not if it was bruised and sore or soft and welcoming.

Jeez. Get a grip, Hoffman.

Holding the camera in his hands, Leo thought about going home. Just for tonight. It would feel amazing to sleep in his own king-sized bed that actually fit his long body. And he could get these latest prints uploaded and maybe even get started on editing them. But Dad had already put his famous Hoffman chili into the crockpot this morning before he left for work. Leo couldn't disappoint him. This week was probably as important to him as it was to the Whitley's. Without Mom here, Leo felt the added pressure to be completely present.

This house had warm memories filled to the brim. His mom had always made sure holidays were memorable. She'd planned fun family game nights and themed parties. In wintertime, she'd woken him and Landon up every Saturday with hot cocoa in an effort to bribe them to go outside and shovel the driveway.

While Leo held those memories close to his heart, he mostly tried to not think about them. Without Mom in this house, it felt drafty, and empty. The wood-paneled walls, red brick around the fireplace, and brown living room furniture made it dark. She'd been the one to breathe life into the house.

He wished she was here. Not only because she made the holidays authentic and memorable, but he could use her expertise right now with Isabella. He didn't know how it was possible, but he was more confused about their relationship than ever before. If you could even call it a relationship. Throwing an arm across his face, his eyes fluttered closed.

"Hey." Landon nudged Leo in the shoulder, waking him out of his near comatose state.

Leo pried open one eye. Landon held out an old mug with a bear printed on the side.

"Coffee?" Landon said.

Leo sat up, his cold body slow to respond. He took the mug and nodded his thanks.

Landon sat across from him, perching on the edge of Dad's worn leather recliner, his own mug held in both hands.

Leo had a sneaking suspicion Landon had something on his mind. And he was fairly certain he knew exactly what it was. Or rather *who* it was.

"What's up?"

"Nothing." Landon hunched both shoulders.

Leo took a sip and allowed the coffee to work its magic before prodding Landon further. But the two of them sitting there in silence drinking their coffee grew increasingly more awkward as each second passed.

"Nothing, huh? Because it looks like you've got something on your mind."

Landon studied his thumb as he rubbed it against the ceramic handle.

"Out with it already."

Landon glanced up. "Fine. I sort of have a favor to ask."

"Why do I feel like this favor is going to involve a certain Whitley woman? And not the one you're engaged to."

Landon winced.

"Because I sort of haven't accomplished the last favor you requested." He'd have it done in about five more days, when this extreme Whitley tradition was over, and he wasn't forced to spend nearly every waking moment with his high school sweetheart.

"Yeah, I know. This favor isn't as big of a commitment, I swear."

"So what is it?"

"Isabella is taking Norah out for a bachelorette party tonight—"

"Yes," Leo interrupted. "I'll do it."

"But you don't even know what I was going to ask."

"You want me to take you out for a bachelor party? Man, I thought you'd never ask." He perked up, scooting to the edge of the couch cushion. "I'm in." This could be exactly what Leo needed to take his mind off Isabella. A guys' night.

"Not exactly." Landon rubbed his hand over his short brown hair.

Leo pinched his brows together. "Then what?"

"They're just taking Norah to O'Henry's. And Norah doesn't want to go alone."

"But she won't be alone. She'll have Nina and Isabella and I'm assuming Maddie and Taylor."

"Right," he stretched out the word. "She doesn't want to go without me."

Leo blinked at his brother. Was he serious? Norah couldn't even go to her own bachelorette party without Landon? He was no therapist but that sounded like all kinds of messed up.

"So what exactly do you need from me?"

"I want you to come with me."

Leo pumped the imaginary brakes in his brain. "The last thing I had on my agenda tonight was hanging out with Isabella Whitley and her crew at a bar." He gulped his coffee. Sure, he wouldn't mind a glimpse of Izzy dressed for a night out on the town, bending over a pool table with a stick in hand, shimmying her hips to the music. Just the picture in his mind was enough to instigate a spark moving south. "C'mon, Landon. Don't you think you've asked me to sacrifice enough?"

"You don't have to hang out with her," Landon insisted. "Just hang out with me. We'll have a beer or two, shoot some pool, play some darts, and I can drive Norah home when the night is done."

"It sounds a lot to me like you don't trust your fiancée and you want to babysit her."

Landon stood abruptly and took a swig of coffee. "Never mind. I don't expect you to understand. Just forget it." He crossed the room in a hurry.

"No, I don't think *you* understand," Leo called after him. When Landon didn't stop, he said, "She came back, ya know?"

Landon froze.

Standing, Leo said, "Did you know?"

Landon turned slowly and faced him. He shook his head. "No. I didn't know. When?"

Leo's heart heaved at the memory of the words Isabella spoke up on the mountain. He glanced at the nearly empty mug in his hand before looking back at his little brother, not fully sure he could believe him. "I guess sometime after college and before Mom passed."

"Wow," Landon said, breathing out a long sigh.

"Yeah. So you didn't know?"

"Honest, man. I had no idea. And I don't think Norah knew either. She would've told me."

"But that's what I don't get. How could she have come home without anyone knowing?"

The rumble of Dad's old work truck sounded outside and pulled both of their attention toward the front window.

"Like I said, just talk to her." Landon made it sound so easy.

Leo rubbed the back of his neck. Talking to Isabella wasn't easy. It seemed like any time they talked, other things happened too. Sexy, tempting things. Things they had no right doing when things between them still weren't clear.

Dad came inside, a whirl of cold air entering with him, stomping the snow off his boots in the entryway and setting his lunchbox down. "One would think having two grown men around the house would mean the front walk would get shoveled, but what do I know?"

"Sorry, Dad." Leo snatched his knit beanie from off the arm of the couch. "We were out most of the day. I'll go do it now."

"No, no, I got it." Landon rushed to the entryway.

Generally, Leo would argue, and he'd win—resulting in him doing the chores around the house that didn't even belong to him anymore. But with the latest favor Landon asked of him, Leo figured his brother owed him.

"You're home a little early," Leo stated.

"Yeah, finished the job sooner than expected. And the Whitley's invited me over tonight for some of Sue's special eggnog."

Leo arched a brow. "Yeah?" He was all too familiar of Sue's special eggnog and a night off the hard stuff was probably a good idea.

His dad hunched a shoulder, forming his lips into a pout. "Why not? I'm feeling festive this year." He smiled. "I'm thinking I should put up a tree. Maybe even hang some lights outside."

Warmth ballooned in Leo's chest, unthawing his frosty heart with old, harbored feelings over family Christmas and traditions. He patted his dad's back. "I could look for the menorah in the garage if ya want?"

"Great idea, son."

"I'll help with whatever you need."

CHAPTER SIXTEEN

ISABELLA

PINERIDGE DIDN'T HAVE MANY OPTIONS FOR BACHELORETTE PARTIES AS far as venues go, especially at the last minute. They'd have to settle for O'Henry's. It was rustic, to put it nicely, but it was the only local brewpub that had both dancing and live music.

Isabella was more than ready to relax and let loose. She'd been uptight ever since she stepped foot on the airplane several days before. But of course, this night was about Norah, who seemed as though she needed a break from all the holiday shenanigans just as much as Isabella, if not more. Planning a wedding was ultra-stressful, much less a Christmas wedding.

O'Henry's hadn't changed a bit. The bar was flanked in old, barn wood siding and had neon signs hung above blacked-out windows. If it wasn't for the multitude of cars parked out front, it would have appeared deserted. Back when she was in high school, the owners, Ricky O'Henry's parents, would occasionally allow some of Ricky's friends to hang out there in the winter so they'd have somewhere safe and warm to go.

The sound of the instruments, the beat of the drum, and the hollering of patrons boomed outside when Isabella stepped out of the

Norah's SUV, her wedged ankle boots crunching onto the snow-compacted parking lot.

Isabella ushered Norah, Maddie, Taylor, and Nina into the cozy bar. "Okay, ladies, shots all around?" She asked on their way inside.

Nina adjusted her boobs in the burgundy scoop halter dress after stripping off her wool coat. "Do you even have to ask? Yes, please."

"Woohoo!" Maddie, one of Norah's bridesmaids and her best friend since kindergarten, shouted. She took off her winter coat, shaking the snow off her blonde highlighted hair and hung it on a hook by the door. Maddie smoothed the black cotton midi dress over her hips. "Norah, your sister knows how to party. Why did I never know this?"

"Probably because when she was partying at seventeen, we were in middle school."

"Right," Maddie observed.

"And we aren't going to party too hard. We have a big day tomorrow." Norah passed Isabella a look of warning. She had on an adorable oversized black sweater paired with a black and white floral skirt, black tights, and black chunky ankle boots.

"Right, right, right. Day four of Christmas…" Isabella scrunched her face, thinking about what holiday activity awaited them tomorrow. "Cookies. Oh, we can totally do that a little hungover," she teased, shrugging out of her tweed coat, revealing a red dress with tank straps, a square neckline, and a flared skirt.

"Ha, very funny. But there's no way I'm getting drunk. Mom and Dad have never seen me hungover."

Norah was such a goody-goody. She'd always been Mrs. Perfect. Isabella seemed to forget that detail since there was such an age gap between them. When Isabella was going to O'Henry's with her best friend Kelsey Sanders, Ricky, and Leo, Norah had been at home in bed or at the ice rink skating.

Ugh, Leo. Tonight, she wanted to drink enough to forget all about him. Past Leo and present Leo. And all the harbored feelings that had recently inched to the surface of her heart.

"C'mon, ladies. Let's get drinks and snag a table." Isabella headed toward the bar, the other girls following behind.

When she reached the bar, she leaned over the counter, waving to grab the bartender's attention. "Excuse me, barkeep, five shots of tequila for me and my friends, please," she said, using an exaggerated Irish accent.

"Tequila?" Norah groaned.

Isabella turned to her. "One shot. It won't kill you."

"Oh, lighten up." Maddie smacked Norah on the back. "Have some fun for once."

"I have fun." Norah pouted.

"I'm game," Taylor said, her black hair pulled into a tight topknot.

The bartender, a guy around Isabella's age, with a reddish, thick beard shuffled toward them, his eyes widening. "Isabella Whitley."

"Ricky?"

"In the flesh." He raised his arms at his sides and stuck out his beer gut, as though he were a grand specimen to behold.

Isabella couldn't help but smile. "Oh my gosh, you're so…grown up. Look at that beard."

"Yeah, well," he said, mindlessly scratching the scruff on his chin. "And you, look at you. You look great." He stretched across the bar and pulled her in for an awkward hug.

"It's so good to see you."

"You too," he said into her hair.

"Izzy?" Her name floated over the music in a high-pitched shriek.

She and Ricky released their embrace, and it seemed as if everyone in the bar turned in the direction of the shrill voice. And there stood Kelsey Sanders, Isabella's childhood best friend, slack-jawed, hands pressed to her hips. But the most obvious and pressing appearance was her protruding belly.

"Kelsey?" She had to question it. Because even though she knew it was her, with the same black bob and bright blue eyes, Isabella's brain couldn't comprehend the fact that Kelsey was pregnant. She hurried to greet her, shuffling around people crowding at the bar.

When they reached one another, the women hesitated, the awkwardness of the time apart obvious and stretching between them.

"Holy hell," she breathed out, without intending to speak the words aloud. "I mean…I can't believe it's really you."

"Wow," Kelsey said, her gaze trailing up and down Isabella's body.

"You look amazing. Gosh, New York has been good to you." She put her finger on Isabella's shoulder and retracted it quickly, shaking out her hand dramatically. "Ooo, you're hot."

Isabella laughed, though it came out sounding forced. "You look great, too." She tried to end the awkwardness by wrapping her old friend in a tight hug, though the round belly in between them was a reminder. "And you're pregnant?"

"Oh, yes…you noticed?" She laughed, pink highlighting her round cheeks.

Isabella's jaw dropped, and she blinked. Was she wrong? She hadn't spent much time around pregnant women, but she knew a pregnant belly when she saw one. Didn't she?

"I'm teasing, Izz." Kelsey waved her off. "Obviously you would notice. I'm nearly full term. This baby may just make an appearance on Christmas. Can you imagine? A Christmas baby?"

Isabella shook her head. She couldn't even imagine having a baby on any day, never mind on Christmas. "A baby. Wow. You're going to be a mom."

"Oh, no," she laughed, tucking her short hair behind both ears. "I've been a mom for a few years now. I've got two more at home with Grandma."

"Really?" Isabella's voice strained. She cleared her throat, attempting to recover. "How's your mom doing?"

"Oh, not my mom. My mom couldn't last five minutes with those two before she'd be heading to the liquor cabinet. We still haven't been able to get her off the juice, if you know what I mean?" She made a drinking gesture with her cupped hand to her lips.

Isabella did know. Kelsey's mom had been an alcoholic since the girls were young. It was part of the reason why Kelsey had spent numerous nights curled up on the trundle under Isabella's daybed.

"They're with Ricky's Mom."

Isabella whipped her head back to Ricky who was serving Norah and the other girls their shots but eavesdropping on their entire conversation. He grinned wide, giving her a proud nod of assurance.

"You and Ricky?" Isabella asked.

"Yep. Going on six years now."

"Wow, that's crazy." Though that didn't come out right. She bit her lip. "I mean, I just didn't know you two, you know, were ever involved."

"Oh, we weren't. You know he drove me crazy in high school. But I guess that's when you know you're meant to be. When someone drives you that crazy, it's gotta be love, right?" She gazed at Ricky, a dreamy haze in her blue eyes.

"That's great. So great. I'm just so happy for you."

"Thank you. That really means a lot." Kelsey took Isabella's hand and squeezed it before letting it go. "And how about you? I heard you're some big reporter in New York and work in a fancy office."

Isabella tucked her chin to her chest, glancing at her ankle boots. She typically didn't like to brag. But she had worked extremely hard to get to where she was. "Well, not a reporter. I'm actually a journalist."

"Oh," Kelsey nodded. "So do you know Hoda Kotb?"

She blinked at her. "Um, no. I write for *The New Yorker*." Typically when Isabella gave out this information, she received a wow in response. But Kelsey just stared at her blankly. "You know, so there's lots of meetings and traveling and deadlines."

"Whoa. Sounds intense. I could never do all that…all that pressure." She rubbed her belly.

"Well, I mean, you have other intense things going on. Like, getting ready to push that watermelon out of your hoo-hah." She smiled, but her cheeks burned. She seriously wasn't getting this right.

"Gee, I guess that's one way to put it." She hunched her shoulders. "Anyway, I should get home. I just came to pick up dinner for Ricky's parents. It was good catching up with you."

Isabella's chest tightened. At one point, Kelsey had been her best friend. All of those nights when the two would whisper secrets into the dark and talk about their dreams. But when Isabella left for Ithaca, Kelsey had stayed in Pineridge and helped her mom in the bakery. They'd lost touch a few years later. "Hey, Kelsey? Why don't you stay?"

"Oh no, that's okay." She dipped her chin, her round cheeks blushing.

"It's Norah's bachelorette party. You should stay. It'll be fun." Isabella touched her arm.

"I'm afraid *I* won't be much fun." She gestured to her stomach.

"You guys have a good time, though." She waved. "And I'll see you at the wedding."

"Oh, right. The wedding. Sounds good." Isabella waved, her chest heaving as she watched her old friend weave out of the bar.

Norah strolled up alongside her. "Well, that was awkward." She handed Isabella a shot glass.

"Yeah," she agreed. "I feel terrible. I've missed so much. I didn't even know about her and Ricky. Why didn't anyone tell me?"

Norah shrugged. "I thought Mom did. Kelsey said they invited you to the wedding."

"What? I don't remember that." Isabella clutched her chest.

"I think Mom said you were in Russia then? I don't really remember." Norah was distracted, scoping the crowded bar, bright Christmas lights strung along the ceiling. "Look, empty table."

"Sweet," Taylor said, sitting in an open chair and smoothing down a black designer A-line skirt. "Let's take these shots already."

Isabella tried to shake off the feelings of running into Kelsey. She came here tonight to relax. To get out of her head. To celebrate Norah. And not think about Leo and her past. She supposed it was impossible to escape the past when she'd literally walked right into it.

"Alright, ladies," she said. "Bottoms up."

They each slung back their shots of tequila. The malt liquid burned her throat and warmed her stomach, assuring her comfort in due time. Yes, this was exactly what she needed.

Nina slammed her glass to the table. "Let's do another!"

Isabella was just about to agree with Nina, after she finished sucking the juice from a lime wedge but was interrupted when Landon passed by their table. She turned, clenching her jaw.

He waved. "Hello, ladies."

What was Landon doing here? And if he was here—she glanced over her shoulder, sighing when she spotted his brother shrugging out of his jacket near the door.

So much for not thinking about Leo.

CHAPTER SEVENTEEN

ISABELLA

Norah!" Isabella hissed. "What are they doing here?"

Norah winced. "Sorry, Izz, did I forget to mention the guys were coming, too?"

"Yeah, ya did," Isabella scoffed.

"I didn't want to drink without Landon. We just don't do that kind of stuff without each other, ya know? You understand, don't you?"

No, she didn't understand.

She ground her jaw as her skin burned. This was bullcrap. Did Landon have to babysit Norah? Could the two ever be apart? That couldn't be healthy.

"But this is your bachelorette party," Isabella argued.

"C'mon, let's get another drink and just forget about them," Nina suggested.

"They won't bother us. Landon promised. We won't even know they're here," Norah said.

"Yeah, right." Isabella glanced at Leo who now stood at the bar talking to Ricky, laughing like old pals did. It wasn't that she didn't want to see Leo, but tonight was supposed to be about Norah. With him there, leaning against the bar, stroking the scruff on his face, a sexy grin playing on his lips, she'd definitely be distracted. She needed to put space between them. "I'm going to the lady's room."

When Isabella returned, to Landon's credit, he and the guys were seated at a table across the bar. *The guys* consisted of Leo, Finn—that traitor—and two of Landon's friends Isabella didn't recognize but assumed to be groomsmen.

"See?" Norah said proudly. "Harmless."

"It's fine, Norah," Isabella huffed. "If you want your fiancée here, that's your choice."

"Thanks for understanding, sis."

Isabella ignored Norah and glanced around, searching for the waiter. She needed another drink.

Isabella had downed two beers and the buzz from the alcohol hummed its way through her bloodstream. Her usual libation was either whiskey with her coworkers or wine with Harrison, and she typically stopped after two drinks. But tonight, she wasn't thinking. Because that was exactly it. She didn't want to think. Not about Leo or Kelsey or the past—at all.

"Should we dance?" Maddie asked, nursing her first beer.

Isabella scanned the bar. At some point, Norah had drifted across the bar and was now sitting on Landon's lap. Isabella shook her head and groaned.

"Or karaoke?" Taylor suggested.

Isabella perked up. "Now that…sounds interesting."

"Really?" Maddie said. "Because I think I'd rather dance."

"That's because you're a fantastic dancer." Taylor picked a piece of lint off the front of her dress.

"I'm a fantastic singer too," Maddie said, brazenly. "But I'm not drunk enough yet to embarrass myself in front of Landon and his friends by singing some lame version of 'Total Eclipse of the Heart.'"

"But it's fun. And Norah loves karaoke."

"Truth," Maddie agreed with Taylor. "And then maybe we can get her back over here."

"Exactly." Isabella pointed her beer bottle at Taylor. "I'm putting us on the list." She pushed away from the table and went to the karaoke organizer, adding their names to the list, and choosing "I Wanna Dance With Somebody" by Whitney Houston.

She strolled toward Norah. "C'mon. We're up next for karaoke." She tugged her sister by the arm.

"Really?" Norah squealed, jumping off Landon's lap. "Oh, I love karaoke."

"Hello, boys." Isabella smiled, waggling her fingers at them.

"Sorry for intruding on your ladies night," Landon apologized.

"It's not a ladies night. It's a bachelorette party. But whatever, it's fine." She started to saunter away, an extra sashay in her step, but...

"Can't wait to hear what you chose to sing," Leo said, his voice a rumbling tone that hit her low in her belly. "Any of my favorites?"

Isabella twirled around. Leo's alluring dark eyes made it impossible to not be captivated. "Probably not."

"Let me guess, 'Man! I Feel Like a Woman'? I know you always loved that one."

Her face heated. "I did." She dipped her chin to her chest. "You remember." It came out like a question.

"Ooo what about, 'Endless Love'?" Norah interrupted. "Izzy said that used to be your song."

"Norah." Isabella groaned, tucking her hair behind her ear. Her skin felt sweltering. Why was it so hot in here?

Norah shrugged a shoulder. "C'mon, it'll be fun."

ISABELLA FIDDLED with the pendant dangling from her neck. It felt like it was about a thousand degrees in the bar with too many intrusive eyes on her and Leo.

Clearing his throat—and drawing her attention—Leo mumbled, "I know I wouldn't mind hearing you sing that song." He smiled, bringing his beer bottle to those luscious lips.

Isabella's heart shifted in her chest. She rested a hip against the guys' table, leaning in closer to Leo. "Just how many beers have you had tonight?"

Because he must be drunk if he wanted her to sing that song.

Their song.

"Who me?" His brows lifted. "This is my first. How many have you had? That's the question. We both know what alcohol does to you." He winked, and his intense gaze fixed on her.

Her already overheated skin ignited, and her limbs felt weak.

Fine. He wanted to flirt? To take a stroll down memory lane?

Two could play at this game.

"I dare you to sing with me," she said. "After me and the ladies are done."

He looked like a deer in headlights. Leo never could say no to a dare, and when the guys started laughing and ribbing him about singing, Isabella knew she had him exactly where she wanted him.

"You in?"

Landon elbowed his brother, wearing a bright smile. "Yeah man. You in?"

Leo rolled his eyes and glared at Isabella. "You are evil."

She fluttered her eyelashes. "I do try." Isabella tugged her sister's arm, pulling her back toward the girls. "C'mon, Norah." She couldn't help but shoot a seductive smile over her shoulder at Leo though. "See you in a bit. Can't wait to hear those rusty pipes."

The girls were up next. The organizer called them onto the stage. Isabella downed half of her third beer before she hustled up the step. She hadn't done this since she was eighteen. Back with Kelsey, Ricky, Leo, and Joey Moretti.

The four other women followed her, plucking microphones from the stands and waiting for the song to begin. Isabella's body stiffened while butterflies thrashed around in her stomach and a couple dozen sets of eyes focused in on her.

The words popped on the screen and the music played through the speakers for "I Wanna Dance With Somebody" by Whitney Houston. The women sang the entire song, even adlibbing some dance steps as well. They missed a few words here and there because they'd been too busy laughing. But they had fun. And it was good to be with Norah and laugh with her. To see her happy.

Isabella missed this. Her heart missed this.

When the song ended, she hopped off the stage as applause filled the bar. People fist-bumped and high-fived the women as they weaved their way back to their table. Isabella breathed heavily, her body hot from adrenaline.

But she didn't have much time to rest before her and Leo's names were called in a tinny voice through the microphone. The organizer had scheduled her sets back-to-back. She snatched Taylor's beer from the table and took a long swig.

"Alright, Norah, if this ends badly, it's on you." Isabella curved her lips deviously.

"Yay!" Norah clapped her hands.

The crowd cheered as she and Leo made their way to the stage.

"They're playing our song, babe." She glanced at him, a sly smile sliding into place.

"I said I wanted to hear *you* sing this song," he said, gritting out the words, voice low.

She arched her brow. "You also said that you like competing with me, didn't you?" The karaoke organizer jumped off the stage, giving them a double point with shooter fingers. The music began, and the familiar tune danced through Isabella's soul. With the words plastered on the screen, her mind traveled back with ease. But she didn't need the lyrics. She knew them by heart.

Leo smirked, his mischievous brown eyes sparkling.

She turned her attention to the crowd and smiled. The song was a duet with a female part first, so she began, singing out the familiar lyrics to "Endless Love" by Diana Ross and Lionel Richie. As far as karaoke voices went, hers was decent, but Leo was still a nice tenor. Together, they harmonized fairly well.

Isabella stood close to Leo. She pouted her lips, singing into the mic, and peering up at him in between glancing at the crowd every few beats. If he wanted a competition, she'd give him one. She sauntered across the stage, shimmying her hips, the flared skirt of her red dress fluttering.

When Leo looked at her, his eyes darkened and dragged up the length of her. Heat bloomed in her chest, and she shivered. He bit on his lip, tripping on a few lyrics and provoking a giggle to escape from her throat.

He wouldn't go down with a fight. He pushed her aside and strutted in front of her, shaking his backside that looked mighty fine in a pair of dark jeans.

This song—their song—was a poignant memory of the relationship they once had shared. As the song ended, the nostalgia wrapped around her heart. She had the urge to do both—yank Leo into her arms and push the emotions away.

Isabella smiled at the crowd while they clapped. She glanced at Leo and he winked at her, a thrill skidding into her depths. She dropped the mic into the stand and rushed off the stage, fighting back the moisture building in her eyes. She headed straight to the bar, taking a seat on an empty metal stool.

Ricky caught her eye. "Beer?"

"Yes, please," her voice managed to croak out.

He cracked the top off before placing it on the bar for her, eyeing her. "That was, um…interesting."

"That's an understatement." She laughed and chugged her beer.

"Okay, that was hot."

Isabella snorted, nearly choking.

A customer called for Ricky.

"You might want to go easy on that," he said to her before hurrying off.

Leo sidled up next to her, dropping on the open bar stool. "That was cruel."

His voice buzzed in her ears as she wiped at the condensation on her bottle. A playful smile pulled at her lips.

"Guilty." She took a sip of her beer. "But it was fun."

"It was," he agreed.

"You up for a rematch?"

"Maybe later." He swiveled to face her, and she lifted her chin to look at him, her face warming. "Look, I know my timing sucks, but after you told me the other day that you came back, my head's been going crazy. I've been racking my brain to figure out when. And why no one knew. Talk to me Izz. Please."

Isabella's breath caught in her throat. The conversation was inevitable, but she didn't want to do this now. Not in the middle of her sister's bachelorette party.

"How about we talk later? When we get home?"

Leo rested his hand on her thigh, heat radiating there. "Please, Izz."

His words, the plea, the look of desperation in his shimmering, brown eyes nearly broke her.

Isabella glanced in the direction of the girls. "Let me grab my coat. Let's go talk in your truck."

After shrugging on her jacket, telling the girls not to leave without her, they stepped outside into the dark, cold winter night, a terrible rendition of "All I Want For Christmas Is You" trailing behind them. Leo led her to the passenger side of his truck where he brushed the snow off before opening the door for her. He hopped in the driver's side and turned over the ignition, powering on the heat.

But between the alcohol in her bloodstream and the tension building in her chest as she prepared to release the words she'd been holding in for so long, she wasn't cold.

Leo cupped his hands into fists and breathed hot air into them. She turned and studied the straight lines and facial hair on his familiar, handsome face.

Replaying the words she planned to speak over and over like a broken record in her mind for the last several years didn't help. Because sitting there with him now, finally about to say them aloud felt impossible.

Isabella scooted closer to Leo, propping her knee on the seat. He rested his hand on her leg, his touch sending warmth traveling through her.

She sighed. "This is a million times harder than I thought it would be."

He brushed her cheekbone with his finger before tucking her hair behind her ear, sending goosebumps dancing across her skin. "I always loved this face."

She melted into his touch, pushing her cheek into his palm and closing her eyes. Why did he have to make this harder? She needed him to be a jerk. So that when he got mad about what she told him, it would be easier after they parted ways again.

"I wish—" she began, fighting to keep her voice even, "—I wish I'd done things differently. I need you to at least believe that." She needed him to know how sorry she was. That now, looking back, and after spending these last few days together, she regretted how she handled things. Maybe she should've never gone to New York. Maybe that hadn't been her dream after all. Maybe Leo had been her dream all along and she was just too anxious to get out of Pineridge to realize.

And maybe the alcohol was *messing with her brain*. Because of course Ithaca College and working at *The New Yorker* had been her dream.

"Listen, there's no easy way to say this. So I'm just gonna say it. Then, you can go back to hating me."

"Izz, I've never hated you. I mean…" He rubbed his hand over her thigh, the friction stirring something low in her belly. "I never wanted to hate you."

"I came back after college graduation," she finally blurted. "I had all these plans to tell you about. There was this fantastic apartment I found for us. Decent rent and right over a second-hand music store. You would've loved it. And I'd been talking to these friends of mine who were in a photography class who had a position open on their team. I instantly thought of you and how it would've been perfect for you." She was rambling, she knew. But he needed to know—she really did have plans for him to come to New York with her. "Anyway, your mom was sick." She paused, making eye contact. The light pouring into the cab of the pickup from the parking lot glassed over his eyes. "I knew I needed to see her before…well, before she passed. So I did."

"Wait. You saw my mom? When?"

"Right after college graduation."

He gave a slow shake of his head. "She never told me."

Isabella nodded. She'd always assumed this, but it still hurt having Leo confirm her suspicions. "She never told you because she didn't want you to know I was there."

"Why would she do that?"

"Because Leo, she loved you so much. She wanted the very best for you. She wanted you to strive for your dreams. And your dreams were to stay in Pineridge. To take pictures of the mountains. To raise a family here. She wanted you to take over your dad's company and to be here for Landon."

His brow crumpled. "So what are you saying?"

She dropped her head, tucking her chin to her chest, unable to look at him anymore. The memory of that day flooded into her mind, and the grief of all she lost caught in her throat. "I think you know what I'm saying."

"My mom?" He scrubbed a hand down his face. "My mom is the reason you never came back to me?"

She hadn't believed her heart could break any more over this, but in that moment, his words sent fissures spreading. He hadn't said *to Pineridge*. He'd said *to me*. "No, she wasn't the reason," she was quick to say, her throat constricting. "Not exactly. I'd never blame her."

"Then what?"

"It was her reasons for why you and I shouldn't have a future together. Her not being able to give us her blessing." She reached for his hand, but he didn't allow it, clenching his fingers into fists instead. "Leo, I just couldn't. I couldn't do that to her. To you. My future was in New York. Yours was here." Tears slid down her cold cheeks.

"I don't believe this." He shook his head. "All these years I had myself convinced I'd done something to push you away." He shoved both hands through his hair, resting them against the back of his neck. "You're telling me that my mother caused all of this?"

She was desperate to comfort him, to ease his confusion and his pain. But he wasn't hers to comfort. "She was sick, Leo. I couldn't take you away from her. I couldn't make you choose between us, and I...I had a life I didn't want to lose. I'm so sorry, Leo. I didn't mean to hurt you."

"Yeah well, you did," he muttered, adjusting in his seat. Facing forward, he stared out the frosty windshield as the snowflakes sprinkled it like confetti. "You obliterated me, Izz."

Her chest ached unforgivingly. She swallowed against the tightness in her throat, tears stinging the backs of her eyes. "I wanted to tell you. So badly."

"Well, now you have," he said.

"What can I do or say to help fix this?"

He gripped the steering wheel. "I don't know. I just need to be alone. You should go."

"Are you sure?" She rested her palm on his firm chest. He winced and shook off her touch, causing her to reel back.

Instead of breaking her heart even more so, it simply grew another layer of protection. Because that's how her heart worked. It was the only way she could protect it, the only way she could survive.

"Please, just go."

And she did—listening to and respecting his words but not at all unscathed by them. She jumped down from the truck and shut the door. Within seconds he backed out of the parking lot, leaving her shivering and enveloped in a plume of exhaust smoke.

CHAPTER EIGHTEEN

LEO

As soon as Isabella shut the door of his truck, Leo took off out of the parking lot of O'Henry's, his tires sliding on the ice, and headed in the direction of home. *His* home. He needed to be surrounded by his own things. He needed a reminder of what he'd worked so hard and tirelessly for. The life he created after his mom pushed him in the direction of pursuing his dreams right before she passed away.

He couldn't fathom his mom pushing him in the complete opposite direction of Isabella. But had she? His mom always wanted him to be happy; she told him a million times. And she knew Isabella made him happy. So no, he couldn't believe Isabella. He wouldn't.

Leo eased up the long asphalt driveway covered in several inches of snow, revealing the amount of time he'd been away. He hopped out of the truck, the snow reaching the height of the top of his boots.

Gazing at the log house, an aching anxiousness filled his chest. Usually, when he arrived home after being out of town on a job, he felt an overwhelming sensation of relief. Tonight he only felt confused. He could've had such a different life. Was he even where he was meant to be? Or had this path been carved and crafted by other hands? Without him even realizing it?

He stomped the snow from his boots and unlocked the front door. Glancing around, he found everything in its place, things he'd once shared with Talia. For a while, he imagined having a dog run to greet him every day when he'd come home, but since he did so much traveling these days, owning a dog didn't make sense.

He and Talia had talked about getting a pet when they were married. Leo told her a dog would keep her company when he was away. But a dog as a companion wasn't enough. Talia apparently needed male companionship. Someone who would let her make all the decisions and who would take her along with him on jobs, not leave her home alone.

They should've never gotten married. He just wanted to be happy again. He wanted to share his life with someone. If he was being honest, he didn't really care who with. But even then, even though he tried to deny it, he'd had an Isabella-shaped hole in his heart that eclipsed all else.

Leo flipped on the lights and strolled into the kitchen. He opened the fridge and found an old takeout container of Chinese food, a box of leftover pizza, and a six-pack of beer with only one bottle remaining. He snatched the beer and popped it open, making his way into the living room where he loaded the wood stove with newspaper and a few logs. Kneeling, he used his free hand to strike a match and held the flame to the paper until it lit and caught the wood on fire.

He reclined on the sofa, taking a long pull from his beer. The prints in frames surrounding his vaulted wood-lined walls mocked him. They reflected mountainous landscapes from all over the country. Incredible places he'd been. Landmarks that were unforgettable because they were that picturesque. A knock sounded on his door. He went to the front window and spotted the Hoffman and Son's truck in the drive.

It had to be one of two people.

He swung the door open, not at all surprised to find Dad standing on his welcome mat. Dad pulled his hat from his head and shook it out before coming inside. "I thought I might find you here."

"What's going on? Everything okay?"

"I brought this for you." He handed Leo his black canvas bag that held his camera gear. "Thought you may want it. Though I'm not sure why you didn't stop by the house first to pick it up."

"Thanks." Leo took the bag and carried it to his desk positioned underneath the wide A-frame windows in the living room. "I hadn't planned on coming here," Leo called over his shoulder to where his dad still stood in the front entryway.

"Yeah, that's kinda what I figured." Dad ran his rough hand over his wrinkled forehead and graying dark hair.

Leo left the bag on the desk, his fingers itching to unzip it and hold the camera in his hands. He propped his hands on his hips. "I'd offer you a beer, but the fridge is empty."

His dad waved him off, glancing around inside the house but not stepping too far from the entryway. "I'm fine."

Leo's brows knitted together. "You got something on your mind?"

His dad nodded a few times before ultimately giving in, his shoulders slumping as he shuffled toward the sofa, not bothering to remove his boots. "Mind if we sit for a minute?" He sat, leaning forward and holding the hat in between his hands, resting his elbows across his thighs.

Leo walked over and perched on the edge of the leather armchair, running his palms over his jeans. "What's up? You okay?"

"I am, but I'm worried that you're not." He squeezed the hat in between both fists. "Just thought it was about time I cleared something up."

Leo didn't like the sound of his father's voice just then. He knew that sound. It meant this talk wasn't going to be an easy one.

"Landon mentioned you've been revisiting your past with Isabella."

Leo's throat went dry. "What about it?"

"Boy, anyone ever tell you that you ask too many questions? I can't get a word in edgewise." Dad shook his head. "And you wonder why I'm so quiet. You say enough for the two of us."

Leo's chest expanded and he sat up straighter. "Well if I didn't, we'd never have a full conversation."

"C'mon, don't go getting on the defensive. I came here to say something."

"Then say it already."

"I'm trying," Dad blurted and stood abruptly. He paced in front of the sofa before heading toward the windows and stopped. "Isabella is telling you the truth. She did come back here. Right after you two graduated college."

Leo's breath caught. He shook his head mindlessly. He wanted to drill his father with questions, but he folded his lips in between his teeth instead and waited eagerly.

"She was excited. Didn't even go see her family first. Mom said she looked really pretty. But you know she always looked pretty. Hell, your mom and I both knew we were in trouble the day the Whitley's moved in next door." He chuckled to himself, turning away from the window with brown glossy eyes that matched Leo's.

Leo bounced his knee and furrowed his brows, his mind spinning.

"Your mom told me all about the conversation the two of them had that day. She felt horrible meddling the way she did. You gotta realize, son, she meant well. You were her child. She needed you to follow your own dreams, not some girl's. She wanted you to have a future you chose."

"But she wasn't just some girl," Leo spat, unable to bite his tongue any longer. He stood jerkily. "It was Izzy."

Dad dropped his chin and gave a half nod, switching the hat back and forth between his hands. "I know that. Your mom knew that too."

"That wasn't her decision to make. That was my life. My future. My choice."

Dad raised his head, eyes meeting Leo's. "Your life isn't over. Leo, you're still young. You still got your whole life ahead of you."

Leo threw his hand in the air. "But it's too late now, don't you get that?"

"Nothing's too late, son. Nothing's set in stone."

"She made her decision. To leave. To not come back. And I moved on, too."

"Oh, you mean Talia? She left you. She ain't coming back."

"I know that. You think I want her back? I think I'm smarter than that, Dad."

"Well, if you're so smart, then tell Isabella how you feel."

"What?" Leo swiped his beer from the coffee table. "I don't feel anything for her anymore."

"Fine. Keep lying to yourself." Dad yanked the hat over his head, covering his ears. "I came, I said what I needed to. I'll let myself out."

Leo groaned. "Dad."

His father swiveled to face him, his hand on the doorknob.

"I have a business here," Leo said. "I have you and Landon. I have responsibilities."

"Yeah? Sound like excuses to me."

"Well, they're the same damn excuses Mom used to send Izzy away in the first place."

"Well, your mother isn't here anymore, Leo. Landon has Norah, and I have them both. I have the business. I have the house. I have my own life. Listen, I don't think it's necessary, but if you need it, this is me letting you off the hook. You have our blessing. Mine and your mother's. If she were here, I know what she would say to you. That she's sorry, and that you need to go get that girl."

With that, Dad slipped into the cold night.

Leo took a few hurried steps toward the front door, wanting to scream into the night that it was too late, but Dad was already hopping into his truck.

Leo shut the door and leaned against it, running his hands over his head. His mind raced. Dragging himself to the sofa, Leo dropped down, his body heavy. Part of him couldn't believe his mom would do such a thing. But when he thought back to that time, pieces started to fit together like a puzzle. Moments when his mother would say little things about why Isabella wasn't there, why he was better off without her, how bright of a future he had in Pineridge.

He leaned forward on his knees, his face pressed in his palms, and let the guilt of all the hateful thoughts and feelings toward Isabella spill over him. All this time, he'd blamed her for leaving him, for not coming back, when his mom had played a hand in it, too. Isabella's sacrifice of assuring his family stayed together and that his mom's wish was fulfilled hit him like a punch to the gut.

He'd been oblivious. For years.

Well, no more. Isabella was here now, and while he couldn't undo their past, couldn't get that time back, he could change things from here forward.

CHAPTER NINETEEN

ISABELLA

Isabella took her time coming downstairs for breakfast. Not only because she was dreading seeing Leo today but also because of all the alcohol she'd consumed the night before. It left her with a pounding headache. Her tongue felt like sandpaper and her stomach was a bit woozy.

She trudged downstairs in her slippered feet, hesitant but on a mission—coffee. It could be the only thing to get her through day four of Christmas: cookie decorating.

Finding the kitchen and dining room empty, Isabella's shoulders relaxed. Her stomach had been full of knots all night and morning, anxiety over seeing Leo. As much as he had a right to be angry with her, she wished he wasn't. She wished there was something she could've done to ease the pain, to ease the tension. But she'd given him the space he requested.

Which only made seeing him more worrisome.

She poured a mug of Magical Hangover Brew, threading her fingers through her tangled hair before taking a sip.

"Morning, sis," Norah said, strolling into the kitchen, still wearing her pajamas too. "How ya feeling?"

Isabella grunted, shuffling into the dining room and plopping onto a chair. "Been better."

"Same." Norah filled a mug and joined her sister. "You were so quiet last night after your chat with Leo. Ready to talk about it?"

She wasn't. Between her pounding head and the tightness in her chest, she feared a panic attack was on the rise. But she'd wanted to confide in Norah about this for so long. Wanted to explain why she'd missed out on so many birthdays and Christmases.

"I told Leo why I never came back to Pineridge like I'd promised."

"Whoa." Norah's eyebrows shot to her hairline. "This is huge, Izz."

Isabella wiped the sleep from her eyes, anguish building in her chest. "I'm going to tell you too, but I need you to swear not to tell Landon. At least for now. He's got enough on his plate with the wedding and moving out of Howard's."

Norah made an X over her heart. "Okay, I swear."

Pinching her eyes shut for a moment, Isabella inhaled a deep breath before releasing it. "After college graduation, I came home. Mrs. Hoffman was really sick, so I went straight to their house to see her. I had planned to convince Leo to come back to New York with me, but I knew he wouldn't go without his mom's blessing." Her eyes burned. "And she didn't give it to me. To us."

"Oh, Izzy." Norah took her hand. "I had no idea."

Isabella swiped at a fallen tear. "You know how Mrs. Hoffman was, her family was so important to her. She was very vocal about wanting her boys to stay in Pineridge. She knew if Leo stayed with me, he'd leave." She hunched her shoulders, her eyes filling with more tears. "So I made the decision for him."

Eyebrows furrowed, Norah squeezed Isabella's hand. "Sweetie, you shouldn't have gone through that alone."

"I was young and didn't know what to do. Even now, I have no idea if I made the right decision. But I was trying to do the right thing."

"I know." Norah brushed away another rogue tear from Isabella's face. "How'd Leo take it?"

"How do you think? He's upset. Confused." She shook her head.

Norah plucked a napkin from the lazy Susan on the middle of the table and handed it to Isabella. "I think if you just give him some time, you guys will be okay."

"I don't know, Nor, this is big." She swiped the napkin over her wet cheeks.

"Well, I do know. Leo is a reasonable guy. And I can see the way he looks at you. Everyone can see."

Isabella didn't really know how to respond to that, and thankfully she didn't have to. Nina shuffled into the dining room, her hair a mess on top of her head, and still dressed in pajamas.

She held up a palm. "Remind me to never go out drinking with you girls again." She dropped onto a chair and smashed her forehead against the dining table.

Isabella and Norah shared a look.

"Not feeling great, huh?" Norah asked quietly.

"I only had that one shot of tequila and two beers. I used to be able to drink all night long," she muttered. "Now I have Mom Blood. I can't handle this."

"If it makes you feel any better, we're both dragging today too," Isabella said, tossing the tear-stained napkin onto the table. She grabbed her coffee, happy to drown her sorrows in coffee and caffeine.

"Where's Ava?" Norah asked.

"Outside." Nina lifted her head, resting the weight of it in her hand. She looked like she might slump over any minute. "Finn took her to play in the snow."

Isabella's phone rang, the sound and vibration making her jump.

She glanced at the screen.

Harrison. Again.

She still hadn't talked to him but knew she needed to. Yet since she'd just come clean with Leo about everything, he was the only person she wanted to focus on right now.

"Ugh, make the ringing stop," Nina whined.

"Sorry." Isabella snatched her phone off the table and hopped out of the chair. "I'm gonna take this outside."

"Good luck," Norah whispered.

Isabella pressed her phone to her ear and slipped out the back door. "Hello?"

"Isabella? My God, I was beginning to think something happened to you." Harrison sighed, and she could just imagine him tearing off his glasses and scrubbing his eyes.

"Nope. I'm fine. What do you want?" She realized too late her mistake of coming out to the deck when the biting cold sliced through her pajama pants and sweatshirt.

"Haven't you been getting my texts?"

"I have."

"So you should know what I want."

Silence.

She took a deep breath and stared into the snowy tree line behind her parents' home. "And what made you change your mind?"

"I don't know." His voice came out softer than she'd heard it in a long time. "Maybe our time apart has given me the space to think. Or…or maybe because our place doesn't feel like "our" place anymore. Not without you. Your things are gone. Your scent is gone."

Isabella shut her eyes tight. His words should've been a comfort. They were the kind of words that screamed commitment, that told her he was ready to take their relationship to the next level. The very words she'd been waiting for him to say for so long. And yet, now, listening to them from over 1,800 miles away, they felt all wrong. Something had changed since he'd broken things off. And even more had changed since she arrived in Colorado.

She felt different.

She *was* different.

"Maybe," Harrison continued when silence remained on her end of the phone, "it's the thought of not spending Christmas with you for the first time in four years."

Isabella exhaled, watching her hot breath puff into the cold winter air. "Are you trying to tell me you're ready to commit?"

"I'm trying to tell you…that I'm willing to try."

"And what about all the other issues we have? They don't just go away because people decide they want to be together. One of us will have to compromise. Maybe even both of us."

"We can figure out all those details later. After you're home."

The word *home* in reference to the stylish Manhattan apartment she shared with Harrison felt eccentric now. For nearly four years it had been her place of dwelling, but it no longer felt like home. Not since she'd been back to Colorado.

"So what exactly are you saying?"

"I'm saying that I want you to move back in here. Back into our apartment. To make this place feel like home again. Bella, I miss you."

"I need more time," she said. "I think *we* need more time. Apart."

Footsteps crunched on the snow-covered deck behind her, followed by the sound of a throat being cleared. She spun around, hugging her body with one arm and clutching her phone in the other. Her breath caught. Leo stood there, dressed in a heavy winter coat, a beanie and jeans, his large hands stuffed into the pockets.

"I don't need more time," Harrison said, his voice cutting, "I want you to come home. I don't want to spend Christmas without you."

Isabella spun away from Leo, unable to look him in the eyes while having this conversation. "Well, I can't come home yet," she replied, lowering her voice. "Norah's wedding is on Christmas Day."

"I'm sure she'll understand."

"What? I'm not doing that. How can you even ask me to?" she snapped.

"I'm sorry, I just miss you so much." She could hear the strain in his voice, feel the tension in his sigh. Even with all the miles separating them.

She glanced over her shoulder and watched as Leo turned toward the back door of the house.

She reached out and grabbed his sleeve, heart racing when his eyes met hers.

"I gotta go," she said into the phone.

"Will you at least call me later?"

"Sure," she muttered.

But she wasn't sure at all.

"Love you, Bella."

She couldn't say it. Her lips wouldn't form the words, like her body knew they weren't true, not in the way they should've been.

She ended the call without a reply and slipped the phone into the front pocket of her hooded sweatshirt. Her chest tightened, her stomach like a crashing wave.

"Hey."

"Hey," Leo said, stomping the snow from his boots.

She didn't know how to do this with him. What if he didn't believe her? What if he couldn't get over this? Everything inside her felt twisted up.

"You must be freezing." He shrugged out of his jacket and wrapped it around her shoulders.

Isabella wanted to resist, but the biting cold felt as if it had seeped into her bones. And if this was an olive branch—she'd take it.

She swallowed, trying not to bury her face in his coat. It smelled like him.

"Thanks," she said. "Can we sit for a minute?"

He nodded, joining her on the top step of the deck. It was the only one the roof overhang kept clear from snow.

She wasn't positive how to begin the conversation, only that they needed to have one. "Are we…okay?"

He stared down at his boots. "We will be."

"What does that mean?"

"I just need time."

The irony of hearing the same words coming from Leo that she'd just spoken to Harrison was almost too much to bear. Time could do wonders. But it could also do absolutely nothing. She had held onto that lie for years, telling herself that if she only waited a bit longer, she'd get over Leo. From the moment she'd turned around and taken in one glance of him at the airport, she was done for. All those feelings and desires had come rushing back.

They stared out at the backyard where glistening snow covered the grass, gardens, and the old swing set her, Finn, and Norah used to play on.

"I really am sorry, Leo."

"Me too…me too," he repeated on an exhale.

He reached an arm around her, and she cautiously rested her head on his shoulder. When he laid his head against hers, the worry whirling around in her chest eased ever so slightly.

Maybe they would be okay. Eventually.

"So what was that about?" he asked.

She didn't have to ask what he was referring to. "He asked me to come back," she said.

"When?"

"Now, I guess."

"He actually asked you to ditch your sister's wedding?"

"Basically."

"Are you gonna go?"

Isabella lifted her head. "What do you think?" she asked, incredulous.

He pinched his lips together and raised a brow at her.

"You think that low of me, that I'd miss Norah's wedding? That I'd miss Christmas with my family?" She wanted to add, *miss Christmas with you*, but didn't.

She stood abruptly and shrugged out of his coat. She wasn't angry. She was...hurt. She wanted so badly for him to know her better than that, to believe in her. But she supposed she'd given him little reason.

"I didn't say that." He pushed off his knees and stood on the step next to her. "Jeez, Izzy, don't cry."

She wasn't crying. Almost, but not yet.

"Just forget it." She sniffled. "You just really don't know me. At all." She shoved his coat at his chest before heading toward the back door of the house.

"You're right," he said, just a bit too loudly. "And who's fault is that?"

She turned back around, slow and measured. "Seriously, Leo? We're seriously gonna do this again? Now?"

"Look. My dad came by my place last night." He paced the length of the deck. "He told me about you coming back. And about what my mom said to you." He faced her. "To be honest, I don't think she disapproved of us as much as she disapproved of you taking me away. Death is hard. She knew she was sick, and she didn't want to lose me before she had to."

Isabella blinked at him, her chest rising and falling in quick succession. "I knew that, too. I knew she just wanted to keep her family together. But I was young, and her words stung. She didn't want me for you. She said New York would never be where you belonged, and I...I could see that. I didn't want to be the reason you left everything you loved, Leo."

He looked down at his boots, his hands buried in his coat pockets again. "Because I would have. For you, you know I would have."

She crossed her arms, rubbing warmth into them, her chest hurting so damn bad. "I know."

He glanced up at her, his brown eyes studying her face. "So the question is, what do we do now?"

She remained quiet. She didn't know the answer.

"I know things between you and Harrison are a mess right now. And I don't want to cause more problems for you. But I'm gonna be real honest. I still care about you, Izzy. I didn't want to. I wanted to hate you. But I don't think that will ever be possible."

Heart racing, Isabella's skin tingled. She had planned for the worst, expecting Leo to tell her that he never wanted to speak to her again, or that he didn't believe her. Or worse—that he wouldn't forgive her. Instead, he was laying the cards on the table. Confessing that he still had feelings for her.

"I care about you, too, Leo. So much," her voice came out soft.

He gazed at her, eyes dark and intense, and her breathing quickened. She had a strong desire pulsating through her to move closer to him.

Leo reached for her hand and, like he could read her mind, pulled her close. "It's freezing out here, let's go inside, bake the hell out of some cookies, and we can talk more tonight."

Cheeks warming, she smiled. She liked the sound of that.

So sweetly, and unlike anything she expected upon seeing him again, he pressed a kiss to her forehead. "I've missed you."

She slid her hands up his back and met his gaze. "I've missed you, too."

CHAPTER TWENTY

LEO

Sitting at the Whitley's dining room table with Isabella directly across from him, Leo looked at her with fresh eyes, noticing the beautiful, confident woman she'd grown up to be. Before last night, he'd had a difficult time seeing it. But now, with the air cleared between them since her confession and the conversation with Dad, he felt the eagerness to win back her heart. He couldn't let her go back home to that city prick. Leo was going to shoot his shot.

He just needed her to see that he was the solid choice.

Finn, Nina, Landon, Norah, and Ava sat around the table as well, while Mr. and Mrs. W. sat at the kitchen island. They each had a pile of flour, a rolled-out ball of dough, and they worked on cutting out a variety of Christmas-shaped cookies. Even though it had been several years since he and Isabella participated in this tradition, he couldn't help but be warmed by the memories that rolled through his mind.

Now, they were making new memories.

Christmas music played in the background while Mrs. W. hummed along, and Ava chatted a mile a minute. Through the windows and back door, snow fell like confetti.

Leo reached for a snowman cookie cutter at the same time as

Isabella, their fingers touching, lingering. He glanced up to find her eyes bright and glossy, her skin flushed.

"Sorry," he was quick to say, "you can have it."

"No, it's fine. I can use a different one." Pink tinted her cheeks.

He knew that blush. It was the same blush that spread over her when they kissed—or did other amorous things. It was so intoxicating, even now.

She picked up the tree cutter instead and flashed him a faint smile. To say he was shocked by her giving up so quickly would be an understatement. This was a new side of her he wasn't familiar with. While it was placating dealing with an easy-going Isabella, he preferred his feisty girl.

A mischievous grin tugged at Leo's lips. He snatched the tree cutter before Isabella could press it into her rolled dough.

"Hey!" she barked.

"Oh, I'm so sorry. Were you using this one?" He gave her a mock frown of confusion and held the cookie cutter just out of her reach.

She opened her mouth to speak, but then recognition took over her face.

She narrowed her eyes, and with that perfectly angled brow arching like the devil himself, she stretched her hand further, but Leo only wrenched back even more. Smirking, she hopped out of her chair and pounced, leaning across him, her body brushing against his.

A tingle shot straight through every one of his nerve endings.

Now *this* was the Izzy he adored.

Finally, she grabbed hold of the cookie cutter and tore it from his grasp, releasing a satisfied, "Ah-ha," a smug smile curving her lips.

He raised his palms, chuckling. "Alright, alright, I'll use a different one."

But then she met his stare, and the moment stretched like time could stop. He let his hand settle on her hip, feeling her softness through the thin material of her pajama pants. It was impossible to keep from glancing at her mouth. She was so close.

Finn cleared his throat. A simple reminder that they were not the only people in the room. Isabella bit her lip and gave Leo a playful wide-eyed look, then slipped back to her seat. A little competition, a bit of flirting, was harmless.

Wasn't it?

Leo needed to remind Isabella what they were like when they were a couple. How their relationship used to be and what it could be like now. They'd always had so much fire.

After he used almost all of his dough, Leo realized that his mind had clearly been elsewhere, like imagining what might've happened had he and Isabella been alone. He'd missed the unspoken conversation surrounding the table. He glanced at Isabella who looked distracted as she eyed Finn and the cookie shapes he'd already cut out as well as the ones Nina was currently working on.

"Don't even think about it," Finn warned, glaring at Isabella.

"What?" Her tone rose.

"I see what you're doing. You're trying to size up your competition."

"Am not."

Leo looked back and forth between Isabella and Finn.

"Wait," Nina said, "*this* is a competition, too?"

"No," Finn confirmed. "This is just Izzy being Izzy."

"You're just paranoid." Isabella rolled the dough, then bent and admired the thickness.

Finn arched a brow. "Oh, am I?"

"Please tell me this *isn't* a competition." Nina rubbed her forehead. "My head is pounding too much for this."

"It's not," Finn and Isabella announced in unison.

"I like competitions," Ava said, patting her ball of dough.

"Of course you do." Isabella winked at her. "Because you're my niece."

Leo chuckled and shook his head. Was he positive he wanted to get even more bonded to this family? They were borderline characters on *Survivor*, without the ally portion. Because this was definitely a competition. Why Nina didn't know this by now was beyond him.

Finn puffed out his chest. "I think it has more to do with me being her father."

"Oh, she's definitely a Whitley," Nina said.

Finn leaned toward Ava. "But this is not a competition. Cutting out the cookies and then decorating them is one of the best Whitley Christmas traditions."

Isabella whispered, "Especially if you win."

Finn gave her a death look.

Leo caught Isabella studying his rolled-out dough next. When she dragged her eyes upward, he peered into them in a way that let her know that he would be her biggest competition today. It was on.

While Mrs. Whitley rotated the pans of cookies in and out of the oven, and the rest of the family crowded around the TV to watch *A Christmas Story*, Leo pinched the back of Isabella's sweatshirt, pulling her into the hall with him. He craved being near her. He just wanted even one second alone with her. "Hold up a sec," he whispered, taking her hand.

She glanced at their hands, then gazed up at him, biting that beautiful lip. "What's up?"

He peered down the hall toward the living room, then the kitchen. "When do you think we'll have a chance to be alone?"

She leaned in closer and stroked her throat. "Alone?"

"Yeah. We said we would finish our talk tonight."

Though he wanted to do more than talk. His fingers ached to touch her, so he scratched at the scruff on his chin instead.

She glanced over her shoulder. "When everyone goes to bed and Landon heads home, you could stay?" Her words came out subdued, almost raspy and it did very little to quell his craving for her.

"Sounds like a plan."

The thought of being alone with her enticed him but also forced an ache in his gut. Falling back into a pattern of stolen kisses would be easy. But he couldn't get his hopes up. Not until they finished their conversation.

Isabella took a step away from him, and he sucked in a deep breath.

"Until then." She flashed a coy smile over her shoulder and started for the living room but then she turned around, a sexy smirk on her face. "And you do know I'm going to have the best cookies."

He smiled, taking her in from head to toe. She was so damn adorable.

"Oh, I have no doubt that you have the best cookies."

She grinned. "*Will have.*" She took a step closer and lowered her voice. "Are we even still talking about cookies?"

He took a step closer too, shoved his hands into his pants pockets so he didn't grab her the way he wanted to. "I don't know, Miss New Yorker, are we? Because I've tasted your cookies, and they blow my mind every time."

She took a long breath, looked up at him, her eyes resembling firelight. He could kiss her right now. Kiss her and forget about everything else.

He leaned forward.

"Auntie Izzy, come on!" Ava shouted, startling them from their daze.

They stepped away from each other and turned to look at the little girl at the end of the hall, frustrated that her aunt was a slow-ass.

"Kids." Isabella laughed and headed that way, walking backwards. "You coming? Or are you dreading the smackdown I'm about to deliver?"

He just smiled and shook his head. "You should know better than to challenge me, Isabella Whitley. It's on now."

With a laugh he felt down to his toes, she turned and disappeared into the kitchen.

He clutched his heart, his blood running hot. *Trouble* just sauntered away from him in the form of a beautiful brunette.

And he was eager to discover just what kind of shenanigans she could get him into.

CHAPTER TWENTY-ONE

ISABELLA

Squeezing a piping bag stuffed full of green frosting, Isabella tried to focus on decorating a tree shaped sugar cookie. She was still in awe that Leo had forgiven her. And maybe even more shocking, he'd confessed he cared about her.

Now, he stood so close to her, brushing all manner of body parts against her when no one was looking. After their conversation in the hall, he was making her so hot she worried she might spontaneously combust, and she had no doubt that he knew exactly what he was doing. But she wasn't going to think about Leo. Not about his nearness, and certainly not about the impending talk they were going to have later.

Alone.

Which was a lie. He was all she could think about, damn him.

Ava's giggle snapped her out of her Leo stupor. Isabella glimpsed at her niece's star-shaped cookie that she was currently piling high with gobs of yellow frosting. Isabella glanced back at her own, about to add a bit of yellow frosting to the top of the tree cookie to act as a star, when Leo's arm swooped in front of her, piping red there instead. She inhaled a sharp breath.

"*What* did you just do?" She shoved his arm out of the way to get a better look at her cookie that moments ago was close to perfect. "Who puts a red star on top of their Christmas tree?" She narrowed her eyes at him.

Leo gave her a playful smile. "I thought red would look nice."

"Now who's evil?" she grumbled.

"Did you forget, Leo?" Norah asked from the other side of the table. "Izzy is super particular about her decorating." She winked at her sister.

Isabella picked up the piping bag full of blue frosting, narrowing her eyes deviously, and squeezed a giant pile right in the middle of Leo's flawless white snowman.

He gasped. "Okay, okay, so you want to play dirty, huh?"

With a sly smile, Isabella rushed to cover her precious cookie with her hand, but she was too late. Leo spread white icing all over her once perfectly green, frosted tree. She shrieked, then squeezed more blue onto his cookie, snickering.

Leo took hold of her wrist and held the frosting bag over her face. She squealed, attempting to back up and struggling against him. "Ack! Leo!"

"Just hold still for a sec," he teased.

Isabella bent, nearly out of his reach but he caught her, arm around her waist, pulling her closer. Leo compressed the bag, releasing a glob of icing on her nose. She screamed and snorted a laugh.

"Oh, you are so dead." Picking up the blue frosting bag, she narrowed her eyes, her lips curving wickedly. She aimed the bag straight at him and squeezed. Blue splattered the front of his flannel.

Ava whooped. "Ooo, Auntie Izzy. You're gonna be in *big* trouble."

Leo snatched two bags of icing. He offered her a bemused smile and wiggled his brows. "Oh, yes she is."

"Leo, no." She stuck up her hands in surrender, laughing, backing away. "Don't you dare."

Red and white frosting smeared her face, her neck, and her sweatshirt. Leo chuckled as he swiped a finger across the icing on the tip of her nose.

He brought his finger to his mouth and sucked it off.

Focusing on his mouth was very bad. Thinking about his soft lips and tongue was even worse. Their eyes darted to one another's, making the kind of contact that could be really problematic. Her skin flushed, and an intense longing strummed through her.

Ava squeezed in between them, studying their sugar cookies. She spun back around and pumped her small fists into the air. "Yes! No way your cookies are gonna win." She skipped back to her spot at the table where she dropped a mass of gold sprinkles onto her star-shaped cookie.

Isabella cleared her throat. Leo's eyes darkened, not breaking contact as he brought a dish towel to her face, ever so gently wiping the frosting from her cheek, her neck, and lower. She swallowed, her body craving more than this lingering touch of his, but dang the intrusive audience always lurking.

AFTER EVERYONE HAD GONE UP to bed, Isabella shut the door behind Landon, shivering against the cold air that snuck in a moment before. Hugging herself, she turned to find Leo sitting on the couch, staring at her like he had all night. Only now they were alone, and that stare felt more intense.

He grabbed a blanket out of a basket and spread it over his legs, then lifted one corner. "Come on," he said, his voice all warm and soft and way too inviting.

She went to him, nestling under his arm and tucking herself against his side. He covered her with the blanket and said, "Are you comfortable?"

She swallowed. Hard. "Mm-hmm," she mumbled.

The fireplace crackled, the wood still fiery red and burning. A continuous string of country Christmas carols played softly from YouTube on the TV. None of this seemed fair. To be sitting here, back at her parent's home, next to Leo, but not *with* him. She couldn't hardly remember how to do Christmas here in Colorado without being with him. And even though they were together physically, they weren't technically *together*.

She fantasized about climbing into his lap and pushing her fingers through his hair, but instead of giving into a fantasy, she said, "Hey, do you wanna dance?"

Leo arched his brow. "A chance to hold you? How can I say no?"

He accepted her awaiting hand, tugging her off the couch and leading her across the room before coming to a stop in front of the Christmas tree.

Gazing into Leo's eyes, Isabella hooked her arms around his neck. Leo pressed his palms against the small of her back, sending a jolt of electricity gliding down her body. They moved and swayed to the sweet tune of the music.

Christmas had always been extra special to the Whitley family. In New York, Isabella tried to recreate some of the traditions and magic. She made her friends have gingerbread house contests with her, exchanged white elephant gifts, built snowmen on the city apartment's roof—but it wasn't the same. None of her friends got into it quite like the Whitley's. The first year she and Harrison celebrated Christmas together, she thought about telling him about the Christmas Eve boxes that her parents used to give them. But since that was something she and Leo shared after they began dating, it didn't feel right. Exchanging the boxes with Harrison somehow felt as if she'd be betraying Leo.

When the song ended, Isabella didn't want to part from Leo. She hadn't felt so at peace in quite some time. Being in Leo's arms felt like protection. She was exhausted from fastening the several layers around her heart and from the guard she'd been keeping up since she left him all those years ago. Secure and safe in Leo's arms, she could finally let her guard down.

Being in Leo's arms felt like home.

"Can you just…hold me. A little longer?" she whispered against his chest. She felt vulnerable saying it out loud; it caused anxiety to pinch in her gut.

But then he responded, "Of course."

And she inwardly exhaled the pent-up dread. This was Leo. She didn't need to feel anxious about what he would think of her.

"Are you okay?"

Tears worked their way into her eyes. She didn't know why exactly. Her crying always made Harrison nervous. He never really knew quite what to do with her, so he usually left her alone.

But what Isabella desperately needed at those times wasn't to be left alone. But instead, she needed a hug. She needed someone who cared about her enough to be there. To show up. To comfort her.

"I'm fine." She raised her chin and swiped at a traitorous tear.

"What's wrong? Did I do something?"

She gave a slight shake of her head, gazing up at him again, staring into his familiar brown eyes. "No, you're wonderful." Her voice came out uneven.

He bent down, holding her gaze. "Hey. Talk to me."

She unhooked her arms from his neck and sat down on the edge of the hearth's stone ledge, propping a knee up as she stared into the remaining flames in the fireplace.

Leo joined her.

"It's just, I don't know. Being back here. With you. Our conversation on the deck this morning." She pushed her hair away from her face.

"Yeah," he said, rubbing the back of his neck. "I've been wanting to continue that conversation."

"Me too." She smiled, wiping her wet cheeks. "Because I gotta admit, I'm a little confused."

"You're not the only one." He winked.

"I just have so many unfinished feelings that clearly never went away."

He nodded. "I don't think either of us ever really got that closure thing people are always talking about."

She looked at him with a soft smile, though she felt so much sadness for both of them. "No. I guess we didn't." She studied his face. She didn't want to forget the angle of his cheekbones, the scruff on his chin, his mesmerizing brown eyes. "I know I had a choice in the matter, and you didn't," she said, "but I need you to know that it didn't make the pain any less or the situation any easier. I thought I would die without you, Leo. It hurt so much, but I thought I was doing the right thing."

He rested a firm hand on her thigh, sliding it up and down, sending soothing warmth flooding into her. "Hey." Again, he bent low and caught her gaze. "I'm glad to know that I wasn't easy to leave. But I'm sorry you went through that. Being alone…it had to have been tough. I had my family. If I had just known." A sigh left him, and the obvious lingering hurt she'd caused him streaked his beautiful face.

An ache formed in her gut that wouldn't ease. She had caused his pain—caused the wedge between them.

"You could never be easy to leave." Tears welled in her eyes again. "I wish I would've done things differently. But to be honest, I don't know if I would have. She was your mom, Leo."

"I know. I get that…now. And really, you respecting her that much means a lot. A hell of a lot." He ran his palm down her leg and her fingers itched to touch him. "But I can't lie and say that I don't wish you would've done things differently."

"And now that you know everything, what do you think I should've done?"

He tucked a strand of hair behind her ear. "I don't know. Maybe given me all the information and let me decide."

She shook her head. "I couldn't let you do that. You would've had to decide between me and your family. I just couldn't. I thought it would be easier if I decided for you."

"Yeah, but that should've been my call, Izzy."

Tears slipped out of her eyes, and she wiped at them quickly.

He leaned into her, pulling her face toward his while his eyes danced back and forth between hers. Her mouth watered, and her breath quickened. With their lips hovering over one another's, grazing slightly, he confessed in a whisper, "I told you this morning. I would've picked you. And I meant it."

She blinked out more tears and he wiped them away before kissing her. This time, their kiss felt different, more earnest, and without alcohol insisting they needed one another. Instead, the craving was raw and real, and she couldn't deny it. The desire was like a dull ache in her chest.

Isabella reached her arms around him, pulled him closer, and he kissed her harder and with more fervor. The kiss resembled a hundred of their teenage kisses all wrapped into one gigantic explosion. It felt more grown-up and yet, that familiar childlike nostalgia was still there, lingering. And it only made her want him more. To never stop kissing the Leo she fell in love with all those years ago. He was still in there. And the man he'd become was a highlighted version.

His teeth tugged softly on her lower lip as he pulled back, causing her depths to hum. He pressed his forehead to hers and gazed into her eyes, the two of them breathing heavily. They shared a smile. One that said unspoken words of yearning and adoration. They kissed again, lingering in the moment, and she wasn't sure how it was possible, but it was an even more passionate kiss than the first.

When Leo pulled away again, he said, with a shortness of breath, "That was…that was pretty amazing."

"Pretty amazing?"

"Okay, that was mind-numbingly amazing."

She snorted a laugh.

He grazed his hands over her face, her neck, the pads of his rough thumbs running over her collarbones, causing her to shiver. "Please don't ever stop laughing."

"What?"

"I've really missed your laugh. I've always loved your laugh. Your smile. It was everything."

Her cheeks warmed. She loved his laugh, too—all throaty and resounding. But now, his laugh was even deeper, even sexier.

"Izzy?" he whispered, taking her hands in his. "I gotta be honest, I want you. I can't explain to you how much I just want to take you home with me and get lost in you. But it took me a long time to get over you. A crazy long time. You're leaving in a few days. If we hook up, I just don't know if I can go through that again. You leaving."

She sulked, and her heartbeat felt hollow in her chest. He wasn't wrong. She *was* leaving in a few days. Things between them were already complicated enough.

"I don't want to hurt you again. And," she stared deep into his eyes, her fingers grazing his cheek, "I don't want to leave you again either."

He took her in his arms, taking charge of her mouth again. He kissed her stronger, deeper, sending an ache between her thighs.

They weren't going to make it to his house.

She thrust her fingers through his hair and tugged, eliciting a strangled moan from his throat. They stood at the same time, and she moved backward, pulling him with her toward the stairs. He came willingly, hunger indisputable in his darkening eyes.

Once inside her room, Leo tore off his shirt, giving her a second to drink in the sight of him. So hard and beautiful. He was on her then, mouths crashing, teeth nipping at her bottom lip, sucking on her tongue. He tugged at the hem of her sweatshirt and pulled away just long enough to rip the garment over her head. He tossed it to the floor, and his mouth met hers again, his hands roaming up her waist, cupping her breasts, teasing out a moan she prayed her family didn't hear.

"Off," she muttered against his lips, and his hands slid around to her back, deftly unclasping her bra, and stripping it away. Her pants came off next. She wriggled them down her hips and sat on the edge of the bed. Leo yanked them the rest of the way, his hooded, dark eyes never leaving hers.

He wrestled his wallet from his pocket and plucked a condom free before stepping out of his jeans.

Isabella inched herself up the bed, a frenzy of nerves fluttering in her stomach as he climbed on top of her. Holding up his weight by his forearms, he clutched the packet between his fingers. She hooked her legs around his waist, digging her fingernails into his back and craving his touch.

He raised his brows. "You sure about this?"

She propped herself up on her elbows, bringing her mouth to his, answering him with a fiery kiss.

Unlocking his lips from hers, he grazed the pad of his thumb over her lower lip. "I think that's a *hell, yes,* but I'm gonna need you to give me a straight answer here."

She gazed deeply into his brown eyes, her body on fire with desperation for him. "It is definitely a *hell, yes*. Please," she whimpered.

His eyes darkened and he grinned, nipping her shoulder before tearing the packet open with his teeth and quickly rolling on the condom. Then he looked at her one more time, and she knew he was waiting for assurance. She nodded and rocked her hips, helping to guide him. She gasped and gripped his back as he moved over her. He whispered incoherent words in her ear, but the hot, breathy mumbles were enough to send her skyrocketing with pleasure.

She closed her eyes and sucked in a breath, clutching the iron spindles of her headboard, praying her bed held up against a very adult Leo doing very adult things to her body.

It did, but only because Leo had become a master of control during their time apart. His body was all hard lines, so strong, holding her through every movement of skillful and strategic work of art.

It didn't take long until she felt his release building, almost in time with her own.

"Leo," his name was a plea, followed by a moan she couldn't contain.

"You have to be quiet," he whispered, kissing her, grinning the entire time.

"God, Leo! I'm—"

He clamped a hand over her mouth, a delicious smile curling his lips.

Forget about "Silent Night." After ten years, they were about to bring down the house.

She teetered on the edge of a place she realized she hadn't been in so long—that place of complete rapture that echoes in the bone—until she was plunging into a splintering eruption of bliss. He removed his hand from her mouth and kissed her while she let go of all restraint, swallowing her cries.

Wrapped in Leo's arms, deliriously satisfied, Isabella pressed her cheek against his chest as their ragged breathing returned to normal. She stroked her finger up his bicep and across his smooth pecs, trying to stay in the moment and not allow herself to question what had just happened.

He kissed the top of her head, and she raised her chin, resting it over his thrumming heart before he smiled, leaned in, and kissed her again.

CHAPTER TWENTY-TWO

LEO

Isabella's phone vibrated on her bedside table. Leo wanted her to ignore it. He wanted to make love to her again. And again, and again, and again. He felt starved—starved of Isabella. Once wasn't enough. He wasn't sure forever would be enough.

But the buzzing didn't stop. Which meant several texts were coming in, one after another. The distraction was enough for Leo to pull away and put a halt to their delirious kissing.

"Do you need to get that?"

"I'm sure it's nothing." She kissed a path from his lips toward his ear, making him momentarily forget what a phone even was.

But the dang thing buzzed again.

"It could be important."

She groaned and trailed her hand down his stomach. "Doubtful."

He could barely think with her touching him like that, but...

"Work?"

She looked up at him. "This late? No."

Another buzz.

Leo reached for the phone while she continued teasing him with kisses, from the hollow of his throat down to his chest. He intended to hand it to her, but his eyes snagged on the screen.

A string of texts filled Isabella's notifications.

His gut wrenched, just enough to make him feel a little nauseated.

Harrison: I'm ready to make a commitment.

Harrison: Come home so we can figure this out.

Harrison: I want to be with you. Forever. I love you.

"You might want to take a look at these." Leo pressed the phone into Isabella's hand. He sat up and scooted to the edge of the bed, trying to give Isabella space. He stabbed his fingers through his hair and let out a silent breath.

He didn't know what would happen in a few days when Izzy had to get back on a plane to New York. He didn't know if she'd do so willingly, ready to meet Harrison halfway, or if she'd struggle to leave, or even choose to stay in Pineridge a while longer.

Granted, the last damn thing he needed was another crack in his heart, but how could he let this moment in time with Isabella slip away? He'd let ten years slip away already.

Sure, his mom had made the choice for him, but he hadn't had the balls to go to New York regardless. He imagined it like some scene in a romantic movie, where the hero rushes across the country to be with the woman he loves, come hell or high water.

But he hadn't done that.

He'd been the man who bottled up his rejection and worshipped it every day for a miserable decade.

No more.

Leo couldn't see the future, much as he wished he could, but he could control the now. He could treat Izzy with the respect Harrison so obviously didn't know how to give. The respect Leo hadn't known how to give.

Until now.

He could make love to her for days if that's what she wanted. He so hoped that's what she wanted. Or he could give her space. Whatever made this easier on her.

Isabella moved across the bed to sit next to him, clutching her phone to her chest. "Leo," she sighed. "I'm sorry. I wish you hadn't seen those."

"Maybe I should go." He stood, hands on his hips, searching the floor for his clothing.

She scrambled off the bed, taking his hand in hers. "Please don't."

With her hair messy and her lips swollen, she was more than enticing. He wanted to sweep her up in his arms and yank her back down on the bed with him. But he was not making decisions on impulse. He needed to let her call the shots. To show him what she wanted. What she needed.

"Things are…complicated," she said.

He sighed and tugged the phone from her grasp, returning it to the nightstand. "It's okay. I know you have a life, Izzy. I don't expect you to walk away from everything just because…" He glanced at the bed, then met her eyes again. "But I'm not ready to let him just have you either. If you aren't sure about me, I want to try to make you sure." He took her hand, kissed her fingertips. "Ten years is a long time. I don't want a lifetime to pass knowing that I didn't at least try for the one thing I want most in this world."

Her gaze traveled up the length of him, lingering and taking him in, and his stomach clenched. Her brown eyes darkened, and she said, "Then make me sure."

Her lips curved devilishly, and she dragged him back to the bed. He not only went with her willingly, but eagerly.

God help him.

It was midnight, and snow was falling outside her window. He was falling, too. With every kiss, every touch, every new taste of her, he felt himself tumbling into Isabella's universe all over again.

He took her until his arms wouldn't hold him anymore, then she led the way, planting images of her ecstasy in his mind that he prayed would never leave.

CHAPTER TWENTY-THREE

ISABELLA

ON DAY FIVE, ISABELLA OPENED HER EYES TO THE SUN PEERING THROUGH the sheer curtains, glowing against the mauve-colored carpet, giving it an orangish hue. As a teenager, Isabella loved to wake up slowly, take in the sights of her room as it awoke with her. Her bedroom had been one of her favorite places while growing up. She spent plenty of time perched at the window seat, daydreaming about her future, traveling, and story ideas.

But today, as she woke lazily, she realized too late that she wasn't alone. Next to her lay a very hard body. A very naked, mouth-watering, tempting body.

Leo. In her childhood bedroom.

She reached for her phone on the nightstand—8:55 a.m.

She'd slept late. *Crap*.

With only an unfair moment to take in the view of Leo's bare, solid chest, Isabella shoved him in the arm. "Leo, wake up! We fell asleep."

He jolted awake, then zoned in on her face, a sleepy smile spreading on his lips. "Good morning," he said, all husky and sexy.

"Not good morning, Leo. You can't be here."

There was a knock on the door. Isabella's heart jumped. She put a finger to Leo's lips, giving him a look of warning.

"Izzy?" Dad called from the other side of the door. "It's almost nine o'clock. You feeling alright?"

Isabella leapt out of the bed, naked as the day was long, yanking on Leo's arm. "Hurry, get up!" she hissed quietly. Then hollered over her shoulder, "Yeah, I'm fine."

She wrapped up in a blanket and raced around the room searching for Leo's clothes as he hopped around yanking on his jeans.

"Are you sure? What's all that noise?" Dad asked through the door.

She thrust Leo's T-shirt and flannel at the exposed chest she wished she was still kissing.

"You're gonna have to go out the window," she whispered. Isabella shoved him forward, reaching around him to pry open the nearly frozen shut window, and tossed his boots outside. "It's nothing," she called. "I just slept in. I'll be right down."

Leo stared at her, incredulous. "But it's like ten degrees out there!"

"I'm sorry! I'm panicking!"

Leo grabbed her and kissed her. Hard. It was so good it made her toes curl.

"You are the only woman on the planet that I would do this for, Isabella Whitley." Just like when they were kids, he crawled out the window.

She tightened the blanket around her shoulders, her cheeks burning.

"Wouldn't be the first time I nearly froze to death climbing out of your window."

Isabella giggled and threw on an Ithaca College sweatshirt, leggings, and a pair of slippers, then padded down the creaky, wooden steps, heart hammering in her chest. She just hoped she overslept so long that everyone had already finished breakfast.

No such luck. She turned the corner into the kitchen and was greeted with several pairs of eyes trained solely on her.

Perfect. Gang's all here.

"There she is," Dad said, practically in singsong.

Dad's morning-person vibe was usually a real nails-on-the-chalkboard irritant until Isabella had some caffeine pumping through her veins.

But today, she welcomed it. Nothing was going to bring her down.

She was light as air, floating from a night of earth-shattering sex. She felt invincible, even with the moment of tension they'd shared over Harrison's texts. Leo wanted her. And he wanted to fight for her.

Not that he even had to.

"Morning, sleepyhead," Norah crooned from her spot on a stool at the kitchen counter next to Landon.

"We thought we were gonna have to blow a foghorn to wake you up today," Finn said.

Norah eyed her suspiciously. "Rough night?"

Isabella ran her hand over her tattered hair, her face warming. "Just didn't sleep good."

"Don't worry, Auntie Izzy. I wake up with messy hair every day," Ava said, a hot cocoa mustache coating her upper lip. "Just don't let Daddy brush it out for you. Mommy is better."

Isabella smiled at her niece. "Thanks for the tip."

As she poured a mug of coffee, the back door swung open, a gust of cold whooshing in with a frazzled Leo, like the outdoors themselves were delivering him at her doorstep.

He paused just inside, his eyes like a deer in headlights. "Oh, hey, everybody." He looked frantically at Isabella, and she winced. He cleared his throat. "Am I too late for breakfast?"

"Absolutely not, hon." Mom abandoned her spot at the table. "Let's fix you a plate."

He rubbed the back of his neck, following her into the kitchen. "Thanks, Mrs. W."

Leo passed Isabella as she made her way into the dining room. Her eyes fluttered up from her mug to meet his. He gave her a conspiratorial smile and her body flooded with warmth. She sat in her spot on the stool next to Norah.

"Okay, after everyone's done eating, I think we have a movie planned, followed by the notorious gingerbread house competition," Dad said. "I just love day five." He rubbed his hands together.

Isabella took a sip of her coffee, trying hard to not watch Leo as he leaned on the other side of the island, shoveling scrambled eggs into his mouth.

"With all of these traditions, I feel like I'm stuck in the same repeating day," Isabella muttered over the brim of her mug.

"That's just the charm of Eight Days of Christmas," Dad said wistfully. "They're like magic."

"You might be right, Isabella," Landon said, narrowing his eyes at Leo. "Aren't those the same clothes you had on yesterday, bro?"

Isabella choked on her coffee.

"They sure look the same," Norah piped up, eyeing her sister. "Looks like Leo didn't sleep well either."

Awkward silence filled the kitchen, gazes darting around, no one knowing quite where to look or what to think, especially Mom and Dad who thankfully looked lost. Still, one too many smirks were being directed at Isabella and Leo.

"I'm sure Leo has plenty of flannels," she said. "I bet some of them are even the same. He has the style of a lumberjack."

"Right. Exactly." Leo cleared his throat, but then, as if just now realizing what he was agreeing to, he gave Isabella a narrowed look. "Hey. Wait. I don't dress like a lumberjack, thank you very much." He turned to Landon. "And you, you don't even know what the hell you're talking about. Go away."

But it was obvious that Landon knew exactly what he was talking about.

They were caught.

Norah nudged her shoulder into Isabella's playfully, passing her a knowing smile.

Yep. Before long, the entire Whitley/Hoffman clan would be buzzing about their hookup.

As soon as *Home Alone* finished and they'd scarfed down a quick lunch of Mom's leftover stew, the family was back in the dining room for another Eight Days of Christmas tradition: the blindfolded gingerbread house competition.

"I get to choose the teams, right Dad?" Norah asked, flashing Isabella a wicked smile.

Here we go again.

"Absolutely. It's your week." He helped Mom finish spreading the supplies out on the table.

Norah divvied up the teams. Isabella and Leo, Finn and Nina, Norah and Landon, and Mom bowed out so Ava could team up with Dad.

"I'll be the judge," Mom announced, passing out blindfolds for one member of each team.

The teams gathered around their bare gingerbread houses that waited to be decorated. The rules were simple: one person stood behind the other, blindfolded but hands ready to decorate, while the person in front had to be the "eyes."

When Isabella moved next to Leo, she was already distracted by the closeness of him. He bent so she could tie the blindfold over his eyes, giving her one last lopsided grin.

"Are you sure you're ready for this?" she asked him.

"Oh, you have no idea. I have never wanted to decorate a gingerbread house so badly in my life."

She couldn't help but smile.

When Leo maneuvered behind her, reaching his hands around her waist for the decorating supplies, she sucked in a breath. Her insides burned with the press of his body against hers.

"Ready?" Mom asked. "Set, go!"

"Okay, listen to the sound of my voice and try to block everyone else out," she said. It would be difficult. Despite being small, Ava packed a loud, booming voice as she blurted instructions for her blindfolded grandpa.

Leo nuzzled Isabella's neck, goosebumps gliding across her skin at the feel of the rough stubble on his cheeks. "I could listen to the purr of your voice all night."

She nudged him gently in the gut with her elbow. "Leo, focus." She glanced at their pathetic gingerbread house that only had a strip of icing dripped down the middle of the roof and a couple globs on the front. Finn had already advised Nina exactly where the red and green M&M lined walkway should go. They had to pick it up if they wanted to win.

And Isabella did.

Leo held out the bag of white icing. "Which way?"

"A little to the left. A little more. No, no, too far. Okay, just a smidge to the right. There," Isabella said. "If you could just smear a bunch of frosting on the roof, I'll talk you through adding the Chex cereal as shingles."

"That's rather ambitious, don't you think? Shouldn't we keep it simple?"

"You remember who you're talking to, right? I don't do simple. I want to win."

"Right," he stretched out the word. "My mistake." He chuckled.

With a bit more frosting on the roof, and a couple globs draping down the sides, she directed Leo to the bowl of Chex cereal. "Okay, and now for the shingles."

"I will do my best."

Next to them, Norah and Landon's house looked like Christmas had thrown up all over it. Icing had been sporadically squeezed out, and red- and white-swirled peppermints stuck to the sides while M&M's and sugary gumdrops sat in piles, not even attached, and mini marshmallows drooped from the roof.

An agitated Landon put his face in his palm, muffling a groan.

"I'm sorry, but maybe if you gave me better directions…" Norah was saying.

Isabella studied her and Leo's house again. It didn't look so bad compared to the competition. "It's looking good," she told Leo.

"That's because we make a good team," he said, his voice low and growly.

Her chest fluttered. They did make a good team. They'd always made a good team.

With icing on his fingers, Leo reached his hand around to her face, smearing icing on her cheek and nose, a clump of it landing on her chest and rolling down her shirt. She squealed, shoving his hand away.

"Ack! The icing goes on the house, Leo, not on me. It's all over my shirt." She laughed, attempting to wipe it off.

He nudged the blindfold up a bit, sneaking a peek at her. He leaned in close, whispering, "Somebody's gonna taste sweet tonight."

She tucked her chin to her chest as a tingle swept up the back of her neck, making her heartbeat race. When she glanced up, Finn watched her with a curious stare.

Uh oh, caught again.

Despite them making a good team, Isabella and Leo lost, beaten by a five-year-old. Mom was definitely playing favorites.

Or maybe their house hadn't been so marvelous after all. Was she losing her touch, or were she and Leo not working together as well as she thought? How could they even think about getting back together if her life was in New York, and Leo's was in Pineridge? Where would home be?

Isabella didn't know how or if they'd ever be able to compromise. And if she was being truly honest with herself, she wasn't positive which she could give up—New York or Leo.

BESIDES THE CRACKLING fire and the volume low on the TV playing the animated version of *How the Grinch Stole Christmas*, the Whitley house was peaceful. Leo and Landon left after the competition to hang Christmas lights on the outside of their dad's house to surprise him when he got home from work. Finn and Nina drove into town to do Santa's Christmas shopping, leaving Ava with Mom and Dad and Norah had gone to the indoor skating rink.

Wanting to take advantage of the calmness, Isabella padded into the living room. A bit of the heaviness in her gut subsided when she found little Ava asleep, her head rested in Mom's lap. The last people who deserved an explanation of why she hadn't been home for so long should've been higher on her list. Mom and Dad had been so patient with her this week, waiting for her to come to them.

When Isabella sat on the loveseat, tucking her feet underneath her, both parents fixed their eyes on her, almost as if they knew. But didn't parents always know?

Her throat thickened, and she inhaled a deep, pained breath.

"You okay?" Dad asked.

"I'm fine," she mumbled.

Mom gave her a skeptical look. "What is it, sweetie?"

Ava stirred, and Mom swept her fingers over her rosy cheek before pushing them through her granddaughter's curly brown hair.

"I've been wanting to explain…about why I haven't been home for so long," Isabella began.

Dad scooted to the edge of the sofa. "It's okay, Izzy. Howard already told us."

Her breath caught, and she touched her throat, her fingers grazing the pendant necklace dangling there.

"We've just been waiting for *you* to tell us." Mom tucked her short hair behind her ears. "You never should've had to go through that alone. To make that decision on your own. That's what we're here for."

"That's what *family* is for," Dad confirmed.

Tears pooled in Isabella's eyes. "I know, I know, I just…I didn't know what to do. I'm so sorry."

"Well, you're home now. And I'd say it feels practically like old times," Dad said.

She pressed her lips together, a sinking feeling in her stomach. "There's more," she admitted.

Mom frowned.

She needed to get it all out. Like ripping off a Band-Aid, once and for all.

"Harrison and I broke up. A few months ago. I've been crashing on a friend's couch."

"Oh, sweetie." Mom clutched her chest where Rudolph's red nose blinked distractingly in the center of her sweater.

"Harrison wants to get back together. But now that I'm here, at home, with all of you—and Leo—everything feels familiar and…right." She pinched the bridge of her nose.

"Maybe that's not a bad thing," Mom whispered.

"But nothing has changed. We have the same dilemma. Leo is Colorado to the core and I'm New York."

Dad stood and came over to wrap an arm around her shoulders. "I think you need to take these next few days to think about this Harrison fella, and Leo, and what you want your life and your future to look like."

He lifted her chin with his finger. "And if that vision coincides with your dreams."

Tears burned at the corners of her eyes, and she swallowed the lump in her throat. "Thanks, Dad." She exhaled a haggard sigh, standing and reaching her arms around his neck, hugging him close.

She went to Mom next and wrapped her up in a tight hug over Ava's sleeping form. When Isabella pulled away, Mom cupped her cheek and whispered, "You'll figure it out, honey."

In her bedroom, freshly showered after the icing fiasco and conversation with Mom and Dad, Isabella sat at the window seat, toweling her damp hair. Dressed in Leo's old hockey jersey and a pair of leggings, she gazed out the window. If you looked straight out, there was a perfect view of the Hoffman home. But if you sat at an angle, you not only saw the street with snow covering everything like a blanket, but you could also see the ice rink at the elementary school.

In the spring, once all the snow had melted, the field was used for soccer. But in the winter, it was turned into an ice rink. That's where the Whitley kids and the Hoffman boys had first learned to ice skate. On Saturdays, Mr. Hoffman usually had to work so Dad took all five kids to the rink and let them skate for hours.

A knock on Isabella's bedroom door sounded before it opened. Norah peeked her head inside.

"Hey," Isabella said. "What's up?"

Norah joined her at the window seat, tucking her legs up to her chest like she used to do when she was little. She arched a brow at Isabella. "Nuh-uh, what's up with you? And Leo?"

Isabella's eyes flickered away, and she felt her cheeks heat. "Nothing. Nothing at all."

When Isabella looked back at her sister, Norah's eyebrow only rose even more. "Seriously? I may have been blindfolded for the competition, but I heard all the flirting going on between you two. And I can see. The sexual tension between you two is literally visible in the air. C'mon, spill it."

Isabella wanted to keep this special, new thing between her and Leo hidden, protected for as long as possible. But maybe if she came clean with Norah, she could get some advice on what to do.

"Fine. But you have to swear not to tell *anyone*."

Another knock sounded at the door. Nina pushed through without invitation. "Hey, ladies." She strolled across the room and plopped down on the bed. "The guys are talking about snow blowers and whose is better, and Ava is all wired up after the gingerbread houses and a nap so your mom is stuffing her full of whole wheat toast and, man, I just can't deal with the chaos anymore. I need to hide out for a bit."

Isabella and Norah blinked at her. Nina looked back and forth between them, straightening. "Uh...what did I just walk in on?"

"Izzy was just about to confess what's going on with her and Leo," Norah explained.

Nina's eyes widened, and she grabbed a pillow, clutching it to her chest. "Oh yeah, give mama the good stuff." She crossed her legs and grinned.

"Gah, okay, but no running off to tell your husbands." Isabella pointed a warning finger at them both.

"Deal. Now go," Nina said.

Norah drew an X across her chest.

Wincing, Isabella exhaled. "Leo and I hooked up last night."

Norah gasped, swatting Isabella's leg "Shut up!"

Nina threw her head back and raised her fists in the air. "Yes!" She drew out the word. "I knew it would happen."

Isabella was delighted that her sisters were clearly thrilled by this news, but at the same time, she needed an opinion that was neutral. Not so obviously #TeamLeo.

"But then Harrison texted me," she said. "Literally minutes afterward, telling me he wants to work things out."

"Wow, this is huge," Norah said.

"He said he's ready to commit."

"Of course he is." Nina threw a dramatic hand into the air. "Now that you're into Leo again."

Isabella groaned. "I don't think I was ever *out* of him."

"What are you gonna do?" Norah asked.

Isabella lifted her gaze to meet Norah's. "I don't know."

"I know you don't love Harrison. You love Leo."

"Sorry, sis. But it's pretty obvious." Nina gave her a half-smile, all crooked and knowing.

"But nothing has changed," Isabella continued. "His life is in Colorado and mine is in New York, and I don't know how to overcome that."

"I think," Norah paused as if measuring her words, "that if you just talked to Leo about all of this, it would help."

"How? One of us has to give up a life we love."

Nina shrugged. "Home isn't always a place, Izzy. Sometimes home is with the right person, no matter where they live. I think the two of you could find a way to make things work. You just have to try."

"Maybe," Isabella said, but it felt hopeless.

She threaded her fingers through her damp hair, gazing out the window at the falling snow, a heaviness in her stomach.

"There are ways to get over the obstacles of distance and careers," Nina began, "but not many when it comes to the heart. If you two are meant to be," she coughed out the next words, "which you are," and she smiled slyly, saying, "you'll find a way."

Nina's words hit Isabella in the center of her chest, radiating there and making more sense with each passing moment. Leo *was* home. She knew that already, especially after last night. She just didn't know how to have the life she'd built *and* him at the same time.

CHAPTER TWENTY-FOUR

LEO

WHY DID LEO REMEMBER IT BEING SO MUCH EASIER TO CLIMB THE trellis and hoist himself onto the Whitley's roof? Maybe it would've been if it wasn't snowing and there wasn't an inch of ice coating the shingles.

He perched in front of Isabella's window, the early afternoon wind whipping at his back. He tapped on the glass. Breathing hot breath into his cupped hands, he waited.

The sheer curtains lifted, and Isabella peered out. She flashed him a wide smile while she yanked the window open.

"Leo," she whispered, though not very quietly, dragging him inside. "Why didn't you just use the door?"

He dropped inside, tumbling onto the floor.

She giggled. "Shh."

"I wanted to see you without running into every single Whitley along the way," he said, standing.

He ran his hands over his jeans, trying to rub warmth back into them. His eyes scanned her body, paying close attention to the shirt she wore. His hockey jersey. No question, she definitely wore it better. So much so, he couldn't wait to tear it off her.

Leo gazed at her, pinching the sweater and pulling her into him. "The mystery of my missing hockey jersey has been solved."

"You caught me." Pink tinted her cheeks. "Do you want it back?"

"Not a chance. It looks way better on you."

She smiled but her eyes shifted.

He bent to get a closer look at her. "What's wrong?"

Hesitation played out on her face, and she scrunched her lips into a thought before speaking. "So I was all set to finally tell my parents about what happened."

"Oh wow, really?"

"But apparently your dad already told them. They were just waiting until I was ready to talk to them about it."

His eyes widened, and then with a shrug he said, "I'm sure knowing everything helped them understand why you haven't been home."

"It did. But it made me realize something. You and I still have the same dilemma. You're Colorado, and I'm New York."

He pulled her in closer, pressing her body against his, and breathed in the intoxicating scent of her freshly washed hair. He grazed her lip with his thumb before he planted a kiss there on her soft mouth.

When he pulled back, he said, "Maybe we could learn to be something else. Maybe, just maybe, things could work out for us for a change. We just have to be open to it. Not scared of what might or might not happen."

"I'm trying, I'm really trying." She sucked her lower lip in between her teeth.

"I know. Me too." Then he tugged her toward the bed, and she giggled against his chest as they crashed together.

They made love until they were both exhausted yet utterly exhilarated from one another's touch, kiss…presence.

Leo held Isabella, touching her in ways he hadn't been able to before—a caress along her sleek throat, admiration of her beautiful writer's hands, kisses down the curve of her hips that made him absolutely wild.

He gazed at her even after she'd fallen asleep in his arms.

His phone buzzed, interrupting him.

Was this going to happen every time they were together?

A soft glow from the low-sitting sun slanted through the sheer curtains cascading her in half shadow. She looked beautiful as she slept, one arm tucked possessively over his. He could stay here for the rest of the night, draw her into him, and just hold her until morning.

But his phone buzzed again. He reached for it, checking the time. Four-thirty in the afternoon. The sun would set soon, then the Whitleys and Hoffmans would all meet in town for Pineridge's Tree Lighting Festival tonight. Blowing off the family *and* tradition wasn't an option.

Leo scrolled through the notifications on his phone. There was an email from a client for an urgent order for prints by Christmas. The New York-based customer was interested in ordering four prints and wanted assurance they'd reach the recipient by Christmas Day. He checked the calendar app on his phone. If he drove out to his home, printed the images, and prepared them, he could swing by the post office on his way to the festival and ship the order overnight. Overnighting was expensive, but even choosing two-day shipping and hoping the order would arrive on Christmas Eve was risky.

Leo emailed the customer, letting him know the price difference for overnighting the order and returned his phone to the nightstand. He gazed at Isabella again, her dark hair spilling over the pillow. He traced his finger ever so gently over her bare skin and the curve of her back.

His phone buzzed again.

Leo checked his email, surprised to find a response from the New York customer. And even more shocking—the order had already been paid for. He tore his eyes away from the captivating woman next to him and slid out of bed and yanked on his jeans. Seeing her so peaceful, he couldn't bear the thought of waking her. But he didn't want to just leave without saying anything like a jackass.

He padded over to her desk where he found a small notebook and a pen. Tearing off a piece of paper, he hovered over it, glancing at her again. His mind was an explosion of reality and fantasy as he remembered their lovemaking from only hours before. He jotted down a quick note to her, folded it, and slipped it underneath her phone on the nightstand. After he'd dressed, he pressed a kiss to her forehead and hauled himself out the window once again.

By the time Leo made the winding, snowy drive, it was dark when he finally parked his truck in the driveway of his home. He headed inside, stomping the snow from his boots and hurrying into his office to get to work on filling the order.

His office had a black, modern glass desk with a desktop computer and state-of-the-art professional printer used for giclee and top-quality archival printing. He prepped the machine for printing the order. The four images the customer had chosen from his website were some of Leo's favorite landmarks in Colorado. Two from Denver and two from the Rockies.

While the printer worked its magic, he prepped the mailing stickers for the Kraft mailing tubes, silently grumbling as he read New York City as the ship-to address. He couldn't help his mind from traveling from the thought of New York to Isabella.

An incoming text chimed on his phone, and he pulled it from his jeans pocket.

Ricky: Tree Lighting Festival tonight at 8:00?

He usually met up with Ricky and Kelsey at the festival, along with a few other friends from high school. The last two years, Landon and Norah had joined them.

Leo: I'll be there.

Ricky: Right on. I'll bring the beer.

Leo: Sounds good.

He chuckled after sending the text. Pineridge's Tree Lighting Festival was an alcohol-free event, only serving hot cocoa and kettle corn. But that didn't stop Ricky from sneaking booze in anyway.

The Tree Lighting Festival had live music, dancing, and the lighting of the town's tree. It was all very simple, but Leo embraced it; he found it familiar and comforting and God knew he needed both things right now. But the best part of the evening was when they all ditched the festivities and went out on the local rink for a game of beer ice hockey.

His phone chimed again. He groaned. Probably Ricky again, asking him how much beer was too much. But a smile tugged at his lips when he found Isabella's name on his screen.

Isabella: Not gonna lie, I was so sad to wake up to an empty bed.

Leo: Sorry. I had some work things to take care of. Trust me, I didn't want to leave.

Isabella: The note was sweet.
Leo: Just sweet? I was going for sexy.
Isabella: Fine, it was both.
He chuckled out loud.
Leo: Still meeting me at the festival?
Isabella: Wouldn't miss it.

FRESHLY SHOWERED and bundled up in his dressiest flannel, peacoat, knitted scarf, and double pairs of alpaca socks, Leo searched for familiar faces in the crowd. He waved and nodded hello to a few of his dad's friends, Hannah, an attractive barista who worked at The Local Grind coffee shop, and Joey who played on the high school hockey team with him ages ago and now sat bundled up and confined to a wheelchair. If it hadn't been for that one bad decision senior year to get behind the wheel after drinking, Leo knew Joey could've made it in the NHL. Joey's wife Vanessa held his hand and when she waved to Leo, he headed toward them to say hello.

"Hi, Vanessa." He bent, pressing a kiss to her cheek.

"Hey, Leo. It's good to see you."

Leo shook hands with Joey, leaning into him for a manly hug.

"It's been a while. You're a busy guy to get a hold of," Joey said.

"Yeah, just got back from Michigan. It was beautiful there."

"Made it back just in time for the wedding," Vanessa said.

Ricky jogged toward them. "Hey, man. There you are." He hooked an elbow around Leo's neck.

Leo jabbed Ricky in the gut, causing him to back off.

Ricky chuckled as he moved around to the back of Joey's wheelchair and gripped the handles. "I need to steal this guy for a bit, you cool with that?" he asked Vanessa.

She chewed on her lip, considering. "Fine. Just don't get him in any trouble. I'm still trying to butter up Mrs. Chen after you guys plowed through her sunflower field and blamed it on Joey."

"Hey, that was not me." Leo stuck up his palms in surrender. "That was a solo operation."

She narrowed her eyes but smiled.

"I promise to bring him back in one piece." Ricky pushed Joey's wheelchair in the opposite direction as if he was in a race, most likely he worried Vanessa would change her mind.

"As usual, you know where you can find us." Leo winked at Vanessa before hurrying to catch up with them.

"We gotta hurry. They're about to light the tree. And then you know what that means." Ricky waggled his brows. "Beer hockey."

"You ever gonna grow up, Ricky?" Joey asked over his shoulder.

"I work nearly sixty hours a week managing O'Henry's, I've got a wife, two kids, and another on the way. Just give me this, okay?"

"I'm always up for it," Leo said.

Ricky grinned and continued pushing Joey toward the crowd gathering around the tree and the stage where the band was warming up.

"Hey, there's Kelsey." Ricky plowed Joey's wheelchair through the crowd like he was parting the Red Sea, and Leo followed close behind.

"Joey!" Kelsey gave him a huge hug. "Where's Vanessa?"

"She's around here somewhere," Joey said.

"Well, boys, I come bearing gifts." Kelsey held open the bag hanging off her shoulder. "No one's gonna suspect a pregnant woman's smuggling in beer." She snickered.

"It's a Christmas miracle." Ricky planted a sloppy kiss on her cheek and took the bag.

"Now you boys have fun. But not too much fun," Kelsey warned. "My husband has promised me at least one dance tonight."

"We'll be back before too long," Joey said.

Kelsey eyed the men suspiciously.

"You have my word," Leo said.

"I trust Leo, it's the two of you I'm gonna keep my eyes on." Kelsey gestured that she'd be watching them.

An annoying screech sounded out through the speakers, causing all attention to be drawn toward the stage. The mayor stood up front, holding a mic in black-gloved hands. Leo shuffled his feet back and forth, attempting to search for Isabella over the heads of the other townspeople.

And then he saw her, a knit beanie on her head and the same white, puffy winter jacket she'd worn in the rental car that first night. The memory of unzipping the jacket and pulling it off her shoulders created a heat within him.

As he checked her out and visualized her from that night, she turned her head in his direction and they made eye contact. It was too late to look away—he'd already been caught.

She smiled wide, showing off bright white teeth, and shuffled through the crowd, making her way toward him and hauling Norah with her. His heart drummed in his chest. He had never felt more awake than at that moment.

"Hey, there's Izzy," Kelsey said. She flailed her arms, gesturing for Isabella's attention, waving her over.

After a few moments, Isabella, Norah, Landon, Finn, and Nina joined them. It should've felt more natural, having not only his brother there but Norah and Finn too. He'd been spending so much time with the Whitleys in the last two years, they were as close as family to him. But he selfishly only wanted Isabella there. He wanted her all to himself. Being in such close proximity to her and unable to touch her drove him wild.

"Isabella, you haven't changed a bit," Joey said when she gave him a lingering hug.

"Now that's just mean. I got rid of my crooked teeth since you last saw me. And you're also now looking at a successful journalist for *The New Yorker*." She straightened, squaring her shoulders.

Joey, Ricky, and Leo all shared a look, brows raised.

"All right then, you hoity-toity, New Yorker," Joey teased.

"That's more like it." Isabella swatted Joey's shoulder. "So, what are we drinking?"

Joey grinned wordlessly.

"Shh," Kelsey warned, pressing her finger to her lips. "Mayor Freeman is getting ready to light the tree."

Their attention moved to the still-dark, large pine tree situated in the middle of town, awaiting the Mayor's move. But Leo couldn't help staring at Isabella while she watched the lighting of the tree. From the corner of his eye, a white, gleaming blur appeared in an instant. At the same moment, Isabella's eyes widened and glistened. Her soft lips curved at the corners, pulling into a sweet, genuine smile.

Her head swiveled in his direction, and she caught him staring at her once again. She eyed him seductively, and his heart pounded against his chest unforgiving.

He gave her a devilish grin. The sound of the crowd cheering and clapping broke their spell and they both joined in the celebration.

The live band began with an upbeat version of "Colorado Christmas," so they stuck around for some dancing before ditching the festival for beer hockey. When the band led into a soft rendition of "Have Yourself a Merry Little Christmas," Leo watched as his friends coupled off. He felt the itching underneath his skin, the spring underneath his feet propelling him forward, and the magnet drawing him closer to Isabella. While she chewed on her lower lip, he advanced, taking a risk, and set an open palm out to her.

"What do you say? Wanna dance?"

She smiled. "I was wondering if you were ever gonna ask."

Holding her close, Leo nuzzled his face into her neck and inhaled her intoxicating scent. Tonight, he caught floral with a hint of citrus on her skin. He closed his eyes and slowly spun her around, her soft body still pressed against his.

When the song ended, he didn't want to release her. But when he gazed down at her, he caught Ricky in his periphery.

Ricky cleared his throat. "What do you say we get out of here?"

"I'm ready," Joey replied.

Leo released Isabella, smiling. "C'mon."

He led the way, pushing Joey's wheelchair to the parking lot. Landon, Norah, and Kelsey followed close behind. Ricky grabbed the sled he'd thrown in the back of his truck and set it on the snow. The guys each took a side of Joey's wheelchair, lifting and resting it on the sled, adjusting his brakes into position. They pulled the hockey bags from the back of the truck, and each took turns pulling the sled through the snowy trail from the parking lot to the outdoor ice rink. With the glowing lights from town and the live music streaming from the band, the old shiny rink never looked more inviting.

After Leo and Ricky moved Joey's wheelchair to the ice, the rest of them sat on the bleachers chugging beer while they laced their skates. Leo's chest thrummed with the excitement of getting out on the ice and slapping the puck around. Not only because it was one of his most treasured pastimes with his boys, but because Isabella was there, too. He couldn't let go of the desire to recreate the memories they shared in some desperate hope it would be enough for her to choose him.

Isabella sat on the bleachers next to him, hugging her arms to her chest.

"You sure you don't want to go back to the house and grab your skates?" he asked her.

"Nah, you know me. I'd rather keep my feet out of skates as much as possible." She snorted.

He handed her a beer. "To help keep you warm then."

Norah plopped down next to Isabella. "I'm sitting out too. We'll huddle together."

"Better make it a threesome," Landon said, chuckling and sitting on Norah's other side.

"Fine, you wuss," Leo teased his brother.

Kelsey climbed down the bleachers carefully, pressing a hand to her round belly. "Let's get this going. I'm freezing for two." She shuffled onto the ice, carrying a couple empty beer cans in her arms.

"Be careful, babe. I'll help you." Ricky collected the rest of the empty cans and skated to one side of the rink. He lined the empty cans on the ice and pulled several hockey pucks from his pockets. He cupped his hands around his mouth and called, "Alright, I lined up the cans so I'm going first."

"Go, baby!" Kelsey hollered.

Ricky dropped the pucks about halfway from where the cans were lined up, skated around the rink a few times, and then started swinging his hockey stick, the pucks coming in contact with five out of the six beer cans.

Kelsey cheered from the sidelines.

Ricky skated toward them, skidding to an abrupt stop and spraying ice in Leo's face. "Beat that."

Leo narrowed his eyes. "You got it." He repositioned the cans and gathered the pucks, taking a few slap shots to move the pucks back toward the middle of the rink. After lining them up, he sucked in a deep breath and ignored Ricky and Joey's smack talking. He swung his stick repeatedly, sending the pucks sliding against the ice and slamming into the cans with a crash each time. Flashing a conceited grin over his shoulder at Ricky, he handed his stick to Joey. "Six. Think you can measure up?"

Joey snatched the stick. "Always."

"Alright. We'll see." Leo pushed Joey's wheelchair to the middle of the ice while Ricky lined up the cans and delivered the pucks to Joey.

A pinch of guilt twisted in Leo's gut for giving his all. But the one thing Joey had made all of them promise after his accident was that they could never go easy on him. He didn't want them to give him special treatment because of the chair. His attitude made Leo respect him more than he ever did before the accident.

Leo gripped the handles of Joey's wheelchair and leaned forward, whispering in his ear, "You got this."

He wouldn't go easy on him, but he'd never stop encouraging him.

Leo pushed his skates against the ice and propelled forward, hustling the wheelchair, gliding around the rink, this way and that while Joey slapped the puck back and forth with the hockey stick. About midway from the cans, Leo stopped and lined up the wheelchair, then Joey took a swing. The puck struck the can in a loud thrash and their friends cheered from the sidelines. Leo did this with each puck until Joey had taken out and smashed all six cans.

Leo spun Joey's wheelchair in circles while he held his stick above his head cheering. Isabella and Norah cheered and whistled from the bleachers.

"Show-off," Leo said.

Ricky high-fived Joey. "Both of you are show-offs."

"Let's agree to disagree, you're all show-offs," Kelsey said. "Now, can we please get Joey ready so you can take me home? This baby and I are freezing."

"Sure thing," Ricky took her by the cheeks and gave her a sloppy kiss before sitting and unlacing his skates.

At the edge of the rink, sitting in the bleachers, Leo caught the sight of Isabella. His heart rate picked up. For a moment, he was taken back to a different time, an easier time. When Isabella used to sit in the bleachers and cheer for him. A time when they loved one another more than stupid hockey, photography, or articles.

"Hey, Landon?" Leo said. "You mind helping them get Joey back to Vanessa? I'll stay and clean up the pucks and cans."

"Sure thing." He smacked Leo's arm. "C'mon, Norah, you ready?"

Norah gave Isabella a side hug before climbing down the bleachers and meeting up with the rest of them.

"You better get him back safely. I promised his wife," Leo called to his friends.

"No promises, man," Ricky teased.

"Don't worry, I got you," Kelsey said, winking at Leo.

Leo watched his friends and his brother go before he picked up the demolished cans and searched for the pucks. After he finished, he skated to the bleachers and sat next to Isabella, unlacing his skates with freezing, hurried fingers.

"I can't believe you all still come out here and do this every year," she said.

Leo shrugged. "If something ain't broke, why fix it?"

"I guess."

Maybe that motto of his didn't work for Isabella and her city life. But it had been something that had helped him get by all these years. The one time he'd gone against it, he made the biggest mistake by thinking his single, simple life needed to be shaken up. He married Talia.

"It's sweet. You guys including Joey the way that you do. Really sweet."

He raised his chin to look at her, finding her eyes glossy and her cheeks pink. "Like I said, if it ain't broke, why fix it?"

"I heard about his accident. I wish I could've been here."

"Yeah, well," he let his words taper off because he didn't know what to say to that. He wished she could've been there too. Isabella leaving had seemed to leave a giant hole in everything around this town.

"I wish I could've been here for a lot of things," she said wistfully.

"Me too," he admitted, caressing her thigh. "But we figured out a new rhythm. We all just missed you."

"I missed everyone too. So much."

Leo wrapped his arm around her and pulled her close against him. "I can honestly admit, Pineridge feels more like home since you've been back."

Isabella reached her arm around his waist, burrowing her face into his neck. "Being here feels right. In Pineridge, and with you."

Her affirmation of what he'd been hoping for rejuvenated his tattered heart. It was like a kick drum in his chest, and all he could do was hold onto her words and to her for as long as she would allow him to.

CHAPTER TWENTY-FIVE

ISABELLA

The next morning, after a quick breakfast, Finn and Dad tossed the sleds into the back of Landon's and Leo's trucks. Isabella knelt in front of Ava, helping her with her gloves and zipping her coat.

"There you go, you're all bundled up." Isabella stood and smiled down at Ava.

"Thanks, Auntie Izzy." She ran outside, clomping toward the driveway.

Isabella laced her boots, grateful Norah had let her borrow her old pair so she didn't freeze her toes off in her UGGs again. She hurried out the front door, hoping to land a spot in Landon's truck. The last thing she wanted was her family witnessing her and Leo's unlabeled relationship and all the sexual tension buzzing between them.

Day six had always been a favorite of Isabella's. A few hours of sledding at the mountain followed by an evening shopping for gifts for the white elephant gift exchange. Besides racing to the bottom of the sledding hill, there wasn't much competition on this day.

Scoring a seat in the back of Landon's truck, Isabella stayed quiet. Norah sat in the front with Landon which left her sandwiched in between Mom and Dad. She checked her phone for any missed texts, surprised Harrison had respected her wishes of giving her time to think.

Isabella set her phone upside down on her thigh and glanced out the window. The views on the way to the mountain were beautiful. Bright white snow covered the road and blanketed the trees. She hadn't taken this drive for several years, and she missed the way the excitement from it bubbled in her chest.

When they reached the turn off for the sledding hill and all climbed out with their gear, Isabella stared down. She clutched the handle of the sled while the wind whipped at her face and adrenaline pumped through her veins. She didn't recall the hill being this steep. Or this crowded. Every Pineridge resident along with every single person from here to Denver had to be out sledding today.

"You ready to do this?" Finn asked, standing at her side.

She swallowed and faked a brave face. "Of course."

"Right on." Finn smiled. "She's ready," he called over his shoulder.

She backed up and turned around, hoping to find some saving grace. But her family, along with the Hoffman's, looked as if they were a football team ready for game day—maybe the playoffs even. At that moment, she wondered for the first time, probably ever, if her family took their traditions just a little too seriously.

Even Ava was raring to go. There she was, in a snowsuit, puffy jacket, and clumpy snow boots, jumping up and down once again. "I wanna go with Uncle Leo!"

"Fine by me, if it's okay with your mom and dad."

"Please, Mommy! Please, Daddy!" Ava pleaded.

"Sure, it's fine," Nina said.

Isabella looked at her, slack-jawed. It's fine? She's going to allow her five-year-old to go sledding down this steep of a slope?

"Are you sure you want to, Ava? It's really high," Isabella said.

"I'm sure, I'm sure." She bounced around, heading toward the hill's highest point.

As Leo passed her, he leaned over and said, "She's in good hands." He smirked.

"Don't I know it." She bit the inside of her cheek.

Leo followed Ava, and Isabella followed Leo, watching with jitters as he set the sled at the top of the hill and sat down. Ava climbed on next, scooting in front of him while he braced them with his hands in the snow.

With a wide, cheesy grin on her lips, Ava shouted, "Ready!"

"You mind giving us a push?" Leo asked.

Isabella wrung out her hands. "It's not too late to change your mind, Ava."

"No way, I'm ready!"

"Hey, Izz?" Leo said, his tone smooth and low. "Ava has ridden this hill for a few years now. She'll be fine." He gave her a reassuring smile.

Despite knowing she and her siblings were sledding down this exact hill when they were Ava's age, she still worried. But Leo was right, Ava could do this. And who better than Leo to take her?

Isabella exhaled a pent-up sigh and pressed her gloved hands to his back, giving the two of them a push, albeit a small one.

The sled went sailing down the snowy hill in a *swoosh*. Isabella bit her lower lip, chanting a prayer while she hovered on the hilltop and waited for them to reach the bottom safely. When the sled came to a stop, Ava climbed out and pumped both fists into the air and shouted while the rest of the family stood at the top clapping.

Leo made the trek back up the hill with Ava on his back, dragging the sled behind him. It was sweet, him carrying Ava so she didn't have to make the climb on such little legs. The gesture, and the look of pure joy on Leo's face, gave her the warm fuzzies. If she could be wooed any further, he'd just done it.

When they reached the knoll, Leo set Ava down.

"Again!" Ava shouted.

"Okay, why don't we let Uncle Leo catch his breath. You and Daddy can take a ride next," Nina said.

"Yay!" She bounced.

Leo carried the sled, and when he reached Isabella, he handed it out to her. "Your turn."

"Oh, I don't think…I mean…I can wait. How about we let Ava and Finn go?"

Leo persisted for a moment longer, still holding the sled out. But when she didn't accept, Finn swooped in and snatched it.

"We'll go next. Isabella can have a few more minutes to psych herself up. Then it's time for a little friendly competition."

"How do you compete with sledding?" she asked.

Finn just laughed while he positioned himself on the sled.

Isabella turned and looked at Leo. "Or should I be afraid to ask that?"

Leo quirked a dark brow at her. "Did you forget? You're a Whitley, everything's a competition."

"Right," she answered thoughtfully.

Great. Not only did she have this sense of crippling fear that came from out of nowhere, but now she would have no choice but to get on that sled.

"Okay, Finn. You asked for a little competition?" Norah raised her brows playfully. "Count Landon and I off." She waved Landon over and the two hopped on a second sled.

"Oh, it's on," Finn said. "Ava and I have this in the bag."

When Isabella glanced in Leo's direction, her stomach plummeted to the snow at her feet at the sight of him holding a sled and gesturing with his chin.

"You go ahead," she insisted.

"I need you," Leo said with a wink.

Her face heated. His words ballooned in her chest, and she let them float there for a moment.

"C'mon, Izzy. I've never seen you back down from a little family competition," Finn coaxed.

He wasn't wrong. And she couldn't ruin her reputation now.

She sucked in a breath and pranced toward Leo and the sled. "Fine. Let's do this."

"Alright!" Leo climbed into the sled, positioning himself in the back, his legs spread open. "Okay, c'mon." He held an open palm out to her and she accepted, taking her place in front of him.

She scooted her backside closer into him, and he let out a grunt in her ear. "Sorry," she mumbled.

"Believe me, I don't mind," he said, low and quiet, tightening his legs around her body. "Hold the strap and don't let go. I don't want to go flying off this thing."

"Got it."

"And lean forward, it will help build momentum." He adjusted himself behind her.

"Yeah, I remember."

"You two finally situated over there?" Norah called to them.

"Yeah. We're ready," Leo replied.

"Are we?" she whispered.

As if they couldn't get any closer, Leo scooted into her and squeezed his thighs around her body, cocooning her. He grabbed a hold of the strap, his hands over hers, gripping tightly. His balmy breath collided with her face, and a shiver coursed through her as a result.

"I've got you, always," he whispered in her ear, sending a craving zinging to places that had no business being zinged at the moment.

With a heady feeling having Leo embracing her, adrenaline pumping in her blood, and the cold air whipping at her face, she nearly missed hearing Mom holler, "Go!"

Leo pushed them off the teetering edge and they flew down the hill, swishing over the snow almost as if they were flying, the ice-cold wind biting at her bare cheeks. Leo's words rushed into her mind, and she leaned forward just as she felt his taut chest push into her back. The entire length of the sled ride finished so quickly that she barely had a chance to glance over at her competition. But she and Leo were winning.

Right when she drew her attention back to forward, she could see they were in trouble. A man had walked directly into their path, and they'd picked up so much momentum, they wouldn't stop before reaching him.

With no time to discuss a plan, the two tugged the strap to the right, veering the sled off course and resulting in them flying off in the jolt. Isabella hit the snow with a thud, landing on her side, Leo tumbled and ended up on his back, lying near to her.

Her chest rose and fell in rapid succession, and she groaned from the impact. But ultimately, she didn't feel injured.

Leo scrambled to his knees and rushed toward her in a sort of half crawl. He tore off a glove and brushed the hair out of her face, his worried eyes searching her for a sign of recognition.

"Izzy, are you okay?"

Still panting, she began to laugh. "That was…amazing."

A slow smile stretched wider on Leo's scruffy face, and he laid back against the snow and chuckled. "See? A little risk is good for the soul. Sometimes you just have to close your eyes and go."

Isabella closed her eyes and inhaled the crisp air into her lungs, reveling in the thrill and joy of the moment. Leo's words settled inside her. It felt freeing to do something that had no guaranteed ending.

"You guys okay?"

She opened her eyes, blinking and finding Finn, Norah, Landon, and Ava's faces hovering over her. "I think so."

"Well, you won." Instead of appearing defeated, Finn smiled at her.

"Congrats, sis," Norah said.

Isabella pushed herself up, leaning back on her hands. She didn't even care that she'd won. The rush from that one sled ride gave her the kind of thrill she hadn't felt in years. Not even when she'd been in Europe, conducting interviews. Or when she worked late into the night, turning in a story right before the deadline. Or when Harrison had surprised her with tickets to The Met.

Leo stood over her and held out his palm. She slipped her gloved hands into his and beamed up at him.

"You wanna go again?" He raised a brow at her.

"Yes, please."

SHOPPING FOR A GIFT for the white elephant exchange was one of Isabella's favorite things. But this was one competition she never won. Finn somehow had an eye for the under-ten-dollar item that everyone seemed to not only want but also fight over. Regardless, it never stopped her from trying to win. She would search for that perfect gift until the last minute possible.

That night, they piled into Landon's and Leo's trucks, driving on the freshly plowed streets toward the shopping center in the middle of town. Pineridge didn't have a typical mall. Instead, their shopping center was outdoors. It never made much sense to Isabella to have an outdoor shopping center when they got snow five months out of the year, but tourists seemed to revel in it.

"Izzy," Norah called after they climbed out of the trucks. "Where you heading first?"

"I'm thinking Bath and Body Works. A white elephant gift from there would be a favorite for at least half of us, right?"

"I know I'd love it."

"I'm thinking, maybe a scarf," Landon said.

"Oh, I'd love that too." Norah smiled brightly.

"What about you, Finn?" Isabella wrapped her own scarf around her neck to fight off the biting winter air.

He waved a finger in her face. "No way am I giving you any hints. Or tips for that matter."

Nina laughed and took a hold of his hand as they crossed the street from the parking garage toward the stores.

"Don't you worry, I don't need any tips. I've got a few tricks of my own," Isabella sneered.

"Yeah? Like fruity scented body lotions?" Leo teased.

She tried to glare at him, but a smile broke on her lips instead. "Forget it. I'm not telling any of you my ideas. And I'm going shopping by myself just so none of you can steal any of them." She shoved Leo with her shoulder playfully.

"Seriously? You're gonna go by yourself? I thought we could shop together," Norah said.

"I'll be fine. You go with Landon. Besides, I have a few last-minute gifts I need to pick up anyway."

"Gifts?" Norah perked up.

"You know I already got you something. I saw you snooping under the tree. You're worse than Ava."

"She must need to buy me a gift," Leo said smugly.

"You wish."

"Aw, c'mon, wouldn't you feel bad if there was a gift under the tree from me with your name on it?" He tickled her waist, and she squirmed away, fighting off an impending giggle.

"No. Because I know you didn't get me anything."

"We'll see," he called over his shoulder as he passed her.

"Leo," she warned, "you better not have gotten me anything." She stopped walking. She, of course, had planned to get him something, but she didn't want him to feel obligated to return the gesture.

He faced her, waggling his brows. "Guess you'll have to wait and see."

"Leo," she called. "I'm serious."

Suddenly he rushed at her, grabbing a handful of snow off a bench along the way. He was in her face before she could blink.

"Maybe I'll head to Victoria's Secret," he whispered with an evil grin. "Or is that really a gift for me?"

He stepped back and threw the snow in his hand right at her.

She gasped, standing there, mouth agape.

Oh, he knew just how to push her buttons. Glancing at the snow, she looked back at him and narrowed her eyes. On impulse, she grabbed a handful of the cold and wet white stuff, packing it into a snowball and chucked it at him. It caught him right in the side, and he did a silly wide receiver move to dodge it, but she landed the hit regardless.

"Aw, poor Leo," she said, puckering her lips. "Getting too old to play?"

He gave her a devious smirk. "Oh, so that's how it is? You wanna go? Okay, let's go."

Leo hustled toward the snow piled to the side of the shoveled walkway and packed a snowball faster than she had, throwing it at her. It flew toward her at what had to have been record speed, hardly giving her the chance to blink.

It smacked her in the chest, nearly knocking the breath out of her. He threw another one, almost right after the first one, hitting her in the thigh. It burned on impact.

Without a second thought, she retaliated with another snowball of her own, but Leo jumped to the side just in time. When he threw his next one, she tried to duck but wasn't successful, and it hit her directly in the head.

She shrieked.

Leo gasped, cupping his hands over his mouth looking genuinely worried. "I'm so sorry." He strolled over to her, trying to get a look at her face. "Are you okay?"

"I'm fine." She took off her hat, fighting against a smile trying to break free, and shook the snow from it, then ran her fingers through her hair.

"Do I need to kiss it? Make it better?" He put on his sweet face, the innocent one that was so obviously fake.

She gave him a look. "Don't think I won't get you back. It doesn't matter how cute you are. Just you wait, when you least expect it, I will get you."

Smiling, he leaned in close, pulling her hips toward him, and kissed her on the forehead. "Thanks for the warning," he said, his voice low and husky.

With a shuddering breath, she shoved him away and tugged the hat back on her head. "Okay, enough of this childish behavior. I have shopping to do."

Leo scrubbed his hands together. "So do I."

She walked backward, cupped her hands around her mouth and called, "I hope you know this isn't over, Hoffman."

He simply laughed and continued walking.

Piles of snow, in heaps taller than Ava, surrounded the shops. Lights wrapped around the trees lining the pathways and big, bulbed lights outlined the wood beams framing the stores. Isabella entered a smaller department store and crossed her fingers, hoping they had what she needed to fill Leo's box. She needed a pair of Christmas pajamas, a festive mug, hot cocoa, and a holiday movie.

After searching a few stores, she began to doubt she'd ever find the specific movie she was looking for until she made the trip to the drug store across from the shopping center. She found it. A brand-new Blu-ray Disc of *National Lampoons Christmas Vacation*.

When she and Leo were dating, she somehow ended up with his DVD in the boxes she packed for college. When she couldn't make it home for Christmas that first year, she suggested mailing it to him, but he told her to hold onto it until the next Christmas when they were together. That following Christmas, however, she lied and said her flight home had been canceled due to bad weather conditions. The Christmas after that, Leo didn't even ask for an excuse for why she wasn't coming home, and neither of them mentioned the movie again.

This year, they'd finally be together. She knew it was a few years late, but she hoped that when she gave him the traditional Christmas Eve box, it would make up for the missed years.

CHAPTER TWENTY-SIX

LEO

It wasn't a question of *if* Leo would give Isabella a gift, it was a question on *what* he would give her. He had some ideas, but it needed to be perfect. He wanted to get her something that would make her smile.

The only problem was, after searching for over an hour, he still hadn't found anything. He wandered through a boutique that sold local merchandise like Pineridge, Colorado magnets, bumper stickers, T-shirts, and beer koozies. A magnet on a spinning display boasting a snowy mountainous backdrop and a sled gave him a chuckle. He couldn't resist and swiped it off the display carrying it to the cashier.

On his way to the front counter, Leo spotted Norah and Landon perusing a table of T-shirts and sweatshirts. He eyed them suspiciously as he approached. "Hey, aren't you two supposed to be shopping separately?"

Norah whipped around. "We were…we did…I mean, we're done," she stammered.

"Already?"

"Yep." Landon puffed out his chest. "And let me tell you, brother, don't even bother. We found the best gifts. Even with the ten-dollar cap."

"Yeah, okay. We'll see about that." Leo flipped the magnet over and over in his palm.

"What'cha got there?" Norah arched her brow.

"Just a small gift for Izzy."

Norah's face brightened. "Really?"

"Alright, simmer down. It's nothing." He closed his hand around the magnet.

"Did you ever think that maybe she's waiting for you to do more than nothing? Maybe she's waiting for a grand gesture."

"Izzy's not like that." The girl he knew preferred simple.

"Look," Norah touched his forearm, leaning in closer to him, "I promised I wouldn't say anything to you but enough is enough. You two are the most stubborn people I know." She shook her head. "She's not in love with Harrison. She loves you. But you can't expect her to change her whole life for nothing."

"I'm not asking her to change anything about her life."

"No, which is good. But Leo, change will have to happen. From one or both of you, if this reconnection is going to be anything permanent anyway. Have you even tried a grand gesture? Have you thought about changing your life? Considered moving to New York to be with her?"

Leo rubbed the back of his neck. The idea had crossed his mind. It wouldn't be impossible for him to pick up his life and go to New York, but he hadn't wanted to put that kind of pressure on Isabella. Were they even at that point yet?

"Look, I've let her know how I feel. I'm all-in on this. But I'm also giving her air to breathe."

Norah adjusted her scarf around her neck. "I think that's a mistake."

"Isabella needs time, and to see on her own that I'm the best choice."

"And what if she doesn't? What if she makes the wrong decision?"

He shrugged and stepped back. "I appreciate your concern, but I gotta get back to my shopping."

Leo bought the magnet and returned to the cold night, trying to shake off Norah's concerns. He had enough of his own without her help.

He'd be lying if he said he wasn't scared out of his mind that he'd have to sit back and watch the woman he loved get on a plane in a few days. Just the thought of being apart from her again caused his stomach to ache.

But Norah was right. One or both of them would have to make a change if he and Isabella had any hope of a future together. Deciding to go to New York—if even for a visit, was huge. It would be a risk. They had no idea if what they'd rekindled since her returning to Pineridge would last if they were in New York.

Moving there sounded even more terrifying. It would mean uprooting his business, leaving Dad and Landon, and the only place he knew of as home. The only place where he felt even a smidge of his mom's presence remaining. He was comfortable in Pineridge. His friends were here. His whole life was here.

Except it wasn't. Because Isabella wasn't here.

Leo's body felt heavy, the confliction tight in his chest. He needed to go somewhere to think. He wanted Isabella to come with him, so he sent her a text and waited inside his truck, cranking the heater.

Isabella hopped into the passenger's side a few moments later. "Hey, everything okay?" She breathed warmth into her cupped hands.

"Just peachy." He smirked. "I just needed to get outta there. Thought you might wanna come with?" He raised his brows.

She smiled and nodded, buckling her seatbelt.

Leo parked the truck at the elementary school rink, dragged a large black bag from the back, and sat on the cold metal bleachers. Isabella sat next to him, staying quiet. He slipped his feet into his skates, giving his chest a sense of peace.

"You know hockey has always been the best therapy for me." Lacing his skates had been a focused practice he'd grown accustomed to, a methodical process giving him comfort

"So…what's on your mind?" She fiddled with her scarf.

"Just thinking…about us…and our future."

"Yeah?" She gave him an uneasy smile.

He shrugged. "A lot to think about."

Leo tapped a finger to the tip of her nose before he pushed off the bench and skated out onto the ice. He lined up a puck with an imaginary net at the end of the rink and swung the stick, sending the puck flying over the ice.

Isabella clapped from the bleachers.

"Why don't you come out here with me and give it a try?"

She gestured at her boots. "I don't have skates."

"Are you backing down from a competition, Isabella Whitley?"

She stood and shuffled her fancy boots against the ice, resembling a baby penguin. "Never. I do believe I proved that this morning."

He grinned, waiting for her to reach him in the middle of the rink.

"You sure everything's okay?"

"It's nothing. It's just that, I've been traveling a lot the last few years, meaning I've been alone a lot. Sometimes, after spending so much time with family, I really gotta blow off steam." He dropped a few pucks onto the ice.

"I can think of other, warmer ways we could blow off steam." Her lips curved.

"Oh yeah?" He arched a brow, his hormones revving so easily.

"But if you'd rather play, let's play." She shuffled backward as if she was giving up.

He eyed her skeptically while she penguin-walked herself back to the bleachers, pulled a hockey stick from his bag, and came back to him in the middle of the rink.

"Wait, what?" He straightened and scratched his beard. "I didn't know I had this other option."

She laughed. "We can warm each other up later. Maybe. It's first to two. I win, you give me my gift early."

"But I didn't get you a gift," he teased.

"Pft." She waved him off. "You win, and I'll let you sneak into my window again tonight." She smirked. It was a sexy, playful smirk that warmed his chest and sent his blood pumping.

"This feels like a win-win for me."

She put a hand on her jutted hip. "Those are the terms, buddy. Take 'em or leave 'em."

He drank her in, starting at her beautiful eyes and working downward over the curves of her chest and hips and perfect legs that he would very much like to have wrapped around him all night long. "Fine. You're on."

He set up large rocks as goals and tossed all the extra pucks into his bag. He skated back toward her, stopping in front of her and spraying her with ice. She shrieked, shielding her face. "That was unfair. I don't even have skates on."

"Do you want to give up?"

She stepped close to him, their chests nearly touching, and narrowed her eyes playfully. "I'm no quitter."

He pressed his chest against hers, his heart hammering. "Fine. Let's do this."

He tossed the puck into the air, giving her an additional beat to steal it after it hit the ice with a thud. When she didn't swoop in and take the opportunity, he snatched it, giving it a hard hit.

"Hey," she protested. "I wasn't ready."

He skated after it, unable to hide his amusement. When he reached the puck, she was still several feet away, sliding against the ice under her boots. He chuckled and shook his head before he smacked his stick against the puck again, sending it flying into the makeshift goal.

"And the crowd goes wild," he cheered for himself, pumping his fist and the stick in the air.

"I believe that's grounds for high sticking."

He toed the puck out onto the ice before smacking it and watching it zip past her.

"Okay, you wanna play dirty, huh?" She turned abruptly and shuffled after the puck.

"I always wanna play dirty, especially with you." He skated past her, but gave her a chance this time, waiting for her to catch up.

She stopped in front of him and rested her stick on the ice, lining it up in front of the puck. He set his stick down as well and glared. She bore her gaze straight into his, attempting seriousness.

But when she reared back, ready to take the shot, he snatched the puck, giving it a soft hit and sending it zooming in between her feet. He skated around her and by the time she turned, he'd already sent the puck sailing down the ice and sinking a goal again.

"That's two. I win. It's over, Whitley." He skated around her, cheering over his head again.

"Cute. Real cute." She smirked. "Fine, rules are rules. I guess I'll keep my window unlocked for you."

He stopped in front of her, tugging her against him. "I wouldn't miss it."

Isabella fisted the collar of his jacket in her hands, yanking his mouth closer to hers. She spoke against his lips. "Then you can tell me all about what's been on your mind. About us. And our future."

Their lips crashed together. And that was it. If he wasn't completely unraveled because of this woman before, he was now. He didn't think there was anything he wouldn't do for her.

Including a trip to New York.

CHAPTER TWENTY-SEVEN

ISABELLA

THE NEXT MORNING, ISABELLA WOKE WITH A WONDERFUL ACHE IN EVERY single muscle. She smiled and rolled over, but Leo was already gone. She thought she remembered him leaving, whispering something sweet in her ear before tugging his jeans over that ridiculously sculpted ass and climbing out her window. She'd been too deep inside a blissful sleep to wake up enough to stop him and drag him back to bed.

She buried her face in the pillow next to her, and her stomach flipped.

It smelled like him.

Still groggy, Isabella headed down to the kitchen, only to find it empty. She'd grown used to the sight of Leo perched on her stool at the kitchen island or sitting around the table joking with Ava. Him not being there sent a jolting ache through her chest. Could she actually miss him when she'd only parted from him a few hours ago?

The thought made her heart do all sorts of gymnastics as she strolled to the coffee pot. As if this whole situation couldn't get more complex, she actually felt *giddy*. The feeling vanished though, almost as quickly as she'd felt it, because one glance at the calendar made something very clear. It was day seven already, her favorite day of Eight

Days of Christmas. But it also meant that time was flying, and that her time in Colorado was about to come to a screeching halt.

Then what?

Leo mentioned he'd been thinking about them and their future. But she'd been too scared to pry when they were tangled in each other's arms the night before, too sick with worry over what he'd tell her. Did he think this new thing between them was enough to fight for? Something permanent? Or something temporary?

"Ugh." She closed her eyes and shook the thought from her head, taking a deep, clearing breath. "Not going down that path today," she muttered.

She loved day seven, and nothing, not even thoughts about a future she couldn't quite see yet, was going to ruin it. Tonight, the Whitleys would gather around the Christmas tree and play the white elephant gift exchange, and Mom and Dad would pass out the Christmas Eve boxes. This particular tradition was one of her fondest memories shared with Leo. The first year she and Leo dated, she surprised the usually rough and tough hockey player with a box, and he'd nearly cried. She couldn't wait to see his face tonight, to make him smile, to share another night with him in her bed.

All she had to do first was get through a day of decorating and a wedding rehearsal.

"Morning, sweetie," Mom called from behind her.

Isabella spun around and found her mother dressed in a winter coat and a scarf. It was a bit unsettling after seeing her in strictly Christmas-themed sweaters all week. "What's going on?"

"It's late, honey. We gotta get to the wedding hall. Hurry."

"But I haven't even had coffee yet."

"No time. Pour it into a travel mug. Chop-chop, let's go." She rushed back out of the kitchen.

Isabella searched the cupboard for a travel mug and picked up the coffee pot. Empty. Just great. She sighed and slipped her phone from her sweatshirt pocket, then sent a text to Leo.

Isabella: If you pick me up a coffee from Local Grind on your way to the wedding hall, I'll be your best friend.

Leo: Done.

She grinned, her cheeks warming.

Isabella: Thank you!

Leo: But I thought we already were best friends.

Isabella: The best of the best.

AN HOUR LATER, Isabella was at the wedding hall, chugging a deliciously sweet peppermint mocha, thanks to Leo. Norah was owning her role as a bride-to-be. She was weepy and having a difficult time making decisions. Landon, on the other hand, appeared as calm as ever, prepared to step in and take charge. The two seemed to at least balance one another out.

While Norah was a bit eccentric and anxious, Landon was cool, placid, and had good leadership skills. Norah was prolific and never did things halfway. When she set her mind to something, she accomplished it, but she was so emotional today. Her mind was a bit unsettled.

Isabella had the list of vendors and the ceremony schedule in a note in her Notes app to help keep things running smoothly. She'd tried to review it the night before, memorizing the minister's name, Pastor Tom, who would arrive around five o'clock for the rehearsal, Kelsey's mom with Sweet Cakes bakery, who would deliver the cake in the morning, the servers with Pineridge Eatery, who would be here in the morning as well. But somewhere between the vendor list and the ceremony schedule, Isabella's mind had drifted to Leo, and the next thing she knew, she'd fallen asleep.

Behind the small wedding hall where the reception would take place, stacked white chairs sat underneath a large, draping white tent where the ceremony would be performed. Both locations needed to be completely decorated before they could even begin the rehearsal.

Starting with the wedding hall first, Isabella, Finn, and Landon lugged boxes holding the table centerpieces from the back of Landon's truck. Isabella tried to take some of the stress off Norah by instructing people exactly how the reception tables were to look.

"Tablecloth, burlap, centerpiece, candles around the centerpiece. That's it," she said, spreading a white tablecloth over a round table.

"I think we can handle that." Leo winked at her, a box with branches sticking out of it tucked under his arm.

Her knees went a bit wobbly as she smiled.

"Once we're done in here, we'll decorate under the tent," Isabella called over her shoulder.

Landon stood back, admiring the table Isabella finished decorating, his pointer finger pressed to his pouted lips. "Hmm…"

"What's wrong?"

Landon stayed quiet, his eyes scanning the room.

"Nothing," Norah said. "Everything looks great."

"You sure?" Isabella bit the inside of her cheek. "If you want us to add something, or move something, we can. Like, maybe pinecones around the centerpieces mixed in with the candles?"

"No, no…this is good. I think adding the pinecones would be too much, don't you think, Landon? Less is more, right?"

"Absolutely."

Less also meant they'd be done decorating sooner. And she and Leo would finally be alone. She would give him the gift. They'd be kissing and—

"Maybe we could just see what it would look like *with* the pinecones?" Landon suggested.

Isabella fought back a sigh. "Sure. Sounds good."

Norah shot her a grateful look, chewing her lower lip.

It turned out that Landon did not, in fact, like the way the pinecones looked spread across the tables. But he didn't decide this until after Isabella had finished placing them strategically on all sixteen tables. The wastefulness of her energy was the least of her concerns. It was the wasted time that bothered her. But at least she and Leo were still together, stealing glances and sharing flirtatious smiles and gestures all day.

Underneath the big white tent, Dad and Finn had already placed the white chairs for Norah and Landon's guests in perfect rows. Along with three chandeliers hanging above the middle aisle, Norah and Landon had chosen simple decorations for the ceremony. And as long as Landon didn't change his mind—which was shaping up to be a high probability he most definitely would—they'd be done in no time.

Finn and Landon hauled the potted fir trees from the back of Landon's truck, and Isabella helped assemble them in a nice row across the front near the makeshift platform where the wedding party would stand. Nina helped Mom fill tall cylinder glass vases with water while Norah placed them on the floor at the end of each row of chairs, and Ava placed a floating candle in each one. Isabella draped garland around each vase. Simple—yet elegant. Both aspects she could get behind.

A frazzled man entered the back of the tent, heading straight for Norah and carrying two pathetic-looking bouquets of red roses. After a moment, Norah clutched one of the bouquets, her mouth hanging open, and her brows pinched together. Isabella rushed to her sister's side.

"What's going on?"

Norah's eyes glossed over. "The florist only got half of the roses in his shipment. It's either these or we go with a different flower entirely."

Seeing Norah's pained expression sent a pang of worry to her own heart. "Okay, I'm sure we can figure something out."

"But all the other decorations are with roses," Norah's voice vibrated.

"I can do carnations," the florist suggested.

Norah shook her head. "No, no, Landon specifically said he doesn't want carnations."

Isabella's first thought was, *who the hell cares what Landon wants?* "Okay, sweetie, but what do you want?"

Norah looked at her, eyes brimming with tears, like she didn't have a clue.

Leo approached them, setting a hand on Isabella's back. "What's wrong?"

Isabella held up the bouquet. "The florist only has half of the roses he was expecting. So it's either these, or Norah needs to pick another flower."

"Everything's going wrong," Norah sobbed silently. "First the decorations, now the flowers. What's next?"

Isabella rubbed soothing circles on Norah's back. "We're going to work this out. It will be fine, you'll see."

"I don't know, Izzy. What if this is a sign or something?" Norah wiped her tears.

"Don't be silly. Sometimes these things just happen."

Leo pushed his lips into a thought. "What about a flower that's similar to roses but is still complimentary?"

"Uhh…" the florist said. "We could do a white camellia? I have lots of those on hand."

"That sounds pretty." Isabella glanced at Norah who still looked pitiful.

Norah shook her head. "I don't know."

Leo squeezed Norah's shoulder. "I've been to a lot of weddings, and I can assure you that camellias are beautiful."

Norah peered up at Leo. "Are you sure?"

"I'm so sure. And I bet, if we get extras, we'll even have time to incorporate them with all the other decorations."

"You think so?"

"Izzy and I will make it happen." Leo winked at Isabella and her heart bloomed in her chest. What *couldn't* this man do?

"Okay, white camellias it is." Norah sniffed, wrapping her arms around both Isabella and Leo. "Thanks, guys."

After Norah had shuffled away, Leo exhaled a whistle. "Man, your sister is not handling this wedding stress like I thought she would."

"Right? She seems way more on edge than I ever expected, like something else is wrong." She hated thinking it, that there could be something on a deeper level worrying Norah, or that she could be having second thoughts about this wedding. But maybe it was nothing. "I'm sure it's just nerves."

"Let's just hope nothing else goes sideways. I'm not sure she can handle it."

Isabella's throat constricted as she focused on Norah, smoothing her hands over a tablecloth—she worried about that too.

Once they'd completed the decorating, Isabella stood next to Norah at the back of the tent, and thank God, Norah had a satisfied smile stretched on her face. Mr. Hoffman arrived for the rehearsal, still dressed in his work clothes, and kissed Norah on the cheek.

Isabella was close enough to hear him whisper into Norah's ear, "It looks beautiful. It suits you. And Mrs. Hoffman would've approved."

While the sentiment caused Norah's eyes to water and evoked a hug, it sent an unwelcome ache straight to the pit of Isabella's stomach. She should've been thrilled by his comment. All she'd ever wanted was for her baby sister's happiness. Instead, Isabella had a hard time shaking it from her mind. It brought on the memory of Mrs. Hoffman's last words to her, *You don't have my blessing.*

The rest of the wedding party trickled into the hall and entered the white tent, interrupting the grief working its way up Isabella's throat. Norah rushed toward the front to greet her bridesmaids Taylor and Maddie. The pleasant surprise of Kelsey rushing in was enough to distract Isabella completely.

"Kelsey? What are you doing here?" Isabella called as Kelsey waddled past her.

Kelsey whipped around and the panic on her face rearranged to relief. She wrapped Isabella in a hug. "Thank goodness you're here. You are exactly the person I wanted to see."

"What is it? Is it the baby? Your mom? Oh, please dear God, tell me it's not the cake." Isabella pulled back and pressed her fingertips to her temple.

Kelsey folded her lips in between her teeth before she finally said, "Um...the third one. And sort of the second one. Baby's fine." She plastered on a fake smile.

Isabella took hold of Kelsey's hand and yanked her out of the tent and into the wedding hall, glancing over her shoulder to be sure Norah and Landon didn't notice the disruption. "Okay," she breathed out, resting her hands on her hips. "Just give it to me straight."

"It's Mom. She's real sick."

"How sick?"

"Um...like puking her guts out sick. As in, I-don't-think-anyone-wants-her-touching-the-cake sick."

Isabella paced the length of the entryway of the wedding hall, muttering, "Oh no, oh no, oh no, this can't be happening."

"Listen, I can help. The cakes are already baked."

Isabella froze and spun around, her eyes wide. "I know you used to help cover for your mom from time to time, but do you know how to decorate wedding cakes?"

Kelsey rocked on her toes and held up her chin. "I know my way around a piping bag of royal icing and gum paste flowers."

"But do you know how to assemble red roses on a cake and make the chocolate look all drizzly like in the picture Norah gave to your mom?"

Kelsey waved her off. "Easy-peasy."

"Okay, so if you've got it covered, what's the problem?"

"I'm about nine months pregnant here." She gestured at her round tummy. "I need help assembling all the tiers and doing the final touches. Like a sous chef. Then I'll need help delivering the cake here tomorrow morning. And if I should go into labor or catch the same nasty bug Mom has, I need backup."

"Oh, Kelsey." Isabella planted her palms on her cheeks. "I don't know anything about decorating cakes."

"No, but you are the master at decorating cookies and gingerbread houses."

"That's completely different."

"Well, do you have a better plan? Because I don't think you want me to go tell Norah she's not gonna have a fully-assembled wedding cake tomorrow."

Isabella let her hands fall away and chewed her lip. Kelsey was right. She couldn't do that to Norah. The cake was one of the most important aspects of a wedding. And one of the things your guests looked forward to most.

Going to Sweet Cakes in the morning meant less time with Leo when their time together was already so limited. But Isabella wouldn't allow anything to ruin Norah's big day.

"I'll meet you at the bakery in the morning. Do not mention any of this to Norah."

CHAPTER TWENTY-EIGHT

LEO

ALL LEO COULD THINK ABOUT WHILE SITTING WITH LANDON, DAD, AND the Whitleys in their living room, playing the white elephant gift exchange game, was getting Isabella alone. Not only because it was Christmas Eve, which had him in some weird nostalgic and romantic mood, and not just because watching her bend over a hundred times today had all but killed him, but because he couldn't wait to give her the gift hidden in his truck.

He'd been waiting all evening for the perfect opportunity to get her alone. But between the rehearsal, the rehearsal dinner at O'Henry's, and the gift exchange competition between the siblings, there hadn't been a free moment.

It was torture sitting next to her on the loveseat, unable to touch her. She was too tempting, dressed in a red, fuzzy, off-the-shoulder sweater and black fitted pants. Her mouth became a torture device, drawing his attention every time she popped a peppermint puff. He honestly didn't know how long he could keep their tryst a secret from their families.

"Okay, who's next?" Norah asked.

"Mom is up," Mr. W. said.

"Oh goody." Mom rubbed her hands together conspiratorially.

Mom stood, brows pinched together as she studied everyone's ten-dollar gift they held on their laps.

"Pick mine, Grandma," Ava said, holding out a bottle of gingerbread body lotion.

"Hmm," she pretended to consider. "Sorry, baby girl, but I've got lotion coming out the wazoo."

Leo groaned, running a palm down his face. He leaned in close to Isabella, a hint of her floral scent assaulting him. "Well, I hope you're happy."

She arched a brow at him.

"I got your mom hand lotion for Christmas."

Isabella snorted.

"I guess I'm no longer the favorite Hoffman."

She cocked her head. "You'll always be my favorite Hoffman."

His lips tipped up.

Mom spun around, finally landing on the item Nina held. Toaster Grilled Cheese Bags. She smirked and snatched it.

"Christmas dinner will be a cinch." She winked and then cackled all the way back to her seat.

After the Whitleys determined Finn had once again won for choosing the best gift, Isabella went into the kitchen for a refill of apple cider. She was staying clear of Mom's eggnog tonight.

Leo swooped in and wrapped his arms around her from behind. She rested her head against his chest.

"Hey, you." She turned in his arms, facing him, tethering her hands at the nape of his neck.

"Can I steal you for a few minutes?"

She glanced over his shoulder toward the hall. "What did you have in mind?"

"You'll need your jacket and boots. And probably a hat."

Her brows pinched together. "Where are we going?"

"Just outside. I promise, I only need a few minutes."

"Okay, but we have to hurry. I don't want anyone getting suspicious. We will never hear the end of it, and I have other plans for the night."

He arched a brow and drew her close. "Oh yeah? Am I involved in these plans?"

She couldn't hold back her smile. He could see her trying. "Maybe."

He winked, and she followed him down the hall and into the entryway where they both quickly bundled up in their winter gear and snuck out the front door, her family too busy arguing to notice.

Once outside, Leo took her hand and pulled her along the shoveled path and around the side of the house where he pressed her against the siding and kissed her.

"I've been dying to do that all night." He dragged a long look up the length of her. "You look amazing."

"If you wanted to get me alone so you could kiss me, why didn't you just say so? I'm a very willing participant."

He smiled, pressing one more soft kiss to her lips before taking her hand again. "That wasn't the only reason."

"Okay, now I'm intrigued."

He pulled her along behind him, stopping in front of his truck parked in the Hoffman driveway. "I have your Christmas gift. And I wanted to give it to you tonight."

"You got me a gift?" Her voice went up as she smiled.

"Of course, I did. And I really hope you like it." He let go of her and reached into his truck to grab a box wrapped in Christmas tree-and-snowman-printed paper, complete with a big red bow.

He hesitated before handing it over to her. What if she *didn't* like it?

She snatched the box from his grip, her smile so bright it made his heart squeeze. "Are you sure you want to give it to me?"

"Yes. I'm sure…I think so, at least."

"Should I take my time? Is it breakable?"

"Hmm…why don't I hold it and you tear off the wrapping paper," he suggested.

She smiled even wider and tore into it, trying to keep the paper from falling to the ground. She broke the single piece of tape keeping the box closed and glanced up at him, searching his face before she pulled back the flaps.

When she gently picked up the item from inside, her brows knitted together, and she slid off the several layers of tissue paper.

She held up the gift—a wooden picture frame—and gazed at it, the moment stretching longer and longer without words. The frame held a photo of the two of them when they were young, doing one of their all-time favorite things together—snow angels.

Worry churned in his stomach, his ribs expanding. She was so quiet, maybe she didn't like it. Leo had hoped the photo would remind her of their past, of happy times—in Pineridge and with him. He hadn't taken the photo, so technically, she could argue the gift wasn't his to give. But if he hadn't downloaded it on his computer, edited it, and blown it up, she wouldn't know it existed.

"You wanna say something here? You're worrying me."

She smiled, her eyes glossy. "It's perfect."

"Because if you don't like it, you don't have to keep it. It's fine." He tried to wrestle it out of her grasp, but she gripped it tighter.

"No, no. I love it." She sniffed, hugging it to her chest. "You'd have to tear it out of my cold, dead hands first."

He chuckled, relief filling his chest. "Good, I'm glad you like it."

She held it out again to get a closer look. "*Love* it," she corrected, her eyes tearing up slightly.

"Right."

"How did you find this?"

"It was on an old roll of film I found in my mom's stuff when we went through her things."

"We must've been, what? Ten here?"

"Something like that. Ten or eleven," he said.

She didn't take her focus off the photo. "We've had such a long history."

"We have. Almost all of our lives. Give or take a few years."

Or ten. He wasn't about to say that though.

"Leo…" she bit her lip, and he ran a jerky hand through his hair, his throat constricting while he waited for her to continue. "I go back home in two days. I'm worried about what's going to happen…between us."

His gut ached a little. The same worry had been assaulting him the last day or so as well.

He lifted her chin. "Me too. But I don't plan on wasting what little time we have left being sad."

She stood quiet for a moment, admiring the photo a bit longer before reluctantly placing it back into the box, wrapping the tissue paper over it. "You're right." She took the box from him and put it back inside his truck. "We should spend it doing something fun."

She took his hand and led him to the middle of the yard. "Like making snow angels."

"What?" He glanced at her, then back at the snow, dark brows raised. He could think of many fun things to do with Izzy. Ones that didn't involve him freezing his ass off.

"It'll be fun. C'mon, best snow angel wins."

"Okay, you're on."

She laughed on impact, and he joined her, falling a few inches next to her. The two of them flapped their arms and legs as if they were swimming backstrokes in the snow. When the flailing and laughing stopped, he turned his head to watch her and found her staring at him.

"This was exactly what I needed," she said.

"It's been a long time since I've done this."

"Me too."

"So no snow angels in New York?"

"Not that I can recall, no."

She turned and stared up at the hazy, dark sky. But he couldn't tear his eyes away from her, memorizing her body, her profile, her dark hair spilled across the silvery snow. If memories would be all he'd have from the week they'd shared, he didn't want to forget a single detail.

He rolled to his stomach and crawled over toward her, wrapping an arm over her chest and bringing her close into him. He peered down at her, gazing into her amber eyes, wondering what, if anything, he could say that would make her want to choose him. But he didn't want to push her, and in truth, he was still reeling from Norah's words. Could he leave Colorado for Isabella? Should he?

He kissed her again, right there in the front yard in the snow, in front of God and everybody. He didn't care who saw. He only knew that he wanted more memories with her. They'd lost so much time.

Finally, he pulled away and helped her to her feet. She dusted the snow off her backside, then looked at him. She bit her lip, smiling, staring at him with a glimmer in her eyes, like maybe she…like maybe she loved him.

His heart squeezed so hard it nearly took his breath.

He cleared away the tightness gripping his throat, then wrapped an arm around her shoulders and kissed the top of her head. "C'mon, beautiful. Let's get you inside."

His mind raced as they walked back into the house. Tonight was Christmas Eve. Tomorrow was Christmas, and the wedding. After that, everything would change. Izzy would go back to New York. That was her home. He could tell she wished she could make herself love Pineridge just as much, but whether they liked it or not, she'd made a life in the Big Apple. She'd nailed her dream job there. The only thing missing was real love with a man who truly wanted and valued her.

Leo didn't know what that meant for him. What it meant for them. All he knew was that he wanted to see her happy, and he knew this Harrison guy wasn't the one for her. Not by a long shot. Her life was like an incomplete puzzle.

He wanted to be the missing piece.

CHAPTER TWENTY-NINE

ISABELLA

AFTER THE GIFT EXCHANGE FUN DIED DOWN, FINN AND NINA CARRIED AN already-sleeping Ava upstairs to bed. Mom and Dad followed, and Howard went home. Landon, Norah, Isabella, and Leo remained in the living room, the fire flickering and the lights twinkling from the tree while *It's a Wonderful Life* glowed from the TV.

Isabella wrestled over when to give Leo the Christmas Eve box. It felt too intimate to give it to him in front of her siblings. God knew she didn't need an audience. It already felt like they had one about 99 percent of the time this past week.

Isabella was curled in the chair, her legs dangling over the arm. She made eye contact with Leo from across the room where he sat leaned back, arm slung over the back of the couch and knees wide. He focused his gaze on the TV, but she could tell he wasn't really watching it. She could see his mind moving behind those dark eyes.

He scrubbed a hand through his hair and looked at her from beneath those feathery lashes. Their desire to be alone buzzed in the space between them.

Abruptly, he stood. "I'm gonna head out. It's getting late."

Isabella nearly jumped out of the chair. "Right. And tomorrow's a big day. I'll, uh…I'll walk you out." She followed him toward the entryway where he sat on the lower step, pushing his feet into his boots.

Norah climbed off the loveseat where she and Landon had been cuddling. "Isabella's right. I should get my beauty sleep. I don't want dark circles under my eyes on my wedding day." She pulled Landon up with her. "And it's almost midnight. You can't see me on our wedding day. It's bad luck."

"But you know I don't believe in all that superstition stuff." Landon went to the entryway too and shrugged into his jacket.

"Well, I do, so we can't take the chance," Norah said, following close behind.

After Landon bundled up, Norah kissed him and pushed him outside.

"Hey, bro, you coming?" Landon asked from the porch.

Leo glanced at Isabella and back at Landon. "You go ahead. I'll be there in a bit."

Landon waggled his dark brows.

"Good night, babe. Love you," Norah called before closing the door. She started for the stairs, peering down once she reached the top. "Good night you two," she whispered in a singsong voice.

"Good night," Isabella mimicked.

After the footsteps overhead disappeared and a door closed, Isabella and Leo stared at one another. "Finally," she said.

Still standing in the entryway, he smiled. "But maybe Norah is right. I should go. Tomorrow is a busy day."

She chewed her bottom lip, her stomach tight with desperation. "I was kinda hoping you were going to stay over?"

He wrapped an arm around her back, pulling her in close. "That's risky. Aren't your grandparents coming early in the morning?"

"We could go to your house?"

He cocked a brow. "I like the sound of that."

Leo gazed into her eyes, reminding her exactly what it felt like to be desired. To be wanted and loved. Goosebumps raced down her arms, and she stood on her tippy toes, leaning further into him and pressing a sensual kiss to his irresistible lips. He caressed her back before his hands traveled to her neck and into her hair.

She pulled away, sucked in a breath, and smiled up at him. Now was her chance.

Isabella took Leo's hands and guided him back into the living room. "I want to give you something first."

He smiled, his grin lopsided and goofy, as he toed his boots off. "Oh yeah?"

"Not that," she snorted.

"Damn."

"Not yet," she teased.

Isabella searched underneath the tree for the box she'd tucked in the back. It took both hands to retrieve it and present it to him.

Leo scrunched his forehead. "But it's not Christmas yet."

"You gave me my gift already." She held out the box. "And this can't wait until Christmas."

"And why's that?"

"Because…it's a Christmas Eve box."

His eyes widened. "You're giving me a Christmas Eve box?"

"Yeah. You know, like I used to."

He nodded, slowly, methodically. "I'm just surprised. It's been years since I've gotten a Christmas Eve box." Tucking it under one arm, he swooped her into his side and kissed her on the cheek. "Thank you."

Warmth flitted across her cheeks as she gazed up at him, smiling. "You're welcome."

"You sure I can't open this tomorrow? Because I can think of a better way we could be spending our alone time."

He smiled a wicked grin, and she nearly caved. Getting her antsy hands on that grown-up bare chest of his again hadn't been too far from her mind all day.

"No." She gave him a gentle shove. "If you waited until tomorrow it would totally defeat the purpose. Now, c'mon." She tugged him toward the couch.

They sat—him a bit more reluctantly than her—and he ripped through the wrapping paper and box, grinning like a kid on Christmas morning. Resting right on top was the movie, *National Lampoons Christmas Vacation.*

"No way." He glanced at the back cover. "I haven't watched this in years. This is great, seriously. Thank you." He set his hand on her thigh and gave it a squeeze.

"There's more. Keep going."

He reached in the box and pulled out the Christmas mug with a snowy mountain landscape and a wooden sled resting against a tree. Inside the mug was two packets of his favorite peppermint hot chocolate. The last item was the pajamas. He pulled the pink bunny onesie from *A Christmas Story* out of the box and his facial expression pinched. One arched brow darted toward the ceiling as he looked at her.

"Seriously?"

"Oh c'mon, they're so you." She snorted a laugh.

"Since when?"

"Just put them on."

"Now?"

"Sure, why not? They *are* Christmas pajamas."

"I'm sorry, but I'm not wearing these. Especially not in front of you." He shoved the pajamas back into the box.

"The old Leo wouldn't have thought twice about putting them on and strutting his stuff."

"Then clearly the old Leo was stupidly in love and would've done anything to make his stellar girlfriend happy."

She bit her lower lip. "C'mon please, put them on." She plucked them out of the box and shoved them toward him.

He tilted his head and puffed his cheeks out. "Fine," he said, exhaling.

"Yay." She clapped her hands.

"But," he said in warning, "you're not allowed to take pictures of me in this. And I wouldn't hate it if you were the one to take it off me." He winked and started unzipping his pants.

"Wait. What are you doing?"

"What does it look like? Putting on the pj's like you wanted."

"But not out here. In my parent's living room."

"Oh, now you don't want me to put them on?" he teased.

"I thought you'd put them on in the bathroom or over your clothes or something."

"What's the big deal? Everyone's sleeping. You afraid someone's gonna wake up?"

She pressed her fingers to her chest. "Me? Why would I be afraid? You're the one who would be getting undressed and putting on those silly pj's."

"Look at you. You're blushing." He snickered, twirling a finger in her face. "You just don't want me to get undressed because you know I'll be too tempting to resist?"

She laughed, playing off her attraction and pushing his finger out of her face. "No. I hate to break it to you, but giant pink bunnies just don't do it for me."

"Oh, we'll just see about that." Gathering the hem of his shirt, he pulled it over his head and tossed it next to her on the couch.

Her wandering eyes couldn't refrain from traveling up the length of his torso and admiring the smooth skin over rippling abs. She swallowed. "Wha-what are you doing? Seriously, my parents are right upstairs."

He began shimmying out of his jeans. "I'm calling your bluff."

"Fine," although she could hear the uncertainty in her voice. "Go for it."

Thankfully, Leo stopped undressing when he reached his black boxer briefs. He stood before her, stepping into the pink bunny pajamas. Those few seconds were long enough for her to get a full view of his sexy body and to cause her own to hum with desire.

Dressed in the onesie, he slid the zipper up, but only part of the way, leaving a tantalizing sliver of his bare chest showing. He totally did that on purpose. Well played, Leo Hoffman.

"Well?" With his arms held at his sides, he spun, giving her a full view of him in the silly onesie, complete with a hood and bunny ears.

"Well," she repeated.

He grinned, brows raised. "I'm still hot, right?"

She threw her hands up. "Yep, you got me. Okay? I'm attracted to men in pink bunny pajamas."

He gave a mirthless laugh. "Hopefully not all men. Hopefully only one." Pulling the hood off his head, he took her hands in his and swooped her into his arms, pulling her in close and sliding his lips onto hers, kissing her long and hard.

She whispered against his lips, "Leo? Don't ever let me go."

He kissed her gently this time, slow and sensuous, holding her face in his palms and tracing a rough thumb against her cheek. "Never again," he said, before plunging into a kiss so intense, Isabella's knees nearly buckled.

Maybe they were being crazy, saying these erratic things to one another—making promises in the middle of kisses like that. But she meant it. She didn't want to leave Leo again. Thinking of going back to New York in less than two days seemed impossible.

Leo pulled back, running his palms down the sides of her neck. "I think we have something rare here, Izz."

"Me too."

He pressed his forehead against hers, his breathing fast. "I don't want it to end."

"I don't either." She peered up into his eyes, his dancing back and forth between hers, shimmering against the reflection of the lights. "But what can we do?"

Leo ran his hands over her back, caressing her. "Maybe we actually try this thing? Maybe we try long-distance for a while? You could come back for a visit? I could come there...to see you?"

Isabella's heart squeezed in her chest. Leo had never been a fan of New York. He'd never had intentions to visit her there when she was in college. But now, he was seriously considering it. For a moment, she pictured Leo there, in the city that had become hers, flannel and Carhartts, beanie and scruffy jawline, and a bubble of laughter burst from her throat. Even as tears burned her eyes.

"Not exactly the response I was hoping for," he said after a long exhale.

"I'm sorry." She bit her lip. "Just thinking of you in New York, sitting in my favorite coffee shop, having a beer at my favorite corner bar, taking a walk in Central Park, tanning on the apartment rooftop."

He stiffened in her arms. "I don't fit."

"No, no," she said quickly, squeezing him tight. "That's not it. The opposite actually. I've waited so long to see you in New York, for you to visit me there. To have two of my favorite things in the same place…it would make my heart so happy." She threaded her arms around his neck, smiling up at him.

Leo's lips curved, growing wider with each passing second. She wanted to kiss him there and never stop. But he nuzzled her neck and locked his arms around her.

When he pulled back slightly, his eyes glossy, she feared her heart might just burst straight out of her chest. She couldn't remember being this happy, ever.

"So are we doing this?"

"I think we are."

He kissed her smiling lips, lifting her off her feet and spinning her around while the grandfather clock in the living room announced it was midnight. Setting her back on her feet, he took her by the hand, pulling her back into the entryway. "C'mon, let's go and we can bring in Christmas with a bang."

She giggled, hurrying to put on her boots. "I can't wait."

Then they rushed outside, running across the snowy path, hand in hand toward the Hoffman house, the pink bunny pj's glowing against the moon's gleam.

CHAPTER THIRTY

ISABELLA

THE KISS GOODBYE THAT MORNING WAS QUICK. THEY SLEPT TOO LATE and now Isabella had to sneak back over to the Whitley house when the sun was already shining. As a teenager, she'd climbed out her bedroom window and across the roof to the porch, and then jumped down with ease numerous times. But as an adult, and dressed in her wedged ankle boots, it took a bit more maneuvering.

Dressed in the same clothes from the night before, she slipped out of Leo's bedroom window, padded across the roof, and climbed down the trellis. When she'd almost reached the ground, her sweater snagged on a piece of the lattice, and she yanked on it to free herself.

She tugged too hard, and the next thing she knew she was falling backward, flailing her arms, a strangled cry leaving her throat. She closed her eyes, bracing for impact.

She landed with a *thud* in the snow. Blinking, she groaned and stared up at the early morning winter sky. Thankfully, a snowdrift broke her fall, probably saving her a trip to the ER. What had she been thinking? It was Christmas Day and Norah's wedding. There was no time for sneaking in and out of windows, falling into snowdrifts.

Just as she was about to push herself up, two faces hovered over her. Familiar and yet at the same time, not. Nana and Papa's faces had aged since she'd seen them in person last. But they still had the same recognizable features. Papa and his red bulbous nose and black plastic framed glasses that had come into style again, and Nana with her thin bow-shaped lips and hair so gray it was white.

"Isabella dear, is that you?" Nana said.

Ice cold snow slid up the back of Isabella's sweater, coming in contact with her bare skin and she squealed. She spit snow from her mouth and removed the coat's hood from her head which had come up during her impromptu gymnastic flip.

Welp, it was too late. And not only had she been caught, but she was wet and cold.

"Hi, Nana." Isabella braved a reluctant smile.

"Well, what on earth are you doing?" Nana squinted, gazing up at the Hoffman's trellis.

"Oh, you know me. I just love the snow. Can't get enough of it."

"You need some help, sweetie?" Papa asked.

"No, no." Isabella put up her hand. "I got this." She rolled and stood, only feeling a slight ache in her lower back.

Nana elbowed Papa in the ribs, whispering, "You think maybe she's been, you know?" She made the smoking weed sign. Papa shrugged, his arms full of packages.

Nana pulled Isabella into a hug, sniffing several times.

Isabella made a face. "You okay?"

"We should be asking you the same thing," Nana said.

"I'm fine." Isabella went to the front door, opening it to let Papa inside. "Hi, Papa, how are you?"

"I'll be better when I can set these gifts down. My strength isn't what it used to be." He entered the house with Nana right behind him.

"Well, I think you look great." She took the stack of gifts from his arms.

Dad appeared in the front entryway. "Mom, Dad," he said, holding his arms open wide.

"Isabella, could you please get the rest of the gifts from the trunk of the car? You know Papa and his arthritis?"

"Oh, I remember." She exhaled a light laugh. It may have been years since she'd seen her grandparents, but some things never changed.

Like how Papa's arthritis suddenly acted up when Nana would ask him to do something he didn't feel like doing.

After retrieving the gifts from the trunk of Papa's car, Isabella returned just in time to see Norah, gliding down the stairs. Her face beaming with Christmas morning and wedding day glow. Ava zoomed down the stairs next, nearly colliding into Norah as she ran straight for the tree. She squealed in delight. Santa Claus had been good to Ava, bringing her a few specially wrapped gifts with fancy North Pole wrapping and stuffed her stocking full.

Finn and Nina came down not long after Ava. Finn rubbed at his eyes, then stopped after passing Isabella. He turned and frowned at her. "Dude, Izz, what the heck happened to your pants?"

Isabella chewed on her lip.

"They really are wet." Norah got a closer look.

Isabella backed up. "Okay, can everyone please stop staring at my backside?"

Norah frowned. "Where'd you go this morning?"

"Oh, this one?" Papa hiked a thumb over his shoulder. "We found her lying in the snow by the trellis." He leaned closer to Dad. "Nana and I think she's been puffing the old magic dragon, if you know what I'm saying?"

"Papa," Norah shrieked.

Dad looked at Isabella, frowning.

"I wasn't." She tried to assure him.

"We don't have a trellis."

"What?" Maybe she should've just gone along with Nana and Papa. Even though she and Leo talked about a long-distance relationship, they hadn't discussed if they were going to announce it to their families yet.

"It's fine, dear. Papa and I are hip. We grew up in the '50s and '60s." Nana elbowed Isabella and winked at her. "C'mon, let's get the show on the road." She waved everyone into the living room. "We have a wedding to get to, and it seems an impatient little girl wants to open her stocking."

Ava jumped up and down. Nana was speaking her language. "And one gift!"

"Now, Mom," Dad said, "we talked about this. We're opening gifts this evening when Landon can join us."

"Oh, I know. But you can't expect this poor child to wait all day. She can open the gift from Papa and I."

"It's fine, Dad," Finn said. "Nana is right."

Isabella stood at the entrance to the living room and leaned against the wall watching Ava as she yanked her goodies from her stocking with more enthusiasm than she'd ever seen expelled from one human being. Joy expanded in her chest, and an easy smile tugged at her lips. She'd missed so much, and she didn't want to miss anymore.

Next to her, Norah leaned closer and whispered, "You know we're not idiots, right? You're totally pulling a Leo."

Isabella tried to play dumb. "What?"

"You're wearing the same clothes as yesterday."

Isabella's cheeks burned, and she crossed her arms.

"I hope whatever's going on, it works out this time," Norah said.

Isabella couldn't hold back the smile curving on her lips. "Don't worry about us. Today is *your* day. You're getting married."

With a contemplative look in her eye, Norah said, "I am, aren't I?"

But rather than looking excited or happy as Isabella expected, Norah appeared pensive, maybe even apprehensive.

"Hey, you okay?"

Norah waved her off. "Oh, yeah. Of course. Just nerves is all."

Isabella's phone chimed. She slid it from her pocket, and upon seeing Kelsey's name, hid the screen as she checked the text.

Kelsey: I need you at the bakery. Now.

Isabella's heart dropped.

She turned back to her sister, pressing her lips tight.

"Everything all right?" Norah asked, her brow scrunched.

Isabella let out a deep breath. "Totally. I just gotta step out and take this."

As Isabella rushed out the door, hoping Norah suspected nothing, she typed out a reply.

Isabella: On my way.

Then, she called for backup: Leo. The man who had so easily become her go-to all over again, even after all this time.

· · ·

ISABELLA: Meet me at your truck. Operation Wedding Cake is a go.

"DON'T YOU DARE TRIP, IZZY," Kelsey warned, chewing on her thumbnail and holding the door of the wedding hall open.

Isabella and Leo each gripped a side of the cake board that held the five-tiered confection covered in drizzled chocolate and sprinkled with red roses.

"I'm not gonna trip. As long as you stay clear of that door," Isabella said with a grunt.

They maneuvered the heavy cake into the kitchen where an empty shelf in a commercial refrigerator waited. Isabella, Leo, and Kelsey released a combined exhale once the cake was stored away, safe and sound.

"We did it," Isabella said. She and Leo high-fived one another. "And Norah will never need to know there was ever a problem."

"Mum's the word." Leo pretended to zip his lips.

"Thank you, thank you," Kelsey said, hugging Isabella. "I'm gonna head home now. Lots to do. You two rock." Kelsey stood back, looking back and forth between them with a smile, hand on her rounded belly. "You two really do make a good team." She winked, then headed out the door.

Leo wrapped an arm around Isabella's waist and pulled her in tight. "I think she's right. About the team thing."

Smiling, Isabella slid her hands along his broad shoulders, lacing her fingers together at the back of his neck. "I think so, too."

In one swift movement, Leo lifted Isabella and set her on a stainless steel counter that spanned the middle of the kitchen. She squealed and laughed, but then he was fitting himself between her legs, making butterflies flutter in her stomach. With a low hum in the back of his throat, he leaned down and pressed a lingering kiss to her cheek.

Isabella all but melted into him, holding on to his strong arms, tangling her legs around his. It was an innocent kiss, but Leo could make even the most innocent moments feel like she could lose herself.

He pulled back and looked her in the eyes, wearing that sexy grin. "Had a little chocolate on your face. I couldn't resist." He kissed her then on the mouth, achingly slow, the sweet taste of cocoa still on his tongue. When he drew away once more, leaving her utterly breathless, his eyes glittered. "I had to take the time to do that. Before this day gets any crazier. I love your mouth, Izz."

She bit her lip, her heart pounding. She wanted to say something more, and she'd be lying if she said she didn't wish that *he'd* said something more, too. She wanted Leo to love all of her. Wanted—so badly—to hear him say it.

She glanced down, but he tilted her chin up. "Hey. You're a very good sister, by the way. Norah is going to have a much better memory of her wedding thanks to you."

She tapped his nose, shoving her annoying *feelings* down deep. "And you're a very good soon-to-be-brother-in-law."

He gave her that grin again, along with a sidelong glance. "Whose mouth you also love."

Her heart felt like it was about to explode. She had to will her face not to show disappointment as she said, "Yes. Whose mouth I also love."

Thirty minutes later, Leo pressed a hurried kiss to Isabella's lips before he dropped her back off at the Whitley home. She made it just in time for her and Nina to help Norah with her hair and makeup. Norah wouldn't put her wedding gown on until she arrived at the wedding location. Isabella doubted Norah could even sit in the white, slim-fitted gown once she had it on.

When Norah was ready, Isabella took a quick shower and then hurried into her bedroom to put on the hideous red bridesmaid's dress. At least she only had to wear it for one day, then she'd never have to look at it again.

She rushed to the window, peeking through the sheer curtains, and hoping to catch a glimpse of Leo in his room. But disappointment bloomed in her chest when she found his blinds closed.

"Alright girl, spill it," Nina said from behind her, entering the room.

Isabella spun around. "What?"

"What's going on with you and Leo?"

Isabella's cheeks burned. "Umm…I don't know, exactly."

"Well, he obviously has more than just a thing for you." She didn't say it like a question. "And what are you guys gonna do about it?"

That was the burning question. What *would* they do about it? What *could* they do? Could she sacrifice New York? Her job? She could propose the ability to work remotely, but they could just as easily turn her down. She'd worked so hard to land this job and build this career. And what about her friends? And Todd and Margo? They'd grown so close; they were like family.

Would Leo really come to New York like he'd said? Could he ever see himself settle down there? She wasn't exactly sure how it would work or what their future would look like. But the most important thing was that they would figure it out together. She had to trust everything would fall into place afterward.

"I think we're going to try long-distance," Isabella said.

"Ahh!" Nina shrieked. "You know Norah is gonna flip when she hears this? She's been conspiring for the last few weeks to get you two back together."

"Please don't tell her," Isabella pleaded. "Please don't tell Finn either. Or anyone else."

"Believe me, the last thing I want is to be in on some kind of Whitley family drama." She went back to situating her long, black braids while looking in the full-length mirror. "But for the record, I'm really happy for you Izz."

Isabella's cheeks warmed. "Thanks," she whispered. "I'm happy for me, too."

She slipped her feet into her red pumps. At least *they* were cute. Italian suede with a stiletto heel. And the red sash Norah picked out to wrap around the bridesmaids' shoulders was a nice touch to hopefully conceal the hideous bow, but it did little in the area of keeping them warm.

There was a knock on the door, and Isabella's heart jumped. It took a few seconds for it to calm down and slide back into place once she saw Mom and Ava enter the room. Ava twirled in her sparkly red dress, the full tulle skirt lifting on the ends. They filled Ava's tank full of "ooo's" and "ahh's" and compliments. She really did look beautiful. And maybe, Isabella hoped, Ava's cuteness would be enough distraction for guests not to notice the awful bridesmaids' dresses.

At the wedding hall, Isabella carried Norah's wedding gown encased in a cloth bag, holding it high so it wouldn't drag on the salt-sprinkled icy asphalt. Inside the small tent that had been set up as a Bride's Room, there was a rolling hanging rod where Isabella hung the gown. The tent had a space heater and a few full-length mirrors set up on one side, and a makeshift counter lined with hair products—from hairspray to bobby-pins. The wedding coordinator had thought of everything, including bottles of water and boxes of tissues. Norah had already teared up twice since getting her makeup done. At this rate, she'd have no makeup left by the time the actual ceremony began.

"I'm so nervous," Norah said, beginning to unbutton her blouse.

"What do you have to be nervous about?" Isabella unzipped the gown bag. "You love Landon, and he loves you. It's that simple, right?"

"Right." Norah nodded, though dramatically, causing Isabella to wonder who she was trying to convince.

Isabella wrinkled a brow. "You *do* want to get married, don't you?"

"Of course. Don't be silly." Norah waved her off.

Isabella exhaled. "Good. You had me worried for a second there." She slipped the gown from the bag.

"It's perfectly normal for a bride to be nervous and second guess everything on her wedding day." Norah fingered the waves of her long, sienna hair while looking into the mirror. "So everyone tells me anyway."

Isabella held out the dress to her sister. "That's what I hear, too." She smiled. "It will be great. I've never seen two people more perfect for each other than you two."

That might've been a stretch. Norah was too sweet for her own good. And from what Isabella had experienced in the last week, Landon had a bit of a wandering eye. But she hoped with all her strength that these two kids were gonna make it.

Norah practically jumped into Isabella's arms, wrapping her in a tight hug. Isabella had to hold the dress out so it wouldn't get smashed in between them. "Thank you," Norah whispered.

Isabella's phone chimed. Once she'd handed off the gown to Norah, she slid her phone from her purse, her nerves zipping out of control. But they fizzled fast when she read the text.

Harrison: I know you're busy with wedding stuff but just wanted to say I love you!

Isabella knew she couldn't avoid Harrison forever. She'd asked him to commit, and he was finally trying, it seemed. But now, everything had changed. She needed to tell him as much but having that serious of a conversation by text or phone didn't sit right. She needed to do it in person once she returned to New York tomorrow. She supposed she owed him that courtesy. She sent a reply.

Isabella: I'll be back tomorrow. We can talk then. Merry Christmas.

She sent a text to Leo next.

Isabella: Ready to meet?

Leo: We have a slight problem.

Isabella: What kind of a problem?

Leo: Landon may have had too much whiskey.

Isabella: What? But it's only noon!

Tension kneaded across her shoulders, and anger stirred in her stomach.

Leo: I know.

Isabella: Will he be ready to get married in two hours?

Leo: Um…I'm working on it.

Isabella: Um, how, exactly?

Leo: By keeping him away from the whiskey.

She groaned. Did he have *no* experience in this sort of thing? She tapped out a reply.

Isabella: I'm bringing him coffee. Now.

Leo: Right. Coffee. I should've thought about that.

Of all the people to drink too much before their wedding, Isabella had thought Landon to be the last person. Nerves or not, this was unacceptable. If he ruined her sister's wedding day, she'd kill him.

CHAPTER THIRTY-ONE

LEO

WHAT STARTED AS AN INNOCENT TRADITION OF SHARING A SHOT OF whiskey in the Groom's Room somehow manifested into Leo having a drunk groom on his hands. The Hoffman men always shared a shot of whiskey before any big event. But Landon had poured a few additional shots Leo wasn't aware of. He'd been too distracted thinking about Izzy. Thinking about them. And their decision of trying a long-distance relationship.

Dad hadn't been much help. He'd joined in on the traditional shot and then bowed out, going to mingle with the guests. Leo should've known better than to trust the two groomsmen to keep an eye on Landon. Their cousin Steve could hold liquor better than anyone Leo ever met, and Landon's childhood best friend Riley, who was a new father and had drove in from Denver that morning, kept falling asleep in the corner of the tent.

"Ya know, brother?" Landon said, holding out the whiskey bottle to Leo. "I think you dodged a bullet with Izzy."

Leo snatched the bottle, twisting the cap back on, and setting it out of reach. "Yeah? And why's that?"

"The Whitleys are just so...so...*good*. Ya know?"

Leo clenched his jaw. "Yeah, I know." He wanted to say more, but there wasn't much sense in trying to reason with a drunk person.

"Norah is so...*good.*"

"That she is. You're a lucky guy."

"I know, I know, I know," he muttered. "But sometimes, she's *too* good. Too *innocent.* If you know what I mean?" Landon raised his brows suggestively, and Leo tilted his head.

Their cousin Steve laughed and fist-bumped Landon.

Leo sent another text to Isabella.

Leo: Where are you?

Isabella: On my way.

"I think," Leo spoke slowly, weighing his words, "you and Norah are going to have a long marriage with plenty of time to discuss all the things."

"You and Isabella dated for a while. I'm sure you two had sex, right?"

Leo gritted his teeth. "I'm not having this conversation with you. Especially not now."

"Oh, c'mon, big bro. Fill me in. I need to know if she was as sweet as Norah or if she got a little freaky. Izzy seems like she might be nice and freaky when the lights go out."

Steve snorted into his fist and Leo shot him a fiery look.

"Alright, that's enough."

"Because maybe, Izzy could give Norah some pointers."

Heat bubbled in his chest, setting his skin ablaze. If Landon wasn't his kid brother, he would've punched him. "Landon, I said enough. You're drunk."

"Knock, knock, it's Isabella."

Riley straightened in his chair, rubbing sleep from his eyes.

Leo sighed. Finally, reinforcements. But this was a bad time for Isabella to come strolling into the room.

On his guard, he lifted the curtain, parting it so she could enter. The sight of her nearly took his breath away. She stood there with an airpot cradled in one arm, a single brow arched like she was ready for a battle. Still, the sight of her made his heart stutter. Her dress might've been ugly, but it did nothing to take away from her beauty. With her dark hair falling in curls on one shoulder and pulled up on the opposite side, it revealed a bare collarbone and neck so delicious he ached to taste it.

Landon staggered to standing, a lopsided grin on his face, his dress shirt half untucked, hair disheveled. "Sis," he greeted, attempting to hug her.

She straightened and shoved him in the chest. "Back off, buddy. I'm here to save your ass."

Riley chuckled and stood, stretching. "I'm going to get some air," he muttered as he ducked out of the tent.

"You," Landon pointed at Isabella, his words slurred, "are the bestest sister ever."

"Here." She placed two aspirin in Landon's palm. "Take these and drink this." She shoved a bottle of water at him.

"So bossy," Landon whined but reluctantly took the aspirin.

She *was* being bossy, and Leo found he liked it. A lot. Her no-nonsense attitude was hot, making him crave to snatch her up and take her somewhere they could be alone. "Thank you," Leo whispered.

"Don't thank me yet." She sat the airpot on a table, pumped coffee into a mug, and handed it to Landon. "Here, drink this too."

Landon slumped in a chair, accepted the coffee, and took a sip. "Did I ever tell you that you're my favorite Whitley?"

"No, no you didn't." She crossed her arms and passed Leo a look.

Worry coursed through his veins. If Landon began spouting off his mouth regarding their earlier conversation, Leo would have to do something to shut him up real quick.

"Ya know why?" He sloshed the mug around. "Because you're hardly around. That's one less Whitley I have to worry about impressing."

"I don't mind *any* of the Whitley's." Steve waggled his brows suggestively at her.

Isabella ignored him, keeping her attention on Landon. "Okay, just drink your coffee, will you?"

"With all the family stuff. All the traditions. All the happy, let's-all-be-together-all-the-time-stuff. It gets tiring."

"Landon," Leo warned. "Drink the damn coffee."

"If it's so tiring, maybe you should've thought about that before you decided to marry into Norah's family." Isabella narrowed her eyes.

Leo was about to step in between the two of them.

"But I love her." He tipped back the mug, gulping down the coffee.

"You may want to go easy on that," Isabella warned. "You don't want it all coming back up."

"See?" Landon pointed at her. "Great advice. Another reason why you're my favorite."

"Okay, I should get back to Norah," she said, breathing out a sigh. "You have less than one hour to sober up and get out there and marry my sister. If you screw this up for her, so help me I will rip out your heart, Indiana Jones style."

Landon's facial expression distorted, and he looked as if he might cry.

"I can't handle drunk crying." Isabella turned to leave, handing the airpot to Leo. "I'm leaving you in charge."

"I'll try not to let you down," he said as he followed her to the open curtain, his eyes traveling over her backside. "And we'll talk later?"

"Hopefully sooner rather than later," she whispered, passing him a smile over her shoulder before heading back to tend to Norah.

Less than an hour later, Leo left Landon standing on the platform with the minister—somewhat sober. Thanks to Isabella. He waited with the groomsmen in the back of the tent for the bridesmaids to join them. He caught a glimpse of Norah in her wedding dress, a white beaded crown on her head, and a bouquet of red and white camellias clutched in her hands. Isabella kissed Norah on the cheek before she strolled toward him, her eyes were glossy but a smile stretched on her face.

Isabella linked her arm in his, and he felt a loss for words. When she'd entered the Groom's Room earlier, he wanted to tell her then how stunning she looked.

"You look beautiful."

She winced, shivering a little against the cold. "You don't have to say that. This dress is hideous."

"True, but I didn't compliment the dress. I complimented you."

Her cheeks blushed, matching her red nose.

He leaned into her and whispered into her neck, "You'd look even more beautiful without the dress on."

She turned to him, grinning, and elbowed him in the side, pulling the shawl around her arms.

"So…do you think we should tell our families yet? About us?"

Her lips pouted into a thought. "Maybe. Do you?"

He shuffled his feet, waiting their turn while his shoulders tensed. "I mean, if we're really going to make a go at this, they're bound to find out eventually."

The first couple had already walked down the aisle. Only one more before it would be their turn.

"It might be kinda fun to keep sneaking around for a while?" she whispered.

The thought of that was enticing. At the same time, he also wanted to announce it to the world, to declare their love for one another.

The next couple went.

Leo looked down at Isabella, feeling the weight of the moment. "I will do whatever you want, Isabella Whitley. So long as I'm with you."

She touched his hand with her icy fingers, still holding his gaze, and squeezed, her eyes glassy. She looked like she wanted to say something, opened her mouth like she might, but instead, she bit her lip and blinked back the threatening tears in her eyes.

"Don't cry," he whispered, giving her a reassuring smile. "This is a happy day."

She nodded.

The wedding coordinator gestured for them to begin walking. They took the aisle, their steps in time with one another's. And it felt like something more. As if this was the first moment they were being presented as a couple. Like it signified the beginning of the rest of their lives.

Then, they were being separated. Isabella unlinked her arm from his and pulled apart from him, tightening the red shawl around her body. His chest felt dull and heavy as she slipped away from him.

He took his place next to Landon. Seeing his little brother standing there, dressed in a black tux about to marry the love of his life, Leo's eyes pricked with tears. He couldn't help but miss his mom and think how she would've been so incredibly proud.

He pulled his brother in for a quick hug. "I'm proud of you, little bro." He slapped him on the back. Landon smiled wide and only stumbled slightly.

As Norah and Mr. W. appeared at the back of the tent, the guests stood, and the procession sounded from the sound system speakers. He accompanied her slowly down the aisle. Norah's eyes glistened with tears, but her face radiated happiness.

When she reached the front, she didn't tear her attention away from Landon even for a second. It warmed Leo's soul to see the love Norah had for his brother. After Mr. W. gave Norah away, kissing her on the cheek and shaking the hand of a mostly-sober Landon, Isabella fixed the hem of her sister's dress.

The minister began, speaking about love and commitment and quoting the most popular verse shared at a wedding—1 Corinthians 13:4-8; the one that speaks about love being patient and kind and never failing.

Even though Leo had heard this particular passage numerous times from his wedding videographer days, this time it held larger gravity. Emotions coursed through him while he weighed the significance of the meaning of the L-word. After all that he and Isabella had been through, love had always been the backbone of their relationship. Each of them had made choices out of loving the other.

Glancing across the platform at Isabella, she mouthed something, including brow waggling, and a wink. But he was confused.

"What?" he mouthed back.

She tried again, licking her tongue across her top teeth, and he instantly became self-conscious that he had something stuck there. He ran his tongue along his own teeth, hoping he hadn't been walking around all day since his breakfast smoothie with a lodged strawberry seed.

The next thing Leo knew, the minister had said, "You may now kiss the bride."

Landon and Norah shared a sloppy but moderately intimate short kiss. Something told Leo they had practiced it enough times to get it right today.

The minister declared Landon and Norah as husband and wife, and everyone cheered. Isabella wiped at fallen tears across her cheeks as Leo presented his arm to her. She smiled at him gratefully and linked her arm into his.

As they walked back down the aisle, she said a bit too loudly over the sound of the cheering, "We have a few minutes before the reception, wanna fool around?"

He chuckled, tugging her faster.

They reached the back of the tent, and he yanked her off to the side where they had a bit of privacy while the rest of the wedding party flooded into the wedding hall. His heartrate sped up. Finally, they had a moment to steal on this busy day, and he didn't care anymore if anyone saw them.

He slipped an arm around her, pressing his palm to her lower back and gazing into her familiar amber eyes. He felt giddy being in her arms, a lightness fluttering in his chest as they were risking being caught by family and friends. He dipped his chin, hovering his lips over hers. This embrace was way too intimate to be mistaken as friendly, and he didn't care one bit.

"Isabella," a man's voice called out, interrupting the moment.

She stiffened and spun around, pressing her trembling hand to her chest. *"Harrison?"*

CHAPTER THIRTY-TWO

ISABELLA

SHE STOOD THERE, FROZEN, BLINKING BACK HER DISBELIEF. "WHAT ARE you doing here?"

"You weren't answering my texts. I couldn't let a silly thing like distance keep us apart on Christmas. So, I took the first flight available and then took an Uber from the airport." Tugging her toward him, he shot a glare at Leo, then he swept her up in his arms, spinning her around and nuzzling his chin in her neck. Her world tilted as he gazed down at her with those adoring green eyes, brows furrowed. "What is this horrid dress you're wearing?"

She struggled to get out of his arms, struggled to catch her breath and find words. "You did what? You paid an Uber to drive you to Pineridge from Denver? That's a two-hour drive."

"Yeah. In hindsight, not the best idea. But hey, I'm here." He placed his hands on her face, bringing her in for a kiss. She wanted to resist, but both her mind and body were trying to play catch up.

Harrison was seriously here. In Pineridge. And on Christmas Day.

Kissing her in front of Leo. This was going to be bad.

She had to take control of the situation. Pressing her palm to his chest, she shoved Harrison away and wiped her hand over her lips, but it was too late. When she glanced at Leo who stood a few feet away, his shoulders broad and stiff, a stony expression masked his face.

She swallowed the ever-growing lump in her throat. "Harrison Blake," she said, voice wobbling, "this is Leo Hoffman. Leo, Harrison."

Harrison extended his hand as if accepting an award, but Leo kept his hands fisted at his side. "The infamous Leo Hoffman." He smiled wide, but she could tell it was forced. "You've given a man a notably unattainable image to live up to after being our Bella's first love."

With nostrils flaring and cold eyes, Leo replied, "I've heard quite a bit about you as well, wish I could say all good."

There was a quiver in her stomach, and she pulled the shawl around her arms tighter.

"And I think you mean our *Izzy*?" Leo continued, teeth clenching.

"Ahh." Harrison pointed at him. "That's right. Isabella mentioned the nickname." Placing a confident hand on her lower back, he smiled down at her. "Guess I'll have to get used to it."

Leo only continued to stare him down.

Harrison cleared his throat. "Why don't we grab your things, Izzy, and let's get out of here. There's a flight to JFK in three hours. We'll still make it home in time for Christmas." He tugged on her arm, but she yanked free.

"Wait, just wait a second. I'm not leaving in the middle of my sister's wedding."

"Well, well, well. Who do we have here, Izzy?" Dad asked, coming up from behind them. Mom accompanied him, and Finn, Nina, and Ava brought up the rear. They were like a rat pack. That was her family —always together. Maybe Landon had been right about the Whitleys. She supposed they could come off as a bit intimidating.

"Dad, this is Harrison Blake. Harrison, my dad." She stepped back, allowing room for handshakes and more introductions, and to give her a moment to breathe. "This is my mom, Sue. And over here is my brother Finn and his wife Nina. And this is my niece, Ava."

After Harrison had been introduced all around, he took hold of Isabella's hand, squeezing it. She'd pictured in her mind many times what it might be like to bring Harrison to Colorado. How he would react to meeting her family. What he would think of them and the small town she grew up in. While Harrison was a gentleman, he'd grown up in Manhattan, went to private schools, never had to bundle up in extra layers in the winter when the heating bill needed to be conserved.

Now, he'd come all this way to be with her on Christmas, to meet her family. How could she tell him she no longer had feelings for him? How was she going to tell him she didn't love him and didn't see a future with him?

But with a simple glance in Leo's direction and finding the hurt there, she knew she needed to clear things up—and fast.

She stiffened. "Harrison, we need to talk."

But he ignored her. "Well, I have to say, it's so wonderful to finally meet you all. It's been far too long."

Isabella was distracted by Leo and his uneasiness. He shuffled his feet, and she could tell he wanted to escape—hoping for an excuse to get out of there. She wanted one, too.

Harrison continued, "But I'm especially glad you're all here. Because Bella," he paused, correcting himself, "*Izzy* and I have some news."

She glanced up at him, anxiety coursing through her, crawling up her throat. She whispered, "What are you doing?"

"Don't worry, you're gonna love this. It's perfect," he said in a lowered voice.

"Let's talk first. Just the two of us," she pleaded, yanking on his arm.

He smiled wider, showing off his white teeth to everyone within a fifteen-mile radius. Had his teeth always been that annoyingly white or was she just now noticing? His voice too sounded condescending. Did he always talk to her like that?

"Your family should be here to witness this." He let go of her and pulled a small, black box from his jacket pocket.

Fear shot up her spine, sending a nauseating swirl to her stomach. Maybe puking would be better than what was about to happen. She saw it, could picture it, like a train wreck. A train wreck in slo-mo.

This would not end well.

Dropping on one knee, surrounded by her family, Leo—and now a large group of wedding guests full of extended family and friends and even her childhood pediatrician—Harrison opened the box. He uttered the words Isabella had dreamed of hearing. Only now, it felt more like a nightmare.

"Isabella Anne Whitley, will you make me the happiest guy on earth and marry me?"

With the diamond ring glimmering in the box, his smile stretched out on his face, and with all her family as witnesses, she froze. Her mind, her body—it was as if she'd become paralyzed.

She caught a flicker of movement out of the corner of her eye. Leo—backing up before turning and taking off in the opposite direction.

"Well, would you look at that, she's speechless. That's new?" Harrison teased.

But it didn't feel like teasing to her.

"C'mon, honey, we're all waiting for your answer." He looked at her expectantly.

Her family stared with similar expressions, but all she felt like doing was running—running far away from all of this. It felt as if she'd waited years for Harrison to ask her to marry him. And now that he had, she wanted him to take the question back, to somehow undo the last few minutes.

Tears stung her eyes and worked their way up her throat. She didn't want to hurt him. But she didn't want to hurt Leo either. So she did what anyone would do in her situation.

She stalled.

With almost her entire family, including Nana and Papa, as spectators, she saw only one way out. She'd seen it in movies over a dozen times. How hard could it be? She forced her expression to go still, deadpan, rolled her eyes way up in her head and...

Collapsed.

The crowd shrieked. The fall hurt more than Isabella anticipated. But to make it look believable, she had to let her body drop without trying to catch it—easier said than done.

Within seconds, her family surrounded her head with Harrison at the forefront. He caressed her face and while he, along with the rest of her family called her name, she fluttered her eyes open.

Isabella rested the back of her hand against her forehead, tried to push herself up to a sitting position, and made her voice sound groggy. "What…what happened?"

"Well, sweetie, you fainted," Dad said, rubbing her shoulder.

"I did?" She looked at Harrison, hoping to catch a glimpse of belief there.

"Are you alright?" He took hold of her hands.

"I think so."

"Izzy, sweetie, you want some water?" Mom asked.

"Sure, that would be great, Mom."

"She's so surprised over my proposal, she fainted," Harrison called over his shoulder to the crowd, chuckling.

Finn squeezed in between Mom and Dad and held up three fingers. "Izzy, how many fingers am I holding up?"

"Three." She wanted to reply with a smart aleck remark. Like, is this how doctors check to make sure patients are okay? By holding up fingers? Any idiot could do that without nearly a decade of college under their belt and a degree.

"And how's your head?" Finn felt the back of her skull, but if she'd known better, he was messing up her hair on purpose.

She swatted his hand away. "It's fine."

"Are you sure? I think I might feel a bump." His forehead wrinkled, and his brows raised. He looked at her intently.

"Um, maybe my head does feel a little sore."

"I should take her somewhere she can lie down, and I can get a better look at her," Finn suggested. "Dad, can you help me get her up?"

They both took one of her arms and helped her onto a row of chairs where Finn assisted her with lying across them. Dad assured everyone she was fine. Harrison stood there looking helpless.

He knelt by her side, brushing her cheek with his hand. "Need me to get you something?"

"Hey, man," Finn interrupted. "Would you mind finding her some Tylenol?"

"Oh, sure. I can do that…I suppose." He kissed Isabella on the forehead. "I'll be back."

"Thanks," she muttered.

Once he was out of earshot, Finn punched his fist lightly into Isabella's shoulder.

"Hey." She rubbed her arm. "What was that for?"

"I know you faked it."

"What?"

"You fake fainted."

She bit the inside of her cheek. "How did you know?"

"Oh, I don't know? Maybe because I'm a *doctor*. Or maybe because I'm not a complete moron. If you plan on fake fainting again, you better practice beforehand. That was not an Oscar-winning performance out there."

Dad threw his hand up. "What is going on?"

She buried her face in her palms. If anything, her little performance had only bought her a few extra minutes, and maybe a lot of explaining. But at least it would save Harrison some humiliation from having to let him down in front of all those people.

"You faked it?" Dad sat down in an open chair by her feet.

She pushed up on her elbows. "I'm sorry."

"But...why?"

"I just needed a minute."

"Okay, so you felt put on the spot. I get that. But then why not tell him? Why risk hurting yourself and upsetting your mother?"

Isabella sat up, scooting closer to Dad. "I'm sorry. I didn't want to hurt his feelings in front of all our family and friends."

"So, you're sure you don't want to marry him?"

Isabella nodded, saying, "I'm sure."

"Well, sweetie, I'd say you probably should've told him that before he hopped on a plane on Christmas Day."

"I know." She rubbed her forehead.

"Izzy," Finn said, slumping sideways onto a chair in the row in front of her. "If you don't want to marry this guy, then tell him no."

"I don't want to hurt him."

Dad turned to face her, putting a loving hand on her shoulder and squeezing it. "This is your life, your future we're talking about. What do *you* want?"

Tears worked their way into the corners of her eyes. "I want to be with Leo."

There. She finally said it out loud.

Finn stood, throwing his hands up. "Here we go again."

"What's that supposed to mean?"

"You could've been with Leo. Years ago. Ya see Izzy, this is why men think women are so confusing. Because they are. Because they can't make up their damn minds."

"You don't understand. There are things you don't know."

Nina and Norah rushed into the room.

"Oh my goodness, Izzy. Are you alright? When I didn't see you at the reception, I got worried. Nina said you fainted." Norah threw her arms around Isabella's neck.

"I'm fine."

"Yep, she's fine alright. She's our little Oscar winner, this one," Finn said, incredulous.

"What's he talking about?" Norah asked.

"She faked it."

"What? Why?"

Isabella squeezed her eyes tight and pushed her fingertips into her temples. "Will you all just chill out? Harrison will be back any minute."

As if on cue, Harrison rushed in waving a hand triumphantly in the air. "I've got them. Two Tylenol—as requested."

Everyone turned to look at him. He slowed his steps, his vision darting around to each of them.

"What's going on?" He placed the pills in Isabella's palm.

"Thanks," she whispered.

Norah hovered over Isabella and Harrison acknowledged her. "You must be Norah. I'm Harrison. It's so good to finally meet you."

Norah's jaw dropped, and she took his hand, shaking it limply. "Yeah, you too. I've heard...so much about you." She glanced back and forth between him and Isabella, mouth still hanging open.

Mom rushed toward her. "Here's the water." She handed the glass to Isabella. "You alright? Finn checked you out?"

"I'm fine, Mom, thanks." She set the glass on the floor, the pills on the seat next to her. "You all hurry and get to the reception. We'll be right there." She gave her mom a glance that she prayed said everything she couldn't in that moment. She needed to be alone with Harrison.

Realization dawned on Mom's face, and she kissed Isabella on the cheek. "Sure thing, sweetie."

Dad squeezed Isabella's shoulder but gave her a pointed look. She had finally been honest with herself and her family. Now it was time to be honest with Harrison. And hopefully, Leo—if it wasn't too late.

"If you're sure…everyone is probably wondering where the bride has run off to," Mom said.

"Exactly," Norah said, giving Isabella a tiny wink before she took Mom's hand and led her and Dad toward the reception. Finn and Nina followed behind. Isabella watched them go, staring at the empty space before turning to face Harrison, taking in a deep breath.

"Thanks again for the Tylenol," she said

"I'm just glad you're alright. Do you think you'll be ready to fly today?"

She tucked her chin to her chest. "Harrison, I'm not leaving. Not yet." Her gaze lifted. "This is my sister's wedding."

"I'm sure she won't mind."

She blinked, honestly confused that he couldn't grasp how self-centered he was being, how this was not even something that was up for debate. But maybe part of it was her fault. She'd taught Harrison that her family didn't mean enough for her to even visit for the holidays. She'd taught him that they were not a focal point in her life.

"Harrison, I love my family. I know that seems new to you, but I would never just walk out on Norah's wedding. Not for you, not for anyone. I think…" she paused, considering her words. "I think that you don't really know me. And it isn't your fault. I'd forgotten who I even was until I came home."

He took her hands in his. "Bella. How can you say that? I think I know the woman I've spent four years of my life with. I love her enough that I just flew 1,800 miles, in coach, to be with her on Christmas."

"And I appreciate the sentiment," she replied. "But that doesn't change anything. It doesn't change that I'm a different person now than I was when I got on the plane to come here."

He dropped her hands, pushing his fingers through his hair and turning away from her, then groaning and spinning back around to face her. "What exactly are you saying?"

She stood, the deepest knowing pulsing deep inside her. "I'm saying that you're free to stay if you'd like, but I'm not leaving. And I'm not marrying you just because you finally decided you wanted me. Now if you'll excuse me, I have someone's heart to unbreak." She brushed past him, dashing out of the tent.

Isabella rushed into the wedding hall searching for Leo. A crowd of guests flocked around Landon and Norah congratulating them. She scanned the head table, but Leo's seat was empty. Discouraged, she pulled her phone from her purse and sent him a text. But she had the sinking feeling he wouldn't respond.

He had every right to be furious and feel dejected. But would Leo seriously skip out on his brother's wedding reception? Thinking about breaking his heart for a second time hit her hard in the chest, giving her an unforgiving ache there.

As family members and wedding guests greeted her, she felt disoriented. She wanted to be present for Norah on her special day, but she couldn't stop thinking about Leo and how much she desperately wanted to find him and explain things. Even though she still didn't know what their future would look like, she wanted them to be together.

When she noticed the wedding party begin to take their seats at the head table, she glanced around but there still wasn't any sign of him. She held onto the hope that he would show himself soon.

She rushed to Norah and Landon as they sat. "Hey guys, have either of you seen Leo?"

"Oh, sweetie." Norah grazed her arm and flashed her a sympathetic smile.

Landon slid his phone out of the pocket of the tux jacket and held it out for her to read. "A text from Leo."

Leo: Sorry bro but I can't be here.

Isabella shut her eyes through the pain and pinched the bridge of her nose. "I'm so sorry, Landon." Her heart ached, and she was desperate to console it, but it hurt for Landon too. She'd stolen this from him—having his brother at his wedding reception. He already didn't have his mother there.

She wanted so badly to fix this. To go back to how things were between her and Leo the day before. Or even an hour before. She didn't want Harrison. She wanted Leo—if he still wanted her. They were the ones who made a good team. They could fix anything as long as they did it together.

That's all they needed. Each other. But how could she explain it to him when he was MIA?

CHAPTER THIRTY-THREE

LEO

Leo couldn't hide in his truck forever. He knew he needed to go back inside. Not for Isabella, but for Landon. His brother was counting on him. He was the best man and still needed to do the toast. But if he were honest, all he wanted to do was start up his Chevy truck and drive until it ran out of gas. He didn't care where he ended up.

He'd decided to give her space, to let her work through Harrison's arrival on her own. But in truth, he was terrified. Izzy's choice had flown in on a plane and found her. Leo wanted to think she would say no to Harrison, but he also knew that she had a life before him. A life she'd wanted. Leo wasn't sure he could survive having his heart ripped out of his chest again, and even the chance that he might have to look at her, knowing that she'd chosen Harrison, would do it.

The thing that ate at him the most was that Harrison had been the one to make a grand gesture. He'd traveled all the way to Pineridge, on Christmas Day, and proposed to Isabella in front of strangers. He hadn't let distance stand in the way of them being together.

Ten years and not once had Leo done something like that. He could've gone to New York to see her, and he hadn't. He wasn't even sure why. His mom? Pride? Because he'd decided a long time ago that

Pineridge was his home and nothing or no one would convince him to leave?

He'd been too damn stubborn.

The truth was, Leo wanted to be mad at this Harrison guy for swooping in, stealing what little time he and Isabella had left together, for proposing and being selfless enough to perform a grand gesture. But he couldn't be. He didn't want to admit it, but maybe, the more righteous man had won.

Exhaling a deep sigh, he reluctantly climbed out of the truck and ambled toward the back door of the wedding hall, shuffling his dress shoes against the icy asphalt. He slipped inside just as the servers filled champagne flutes. The wedding coordinator announced into the microphone that it was almost time for the toast and requested that the maid of honor and best man make their way to the front.

Leo hid in the back. Isabella glided to the stage and accepted the microphone. Her voice trembled, but her words were honest and captivating. His heart ached when she spoke of the love between Landon and Norah, about how the two balanced one another out.

In the middle of her speech, she made eye contact with him, and her voice stalled. He dropped his chin, rubbing at the back of his neck, and she eventually recovered, rushing through the last few sentences. The wedding coordinator called for the best man next, and Leo sucked in a deep breath before strolling up to the mic.

Gazing out at family and friends, Leo began by reading off the cards he'd slipped into his pocket that morning. He hadn't planned on going off-script, but when he wrote the toast on Christmas Eve, he'd been hopeful. Love had felt beautiful and possible. His mind had painted a charming picture of reverie and devotion.

When the handwritten words on his cards had run out, he had more to say so he improvised. "Landon and Norah," he continued, stuffing the cards back into the pocket of the tuxedo pants. "When you think you've tried everything, when all else fails, I want you to remember, not only the vows you exchanged today, but remember to never lose hope. Because if it's love, true love, it will always persevere. Anyway, let's raise our glasses to Norah and Landon. Love you guys." He held up his glass, waiting while Norah and Landon kissed, and the wedding guests sipped their champagne.

He handed the mic off to the wedding coordinator and rushed toward the back of the wedding hall, resuming his place on the fringes once again. His heart pounded hard against his chest, and he chugged the champagne in hopes it would ease his vexation and scorching body. Waiting through toasts made by Dad, Finn, and then Norah's bridesmaids had been more difficult than he'd imagined. He couldn't get the image of Harrison kneeling and proposing to Isabella out of his mind.

The wedding coordinator announced that it was time for the bride and groom's first dance. Leo longed to ditch out on the reception now. But if he did, he would be in very few pictures, and he knew Norah would treasure her wedding photos forever. He could set aside his feelings for a while longer.

Or so he'd thought, until he spotted Isabella weaving through the crowd of guests toward him. His heart felt as if it stalled in his chest. He glanced over both shoulders, searching for a clean escape, but it was too late.

"There you are," she said. "I was looking everywhere for you."

"Hey. Sorry, I just needed a breather." He stuffed his hands into his pockets.

"Can we talk?"

"I don't really think there's much to talk about."

She clutched his arm. "I think there's plenty."

"Listen, Izzy." He tucked his chin to his chest. "The plans we made last night, I'm not gonna hold you to them. Things have changed now. I know that."

She shook her head. "Nothing has changed."

Feedback from the microphone screeched through the speakers, followed by the wedding coordinator's voice, "Alright, maid of honor and best man, it's your turn for a dance. Then let's have the wedding party out on the dance floor."

They stared at one another for a beat. Leo held out his palm to her. As much as it hurt to think about holding her, thinking she might not be anything more to him than a friend, he found himself wanting to. He wanted to pull her in close, cling to her, and breathe in her irresistible scent. He hoped she would tell him something different, that she'd chosen him, but she deserved so much more.

She deserved everything.

They reached the dance floor and he pressed his hands to her back, loosening when he realized they had a mind of their own and nearly grazed her backside. She gripped his shoulders, and he was sorry she hadn't tried to tether her hands around his neck, sliding into his hair where they always seemed to go.

"When I told you I wanted to try long-distance, it's because I wanted to be with you. In a relationship. Because I think it's worth it. We're worth it."

He spun them around slowly, regardless that the tempo of the song was faster.

"Long-distance is hard. There's a lot to consider. And it doesn't seem fair to you," he mumbled.

"Fair to me, or fair to you?" She stared up at him, looking pointedly into his eyes. "Because I said I'm willing to put in the work."

He tore his attention away from her. "You know I will always love you, Izzy. You are it for me…" His words trailed as his focus landed on a certain man standing in the back of the room. "I can't let you make a mistake because of me."

She pulled back. "What are you talking about?"

"You deserve better, someone who will perform rom-com-sized gestures to be with you, and maybe that someone is standing right behind you."

He turned her around and then marched across the dance floor and out the door, not looking back.

CHAPTER THIRTY-FOUR

ISABELLA

Isabella turned to see Harrison standing along the room's fringes, hands stuffed inside his trouser pockets. He gave her an unsure smile and waved. When she spun back around, Leo was gone. She didn't know how to feel or what to do. To run for Leo or leave him alone. He wasn't right. Was he?

Isabella faced Harrison once again, her mind reeling. When he told her a few months back that he wanted to take a break, that he thought it best she moved out, Isabella felt as lost as she did right now. She didn't know if they'd ever find their way back to one another.

It wasn't until she returned home that she finally no longer felt untethered. Colorado had always been home to her. A one true north. Here, the fog had cleared. She saw that her life could go on without Harrison. She could finally picture a future without him in it, and it didn't scare her. And when she opened her heart once again to Leo, the hard layers of the shell cracking, she knew Harrison wasn't the answer to her future.

She weaved through a sea of dancing couples until she reached Harrison. "Hey."

He shrugged, sadness tugging at the corners of his eyes. "I couldn't leave yet," he said. "Not without knowing for sure."

Isabella inhaled a deep breath, her throat tight with the words she needed to say. Taking his hands, she looked at him. "Harrison, the last four years with you have been incredible. There are so many things I experienced with you and because of you. But the break we took gave us the time apart we needed. That I know I hadn't wanted, but I ended up needing."

"So, it's really over then?" His eyes flicked away.

Tears formed and fell without intention. She did love this man. And she didn't want to hurt him. "Yes, I can't marry you. You don't even want to be married. Not really," she whispered.

"But I thought..." Disbelief clouded his voice, and his hands tensed in hers. "I thought this is the kind of commitment you wanted. What says commitment more than a marriage proposal?"

"I'm so sorry." Tears rolled down her cheeks—tears of sadness, remorse, and disappointment. No one spends four years in a relationship and expects it to end like this.

"Are you sure?"

She nodded through the tears.

"Because if I walk out of here, get back on that plane, and return to New York without you, that's it. There will be no coming back from that for us."

She knew he meant it. Him coming to Colorado and trying to piece together their broken relationship after being the one to request a break was monumental for him. He didn't usually change his mind. But as much as it hurt, she knew it was the right thing to do.

"I know that, too."

"Okay then." He exhaled a mirthless laugh. "Merry Christmas to me, huh?"

Her chin quivered, and she held a flattened palm to her stomach.

He shook his head somberly. "He's the reason for the wall around your heart?"

Isabella nodded, but what she didn't say was that Leo was also the reason the wall had finally come down.

Harrison exhaled loudly before turning around, holding his head high and pushing through the doors. That was the Harrison she had come to know and love. He had a tremendous amount of pride. Some without merit. But today, he'd shown his vulnerable side. Isabella truly hoped he would open up and let someone else in someday.

But she couldn't be that person for him anymore.

She dragged herself across the hall and slumped into her lonely seat at the wedding party table. She poured a glass of champagne, preparing to drown her sorrows in alcohol while she was being forced to watch the happily married couple dance together, kiss, whisper sweet nothings into one another's ears, and cut cake and smash it into one another's faces. She hoped their marriage lasted and they actually did live happily ever after. She never wanted her little sister's heart to ache with the kind of unforgiving torture hers did right now.

After two glasses of champagne, making small talk with family and friends felt easier to handle. The buzz working through her veins caused her mind to care a little less that her life was in complete shambles. And the more unanswered texts sent to Leo, the more she told herself, they were really over this time.

When Norah handed her a third glass, she did not object. "You gonna be okay?" Her sister asked her.

"You know me, I'm like a cat...I always land on my feet." Isabella held up her glass before taking a big swallow, the bubbly liquid tickling her throat as it went down.

"What are you gonna do now?"

"Go back to New York. It was silly of me to think I could possibly come back here. New York is my home. I've got a great job and great friends." She hoped she sounded convincing. "But I'll need to find a more permanent place to live. I can't sleep on Todd and Margo's couch forever. Besides," she leaned into Norah, "between you and me, I think they're more than just friends. So that puts me in an awkward position."

"Yeah, that would definitely be awkward," Norah agreed. "But you could find work here. And a place to live. It's a little spendy in town but you could always look for a place in Denver. I'm sure Finn and Nina could find you a roommate."

Her throat ached while the anguish permeated there. "I appreciate the sentiment, but I think you and I both know the main reason why I was even considering returning to Colorado. And since Leo practically shoved me into the arms of another man, I think it's safe to say things between us are over." She closed her eyes and kneaded the tension on her forehead with her fingertips.

"Maybe he just needs time."

"I don't know, Norah," Isabella said as she sighed.

"Or maybe you should try to talk to him again."

"I don't even know where he was going." She took another sip, feeling helpless.

"He's supposed to be coming over to Mom and Dad's to open gifts, so I'm sure he went back to his dad's."

"And if I do find him, then what?"

"Tell him you don't want to marry that self-centered prick Harrison. And tell him that you love him and want to be with him."

Isabella gave a slight shake to her head, a hollow feeling in her low belly at the realization things were really over. "He knows. We were going to try long-distance, before Harrison showed up and ruined everything." She slipped her feet out of the red pumps, stretching out her toes.

Norah gasped. "Why didn't you tell me?"

"We were having fun. We wanted to keep it a secret a bit longer." Sorrow pricked her eyes once again. "Ugh. Shouldn't all of this be easier? If two people love each other, shouldn't that be enough?"

Norah shook her head. "I don't know. I wish I had the answer for you."

"Me too." Tears pooled in her eyes.

"The only option you have is to go find Leo and tell him everything before you leave."

"But your reception isn't over."

"Believe me, your doomsday presence really isn't helping the mood." Norah leaned into her, and Isabella pulled her into her side for a hug.

"Thank you." She swiped at her damp cheeks.

Isabella snuck out of the reception, without saying goodbye to friends or family. She took an Uber to her parent's home and ran inside, searching for Leo. When she didn't hear a reply, she ran across the joint yard, the heels of her pumps digging into the snow. After pounding on the front door with no response, she searched for the hide-a-key in the spot it had always been—under the heavy planter next to the front door. She put the key into the lock and pushed it open.

"Leo?" she called, searching through the Hoffman home.

In a way, it felt as if Mrs. Hoffman had never left. Her presence still loomed all around. From the feminine touches of florals to her quilts. But new pictures had been hung on the walls in the hallway and up the stairs. Photos and canvases displaying breathtaking landscapes and destinations that she was positive Leo took.

Her phone chimed in her hand.

Norah: Did you talk to him yet?

Isabella ignored the text, jogging up the stairs. The house had almost the same exact set-up as the Whitley's, but was swapped, making it so that Leo's bedroom was upstairs to the left rather than the right like her own. She pushed open the door, her heart pounding and her feet wet from stepping in the snow.

"Leo?" she called again, searching the room. But the room was completely empty.

Defeated and hopeless, her feet burning from the cold, she slumped onto the window seat. The blinds were still closed, and she pinched the slats, gazing out at her own bedroom.

Her chest felt hollowed out, her heart now completely gone. Leo felt further from her than he ever had before. Even further than those first few months after she'd returned to New York after Mrs. Hoffman had told her to leave and not come back, when she'd felt so heartbroken. But now, she worried her heart would never be revived.

She glanced around the room. The sheets had been stripped from the bed and the quilt Mrs. Hoffman made Leo and given him their sophomore year sat folded at the foot of it. There was no luggage, clothes, shoes, or any other sign Leo had ever been there. Only one thing remained, on top of the folded quilt sat a magnet. She picked it up and gazed at the words: *Pineridge, Colorado* printed on it with a picture of a snowy mountain and a sled. Without having been told, she knew this small gift had been intended for her.

She squeezed the magnet in her fist, pulled herself up, and dragged herself back down the stairs and out of the house. After locking the door and returning the hide-a-key, Isabella went back to the Whitley home and into her childhood room. She took one last look at the space, filling her mind with the memories. All the good and bad. Then she slipped off the wet pumps and began packing her things, tucking the precious magnet into her suitcase.

CELEBRATING CHRISTMAS WENT DREADFULLY SLOW. If she could've, Isabella would've headed to the airport Christmas night after she finished packing her things. But her flight wasn't until nine o'clock the following morning, and Ava had been so happy Isabella was finally celebrating Christmas with them. She couldn't do that to her. But the sympathetic looks Landon continued to pass her all night, along with a gentle hug from Howard as he whispered in her ear, "I apologize for my son, he's a jackass," caused her to crave escape.

After a restless last night sleeping in her childhood bed, Isabella got up before the sun and dragged her luggage downstairs. Besides Dad, Mom was the only other one awake to say goodbye to her. She handed over travel mugs filled with coffee to both Isabella and Dad. And when he headed out to the car to load up her luggage, Mom squeezed Isabella in a tight hug.

"Don't be a stranger this time, okay?" Mom's voice sounded strained.

"I won't." But her words felt like a lie. Isabella didn't know when she'd build up the courage to return to Pineridge again.

Mom pulled back and took Isabella's face in both of her palms. "Remember, you're strong and capable and deserving of love."

Tears worked their way up Isabella's throat, and she tried to clear them away. "Thanks, Mom. I love you."

"Love you too, sweetie."

Dad drove her the two hours to the airport, leaving the house at five in the morning. They sipped coffee but didn't share many words. There wasn't much to say. Everyone knew all that had happened with Harrison and the proposal, then her telling Leo she wanted to stay but he'd told her to go. In a way, when Isabella hugged Mom and Norah and Finn, it felt as if she was not only saying goodbye to them, but to Pineridge, Colorado as well.

For good this time.

"You sure you're gonna be okay?" Dad asked, taking the snowy roads with ease.

"No," she said. She couldn't lie to him. "But what choice do I have?"

Dad shook his head. "I don't know, sweetie. I wish I could fix this for you. And I gotta admit, I saw things going differently."

"You and me both."

"Have any idea when you'll be back?"

Isabella couldn't help but look at Dad, slack-jawed. "No, Dad. No idea. But seeing as things didn't go great this time around, I'm not really in a hurry to return. No offense."

"I get that, I do. But you need to remember. Norah is married to Landon. Landon is a Hoffman. Which means, like it or not, our families will be tied together forever." Dad pulled up to the curb in the airport drop off area.

"Believe me, I haven't forgotten." She picked up her purse and carry-on before climbing out of the car.

Dad got out, pulling her suitcase out of the back. He smiled and wrapped his arms around her in a hug. If she had to be heading back to New York, alone and disheartened, this was the best send-off she could think of. Dad's hugs were full of warmth, love, and repose.

"Thanks, Dad. Love you." She gave him a kiss on the cheek before stepping onto the curb.

"Love you too, sweetie. Take care of yourself. And let us know when you've made it home safe."

Home. Isabella didn't even know where home was anymore.

She stood there, waving until Dad's car had pulled away from the curb. Then she went inside the airport, yanking her suitcase behind her and dragging what was left of her shattered heart.

CHAPTER THIRTY-FIVE

LEO

CHRISTMAS HAD BEEN THE LONELIEST ONE ON RECORD TO DATE, AND that was saying something. Over the last ten years, Leo had spent a few alone. The one after Talia left when he couldn't bring himself to celebrate with Dad and Landon, leaving them to fend for themselves. He'd been selfish. But this year, didn't he have a right to be selfish? To mourn the loss of Isabella and their future?

It only took a day after Isabella left before he realized what an idiot he'd been. That he should've fought for her instead of just giving up and letting her go. He thought he was doing the right thing by stepping aside and allowing her to be happy with Harrison, but since Norah had told him Isabella broke things off for good with him, Leo knew what he had to do.

Go to New York and try. One last time.

Leo had planned to spend most of New Year's alone as well. At least until his flight later that evening. He'd never fully understood the hype regarding New Year's. So what? A year ended and a new year began. It didn't signify anything special in his mind. And don't even get him started on New Year's resolutions.

Ricky had invited Leo to come to celebrate with them at O'Henry's. Leo figured it would give him a chance to say goodbye. Besides, Kelsey would be there with their new baby girl, Charlotte and he hadn't met her yet. She was only four days old. The thought of the little baby sent a pang in his heart. Isabella had missed the birth by two days.

Leo had to park his truck further than usual. O'Henry's was packed. He strolled inside, finding bustling servers and a trio up on stage singing a terrible rendition of "Dancing Queen." He shuttered and approached the bar where Ricky filled pint glasses with beer.

"Hey, man. You made it," Ricky greeted him.

"Yep. You know I wouldn't miss the opportunity to meet the newest O'Henry."

Ricky passed the glasses to a few guys leaning over the bar and wiped his hands on the towel hanging over his shoulder. He gave Leo a fist bump and scanned the nearby faces. "Kels is around here somewhere. Oh, man, just wait until you see Charlotte."

"Can't wait. Congrats, again." He slid onto a barstool and glanced around. He spotted Vanessa and Joey at a table near the front. His attention flicked to one of the women on stage singing karaoke.

Ricky propped his elbows on the bar top. "She's cute, right?"

Leo swiveled on the stool, returning his attention to Ricky, sighing. "Not interested."

"Oh, c'mon. You need to get back in the game."

"When am I gonna get a beer? This place has lousy service," he muttered, teasingly.

Ricky held a glass under the spout of a local pale ale. "How long has it been? Talia?"

When Leo didn't answer, Ricky paused, his green eyes widening. "Isabella?"

"I don't see how this is any of your business."

Ricky chuckled, handing him the filled glass, beer spilling over the edge. "Fine. I'll lay off. I guess it's only been a week."

"A week since what?" a woman's voice asked from behind him.

Leo turned and saw Kelsey, a tiny baby wrapped up and strapped to her front. He was not at all surprised by this. It wasn't unheard of to see the other two O'Henry kids running through the bar on occasion.

"Hey, Kels." He stood and attempted to hug her without squishing the small human attached to her. "She's adorable." He peered down at her, getting a closer look. "Good thing she doesn't take after her father." He chuckled.

"Right. The Lord is good," Kelsey teased, smirking at Ricky. "So," she patted Leo on the shoulder. "How are you holding up?"

He stiffened. "Peachy keen," he said.

She frowned, obviously seeing right through him.

"I talked to Izzy yesterday."

"You did?" His tone sounded anxious, and he hated it.

"She sounded awful."

"Yeah?" Something like hope fluttered in his chest.

"Oh yeah. Depressed as all get out." She shook her head. "You do know she told that Harrison guy to hit the road, yes? How you two couldn't make things work this time around is beyond me."

He wanted to say that he didn't understand it either. But instead, he simply hunched his shoulders in a dramatic shrug. Because what Kelsey didn't know was, he hadn't given up yet.

Not completely.

"Enough of that, Kels," Ricky hollered over the music, pouring a beer for a regular just down the bar. "I invited him here to forget about Izzy."

Kelsey winced, biting her lower lip.

"It's fine," Leo waved her off. "But Ricky did promise me a night I'll never forget."

"Or," Ricky waggled his brows suggestively, sliding another beer in his direction. "A night you *will* forget. Huh? Huh?" He nudged him in the shoulder with his fist.

"You're not children anymore," Kelsey reminded them. "You both have responsibilities."

"I do, for sure. But what does Leo have to do?"

Leo hesitated before speaking. He didn't know if he was ready to let Ricky know what had been on his mind the last few days. "Speaking of responsibilities, I've been thinking it's about time for me to get outta Dodge."

"Hey, a vacation is a great idea. You definitely need it."

"No." Leo shook his head, his chin ducked and his thumb tracing the condensation bubbles on the glass. "Maybe something longer than a vacation."

"What do you mean? Where would you go?"

Leo lifted his gaze. "Maybe East."

"East, huh?" Kelsey side-eyed him, bouncing on her toes when Charlotte fussed.

"You better not be thinking of something permanent. Landon is here. Your dad. What about me, man?"

"Ricky," Kelsey said in a warning tone.

Ricky leaned on his elbows, stretching across the bar, and released a sigh. "Please just tell me you're not considering leaving because of Isabella?"

Leo couldn't lie to Ricky. They'd practically been best friends since before they could walk. But this decision he'd made, to go to New York, was a big one. And if he was being honest, it was scary as hell. He couldn't let Ricky's opinion sway him either way.

He was going.

"She doesn't even live here but you're gonna let her dictate where *you* live?"

"I'm not leaving because of Isabella." Okay so maybe that was sort of a lie.

"Leave the guy alone," Kelsey said, giving Leo a knowing look.

Call it female intuition, but he had a feeling Kelsey knew exactly where he was headed.

Ricky stayed quiet for a beat. "I'd really hate to see you go."

"Like you said, my dad and Landon are here. I'll be back." A voice sounded out from the stage, one he recognized. "Sounds like Joey still has it, huh?"

"That guy has the voice of an angel," Ricky said.

"He really does," Kelsey agreed. "It gets my hormones all amped up, if you know what I mean?"

Leo stiffened and cleared his throat. He rubbed at the back of his neck nervously and glanced over his shoulder. When he did, he spotted Landon and Norah coming inside O'Henry's, Norah shaking the snowflakes from her hair. Their skin glistened with a honey tan, and their faces radiated pure bliss, the kind you only get from an island honeymoon. Instead of their joy rubbing off on him, a bit of jealousy snaked through his core. He wasn't expecting to see them until tomorrow at Dad's for New Year's Day brunch.

"I think that's my cue to leave." He stood, giving a gentle pat on Kelsey's back.

"No, man. You can't go. You didn't even finish your beer. Don't let my wife make you uncomfortable."

"It's not Kelsey. I just can't be here right now." Leo pulled a couple of bills from his wallet and tossed them on the bar top. "I'll catch you tomorrow."

He brushed past Vanessa's greeting and weaved through a crowd by the door, ducking his head as he snuck out without his brother noticing him.

Leo sucked in a deep breath once he was alone in his truck. He pushed his hands through his hair before yanking his phone out of his front pocket and checking his emails. There was a delivery confirmation that the canvases he had sent to Isabella were received two days ago. But he still hadn't heard from her.

Leo wasn't ready to talk to his brother or Norah, or prepared to tell them about his decision of leaving town. He planned on telling them and Dad over brunch the next day. But when Norah had told him about Isabella's New Year's Eve pajama party, he got an idea.

He was headed to New York tonight, to win back the love of his life.

CHAPTER THIRTY-SIX

ISABELLA

Isabella dropped mini marshmallows into mugs filled with hot cocoa that lined the kitchen counter. The apartment was filling quickly with party guests dressed in a variety of styles of pajamas. Some wore barely-there lingerie and others dressed in onesies. Harry Styles's music streamed through Todd's surround sound speakers, bumping through the crowded apartment.

Margo shimmied alongside Isabella, throwing a lazy arm around her waist. "Aww, Izz, everything looks so great. Those mini marshmallows are adorable." Margo plucked one from a mug and popped it into her mouth before resting her hand on Isabella's shoulder. "I just love you, girl."

Tapping her finger to the tip of Margo's nose, Isabella said, "And I think someone is a little bit buzzed."

Margo wrinkled her nose and held her finger and thumb an inch apart. "Just a little." She snorted, straightening. "But seriously, thank you for all of your help. I couldn't have pulled off this party without you."

"You're welcome, it was nothing." Isabella sprinkled cinnamon to the top of each mug, dusting the marshmallows.

"And what a perfect theme—pajama party—after the holidays everyone is exhausted, so this is minimal effort for everyone."

Minimal for everyone but Isabella and Todd. While Mago worked pretty much 24/7 the past week on a big case, she and Todd had three days to come up with a New Year's Eve party theme including food and decorations. But at least the party prep had distracted her from thinking about Leo.

"Is someone still standing downstairs at the door letting guests in?" Isabella asked.

Spinning around, Margo said, "They must be, because look at all these people."

Todd danced his way into the kitchen dressed in a navy-blue silk pajama set. Blank booming through the speakers. "The party's a success. Everyone's having an epic time. We make a great team, Whitley." He held up his fist.

Isabella fist bumped Todd. "You know it, Langston."

Harry Styles's song "Two Ghosts" began and Margo squealed, pumping both fists above her head. "This is my jam." She grabbed Todd's hands and dragged him out of the kitchen. "C'mon, babe, let's dance."

Todd grinned as she pulled him away. "Hey, get out of here and have a good time," he called to Isabella.

She smiled, her heart warming at the sight of her best friends. A few minutes later, she carried a tray of spiked hot cocoa to the living room, setting them on a small table.

She picked up a mug, swiping her finger across the whipped cream and sucking it into her mouth.

"Great outfit," Isabella said to an acquaintance from her office, a young woman wearing barely-there lingerie. Man, did she ever feel self-conscious dressed in Leo's old hockey jersey and a plaid pair of men's boxer shorts.

"Thanks. It was either this or the matching family pajamas my mom gave me for Christmas with a big Santa hat on the front that says, *Dear Santa, They're the Naughty Ones*. Since I decided to go cold turkey and delete my dating apps, I've gone through a dry spell and figured I'd have better luck with the teddy." Her gaze caught the attention of a muscled, shirtless, blonde wearing only boxers. "Ooo, I'll catch up with you later." She sauntered away.

"Get it, girl." Isabella snorted.

Shuffling through the crowded living room, Isabella made small talk with a few people before the stuffiness and boom of the bass got to her. She slipped out onto the patio that had an unmanicured roof garden. The crisp late December air bit at her bare legs and arms and she inhaled a deep breath. An early-season snow had already melted so she padded across the concrete barefoot.

Four floors up, Isabella leaned against the railing, taking in the view of the inky, foggy night. The brightly lit Christmas lights draped across the buildings, the lamp posts shining and lining both sides of the street. Come this time tomorrow, the Christmas decorations would disappear, not being returned until next Thanksgiving. It normally didn't bother her, seeing the holiday end, but this year, it saddened her. She wanted to hold onto Christmas just a little bit longer.

Her phone buzzed and she slid it from inside her bra, glancing at the screen.

Norah: Happy New Year's! Wish you were here!

There was a picture attached of Norah, Landon, Finn, Nina, Ricky, Kelsey, and baby Charlotte at O'Henry's. The instant smile on her face slipped into a frown.

The obvious void of Leo tripped in her mind. Her heart ached, pinching with regret. Each day since she'd returned from Pineridge she stressed over if she'd done the right thing, not staying, not sacrificing everything.

Even now, as she gazed at the beauty of New York, of people celebrating with loud noise makers in the streets, the place that had crept into her heart and became home, she contemplated if she made the right decision.

The noise from inside the apartment drifted outside when the patio door opened. Isabella glanced over her shoulder. Todd strolled toward her, a box underneath his arm.

"Hey, Langston."

He leaned against the railing and bumped a shoulder into her. "I thought I told you to dance and have some fun?"

She shrugged. "Would you believe me if I told you I tried?"

"Not even a little bit." He pushed his hand through his wavy blond hair. "I'm worried about you."

"I'm fine."

He looked at her, incredulous, pushing up his glasses.

"Okay…I will be fine."

"You better be. You're the glue that holds the three of us together," he teased.

She snorted. "If that's true, you guys are in trouble."

He chuckled. "Here." He held the box out to her. "This came for you a few days ago and I forgot to give it to you."

"What is it?" She frowned.

"Not sure. Didn't open it. But the return address is from your hometown."

Isabella stared at the shipping label—LH Photography.

She didn't even have to open it. Just seeing his initials, knowing he'd thought of her, knowing he was alone, it all hit her in a crashing wave.

She needed to go to him. To see him. She couldn't wait.

They could figure out the details later. Whether they dated long-distance or stayed in Colorado or New York. All she knew was she wanted them to be together.

Isabella rushed into the apartment, hurried to the spare room where she'd been staying. She yanked her suitcase from underneath the bed and threw it on top. She unzipped it and pulled random clothes from her closet, stuffing them inside.

After searching online for flights, she called an Uber, pressing her phone to her ear and zipping up her suitcase. She tugged it off the bed and pulled it behind her, rushing out of the room. She weaved in between party guests, apologizing after banging her suitcase into a guy. She needed to find Margo or Todd and tell them she was leaving, but the apartment was even more crowded and loud than earlier.

"Isabella!"

She turned at the faint sound of her name being called. She spun around in each direction.

"Isabella!"

Finally she spotted Margo, hands cupped by her mouth and

standing by the patio doors. Isabella hurried to her, yanking her suitcase behind her. "Hey, I've been trying to find you," Isabella said.

"And everyone's been trying to find you."

Absentmindedly, Isabella continued, "I'm going to Colorado. There's a flight leaving in two hours. I know you told me to move on, but I can't. I love him. I have to see him," she rambled.

Margo gave a dismissive wave. "I'm the last person who should be giving advice. What do I know about love?" She grabbed Isabella's shoulders, forcing her to leave her suitcase and shoved her out onto the roof garden.

"Margo, I don't have time for this. I gotta go," Isabella grumbled.

Margo stopped her in front of the railing. "You don't have to go anywhere."

"What are you talking about?"

Margo gestured at the street and Isabella leaned over, peering down. Below, on the sidewalk and sticking out between the New Year's Eve bar hoppers was Leo.

Her mouth fell open, and her heart all but stopped.

Leo was dressed in the pink bunny pajamas she'd given him.

Her heart restarted, racing, and a smile tugged at her lips, building as the sight set in fully. "Leo? What are you doing here?"

He held his arms up. "A romcom-sized grand gesture."

A bubble of laughter escaped her, and she covered her face with her palms.

He messed with one of the ears on the hood that kept flopping down over his eyes. "Uh…but those romantic comedies don't talk about the embarrassment factor."

She pressed into the railing, gazing at him, ignoring the party guests and bar-hoppers pointing and giggling at him.

"You know I never needed that. I just needed you," she said, her voice vibrating in her chest.

"*Now* you tell me," he teased.

Isabella wanted to jump over the balcony and fling herself straight into his arms. Whatever had changed with him, he'd come all this way to see her.

He was finally here. In New York.

"I can't believe you're here."

"Did you know your buzzer is broken?"

"Yeah." She smiled. "You're supposed to sneak inside with someone with a key."

"Look at me." He lifted his arms from his sides again. "Who's gonna let in a six-foot-four-inch pink bunny?"

She threw her head back and laughed.

"So what do you say, wanna let me into this New Year's Eve pajama party before I get arrested for Disorderly Conduct?"

Her brows pinched together. "How'd you know about the party?"

"Norah."

Of course.

A large crowd of partiers with noise makers passed Leo on the sidewalk just as he opened his mouth to reply.

"What?" she called.

He cupped his hands around his mouth and yelled, "I said, I was an idiot! I shouldn't have let you go!"

A guy on the sidewalk twirling a glow stick in the air stopped, gazed up at Isabella and said, "I agree, you're an idiot. That woman is sexy as hell."

Isabella giggled.

"I know, thanks man," Leo said before turning to face her again. "I don't care where we go or where we end up, whether it's in Pineridge or New York or the moon. I just care that we're together. I love you, Izzy."

Tears streamed down her cheeks. "I love you."

"I choose you. I choose *us*."

"I want to kiss your face off, Leo Hoffman."

"Promise?" He grinned.

"Stay there, I'm coming down." She rushed inside, weaved through friends, and ran out the door, hurrying to the elevator. She punched the button and waited, pacing. "C'mon, c'mon, c'mon," she muttered. "Screw it."

She jogged to the door at the stairwell, racing down each flight, skipping steps. She reached the bottom and rushed through the door. She ran across the lobby, and pushed outside into the night, holding the door open.

"Leo?" She spun in each direction.

No Leo. She panicked.

"Izzy?"

She whipped around, to find Leo standing inside the lobby. Her hand shot to her chest, and her heart squeezed at the sight of him.

He shrugged, smiling. "Someone finally let me in."

She ran back inside and flung herself into his awaiting arms, wrapping her legs around his waist. She held him close, clinging to him and closing her eyes while she inhaled his heady, piney scent. "I missed you," she whispered into his stubbly neck.

"I'm not going anywhere. Ever again. I love you."

Gazing at her as if she was the most exquisite thing he'd ever seen, he tilted his head, and she leaned into him further, their lips sliding against each other's slowly, delicately, and purposefully.

Her heart raced, and she slid her hands into his hair as he deepened the kiss. The taste of him was both sweet and intimate, a taste she wanted to claim as her own for the rest of her days.

He tugged her lower lip with his teeth as she pulled back, trying to catch her breath. She gazed at the face she had memorized, the eyes that had a way of making her breath hitch, and the mouth that was so talented it made her skin burn.

She clasped her hands around his neck. "I love you, the most."

When he returned her to her feet, he winked at her, pinching at his hockey jersey. "I'm glad you kept this. You look so hot in it." He pulled her into his side and pressed a kiss to her temple. "Now, I heard something about a pajama party. Is there a competition? Because I think I have the win in the bag." He presented his hand to her, and she accepted.

Together, they strolled past the elevator and headed toward the stairwell, no longer in a hurry. They didn't need to rush their future. They had all the time in the world. No matter what their future held, or where they ended up, they'd figure it out together, because from now on, they were a packaged deal.

Thank you for reading! Did you enjoy? Please add your review because nothing helps an author more and encourages readers to take a chance on a book than a review.

And don't miss book two of the Pineridge series with TRICKED IN OCTOBER available now. Turn the page for a sneak peek!

You can also sign up for the City Owl Press newsletter to receive notice of all book releases!

SNEAK PEEK OF TRICKED IN OCTOBER

Kelsey O'Henry didn't believe in the traditional five stages of grief. She had her own way of dealing. Push through. No matter what. She was many things—but being a quitter wasn't one of them.

Her best friend, Isabella, often called her bullheaded. She wasn't wrong. But the thing was, Kelsey wasn't only bullheaded, she was short on time.

Who had time to go through the five stages of grief when they had three kids to take care of, a bar to run, and an alcoholic mama to babysit? Denial, anger, bargaining, depression, and acceptance would have to take a backseat.

With a crying baby on her hip, Kelsey filled a pint glass of beer from the tap. A local brewery had just sent over a keg of their newest seasonal brew—an autumn IPA with touches of peach and tangerine. Kelsey hoped it would be a welcomed addition to O'Henry's growing fall menu of beer and hard ciders.

She slid the glass across the smooth bar top to one of her favorite awaiting customers to try. Isabella smiled at Kelsey as she picked up the glass and took a sniff before taking a sip. Typically a wine drinker, Izzy was picky when it came to her beer selection.

Isabella pursed her lips and took another drink before setting her glass down.

"So?" Kelsey's brows lifted, bouncing the still-fussing baby Charlotte on her hip.

Isabella propped an elbow on the bar top. "It's good. Really good. I'm impressed."

The music in the bar was loud tonight, making it hard to hear her bestie's response. A fall playlist the O'Henry's server, Sophie picked out full of cozy and angsty vibes reverberated through the bar's old speakers.

"You actually like it?" Kelsey leaned in.

"Yeah, I mean what's not to like? A citrus IPA…in autumn? Where do I sign up?" Isabella stood from the stool she'd been perched on and adjusted the hem of her dark green sweater.

The tension in Kelsey's shoulders loosened, but only slightly. Satisfied customers of the new beer meant she could cross one thing off her mental to-do list. Now she wouldn't have to cancel the recurring shipments of the IPA kegs from Tapp's Brewery.

That was, if she could afford the recurring shipments. The unpaid bills piled on the back desk haunted her like the Grim Reaper. Outwardly she pretended as if she had it all together, but her worry over the possibility of losing everything threatened to unveil itself.

Isabella reached her hands out for Charlotte who was still crying. Kelsey hesitated before handing her over. Charlotte was a difficult baby to console. She only favored a handful of people and Izzy usually wasn't one of them.

"If you wanna try, be my guest," Kelsey said.

"Shh," Isabella shushed in Charlotte's ear while she bounced her, but the baby continued to fuss. "Where's your mom? I thought she was keeping the kids tonight?"

The tension returned tenfold, and Kelsey's shoulders tightened. "Do you even have to ask?"

Rita, Kelsey's mama, was currently passed out on the small sofa in the back office of O'Henry's Bar and Grill. After years living with the disease, Rita was generally a functioning alcoholic. Meaning, she could be drunk without anyone knowing and a hangover rarely fazed her. But occasionally she went on a binger and Kelsey was reminded how life was like in those first few years after her dad left and the horror began.

Kelsey pushed up the rolled sleeves of her flannel and then filled more pint glasses two at a time now that she had both hands free.

"Why didn't you call me? You know I'd take the kids," Isabella said.

Kelsey snorted a laugh as she set the overfilled glasses onto a tray. "Sorry." She cleared her throat, trying to recover. "I love you, Izz. But you're not exactly Mary Poppins."

Isabella gasped in mock offense, a hand pressed to her chest. "I should be insulted."

Nudging her chin at Sophie as she approached, Kelsey slid the full tray across the bar. Sophie lifted it with a natural ease and carried it to a table of awaiting customers.

Kelsey returned her attention to Isabella. She tugged on the sleeve of Isabella's sweater. "I appreciate you offering, but I need to come up with a more permanent solution. I can't keep bringing them here." She gestured at her two other children who sat at a nearby bar height table stacking salt and pepper shakers into a pyramid.

Her heart pinched in her chest. They didn't deserve this. The two of them used to enjoy coming to the bar and seeing their daddy working. Ricky would make them Shirley Temples with extra cherries. He always introduced them to everyone who came into the bar, he'd been such a proud father.

Charlotte wailed even louder.

Kelsey exhaled a drawn-out sigh. She was so tired. She was pretty sure even the black hair on her head was tired. Taking Charlotte from Isabella, Kelsey pressed a kiss to the ten-month old's head of soft strawberry blonde curls. Out of the three kids, Charlotte resembled Ricky the most. She had his green eyes and red hair. The other two, June and Zach, took after her with dark hair and blue eyes.

"It doesn't help that Charlotte hates everyone."

"She likes my mom. Call her next time," Isabella said.

"Your mama is a saint. She's already watched the kids once this week."

"And she'd be glad to do it again." Isabella smiled.

Kelsey kissed Charlotte on the head. "Thankfully, my in-laws are coming to my rescue—once again." These days, Ricky's parents spent nearly as much time with the kids as she did.

"You better plan ahead and ask them early to babysit on Halloween," Isabella said.

"Already done. While the grandparents take the kids trick-or-treating, I'll be working."

The signs posted around the bar were an annoying reminder of the O'Henry's Halloween Couples Costume Party in a few weeks. Last year she and Ricky dressed as Jim and Pam from *The Office*. This year, she'd planned on dressing in her usual wardrobe of a flannel and jeans.

Isabella pouted her lips. "Kels, no. Please at least dress up."

"What am I gonna wear? Who am I gonna get to dress up with me? The only person other than Ricky I've gone to a couple's costume party with was Davis, and that was so many years ago."

A spark twinkled in Izzy's eyes, and Kelsey shut her down before she could even speak. "No. Davis and I are friends. Best friends. It's not gonna happen." She and Davis Vance hadn't worn those costumes since before there was a 'Kelsey and Ricky'.

That Halloween, nearly ten years ago, the two of them had shared an almost kiss. It was still her biggest regret. It had nearly ruined their friendship.

"Hey, I thought I was your best friend?"

"You're my best girl friend." Kelsey flashed her a smile.

Leo shuffled up behind Izzy, wrapping his arms around her waist and pulling her in close.

Seeing her Isabella happy caused a flutter in her chest.

"Hey, Kels," Leo said, releasing his hold on Isabella.

"Don't stop groping my best friend on my account," Kelsey teased.

Leo hunched his shoulders. "Can you blame me?"

"Not even a little. She *is* the hottest woman in the bar tonight." Kelsey set a beer in front of Leo with a smile. "You better take her out on that dance floor."

"You know I don't dance." Leo chugged his beer.

"That's a great idea. Please, Leo," Isabella coaxed, dragging him away and toward the dance floor.

Leo gave Kelsey a strained look, pushing a hand through his hair.

"Hey, if you don't, I will. And you can watch the three hellions." Kelsey held out Charlotte who hadn't stopped crying, tears and snot streaming down her red, blotchy face.

"Uhh…on second thought, dancing doesn't sound so bad."

Kelsey smirked and returned Charlotte to her hip, squeezing her closer. She knew that would do the trick.

"We'll be back." Isabella dragged a reluctant Leo toward the dance floor.

"Hey, Kelsey?" Julian, the bar's chef called from the kitchen. "The water is still leaking in the kitchen."

A crowd of customers huddled at the bar, signaling her. Even with a baby on her hip, she filled glasses of hard cider and beer one by one as if on autopilot.

"Yeah, yeah. It's on my list," she said, pinching at her flannel shirt to find some relief to her overheated body in between serving the customers.

Igniting the gas fireplace in the corner of the bar to ward off the crisp temperature outside felt like a horrible mistake now as her skin sweltered. The thousands of glowing fairy lights she and Isabella had strung across the ceiling to create a cozy fall vibe seemed like a good idea at the time, too. Now though, they only made her feel feverish.

Sophie approached the bar and slammed down her tray. "Miss Kelsey, there's a tourist at table six who needs to be cut off."

Kelsey shuffled to the computer screen and frowned. "But he's only had one beer."

"Well, I don't know. Maybe he was already drunk before he came in. He's making crude comments and I swear, if he touches me, my jujitsu training might make an appearance."

Ricky always handled the drunk and disorderly customers. It was just another reminder of the things Kelsey had to take care of now that he was gone. But with Charlotte screaming in her ear, the packed bar, and the leaking sink, she felt near the breaking point.

She pinched her eyes shut and swiped the back of her arm across her forehead. She absolutely hated asking for help.

"Hey, Kels. Everything okay?"

At the sound of the soft and rumbling voice, Kelsey's muscles relaxed, and tears nearly welled behind her eyelids. Her throat thickened as her eyes flew open. The sight of the familiar and kind face of her best guy friend, filled her with relief.

Davis.

Despite his over six-foot-tall frame, she felt like tackling him with a hug.

"Thank, God you're here," she said, breathing out a lengthy sigh.

As shocking as his presence was—because he rarely came into

O'Henry's—she was grateful. People who didn't know him might find him intimidating. But to the ones who did know the introverted, shy, Vance twin, he wasn't. When he smiled, his lips practically disappeared and his glassy, blue eyes crinkled at the corners. He kept his facial hair at a permanent three-day stubble that drove Kelsey crazy. Was he growing out a beard or was he just being lazy?

Ugh.

His dark brown hair was unruly, not quite curly but not straight either. He was soft-spoken and often dressed in flannels and oversized sweaters and sweatshirts, hiding the overly fit physique that would make any woman swoon.

Any woman but Kelsey.

Tonight, Davis had on a light blue sweater and his wild hair was tucked beneath a Tapp's Brewery hat.

"What's going on?" he asked, brows furrowed and concern streaking across his face.

"What's not going on? I've got a drunken tourist at table six, a leaky sink in the kitchen, and a crying baby in a bar." She gestured at her hip where the youngster clung on.

Charlotte's crying had turned to a whimper, and she kicked her legs. Charlotte loved Davis. He crouched and leaned in toward her, tickling her underneath her ribs. She didn't react with a full-blown belly laugh, but she did let out a squeal, which felt like progress.

Davis put his hands out for Charlotte, and she went to him easily.

Kelsey's heart shifted in her chest, shoving against her rib cage as Charlotte stopped crying nearly instantly. The girl reached up and tugged on the bill of Davis's baseball hat before yanking it off completely and she giggled.

"Ha, you're a little thief," he teased, his eyes sparkling.

Charlotte smiled wide, her rosy cheeks still dampened with tears.

"You gotta stop giving your mama such a hard time. You hear me?" Davis pressed his finger to the tip of Charlotte's nose.

Charlotte clutched Davis's hat to her chest and giggled.

"Kelsey?" Julian hollered from the open door of the kitchen.

"I'm coming," she called, agitation building in her chest.

"You take care of the leaking sink. Let me go take care of table six," Davis suggested, handing Charlotte back to her.

"You sure?"

A blush swept across Davis's unshaven face as he nodded and chewed a bruised thumbnail, the oversized sleeves of his blue sweater tugged over his knuckles. "What? You don't think I can handle an irate tourist?"

Charlotte began to whine again in between fits of fresh sobs.

"I know you can handle it, it's just that you don't usually like confrontation."

"Doesn't mean I won't handle it. For you." He returned his hat to his head before spinning around on the stool to face the crowd.

Kelsey's chest heaved and her words caught in her throat. She honestly didn't know how she would've survived the last nine months without Davis's friendship.

"Kels?" Julian called again, impatience in his tone.

"Coming," she muttered to Julian.

Rushing into the kitchen, it didn't take Kelsey long to see the problem Julian had warned her about. Water gushed from the shut off under the sink. He had placed a bucket there to catch the water but that was only a temporary fix. Especially by the looks of the wet towels laying on the floor surrounding the bucket.

This was not good. All she could envision was dollar signs flashing in her brain. Money she didn't have.

Julian ran a hand over his tired face. "It's the cold water shut off valve."

She knelt to get a closer look. "You sure?"

"Yeah, pretty sure. I need a wrench to tighten it and I can't find one in Ricky's office. And Kelsey, besides the fact that I don't have time for this, I'm not a plumber. I'm a line cook."

She dropped her head. "I know, I know."

"I told you last week it was leaking. And then I reminded you this morning."

"Damn it, Julian, I know." She folded her lips in between her teeth.

Charlotte stopped crying and sniffed, staring at her wide-eyed.

Kelsey wasn't typically a stressed-out person. Where had the cheerful, easygoing woman she used to be gone? If that woman could come back soon, it would be much appreciated.

"I'm sorry," she mumbled.

Julian sighed, pushing both of his hands through his greasy hair. "I know you're overwhelmed. But you don't have to do everything on your own. You can ask for help once in a while. Or hire someone."

Hiring a plumber would be costly. She knew how to use a wrench. How hard could it be to tighten the shut-off?

"I don't need help. I've got this. I will find a wrench and do it myself."

Julian threw his hands up and cursed under his breath. "Fine. You take care of it. I'll go back to cooking. Or did you want to do that too?"

"Don't be silly. I'm not a cook."

"But you're a plumber?" Julian retorted.

"Tonight, I guess I am," she replied.

Julian backed away, shaking his head but smirking. "Smart ass," he mumbled.

Kelsey rushed to the back office she'd now claimed as her own. She flipped on the light and set Charlotte down on the floor. While she'd left Ricky's posters of monster trucks and 90's grunge bands on the walls, current pictures of the kids now sat in frames on the desk. Orange and white faux pumpkins lined the windowsill and black, hairy spider toys perched in a fake web in the corner of the office.

Kelsey's mama, Rita, stirred on the worn-out leather sofa. She wiped at her raccoon eyes, the black mascara and eyeliner smeared in smudged circles.

"Be a good girl, and turn off the light, will ya, love bug?" Rita asked groggily.

Kelsey ignored her and yanked open the closet door. She rummaged around in the closet, perching on her hands and knees until she finally located Ricky's tool bag in the back on the floor. She lifted it and straightened, tossing the heavy bag onto the desk. The faded green, thick fabric had seen better days. It, along with the tools, had been passed down from Ricky's grandad. She'd given him a hard time about not replacing the old tools, telling him they were rusty. But there were few things Ricky treasured in life, and these tools were one of them.

She dug inside the bag until she found a wrench set. She set it aside before lifting the bag in a hurry, but it was heavier than she'd expected, and she lost her grip. The bag slid off the desk, toppling to the floor with a loud *crash*, spilling an assortment of tools and taking a stack of papers with it.

Her mom, Rita, groaned. "Kelsey, what is all that racket?"

Kelsey exhaled, a hand pressed to her chest upon finding Charlotte out of harm's way. "It's fine, Mama. Just go back to sleep."

Grumbling under her breath, she crouched amongst the fallen tools. She didn't have time for this. There was not only a leaking sink to tend to, but she had a bar packed full of customers and her kids to keep an eye on until reinforcements arrived.

Quickly, Kelsey shoved each tool back into the bag before gathering the papers into a stack and trying not to allow them to distract her. She sat back on her heels, about to push herself up to her feet when something on the top sheet caught her eye. The logo of the bank O'Henry's Bar and Grill had their loan with was reflected in the corner. Bright red words stamped on the page: PAST DUE.

In that moment, her heart skidded behind her ribcage. There was a silent roaring in her ears, and a rumble in her chest as she felt herself losing control of everything. As much as she'd been trying to push this information to the back of her mind, the reality of her financial situation sat staring her in the face. The contents of this letter, and all the rest in the stack, meant things were about to change.

And she hated change.

Forcing herself to focus on the letter again, the date in bold letters caught her attention. If she didn't come up with a solution, in less than forty-five days, O'Henry's would have a new owner.

After Ricky's snowmobile accident the winter before, resulting in his death, Kelsey had taken over the responsibilities of the business. Including handling the finances and managing the bar. In all honesty, it had been a lot to take on. Juggling the bar and the kids the past nine months was exhausting.

Yet, she'd found herself taking to her new role as O'Henry's manager easily. She enjoyed serving the customers, chatting with the

Pineridge locals, and connecting with vendors from breweries all around Colorado.

O'Henry's Bar and Grill wasn't just a bar or a livelihood. And it wasn't only a part of Ricky and his legacy.

It was a part of *her*.

It was a part of Pineridge.

After the accident, she'd closed the bar for a full month which caused her to get behind. But the bills had piled up. She'd had to take a second loan against the business to be able to afford to keep it going. Even though the bar was frequently busy, there was more money going out than what was coming in.

Kelsey wasn't sure how she would fix this, but she had to. She couldn't let this happen. She'd already lost Ricky; she couldn't lose the bar too.

Don't stop now. Keep reading with your copy of TRICKED IN OCTOBER available now.

Don't miss book two of the Pineridge series with TRICKED IN OCTOBER available now and find more from Starla DeKruyf at www.starlawrites.com

In this best-friends-to-lovers romance, mistaken identity leads to a Halloween hook-up that might not be so mistaken after all.

After losing her husband last winter, the thought of hosting a Halloween couples costume party is the furthest thing from Kelsey O'Henry's mind. Besides raising three young children, managing O'Henry's Bar and Grill, and caring for her alcoholic mother, she has more important things to worry about. Like the stack of unpaid business loans that threaten the bar's existence. As well as her newfound feelings she's developed for her best guy friend.

Davis Vance is tired of being followed around by cameras. He misses the days before he and his twin brother became "Renovation Dudes"—hosts of an HGTV show. When Davis learns Kelsey could lose the bar at the end of the fall season, he sees it as an opportunity to not only help his friend, but as a way out of renewing his HGTV contract.

There's just one problem—lately Davis's feelings for Kelsey have been less friendly and more romantic. And on the night of the bar's Halloween party, both Kelsey and Davis can no longer ignore their desires. Will their passionate evening be a one-night stand—only a flicker of heat during the crisp autumn, or will she risk her pride and accept his help?

Please sign up for the City Owl Press newsletter for chances to win special subscriber-only contests and giveaways as well as receiving information on upcoming releases and special excerpts.

All reviews are **welcome** and **appreciated**. Please consider leaving one on your favorite social media and book buying sites.

Escape Your World. Get Lost in Ours! City Owl Press at www.cityowlpress.com.

ACKNOWLEDGMENTS

First, and foremost, I want to thank God. Without Him, I wouldn't be here. I've always said that the ability to write a satisfying story comes from three things: God given talent, passion, and lots of hard work. Everything I accomplish in this life is not I but Him and I give Him the credit and the glory.

To my husband, Jeremy, there's not enough space in this acknowledgments section to say how grateful I am for you. Your endless support and love are what keeps me going. I'm sure I would've given up by now if you didn't push me to keep going, to have a positive attitude, and to believe in myself. You always keep me laughing and keep my dreams in perspective. Your amazing work ethic is what has given me the freedom to keep working at and pursuing my dreams. Thank you for your sense of humor and your epic taste in music. I'm so blessed to share my life with you and be married to my very own romance hero. I love you!

To my kids, Jensen, Jaidyn, and Jace, I am the luckiest mom to have such supportive kids. You encourage me to keep dreaming and to not give up. Thank you for sharing me with my other passion in life. I can only hope that I'm helping to instill in each of you the drive to work hard, fight for what you want, and to never, ever give up on your dreams. All three of you are such talented and kind humans and I love you so much and I couldn't be prouder to be your mom.

To my brilliant editor, Charissa Weaks, without her, none of this would be possible. I will be forever grateful to you for making my dream come true. Thank you for taking a chance on me, believing in this story, and teaching me so much. Thank you for your guidance, patience, and kindness. You are doing the Lord's work, lady.

Thank you to Tina Moss, Yelena Casale, and the entire City Owl team. Thank you for taking a chance on me and for always being available to answer questions and for making this a pleasant process. Thank you to Bailey Potter for your copy edits and MiblArt for the adorable and perfect cover design.

To my parents, Heinz and LaGene Engel, who gave me the freedom to imagine, to dream, to create. Thank you for loving me unconditionally. To my dad who taught me to never stop reaching for my dreams, and to my mom who taught me the importance of keeping my feet planted.

To my in-laws, Marvin and Evelyn, who never missed an opportunity to ask where I was in my publishing journey, for encouraging me to keep going, and for showing their support when my dream finally came true. Thank you!

To my sister, Shellie, who was probably my first reader. Thank you for reading the early, terrible stuff and for pushing me to get better.

To my biggest cheerleader, beta reader, first reader, and bestie, Bethany, words cannot express how grateful I am for you and for your endless support. You encourage me, lift me up when I fail, send me funny gifs, and sweet cards, and you don't let me quit. You learned all about the publishing process just so you could know how to support me and my dream better. I love you and I'm so glad we were born into the same family. God sure knew what he was doing all those years ago!

To my grandma, Merrilee, for instilling in me the love of the written word.

Thank you to my crew of talented CP's: Brittany, Kristine, Lauren, and Tova for your sharp eye and attention to detail, your expertise, and your patience and friendship.

To my ride or die beta readers: Bethany, Lissa, Diane, Janine, and Jodi, I am forever indebted to you and your generous time. All the Starbucks gift cards in the world wouldn't be enough to show my deepest gratitude for you. Thank you!

Thank you to the Bend chapter of Shut Up and Write. Meeting with you all once a week, commiserating, bouncing off ideas with one another, was a highlight of my week, and I will forever cherish that time.

To my online support system, the friends, and connections I've made on Twitter, Instagram, Facebook, and the City Owl squad, I'm incredibly appreciative of you. Thank you specifically to Savannah for your endless support, encouragement, critiques, and friendship. I'm so grateful we met through a Twitter pitch party years ago. Thank you, Rachael, your talent, and success are inspiring. Caroline, thank you for your support and for creating #NightWritersClub with me. Cassie, your talent, and skills, along with your encouragement means everything. JoAnna, thank you for your critiques and friendship and humor that gets me through. To Jess, Maria, Abigail, Angie, Amy, Caitlin, and Kelly, thank you for giving invaluable feedback and support over the years.

Thank you to all my family, my siblings, and sibling-in-laws, from the Engel's to the DeKruyf's and everyone in between, who prayed, supported, encouraged, shared my book news, ordered, and read.

To Emily at Pizza Hut, "Hey, girl, hey!" Thank you for feeding my family on way too many nights to count, and without judgement, so I was able to finish this book.

Thank you to everyone who pre-ordered, purchased, requested my book at your library, reviewed, bookstagrammers, and anyone else who supported and encouraged me along the way. I will forever be thankful to you.

ABOUT THE AUTHOR

Starla DeKruyf started writing when she still had words left to say and everyone stopped listening. Her love of romance novels began when she borrowed her friend's copy of Tiger Eyes by Judy Blume and kept it hidden from her mom. When she's not slinging coffee, volunteering with youth, or taxiing her kids around, you can find her jamming out to her playlists and writing her next swoony romance, usually by hand. She lives in Bend, Oregon, with her husband, three children, Samson, their English Mastiff, and Danner, a rescue pup.

www.starlawrites.com

facebook.com/authorstarladekruyf

instagram.com/starlawrites

twitter.com/starla_writes

ABOUT THE PUBLISHER

City Owl Press is a cutting edge indie publishing company, bringing the world of romance and speculative fiction to discerning readers.

Escape Your World. Get Lost in Ours!

www.cityowlpress.com

facebook.com/CityOwlPress

twitter.com/cityowlpress

instagram.com/cityowlbooks

pinterest.com/cityowlpress

tiktok.com/@cityowlpress

Printed in Poland
by Amazon Fulfillment
Poland Sp. z o.o., Wrocław

26135741R00174